# Tom Bone

# *TOM* BONE

*Charles B. Judah*

William Morrow & Company
NEW YORK : 1944

A WARTIME BOOK

THIS COMPLETE EDITION IS PRODUCED
IN FULL COMPLIANCE WITH THE GOVERN-
MENT'S REGULATIONS FOR CONSERVING
PAPER AND OTHER ESSENTIAL MATERIALS.

TO

JOE *and* CHUCK,

*whose adventure*

*is real*

# Foreword

"I can wait," I told her.

I said it fifteen months ago, and I have kept my promise. But because without her all these past months have been an empty waste, I have sought to beguile time by re-creating the past. The result is the story of myself, Tom Bone.

And it is a story that is done, for tomorrow I leave my fine house in Newport and turn towards the west, and a new life.

NEWPORT *in His Majesty's Province of Rhode Island, 1692*

*Book One*

# I

## I.

I was born in England in the fishing village of Saltash which lies on the west bank of the Tamar, a few miles northwest of Plymouth. I was the twelfth child borne by my mother in eleven years, so it is not strange that no one remembered to record my birth in the parish records. In fact had Guy Barrows escaped hanging I would be hard put to tell the exact date upon which I was born.

Ned Bone, my father, like most of the men in Saltash, was a fisherman. Each year he went to the fishing banks off Newfoundland. The usual time for the departure of the fishing fleets is late February or early March, but in 1645, because of the trouble between King and Parliament which might lead to the impressment of ship and crew for fighting, the fishing vessels sneaked out of Plymouth harbor in January.

On board one of these, dreading the ice and fog of the North Atlantic, but fearing impressment into the navy more, went Ned Bone. It was late November when he returned to England. Good spouse that he was, he went straight to his wife with whom he stayed for two nights and a day. My mother was not a greedy woman but she had learned from experience that if she hoped to get her husband's wages she must do so during those first hours after his return, when he was still so woman-hungry that she would do as well as another. If she failed to make the most of this period of grace the year's earnings might be snatched from her by the whores and tavern keepers of Plymouth. So it happened that during the first flush of my father's homecoming my

3

mother was so occupied that she clean forgot to mention my birth. After his day and two nights my father, taking a few shillings which he had held back for the occasion, went for a walk. He came back a week later satisfied that his return to England had been properly observed. On the following day he encountered for the twelfth time the seemingly inevitable miracle of paternity.

He was sitting in front of the cottage sunning a skin that was more accustomed to being pickled in the sea's brine. Although half asleep he grew aware of someone near him. He opened his eyes and saw his daughter Susan sitting in the dirt a few feet away. She held a baby in her arms.

"That's your father, Tommy," she was saying.

He looked down the muddy highway. No one was in sight.

"He was gone when you got born," Susan continued, "but that's him. He's been drunk."

Ned thought this over.

"Name Tommy?" he asked finally.

"Thomas," corrected Susan gravely, "same as the two that died."

"Maybe it's not a lucky name," observed my father. Then, according to the tale as Susan later told it, he spoke to me for the first time. "Well, Thomas, you're a fine lad," he said, "but a man who's away over nine months on a stretch needs to be cautious, and I'm thinking your birthday will bear looking into."

The task that Ned Bone had set for himself was not easy. Naturally my mother would have known within a week or so the date of my birth, but to ask her was not my father's way. He must find out for himself, and then, if necessary, confront his wife with the facts. Unfortunately for him the villagers of Saltash had been far too busy with their own affairs to heed the birth of another Bone. So in the end it was only a stroke of luck that brought the investigation to a satisfactory conclusion.

On the evening of the seventeenth of August Guy Barrows, known as Black Guy, was hanged. Barrows was tall and swarthy, and undoubtedly a rogue. His hanging was richly deserved, consequently the villagers anticipated the occasion with an even greater zest than usual. Barrows being slender, though of good

4

height, there was speculation regarding the probability of his weight being insufficient to break his neck when the cart should be driven from under him. Wagers on the subject were made freely, the odds being against the group that believed the villain's neck strong enough to stand the shock. Numbered among these latter was one Joe Tinker, or Old Joe as he was called, who having laid sixpence against a shilling that Barrows would die of strangulation rather than a broken neck, hoped not only to see Black Guy dancing furiously on air but also looked forward to a comfortable hour or two in the tavern after the spectacle was over.

The seventeenth proved a balmy day, serene and smiling. Consequently Joe Tinker was in an excellent humor when Jimmy Bone, small and frightened, hailed him. Did he know where the midwife might be found? Joe thought he did, and upon arriving at the scene of the hanging found that his confidence was not misplaced. After some difficulty he persuaded the midwife to forego Black Guy's exit from the world in favor of my entry into it. However, before leaving, she made Joe promise to stop at the Bone home when the affair was over in order to describe each detail while it was still fresh in his mind.

Joe Tinker won his wager. Barrows' neck withstood the weight of his body; and though no odds are more hopeless than those against a man who, with a rope around his neck and only the air under his feet, fights death, Black Guy put up a magnificent struggle. For many minutes after his tongue hung out of his mouth and his swart skin had turned an angry purple, his legs threshed through the air and his toes strained hungrily toward the earth. It was a soul-filling spectacle, one which left Old Joe a shilling richer and at peace with the world.

The benign mood survived two hours at the tavern, so on his way home Joe remembered his promise and stopped at the Bone cottage. The midwife had gone, but a thin wail from the corner of the room told him that she had done her work. Another Bone was in the world. It was to be called Thomas, after the two who had died.

Thus it was that when some two months later my father made

5

casual inquiry at the tavern regarding the date of my birth, Joe Tinker enlightened him. He was so positive that his story could not be doubted. I was born August seventeenth, 1645, the day that Guy Barrows was hanged.

## 2.

Although most of my early childhood is obscured by the ever-thickening cloud of years that separates a man from his past, a few scattered moments, deriding time, gleam bright in the sunlight of my memory. Among these are my first meeting with Polly Bragg and the first time I saw Susan with her gentleman.

Jane Bragg, Polly's mother, was a pretty, frightened creature who had been seduced at an early age. No one in the village knew who Polly's father was, though gossip had it that he was master of the house where her mother worked as scullery maid. Certain it is that, though the squire professed himself a Puritan, Jane was not dismissed when her shame was revealed, but continued to stay at Denham, the squire's manor, where she raised her child. As a consequence Polly was not accustomed to the rough and tumble life of the litter, but reigned in lonely grandeur as mistress of the greasy pots. Her mother was a doting serf.

When Jane Bragg came to the village she brought Polly. While on errands or visiting with gossips she left the child with one or another of her friends. Among these latter was my mother.

It would be easy to pretend, even easy to make myself believe, that I can recall how Polly Bragg looked when I first set eyes on her. But it would not be true. O! I can call a picture of her to mind: a child with heavy sulky lips, a small, slightly receding chin and gray eyes that were cold or hot as Polly willed; she would even then have had the same thin legs and wiry frame that I was to know so well in later years. Perhaps on that day her nostrils quivered and her mouth fell into an incredibly thin line as angry words poured from it. Yes, I can see Polly at seven, just as I can see her at any age, but it is not a memory dating from that distant day when we first met, but rather the recollections of

6

a thousand hours that have seared Polly Bragg into my consciousness, to stay as long as I am alive.

Polly and I quarreled that first day. We had played amiably enough until discord came in the form of a hunk of salt fish that Susan had somehow got for me. Well fed from the squire's kitchen, Polly affected disdain for the precious morsel, and childlike I sought revenge by vowing she could not have it were she starving and mine the last fish in the world. Presently, as I had hoped, Polly asked for a share. I refused; she resorted to force. Despite advantage in age and a strong hulking body it was only after a stout tussle that I emerged sitting triumphantly astride a prostrate but still struggling foe. From my point of vantage I held aloft the now filthy and unsavory hunk of fish, and extolled its luscious taste and belly-filling properties. But even as I boasted I became aware of Polly's eyes. They were hard and fixed, but behind their glass curtain glowed such fury that I grew quiet and scrambled uneasily to my feet. Polly lay silent, staring. Only after I had broken the fish and dropped half of it to the ground beside her did she move. Ignoring my peace offering she got up. A tight-lipped grimace of triumph hovered over her mouth as she looked down at the fish. Then with her bare toes she deliberately turned it over and over in the dust.

"Eat it," she said finally, and I who had watched breathlessly, fearing that she might grind it in the dirt until it was past recovery, fell on the morsel eagerly. And even now it seems to me that salt fish never tasted better than did those foul chunks that I wolfed while crouching at the feet of Polly Bragg.

Polly was probably left with my mother on other occasions, but if so I was away from home on such business as small boys find, and did not see her again for over a year. When the second encounter did occur its impression cut deeper because it was accompanied by my first knowledge of my sister and John Denham.

One morning when I was nine or ten and Susan a full-grown girl of fifteen or thereabouts, I spied her as she was about to leave the house. She was dressed in all the poor magnificence that she could muster. Believing that she was bound for Plymouth I declared my determination to go with her. She rejected my proposal.

I persisted until, in one of her rare lapses of patience, she slapped me sharply and fled. Indignant but unhurt I followed her.

To my surprise Susan did not turn south toward Plymouth, but north into the country. We were soon out of the village and on a narrow lane. Presently she left this too and turned into the woods, thence into a clearing. There, after a rapid glance around, she seated herself on a log. Hiding myself, I waited. Soon a boy about Susan's age appeared. By his dress, though it was sober in cloth and cut, I knew he was the son of a gentleman. His appearance changed Susan from plain Susan of Saltash to a bridling, giggling female creature. But if Susan was coy the newcomer was purposeful enough for them both. Without hesitation he strode to the log, pulled Susan from it, and took her into his arms.

I know now that at this stage they were only a lad and lass playing at love; but the small boy hidden in the bushes was filled with shame. Why should Susan submit to being jerked about and kissed? And why should she seem to enjoy it so much? Angry and hurt, I was soon slinking out of the woods and back down the lane. I had gone but a short distance when I ran into Polly Bragg. She was flushed with anger. Although I knew her at once, she did not recognize me.

"Have you passed him?" she demanded.

"Passed him?" I echoed stupidly.

"Master John."

I knew then that it was Master John whom I had just seen hugging my sister.

"I've seen no one," I lied.

Polly burst into tears interspersed with abuse. The tears it appeared were for Master John, the abuse for an unknown slut who, Polly suspected, had been meeting him in the woods. I stood awkward and uncomfortable. It was Susan who was being abused but I could not defend her. Neither could I entirely understand Polly's rage. As Susan was not her sister, why should she care? Before I could collect my scattered wits Polly's mood changed. The tears ceased to flow, her fists unclenched; smiling, she came close to me.

"I hate him," she declared. "His old drab can have him." She

8

raised a mouth too large for its heart-shaped face. "You can kiss me," she said.

My awkwardness vanished, indecision evaporated. I fled. Floating after me came a taunting voice.

"You're afraid," shouted Polly, pleased laughter bubbling through the gibe. "You're afraid to kiss me."

### 3.

I do not believe that childhood can be measured by a span of years. It is a way of feeling, a manner of living. To be a child is to be care-free and careless, untouched by hatred or bitterness. In such a sense many men and a few women die children, though they may have lived to a great age. By the same measure children are too often shoved into the adult world before their time. Such was my case.

Unlike most of the west country fishermen, my father was not bred to the sea. Born and raised on a farm some miles inland, he had while a lad fallen in with some rogues who, after getting him drunk, had sold him to a sea captain notorious for the ill treatment of his crews. Thus my father's was a hard school for seamen, but it was a good one. When he finally gained his release he found that he could make a better living by sea than by land. He became a fisherman.

Year after year he went to American waters in late winter and did not return until autumn. During the few months of each year spent in England he passed the greater part of his time with his cronies, lounging along the waterfront or in a grog shop. When at home he was taciturn but seldom unkind. My clearest memory of him is sitting in the winter sunshine, hungry eyes fixed on the green country beyond the village.

"It's a good land, Tom," he said to me once, "things grow." He shivered slightly and nodded towards the west. "Not like out yonder."

"How is it there?" I asked eagerly, anxious to hear of the western land.

"Cold," he grunted. "White and green and cold. Even the green is cold and more black than green."

That was a long speech for Ned Bone.

He sometimes worried for fear that he would die in the West. He loved green growing things and wanted to lie in England when he was dead. Next to death in the New World he feared impressment most.

I have met men in America who do not know what impressment is. To one who grew up in the west of England that seems strange. Strange but good. Impressment means forcing men into the navy. And no wonder they must be forced. A man-of-war is worse than a pirate craft, and I who have been among pirates should know something of that. While officers dine off gold plate and swill Spanish wine from goblets of crystal, below deck the carcasses of common seamen, starved or poisoned by rotten food, are shoved out of the portholes; and if the poor devils complain they only die the quicker from being keel hauled, hung up by the thumbs or whipped through the fleet. The prisons are emptied of their worst rogues, the gutters are dragged to man the fleet; but that is not enough: honest men must still be impressed.

In November of 1657 when the fishermen returned from the Banks they were greeted with rumors that impressment was to be invoked to man the fleet for the war which Cromwell was waging against Spain. Seamen all over the West Country met these rumors by binding themselves together to resist. The men of Saltash followed the general example, and among their leaders was Ned Bone.

The weeks passed, however, without the government issuing orders for impressment, so when on the day before Christmas my father took me with him to Plymouth there seemed to be no cause for alarm. Having spent the small sum that we could afford for Christmas gifts we started homeward. On the way my father decided to treat himself to a holiday drink. In the grog shop where we stopped were a scattering of sailors and two constables, quarrelsome from drink. Ordering a pot of small beer my father turned to the seamen.

"A hearty Christmas, lads," he said.

"Don't you include us, fellow?" one of the constables demanded threateningly.

"I drink to my comrades' health; if you are among them I drink to you."

The constable spat.

"Then drink to yourself; I'm none of your seagoing swine."

"Swine mostly stay on land."

The sailors laughed at this sally but the proprietor of the shop looked concerned.

"They're Cousin's men," he muttered.

A shadow crossed my father's face. All Plymouth and its neighborhood knew of and feared Edward Cousin. A fanatical Puritan, he held no office, but nonetheless he always had a constable at his command and some declared that even magistrates obeyed him. It was whispered that he had the favor of the Lord Protector himself. Whatever his authority, his bullies—official and private—ranged the waterfront searching for sinners, they said, and for those who dared murmur against the rule of Oliver Cromwell. So when my father heard the name Cousin muttered, a shadow of fear fell across his face. He nodded understandingly.

"Call me a swine, will you?" roared the constable. "Turn around, I want to see you."

Finishing his pot my father turned slowly. He took my hand in his.

"Time we went home, Tommy," he said.

"Not so fast," cried the bully, "I want to see you."

"Look then, man."

"Aye, I'll look, and I'll remember." He turned to his companion. "Carrion for the fleet," he sneered.

It might have ended there had not one of the men sitting against the wall intervened.

"There's no 'pressment," he protested.

"There will be soon enough," sneered the constable.

The sailor was drunk.

"Aye, and when there is you'll see something. Us seamen will fight but it won't be against the Spaniards; it's the damned stinking jackals that come after us we'll fight."

11

The officer drew a gun. Deliberately he prepared the charge, put the priming in the pan and brought the cock of the weapon up and back.

"Who would resist impressment?" he demanded.

The drunken seaman was frightened.

"Not me, master," he quavered. "I was but speaking of Ned Bone yonder. He's leader of the Saltash men who say they won't sail for the wars."

Cousin's man swung back upon my father. He was grinning as though he had unexpectedly stumbled upon a bit of fun.

"Is that true?" he demanded.

I felt my father's hand clutch mine a little tighter.

"I'm Ned Bone," he said.

That was all. The constable shot him as he stood there, still holding my hand. It was so heavy a charge that it nearly blew his head off. He died almost at once.

I cannot honestly say that I bore great affection for my father. Nonetheless, on that day when they murdered him I first felt hatred. Perhaps my passion was roused by the sight of his great helpless body, or it may have been because when they carried the corpse home my mother, despite bitter grief, was so obsequious to the murderers; but most of all I think it was because his hand clutched mine so desperately just as he died. I could not help him then, but I swore hatred and revenge.

The murderer was not punished.

We buried my father at sunset on Christmas day. Now he is part of the growing things of England. He would like that.

## 4.

Years have passed since Ned Bone was killed. Three thousand miles of water and a fair measure of villainy have made me what is called a gentleman. In this unnatural estate I frequently hear the sufferings of the poor belittled. On such occasions a company is generally gathered in a room which is warm from the fire of sweet-burning hickory logs and bright from the glow of wax candles. More often than not the ladies and gentlemen are sitting around a table littered with the fragments of a hearty meal.

"The lower classes, with their perpetual complaints, do not realize how fortunate they are to escape the burdens and responsibilities of government," someone declares unctuously.

"Perhaps not," I protest, "but they do know hunger and cold."

A lady replies more often than not.

"Oh! but they are accustomed to such things," she says, and her eyes roll soulfully as she strives to conceal the belch that rises from an overloaded belly. "Besides, such inconveniences as you name are mere discomforts of the flesh."

Once I withheld food from such a soulful creature, and after a short time she had so far forgotten her sensibilities that in return for something to eat she was as ready to serve as drab for the seaman as any base-born wench that ever walked the waterfront. But I run ahead of my story.

At the time of my father's death there were seven of us living in the cottage at Saltash. Less than twelve months later only my mother and I remained. One of my brothers went to sea. I have neither seen nor heard of him since. A sister, Kate, close to me in age and next to Susan, my dearest companion, died. We knew as she wasted away before our desperate eyes that she was starving, but there was little we could do. I can still see myself, a child of twelve, creeping into a corner clutching a bowl of pease porridge.

There I would gulp the stuff hastily, looking steadfastly at the floor lest I should see the hollow eyes of my dying sister. Occasionally pity was more than hunger and I gave her my food. Then I spent the night, knees pressed into belly, crying quietly from hunger pains. Perhaps my sacrifices and the greater ones of Susan and my mother kept poor Kate alive a few weeks longer. It could have done no more than that. The parish gave her a pauper's burial.

Another sister, Evalyn, was of sterner stuff. She was there when they brought my dead father home, and neither grief nor shock could prevent her rolling her large, protuberant black eyes. A few days later one of the constables returned and persuaded her to go with him. He kept her for a few weeks, then turned her into the streets. My mother begged her to come back to us, but she preferred to remain in Plymouth where she was soon one of the sisterhood of whores. For all that, she was a good girl, giving my mother a few coppers from time to time.

Susan's turn came.

Susan at eighteen, although small of stature, was a strong wench, well able to bear the burdens of wifehood. But she discouraged the lads who came to court her. Before my father's death this stubborn spinsterhood mattered little; afterward it seemed to my mother a willful withholding of the means of living for the whole family. She nagged at Susan constantly, but Susan, usually so pliant, was obdurate. My mother was both puzzled and angry at such stubbornness. For my part, I thought that I understood. Although a vague sense of shame had prevented my ever following her again, I knew that my sister took frequent walks in the lanes north of Saltash; nor had I forgotten "Master John" who I knew by this time was the young master of Denham, where Jane Bragg was in service.

However my knowledge, or rather suspicion, did not prevent me from being surprised when one morning Master John himself visited us. Jane Bragg, who accompanied him, was the spokesman. Their business was with Susan. She was not at home. Jane explained to my mother.

The squire, having heard of our plight, wished to help us. By happy chance one of the girls who worked in the house had recently married. Susan, it seemed, was to take her place.

Listening from a respectful distance I could guess the source of the squire's knowledge. But my mother was too eager to have Susan earning something, however little, to be suspicious. She accepted the offer instantly. At this point Susan came home.

Poor Susan was never clever at concealing her emotions. Seeing our visitors she gasped; for a moment it seemed that she might flee. But if she had such an impulse she beat it back and after bobbing low as a common wench should to such a gentleman as Master John, she stood there meekly, her mouth trembling, her skin red to the roots of her fair hair. Master John however was cool enough, giving her only an indifferent glance as he asked my mother if this was the lass. On being told that it was, he repeated his offer. Susan refused.

My mother was struck dumb, but only for an instant.

"So you won't work," she protested shrilly. "You who have already driven off half the men of Saltash when they'd marry you." I saw Susan cast a beseeching glance at the squire, but the young man paid no heed. My mother continued in full cry.

"So Susan is too good for the fisher lads, is she? And now she's too proud for honest work. Who, then, is Susan? A fine lady? Or maybe she wants to follow her sister Evalyn to Plymouth and turn whore?"

Susan burst into tears.

"But I can't. You see—that is—I can't—" She gave up what she would say and stood silent.

I had come closer. For some reason not entirely clear even to myself, I joined my pleas to those of my sister.

"Let her be," I muttered; "it's better she stay with us."

Together Susan and I might have prevailed, for my mother was a weak woman; but suddenly we were brought face to face with the power of the gentry. The squire intervened. His brows were creased. His weak mouth had fallen into a petulant pout.

"You're paupers," he declared suddenly, "like to be a charge on the parish. I offer the wench work; there's no more to be said —unless you want a visit from the bailiff."

What he could have done I did not know then nor do I now; but we were a small boy, a distracted woman and a defenseless girl, and above all we were poor. It was my mother who wept now. There was nothing for Susan to do but surrender. Once again she bobbed to Master John as she promised tremulously to scour his hearth and empty his slops at his pleasure.

He came for her the next day. Having his way, he was all smiles, while Susan, the die cast, was apparently pleasantly excited at the prospect of the new life she was about to encounter; but I, who watched with a heavy heart, remembered the threats of yesterday. I hated Master John and all his kind; and though I have since killed their men and possessed their women, I still hate them as I did that day when I watched Master John take Susan away.

15

Thus it was that in a few short months my father was killed, my family was scattered and bitterness and hatred were brought into my life. I was only twelve but the doors that separate childhood from maturity had swung open, and I had been kicked violently across the threshold.

# II

## I.

SOON AFTER Susan left us, my mother and I moved from Saltash to Plymouth. In the larger town we managed to keep alive. Susan helped when she could, and Evalyn contributed now and then. How my mother earned the little money that she brought home I do not know; except that it was by the hardest and meanest drudgery.

As for me, I spent most of my time on the waterfront. There I played with other urchins of my age, earned an occasional copper and stole what I could from the piles of goods that lay on the wharves. Above all else I listened to the yarns of the seamen. Plymouth was a busy port in those days, full of the trade and the tales of the New World. These fascinated me. Of course I had heard of Newfoundland all my life, but disliking it my father had pictured it as cold and inhospitable. Now I learned that far south of the fishing banks lay a land of adventure. Boston, Providence, St. Mary's and Jamestown became names as familiar to me as Bristol, Hull and London. I determined to visit them at the first opportunity. That there would be one I never doubted. Indeed it was not how or when I should go west that plagued my youthful mind, but what I should do when I got there. I spent hours trying to decide whether to snatch adventure from the sea or the wilderness; I suffered agonies of indecision over the relative merits of red men and pirates. Some days I would lean towards one, some days the other, but whatever my rôle the scene remained the same: the land and the seas of the New World.

My passion for stories about America led me to haunt the grog shops on the waterfront. Here, their tongues loosened by liquor, the sailors talked more freely. In such a place I first encountered Edward Cousin.

It was late afternoon. The company of the Blowing Whale was in good humor. The sailors lounging along the wall were still sober enough to enjoy the pervading warmth that rum brought them. Women drifted in, and though some, after an expert glance, left, others stayed to buy a drink or to sit patiently until the liquor should put the men into the proper humor for their services.

Among those who remained was my sister Evalyn. When she saw me she nodded gaily. I felt a surge of pride as I returned her greeting. Even a brother could see that she was prettier than the others. She was young, and so new to her trade that her slightly protuberant black eyes still sparkled as they called their welcome to a man. Knowing that she was doing well I wondered if I could get some money from her. While I was pondering this pleasant possibility a blight fell on the Blowing Whale. The men's talk, vigorous and gusty as a salt breeze, shriveled to a thin whisper; bold eyes turned furtive; roving glances were transformed into stares of sullen indifference. An even greater change was apparent in the women. Terror gripped them, and strangely enough the thing that so affected these men-wise wenches was a man.

He stood motionless in the doorway. He was of medium height, but short legs, a barrel-like chest and broad shoulders made him seem almost squat. His skin was swarthy; his eyes now black and lusterless gave promise of glowing with live hate if he were aroused. His mouth was too small for his broad face, but in compensation nature had bestowed upon him a big nose with wide nostrils and a heavy jutting chin.

Since the day upon which the name Edward Cousin had been muttered as a prelude to the murder of my father, I had learned something of him. It had not been difficult. He was well known in Plymouth.

His grandfather, a Spanish knight, had been made prisoner in 1588 and held by his captor, one Tiviton, a West Country squire, an involuntary though honored and even privileged guest. Awaiting the arrival of his ransom the Señor whiled away the time by taking a prisoner of his own. This captive, who willingly paid tribute, was none other than the squire's lady. So it happened that a few months after his guest's departure, the Englishman, to his indignant dismay, found that his erstwhile prisoner had left more than gold in token of his stay.

Squire Tiviton was a vain man, so rather than acknowledge his cuckoldry he accepted the baby girl as his own. However he avenged his public compliance by private persecution. From infancy the child, christened Margaret, was never permitted to forget the shame of her birth. The erring mother was a poor-spirited creature who, too weak to brave her husband's wrath, attempted to appease it by joining him in persecuting her daughter.

Although Margaret was unable to defend herself, nature avenged her, for year by year she looked more like her Spanish father, until at length the whole countryside was laughing at the discomfited Tiviton. This did not make the girl's lot easier. Consequently, when the chance to escape her tormentors came she seized at it eagerly. Walter Cousin was a lad of good birth and sufficient means, but he was so ugly that all the maids of the county had fled from him and even dissuaded parents from insisting on a match, advantageous as it might be from a worldly standpoint. Cousin, whatever his looks, was kind to Margaret. The only peace that life granted her was during the three years of her marriage.

At the end of that time he died, leaving his widow a comfortable competence and one son, Edward. The child had the dark skin of his mother but the figure and features of his father.

Although well-to-do, Margaret's birth prevented finding another husband; so at length she was forced to return to her parents' house. Here her persecution was resumed. After living long enough to infect her child with the poison distilled from her own bitterness, she died.

By this time Squire Tiviton's humiliation had driven him to lonely morose drinking, while his wife was attempting to find refuge from her shame in religion. To these two the boy Edward was entrusted. Daily his grandmother warned him of his profligate blood and of the corruption and the temptations of the flesh;

daily his grandfather cursed him as the son of a bastard, whose very name stank in the nostrils of respectable people.

Fortune reserved a final blow for Squire Tiviton. Before her lapse from virtue his wife had borne him two fine sons. They had grown to manhood and married, but shortly after Margaret's death both died without heirs. From the day of his last son's burial, Tiviton scarcely drew a sober breath; when he died he left the world drunkenly cursing his wife, her lover, their child and most of all the grandson who was not a grandson, but who was nonetheless the heir to all his property. A few months later his wife followed him to the grave.

Thus Edward Cousin found himself his own master and the possessor of considerable wealth. It was too late. He was already warped beyond redemption. At twenty he was a bitter, cruel man, with his grandmother's sin on his soul, his grandfather's lust in his blood and Squire Tiviton's hatred in his heart. From Spain he inherited vindictive cruelty, from England pious hypocrisy and from both unwarrantable vanity. An Englishman has many virtues and I suppose that even a Spaniard has commendable qualities, but Edward Cousin's heritage was the worst in both races. I admit that he had physical courage, but he was a coward nonetheless. His fear of hell was the obsession of a madman, and he believed that the simplest pleasure was a step thither. Yet he could not resist fleshly sin. He wallowed in it, then attempted to atone for his frailty through merciless punishment of others.

If my portrait of him is wholly black, I can only say that I never found in him a single virtue save that of brute courage, and no gift save a voice that held the listener in black enchantment as harsh Saxon words rolled from his tongue like liquid fire, the music of Spain mingled with English brawn. Such was Edward Cousin as I knew him. Doubtless he was the victim of fate; perhaps he was to be pitied, yet I never pitied him. I believe that I understand the tragedy of Edward Cousin, but for me to understand has never been to forgive.

But I must return to the grog shop. Cousin stood there in the doorway. He was dressed in sober habiliment. Such clothing was not unusual in those days, for since Cromwell had cut off the Old

King's head, and routed the Young King at Worcester, the gentry had hastened to don the dreary garb and the long face of Puritan or Sectarian. But one felt immediately that the dismal garb of this man was fitting cover for a dismal spirit. His small mouth was drawn into a thin line, the wide flaring nostrils twitched, his dark eyes were opaque. He stood impassive until the last whisper died away. Then he spoke.

"Ye serpents, ye generation of vipers! How can ye escape the damnation of Hell?"

He turned to the host of the Blowing Whale.

"Fill their mugs," he ordered, "and bring one to me."

Sullenly the host obeyed. On receiving his mug, Cousin paid not only for his own drink but for all the others. He stared somberly at the mug in his hand before lifting it to his mouth. The host had made the best of a bad business by serving his most expensive rum. It was third run, raw and powerful, such stuff as the sailors loved. Cousin pulled at it long and steadily, before seeming to wrench it from still thirsty lips.

"Oh, God!" he cried, "let these wretches see how Thy servant tastes of pleasure only to renounce it." Throwing the remainder of the liquor on the floor he continued, "Let them witness such strength in Thy bondsman that, weak vessels though they be, they may find courage to follow his example."

His eyes roved over the company. For a moment there was neither movement nor sound in the room; then the nerves of one of the women snapped. With a hysterical cry she threw herself to the floor. Sobbing and writhing she called upon God and Edward Cousin for pity. For the first time I saw the lights burn in Cousin's eyes. But his voice was as cold as his eyes were hot.

"Saith the Lord: I will not pity, nor spare, nor have mercy, but destroy them."

The lights faded as his glance again swept the room. One by one its occupants obeyed the unspoken command. The stout oak flooring was soon wet from the Blowing Whale's finest rum.

There was one rebel. It was my sister Evalyn. She had never heard of Edward Cousin, nor had life yet had time to sap her spirit. And, unfortunately, like most of her sisterhood, poor Evalyn was a somewhat dull-witted creature. Here was a man whose dress, if plain, was still of expensive stuff; clearly he had money. In short, here was a gentleman. Evalyn looked at him and smiled.

"Is it really mine, sir?" she asked archly, as she held up her still full mug. "Did you really buy it for little Evalyn?"

The lights in Cousin's eyes burned again, but he did not reply. A nearby sailor did. If he was full of courage, liquor or pity I do not know, but with an oath he knocked the mug out of her hand.

"Be quiet," he muttered.

Cousin, half turning in the doorway, signaled to someone outside. A half dozen soldiers entered. Cousin waved his arms.

"Jezebels—take them," he said.

One of the soldiers spoke briskly.

"Well, lasses, you heard. Come with us and no trouble."

The poor wenches scarcely hesitated. One by one, like sows summoned to the sticking pen, they arose and filed obediently out the door. Only two showed spirit. One of these—old, ugly and perhaps desperate—muttered unintelligibly, and as she passed Cousin spat. A small fragment of the spittle fouled him. The other mutineer was Evalyn, who, still smiling, sat where she was. The soldier who had spoken approached her.

"You too," he began gruffly. Cousin intervened.

"Leave her," he said sharply.

The soldier looked surprised. Cousin was not accustomed to granting his victims a reprieve.

"She is not repentant," was the toneless explanation. "She will come with me."

Evalyn's smile broadened. The foolish girl believed that here was merely another gentleman with no purpose more sinister than having her in his bed. She had half risen when there was an unforeseen interruption. The sailor who had interfered before jumped up with an oath. Shoving Evalyn back on her bench he turned to Cousin.

"Let her be," he cried.

It was more a plea than a command. Cousin did not answer. Instead he struck. The poor fellow, not entirely sober and still unbalanced from his sudden rise from the bench, fell like a log.

22

Cousin acted deliberately. Aiming carefully he kicked. The sailor was big and accustomed to a rough life below decks, but I have never seen a man who could withstand the agony of such a kick. His knees shot to his chin as if he were a puppet animated by a brutal jerk of the strings. After the first sharp cry of agony he lay there groaning. Finally he relaxed. Again Cousin drew back his foot. With a hoarse sob the fellow scrambled to his knees.

"Take her," he screamed, "take her. But for the love of God, master, not again, not again—" He broke off with an anguished howl as Cousin kicked again.

"He who would thwart the work of the Lord will suffer the tortures of the damned."

Cousin turned to Evalyn.

"Follow me," he ordered.

Docile, but no longer smiling, she arose.

I do not know what it was that forced me to protest. I cared very little for Evalyn, and what I had seen of Cousin inspired me with overwhelming terror, but to see her go away with him was more than I could bear in silence.

"Evalyn!" I cried.

My sister paid no heed but Cousin turned. His eyes fixed themselves on me. My small store of courage ebbed.

"She's my sister, sir," I muttered lamely.

"Is she less impure for that?" he sneered.

Frightened and angry I burst into tears.

"I hate you," I shouted frantically. "May God rot your black soul."

Cousin pointed at me.

"He blasphemes," he said to the soldier. "Take him with the women."

Grasping me roughly the soldier half pushed, half booted me out of the door. Cousin came after us. Evalyn followed obediently in his wake.

2.

I was taken to Plymouth jail. The first days were intolerable. Accustomed as I was to privation I could bear the filth, the over-

23

crowding, the vermin-infested food. But I was desperately afraid of the law.

In the years since, men have told me that the law is just, even benevolent, existing to protect those who respect it. The men who say these things believe them; for them they may even be true, for such men are its masters. But what of the others? What of the wretched boy of twelve who, huddled in a corner of Plymouth jail, sniffled in dismal terror? For I was sure that I would be hanged.

Finally one of the women who had been among those brought from the grog shop found me. It was the crone who had spit at Edward Cousin. Although scarcely better than half witted, Old Jenny, as she was called, gave me what comfort she could. She assured me that neither small boys nor prostitutes were hanged. True, they might be forced to rot in jail for a fortnight, or, if the authorities were in an unusually sanctimonious mood, they might be thrashed, but never hanged. Jenny's cunning in the ways of the law and of the jails was so evident that I took comfort from her.

But no sooner had my fear of the law abated than I was assailed by a new anguish. I was in an agony to be at liberty. The jailers, whose every appearance had at first sent me shrinking into the farthest corner, now seemed angels bearing the keys to freedom. Each time one entered I was hopeful that he came to release me. After about a fortnight one did call my name, ordering me to follow him. Sure that I was to be set free I was overjoyed. Naturally I might be flogged first, but that was a small price to pay for liberty. My optimism was misplaced; I was not released. Instead I was taken before a magistrate.

"Do you know Edward Cousin?" he asked.

At the mention of Cousin's name an unreasoning fear seized me. Once more I saw myself on the gallows. Tremblingly I answered that I did.

"And one Jenny Bush?"

I shook my head. I knew no Jenny Bush.

"He lies," declared the jailer, cuffing me smartly. "He was talking to her just now when I went to fetch him."

24

The magistrate looked at me inquiringly.

"Her, sir?" I said hastily. "Old Jenny? Yes, sir, I know her. I didn't know her name was Bush."

The magistrate accepted my explanation.

"You have been reported as talking to her frequently," he said.

"Yes, sir, I talk to her."

He frowned at a piece of paper that he held in his hand.

"Has this Jenny said ought to you of witches or witchcraft?"

My mouth dropped open.

"Of what?" I gasped.

"You heard me, answer," he growled.

Despite my fear I laughed.

"Lord bless Your Honor, Old Jenny's but half witted. What would she know of such matters?"

"Devil take me if I can say. Ask Edward Cousin," the dignitary exploded irritably. Then he resumed his official manner. "Does she often mutter to herself?"

"That she does."

He grew interested.

"Charms and incantations?"

"No, sir. Just the daft mumbling of a simpleton."

He tacked.

"Was she among those brought by Cousin's orders from the Blowing Whale?"

I answered that she was.

"And did she spit at Cousin?"

"Aye, sir, but—"

"Did any of the spittle go on him?"

"A little," I confessed, "but I am sure that it was not meant in disrespect."

This sounded so foolish, even to me, that I stopped, abashed. The magistrate, a thin smile on his lips, motioned to the jailer.

"Take him away, and bring the woman."

Back in the prison yard the jailer shouted for Jenny. Seeing her as she approached I scuttled to her.

"Jenny," I cried, "don't go! The magistrate—"

She interrupted me with a cackle.

"Wants to see me, does His Honor." She grimaced. "A flogging for Old Jenny, I'll warrant."

We were drawing near the jailer.

"Nay," I shouted desperately, "they'll kill you."

"Fiddlesticks, lad, I tell 'e they don't waste good hemp on such as me, lessit's the knotted end." She giggled. "I know these magistrates. They know us; mayhap they duck or pillory us, but no man ever hanged a wench for just being a whore. God bless your innocence, lad, they need us too much for that."

"But Edward Cousin—" I intervened.

A shadow crossed her face.

"If he's in this I'll no doubt be beat something cruel." She managed a final quavering laugh. "But don't you fret, Tommy. Old Jenny will never hang.

In that she was right.

A number of weeks passed before I was released from jail. As the officials did not disturb me again the fear of the law which had been revived by my visit to the magistrate subsided; and as one long day followed another, even my longing for freedom grew less acute. To the day's usual routine were added the small adventures that an active boy will find wherever he happens to be. The life of a jailbird was becoming tolerable, if not pleasant.

As I look back, only two matters occurring in this period seem worth recounting. These must be recorded even though the memories of one of them still have power to make me hot from shame.

The rigid morals of the Puritans had even reached the jails; consequently an attempt was made to keep the men and women from mingling too freely. For some reason, because I was brought there with them or perhaps because I was so young, I was left with the women at night. Most of the female prisoners were prostitutes who, bored with inactivity, discovered in my innocence an unfailing source of amusement. If I suffered stoically the indignities and familiarities that were thrust upon me, my tormentor of the moment was deluged with contemptuous japes at the expense of her professional skill; if, on the other hand, I gave way to the new sensations that were engulfing me, my futile efforts were greeted

26

with unrestrained merriment, and the slut who had succeeded in debauching me was hailed as a paragon of lechery.

The girls, strong-bodied and weak-minded, as God and their masters had made them, meant no harm. Perhaps no harm was done. This much is certain: as the result of my antics while in jail, it has ever since been impossible for me to regard the so-called rites of love as either mysterious or holy, and the smell of the doxies of Plymouth has remained so fresh in my nostrils that I have never inhaled the perfumed scents of romance without detecting the hot sweating flesh beneath.

But I was not always confined with women only. During the day all the prisoners, male and female, were turned together into the jail yard. One morning we had visitors. One of them was a naval officer, who, because of my experience on the waterfront, I was able to recognize as a ship's lieutenant. With him were half a dozen common seamen. In all probability this meant that some captain, too poor or too brutal to come by a crew honestly, had sent his officer to recruit from the prisons. I could not guess the business of the other stranger. Although he waited patiently until the naval officer was done, a shrewd roving eye indicated that he was interested in the human goods before him. Unafraid, for I knew that I was too young to be impressed, I edged within earshot.

"A mangy lot," grunted the lieutenant discontentedly.

The jailer, who was acting host to our visitors, nodded comfortably.

"Mostly women, too," he ventured, as if proud of the poor quality of his merchandise.

"I can use some of the females," interposed the unknown.

"Trulls," reminded the jailer.

"Men aren't so particular out there. They need women."

Meantime the lieutenant had indicated a score or so of the strongest of the men. These had been herded together by the seaman.

"I'll take these," he said. He turned to the men. "You're for your country's service, my lads; look sharp and you'll find it a fine life."

The hollow joviality of his voice deceived no one. The seamen grimaced; the unfortunate prisoners shuffled dejectedly out, followed by their captors. The jailer turned to his other visitor.

"I hope you can take more, sir; we're cruel overcrowded."

The man shrugged.

"So the magistrate informed me. Let us see first who will go willingly. I prefer them. They make better servants."

Clearing his throat he addressed us.

"I come for volunteers for the New World. Men and women are needed for Virginia plantations. Four, or at most five, years' service for the master who pays your passage is all that is required." His eyes swept the jail yard. "Who will trade freedom and land of his own for this?"

Before he had finished I had made up my mind. Susan, my mother, Edward Cousin, Old Jenny all were forgotten as my fancy swept me to America. Virginia! The very name held magic. I rushed forward.

"I'll go, sir," I cried, even remembering to pull at my forelock in order that he might see what a dutiful servant I would make.

"That's the spirit, lad," he said, smiling down at me. "It's a pity you aren't a few years older."

I tried to protest, but others crowding forward soon shoved me aside. Too downcast to take further interest, I did not learn until evening that some threescore had volunteered, while another half a hundred had been selected and duly sentenced to deportation.

Among those who had gone willingly were all of the girls who had been brought with me from the Blowing Whale. In part, at least, they had gone because of the tales about Old Jenny that were being whispered about the prison. Edward Cousin's name was heard connected with the old woman's, and rumors regarding the fate of those who offended Cousin were revived. To the frightened women who were in prison on his orders, Virginia did not seem too far to go. So of all those who had been taken from the Blowing Whale only myself, Evalyn and Old Jenny remained in England.

A few days after the visitation which resulted in new seamen for the navy and servants for the planters of Virginia, I was released from prison. However, such was my dejection at having missed an opportunity to go to America that I could not savor to the full the joys of liberty. Even the fact that I was not so much as whipped failed to cheer me. I went home, where my mother greeted me as one returned from the grave, where indeed she had concluded I was. For weeks thereafter I moped on the waterfront, watching each sail as it disappeared over the horizon, disconsolately certain that it was going to Virginia.

But if the patient lives, wounds heal. Gradually I resumed my former habits, until one day I even ventured again into the Blowing Whale. At the sight of me the host grunted, but he did not forbid my taking my old place in the corner. Once ensconced it was natural that my thoughts should turn to the last time that I had sat there.

"Have you seen my sister?" I asked the host.

His usually open countenance went blank.

"I know no sister of yours," he muttered.

I knew it was a lie, but failing to heed the storm signals, I continued.

"What of Old Jenny and that devil Edward Cousin?"

The silence that fell on the Blowing Whale reminded me of the time when Cousin himself had stood in the doorway. I glanced in that direction. At that moment my host clipped me.

"Forget Jenny," he growled, "forget your sister, and if you love your life forget Cousin. And don't come back here," he ended as he shoved me into the street.

Startled as I was at this unexpectedly rough treatment, I could not help noting that the host of the Blowing Whale seemed more frightened than angry. It was easy to conclude, and not surprising, that he should fear Cousin; but why was he so concerned over Jenny and Evalyn? Turning the puzzle over in my mind I remembered the blank look and false reply that had followed my question concerning my sister, and recalled the whispered horrors that had swept through Plymouth jail after Jenny had been removed. In the end, as much from curiosity as anything else, I resolved to clear up the mystery.

After a fashion I was to succeed, but before I was done, America and the plantations of Virginia were driven clean out of my mind.

29

My efforts to find out what had happened to my sister Evalyn were for the time being fruitless. The girls on the waterfront came and went without attracting much attention. They were the sailors' women; no one else was interested and even to the seamen themselves one was as good as the next. When, by chance, I did find someone who remembered Evalyn, the bare mention of the fact that she had been last seen with Cousin either closed the informant's mouth or led to uneasy gossip; for Cousin's periodic descents upon the waterfront were well known and as much feared as the plague. If he chose to take a woman away with him wise men forgot her, for few of them returned and dark hints implied that even these few had not been spared. Thus it was gradually borne upon me that it was improbable that I should ever see Evalyn again. At length I abandoned my sister to whatever lot fate or Edward Cousin had assigned her.

My search for Old Jenny proved all too easy, although here too I found people inclined to grow silent and shake their heads, or cross themselves, for Old Jenny was to be tried for witchcraft. Cousin had brought the charge. Remembering my examination before the magistrate I knew that here at least was no idle gossip. I resolved to attend the trial.

At length the day arrived. It was autumn. The vanguard of the Newfoundland fishing fleet had just arrived, so the waterfront was far too busy to concern itself with the trial of a withered old woman who had at best furnished it with occasional sport. Having tried in vain to get company I made my way alone toward the center of town, where the courts of justice were located. The farther I got from the port the faster my heart beat, but I clung to enough courage to keep going. Finally I reached my destination. Once there my fears vanished, for such a crowd was gathered that I knew a lad like me would not attract attention.

Entering the hall where the trial was to be held I squeezed myself into a chair and waited. After what seemed an unbearable length of time Old Jenny was brought in. So far as I could see she had not been mistreated, but it was apparent from the beginning of the trial that her spirit was broken. She was led before the judge, where, after an humble obeisance, she was made to stand or kneel on the hard floor during the whole of the trial.

With suitable pomp and couched in proper language Old Jenny was accused of witchcraft. She denied the charge dully, the denial carrying no conviction. The trial had opened.

The first witness was a countryman named Peter Dingle. He was a stupid lout, the sort of half-wit who occasionally finds his way to the docks, where unconsciously he furnishes sport for the sailors and their trulls. The prosecutor pointed at Old Jenny.

"Do you know that woman?"

"Old Jenny, sir."

"Is that all?"

"Aye, just Old Jenny."

"Tell the Court what you know of her."

"Why, sir, she be the one I'm to say is a witch."

The judge spoke sharply.

"Why were you to say this old woman is a witch?"

"She cozened me, please, Your Honor."

The prosecutor intervened silkily.

"We were about to show that, if the Court will permit."

After hesitating for a moment the judge sank back in his chair. He was frowning thoughtfully. The attorney glared at the witness.

"Tell the Court and jury how you know this woman to be a witch," he ordered.

Dingle grinned foolishly.

"All of it, sir?"

"All of it. Just as you told it to me."

As if these words had jogged his reluctant memory the witness spewed out his tale; and a sordid one it was, though not new to anyone living on the waterfront. Months before, he could not remember the day, Peter Dingle had come to town, where he had fallen in with some sailors. Some time during the course of a wild night Old Jenny had joined them. Half drunk and egged on by his companions, Dingle had offered to take Jenny to bed provided that he pay her only if she satisfied him. She had accepted his offer, but before lying with him had insisted that he drink a hot brew of heady liquor. Having obeyed her they were bedded, where she had scarce taken him into her arms before his money was forfeit.

Someone in the courtroom laughed. The judge ordered silence, but he was smiling himself. He addressed the prosecutor.

"If this be witchcraft, I am afraid the world has long been lost to the devil."

The prosecutor reddened.

"The fellow thinks it was a love potion she gave him," he explained.

The judge grunted. Dingle broke in anxiously.

"Aye, that it was. I be a lusty lad, Your Honor, and it's many a maid's been forced to cry quits of me." He cast a reproachful glance at Jenny. "Bag-o-bones like that could never 'a' done it, sir, 'twaren't for magic."

Peter Dingle was excused. The judge questioned Jenny. She freely admitted the affair, but denied that she had given Dingle a love potion. All he had was a pot of grog. Anyone in her trade knew that drink made men ardent; and, explained Jenny pathetically, a woman grown old and ugly as she needed all the tricks the years had taught her.

The judge appeared to accept her story, remarking with mild humor that though appearances were on the side of the prosecution, the accused's explanation was more in accordance with the known habits of man. The trial proceeded.

Three witnesses were introduced in rapid succession. As they gave their testimony they cast baleful glances at Old Jenny. They swore that after associating with her they became ill. However, it took only a few questions to establish the fact that they were the victims of the pox rather than magic. Jenny admitted having it, but pointed out reasonably that all whores did, and, from what she had heard from various gentlemen, not a few fine ladies. Surely, she pleaded, this did not make them witches. The judge agreed. He instructed the jury to pay no heed to the testimony.

A woman was brought forward. She revived the charge that the accused used love potions. Admitting that she was a prostitute herself, she explained somewhat uncomfortably that Jenny had in

32

times past taken patrons from her. With a malevolent look for her erstwhile rival and a simper for the judge, she submitted that only witchcraft could account for such a phenomenon. The wench was not ill-favored, and had her malice been less evident her testimony might have been damaging. As it was, the jury seemed unimpressed, and when Old Jenny answered in her tired voice that she could not explain men's tastes, but that she supposed they were with women as horses, sometimes leaning toward a young frisky one and at others being better suited by an old mare that knew all the gaits, even the prosecutor laughed.

I breathed more easily. The trial seemed to be going well for Jenny. My relief was premature. The prosecutor was explaining to the Court that owing to negligence, a witness had been released from jail. Fortunately, however, he had been examined; with the consent of the court the jury would hear the evidence of one Thomas Bone.

I was terror-stricken at the mention of my name. I felt that every eye in the courtroom must be fixed on me, every finger pointing at me. I could smell the foul air of Plymouth jail. Gradually, as I realized that no one was noticing me, I again turned my attention to the trial.

A clerk was reading in a sing-song voice. What he read was not far from the truth, but all the same it was unfair. My denials and explanations were omitted. It was made to appear that I had willingly testified that Jenny was in the habit of muttering weird unintelligible phrases, and that I charged her with laying a curse upon Cousin as she spit at him in the doorway of the Blowing Whale.

When the clerk had finished, Old Jenny was recalled. For the first time that day she hurt rather than helped her cause.

"He was just a poor lad in sore trouble, so I helped as much as an old woman could." (The poor thing seemed to believe that her kindness to me would help her.) "And he was that fond of Old Jenny was Tommy," she added proudly.

The tears in my eyes made the room swim dizzily. I wanted to jump up and shriek that it was a lie, that Jenny was no witch, but my knees were as watery as my eyes and my courage weaker than either. The opportunity passed, and though I know that I could have done no good, the memory of my cowardice that afternoon still has the power to throw a shadow across my spirit.

But more damaging testimony was to come. Edward Cousin came forward to give his evidence.

He spoke in a clear, earnest voice. It was impossible to doubt that he believed what he said. He was certain that the woman Jenny Bush was a witch. His account of what took place in the Blowing Whale was accurate in every detail. He told how Old Jenny had cursed and spit at him. He related with obvious sincerity how he felt a malign spirit near when she had cast the evil eye upon him. Finally he swore that a few days later he had suffered excruciating pains in the foot which had been fouled by Jenny's spittle. These pains had spread rapidly throughout the whole leg. Weeks of suffering followed, and it was only after prolonged wrestling with the devil that he had been able to rid himself of the effect of the witch's curse.

It was clear that the jury was moved by the testimony. Here was no jealous rival, half-witted lout or pox-ridden victim, but a gentleman known throughout the countryside for his severe piety. Only the judge seemed dissatisfied.

"Are there witnesses to verify this strange malady and its cure?" he asked.

"My words need no verification," replied Cousin harshly. "God alone is my judge."

"Undoubtedly," agreed the magistrate, "but the jury and myself must judge this woman."

The prosecutor stepped forward.

"We have a witness, if it pleases you," he said.

The new witness came forward. A plain coarse gown hung about her like a sack. Over her head was an ugly hood that half concealed her face. She kept her head bent. Walking slowly she at length reached the bench. The constable ordered her to remove the hood. It must have been a full minute before I recognized her. It was Evalyn. But it was not the Evalyn who had followed Edward Cousin from the Blowing Whale. That Evalyn had been a merry brazen hussy, confident of her ability to give as good as

34

she took, and mulct the man who tumbled her. The woman who stood before the court was a drab broken creature. The large eyes, once bold, were lusterless. The mouth, once so firm and red and impudent, hung loose. The prosecutor began the examination.

"Who are you?" he asked.

"Evalyn Bone, please, sir." Her voice was as beaten and toneless as that of Old Jenny herself.

"Do you know the defendant?"

Evalyn nodded.

"Answer."

"Yes."

"Tell the Court who she is."

"She's a witch, if you please."

Evalyn spoke like an obedient, if somewhat stupid, child. The prosecutor was not satisfied.

"It's the name I want," he barked.

"Her name," Evalyn repeated dully, "her name. Why, it's Old Jenny."

"The rest of it."

Evalyn's eyes filled with tears.

"Please, sir, that's all I know," she whimpered.

The judge intervened.

"You only frighten the girl. We know the woman's name. Permit me to take over."

Turning to Evalyn he spoke kindly.

"Did you hear what Edward Cousin said?"

"Yes, Your Honor."

"Can you substantiate his evidence?"

Evalyn looked at him dumbly. The judge tried again.

"Was what he said true?"

This brought her back to firm ground.

"Indeed, yes." The well-learned lesson was resumed.

She had heard Jenny curse Cousin; had seen her spit. She had even felt the baleful glare of the evil eye. After leaving the Blowing Whale, Cousin had taken her to his home.

"To what purpose?" inquired the judge.

"To cleanse me of sin," Evalyn replied.

35

Someone snickered. Her tale rolled monotonously on. Before many days passed the devil had entered Cousin's foot.

The judge interrupted again.

"How do you know?" he asked.

Evalyn looked puzzled.

"Was there a sore, a rash, a corruption of the flesh?"

She shook her head.

"Then how can you know that he suffered this attack?"

The bawd pitied the ignorance of the magistrate.

"He told me," she said.

With a grunt the judge settled back in his chair and permitted Evalyn to finish without further interruption. I have no doubt that her testimony lacked legal substance, but her evident earnestness carried conviction. She pictured Cousin as a good, if severe, servant of God, who walked in the paths of righteousness and labored over the souls of the damned. On this note the trial ended.

The jury brought in a verdict of guilty. The crowd sighed and was quiet. Jenny was prodded from the floor where she had been crouching and made to stand before the judge. He put on a black hat. His face was impassive, his voice cold. He told her that two weeks from the morrow she would be burned. Jenny collapsed. All in a moment she lay there in a heap before the bench, a pitiful lump of worn rags and scarcely less worn flesh. But at least I thought, in an agony of prophecy, it is still a lump of life, not smoldering ashes whose only warmth comes from a few embers that still feed on seared flesh.

But I had despaired too soon. The judge had done his duty as the law required, but he had not finished. He spoke to the jury.

"You are discharged and the Court thanks you for your zeal in the service of the State," he said mechanically. "And," he added angrily, "you're as addle-pated a crew as ever inflicted itself upon a Court or sent a harmless old woman to the stake." He turned on the prosecutor. "I shall recommend the old woman to the mercy of the Lord Protector."

The lawyer only bowed, but Edward Cousin leaped to his feet.

"Unto Thee, O Lord, belongeth mercy," he shouted, and the malice in his voice made an obscenity of the Holy Writ.

36

"Vengeance is mine; I will repay, saith the Lord," snapped the magistrate.

I do not know if further words were exchanged or not, for at that moment I was caught in the crowd which was surging toward the door, each man trying to be the first to reach the streets with the news that a witch was to be burned. But I did not believe it. I had heard the judge. Surely so great a man could save an old woman. So despite jostling and even occasional cuffs I was happy. I bit my thumb at Edward Cousin.

They burned Old Jenny a fortnight later. All Plymouth must have been there, but I squirmed and wormed my way to the very front. There I stood from morning until mid-afternoon, sweating in fearful anticipation. Yet despite my horror I found the fascination of the crowd infectious. I could hardly wait.

At length the cart rumbled up. Jenny was not a heroine. It took two stout men to drag her screaming, kicking and biting from the cart. She fought with the desperation of the damned. It was of no avail. She was soon tied securely to the stake. Then at last she was quiet and thousands of pairs of avid eyes could feast on the sight of a witch about to be burned. They saw an old woman whose soiled garments hanging in tatters over a gaunt frame revealed as much splotched flesh as they concealed. They caught glimpses of a tear-stained face, twisted in terror, half hidden by an unkempt mass of dirty gray hair. And in all this, many no doubt discerned a witch; I saw only Old Jenny. My knees shook so that I doubted if I could stand.

The public executioner applied the torch. The flames leaped toward her. Jenny strained at her ropes as she let out scream after scream. For my part I sagged to the ground, puking and sobbing at the same time. When I looked again Jenny hung loose in her bonds. She had fainted. I have always tried to believe that she never regained her senses, but I cannot be sure; for although she did not utter another sound the old body twisted and writhed when the flames reached it.

Once the fire was kindled it did not take long. Soon I was dragging myself away, sobbing softly, remembering that Old Jenny had been kind to me. I turned for one last look. Close to the still fitfully burning pyre stood Edward Cousin. Panic-stricken I fled, nor tired as I was did I stop until I arrived at the waterfront.

4.

Christmas Eve. Outside a raw west wind roared, but at the Red Indian Tavern men were warm with rum and good will. I was one of them. True, for a moment I was troubled by a breath from the grave as I remembered that other Christmas Eve when my father was killed, but that seemed long ago. My sense of well-being was scarcely ruffled.

Christmas Eve and the life of a waif on the waterfront was good. A drunken sailor gave me a whole shilling. It was more money than I had ever had at one time. I resolved to have a tot of rum. As befitted the station of a boy with no money I had been crouching in the corner farthest from the fire. Straightening up I swaggered to a bench. Spinning my coin on the table as I had seen the seamen do, I called for a drink. Alas for my dignity, my voice betrayed me as I emitted only a self-conscious squeak. A nearby sailor laughed. This stirred me to greater efforts.

"Have something with me, mate?" I challenged.

I spun the coin again.

The fellow grinned.

"Thanks, lad," he said; then he bellowed with the voice of a bull.

"Two glasses of rum for me and my mate, and mind they're strong for we be two thirsty men."

When the liquor came he would not let me use my shilling, paying from his own pocket.

I took a swallow and straightway fell to coughing and gasping. My new friend chuckled.

"It warms a man's guts."

He tossed off his drink as if it had been nothing more potent than small beer. I looked at him in awe.

"Drink," he bellowed.

38

Holding my breath I downed what was left. Once down the stuff felt warm. A pleasant glow stole over me.

"Two more of rum," I called as loudly as I could, "and mind they're strong, for we be two thirsty men."

When they arrived my friend once more settled the score, brushing aside my feeble protests with one of his gusty laughs.

"And now, my young bully," he cried, "two such men as we need women, and devil take me if two likely queans haven't just come in."

My heart sank. My experience in jail had made me shy of women, though at times I did find myself looking at one with a heady self-consciousness that I had never felt before my arrest. Before I could protest my companion, having gulped down his second rum, got up. Signaling to the wenches who were behind me, he clapped me on the shoulder.

"I'll leave you the skinny one, mate. See that you treat the trollop well."

With that he was gone. I wanted to run, but lacking the courage to do so I spoke as brusquely as I could.

"Well, what's keeping ye, wench, get around where a man can see you."

Someone snickered. I heard shuffling footsteps behind me and realized with mingled satisfaction and fear that the girl was obeying me. An instant later she had, after the fashion of her kind, dropped into my lap. A skinny arm encircled my neck; a listless voice repeated a threadbare formula.

"Lor', my heart, you're the impatient one. A girl—" I felt the arm about my neck tighten convulsively. The voice almost came back to life. "Tommy!" it gasped.

I wrenched my eyes from the floor. The girl in my lap was my sister. For a moment we stared at one another as she sat there, her arm still around me, her soft insinuating body pressing against me.

"Get up," I finally managed to mumble.

Lifelessly, as she had done everything else, she obeyed. She laughed tonelessly as she sank down again, this time beside me.

"You're after the girls young. You'll burn in Hell for it."

39

The rum I had drunk was taking hold of me. I found it hard to concentrate. Talk of burning made me remember Old Jenny.

"Why did you do it?" I cried.

"Do what?"

"Talk in court like you did."

She nodded sagely.

"I helped burn the old witch. He said it might help save my soul."

"Who said it?"

Her tone was reverent.

"Master Cousin."

I forgot Jenny and remembered the rumors I had heard of Cousin.

"What did he do to you?" I asked eagerly.

"Master Cousin—" She was looking far away. If a rabbit that has gazed into the eyes of a snake should survive that awful fascination, it must thereafter be a haunted beast. I had a half-drunken idea of Evalyn as such a rabbit. She began to talk, but it was to herself rather than to me.

"I had pretty clothes, silks and laces. I sat at the foot of his table and had a little country wench who waited on me and called me mistress. For near a month we lived like that, me sharing his house and living like a lady. Only I didn't share his bed. At first I thought that was why he took me there; but he explained that. He said that if I was truly saved that before God I was his bride, but if I let myself go back to my old ways I was only fit to be the whore that he had rescued from the Blowing Whale."

She sighed and was quiet a moment before continuing.

"It was like that for almost a month. Then he went away for a few days. When he came back he was drunk, but not too drunk to talk. He talked beautiful. I've never heard men say things like he did—about love and the pleasure there is in the bodies of women. After a little while he took me to bed."

She stopped again, looking vacantly into space. I've seen the blacks from Africa look that way. Once one of them told me that he was smelling the jungle. I waited. Presently Evalyn went on.

"He kept me there for a long time, two or three days maybe;

40

I don't know. Anyway we slept sometimes, at others he would leave and come back with food and more drink."

Her eyes swept the room. Her tired voice took on a tinge of contempt.

"What do these sailors know? He was right about the pleasure that's in a woman's body." She sighed. Into her eyes had come the bewilderment of a hurt child. "I guess I gave him all the pleasure there was in mine. There's been none since. But I don't understand. I thought it was like he had promised. I had been a good girl and now there in that room it was like being his bride, for three or four days maybe it was like being his bride. Then he went to sleep again, and when he woke up he was different. He said I'd done wrong and that he had warned me against going back to my old ways. But how could I? I hadn't been out of the house while he was gone. There wasn't anyone but him. And with him it was like being his bride. He had said so himself. But he was different now. He said I was wicked and had made him wicked; that I could not be saved and that only chastisement of the flesh remained. I didn't know at first what he meant."

She shivered.

"What did he mean?" I urged.

"Whipping, I guess. Anyway, he took my pretty clothes and tore them up in front of me; he made me put on this instead."

She pointed to the shapeless ugly dress she was wearing. I remembered it. It was the same one she had worn at the trial. "He locked me in a closet off his room. I don't know how long I was there. For a long time I think. Sometimes the little serving girl brought me water and a little bread, but she was afraid to talk to me. She would unlock the door, put the stuff down and leave. But once every day he came to preach to me." There was stark terror in Evalyn's face as she leaned toward me. "He talked about Hell, Tommy. He told me how women like me will be treated in Hell; and I'm going there. I can't stand it. I'm afraid, Tommy, oh, God, I'm afraid!"

Her voice rose to a shrill shriek. Frightened, I pushed what remained of my rum toward her. She drank it eagerly. It seemed to steady her.

"Go on," I urged.

"After he was through talking he whipped me. He used the cat on me every day. Sometimes I thought he would kill me, it hurt so. But I don't think he knew how bad it was. He seemed so excited after he started to whip me. After he got tired and I'd put on my clothes again he would be calmer. He told me that he treated me that way so maybe they wouldn't hurt me quite so much in Hell."

The look of terror came back.

"But it couldn't be much worse in Hell. God! It couldn't."

"When did he let you go?" I asked hastily.

"He let me out of the closet to go to Old Jenny's trial. After that he let me alone, until one day he said that Jenny had been burned and that I'd have to leave. I begged him to let me stay as a servant but he wouldn't. Then I asked him if he could find me honest work in someone else's house. You see I knew if I couldn't get work I'd have to come back here, and all the whipping and preaching would have been for nothing. I explained it to him as well as I could, but I suppose he didn't understand. He said he couldn't put men's souls in peril by sending them anyone as bad as me."

That was Evalyn's story. No doubt a cleverer woman might have found an honest way to live, and a stronger one would have held out longer. But Evalyn was neither clever nor strong; so it was not long before hunger had driven her back to her old profession.

But Cousin's withering blasts had robbed her of the gift of giving herself in pleasure. Men's eager prodding fingers became the devil's pitchfork; hot flashes of love seemed the searing fires of Hell. Sailors are not particular, but they demand a merry wench, so they soon learned to avoid Evalyn; thus she found that whatever virtue she had won was forfeited for lean crusts, and few of these.

We sat for a while after Evalyn had finished. For the first time in my life I was drunk. At length I struggled to my feet.

"Well, my wench, a man likes something roguish abed with

him," I declared owlishly, "so if ye'd please us you'll needs forget Cousin and show some spirit.

With this bit of wisdom, gleaned from the bottom of a tot of rum, I tossed my sister the shilling which I had been unable to spend. Whether it was the sage advice or the silver I do not know, but for a second the old merry twinkle flashed in Evalyn's eyes and a smile played at the corners of her mouth. But light and smile died borning; my last glimpse of her before staggering into the streets was of a dreary drab, listless and worn.

I saw Evalyn once after that. It was early spring. I was sauntering along the dock feeling the blood rise in me as sap rises in the trees. On that morning all the troubles of the winter seemed to have gone with its icy winds; for the first time in months I conjured up dreams of adventure in America. I was so immersed in my own thoughts that, failing to watch where I was going, I bumped into a boy who stood on the edge of a small crowd.

"What is it?" I asked after collecting my scattered wits.

"I saw it myself," the lad babbled. "Threw herself right off the wharf. I yelled loud as ever I could, but she was dead when they pulled her out."

At this moment a constable shouldered his way through the crowd. In his arms he held a body. A coarse heavy dress, no longer loose like a sack, was molded against a figure that was scarce a woman's yet. The heavy hair hung loose, and though it was wet the sea breeze stirred it lazily, giving a fleeting impression that something of life yet remained. But the sea had not washed out the pinched hunger of the face, nor had death erased the look of fear that lingers upon the mouth and in the eyes of a devil-haunted soul.

"Who is it?" someone called.

The constable's reply was in the querulous tone that men use when they have been unreasonably disturbed.

"Just another whore drowned herself," he shouted back.

It was Evalyn's epitaph.

She was not quite seventeen.

# III

## I.

It was the spring of 1659 when Evalyn drowned herself. Oliver Cromwell had been dead for six months and England was beginning to emerge from the Puritan straitjacket which she had worn for nearly twenty years. By summer men laughed again and dared jape at virtue as they gulped strong drink. Fighting cocks, dancing bears, strolling players reappeared on the village green; the market place heard song more frequently than prayer, and round oaths were mingled with bawdy tales; somber garb gave way to peacock feathers; gentlemen let their hair grow and flaunted their mistresses in public; even the priests began to crawl out of the priest holes. Edward Cousin disappeared, and I fell in love.

It was rumored that Cousin had fled the vengeance of certain cavalier gentlemen whom he had helped to ruin; again that he had gone into voluntary exile rather than live in the newly burgeoning England. But if the rumors were true or not no one knew, nor on the waterfront did anyone greatly care. He was gone. That was enough.

In my own case relief at Cousin's departure was tempered by regret; for I had heard that as soon as the Young King came back from over the water, every city gate and every village commons in England would be garnished with the heads of those who murdered his father, and I had fancied myself hurling insults at my enemy's grinning skull. Then softer sentiments claimed me.

Early in the summer I fell ill. For weeks I lay on a pile of rags, wasting with fever. My mother did her best for me, but was unable to give the care or the nourishment that my condition required. In my sickness I longed for Susan. Although she had sent us messages and small sums of money, we had seen little of her for over a year. Day after day I fretted over her absence. At last she came. As she stood before me, her eyes misted with tears, her mouth trembling encouragement, I did not believe it was really Susan. I thought it was a fantasy born of my desire and fever. When her cool hands convinced me of her reality joy surged through my aching body. I was no longer afraid that I was going to die. Then relief gave way to peevishness.

"Why didn't you come sooner?" I demanded.

"I didn't know you were sick."

"You should have known."

She tried to soothe me, but I persisted in my charges of neglect. Susan was incapable alike of either long resistance or subtlety.

"He doesn't want me to come here," she confessed.

"Master John?"

She nodded.

"Do you have to do whatever he says?"

"Why, Tommy, you know I'm his servant."

In the past year I had learned a great deal.

"What are you besides his servant?" I sneered.

Susan's cheeks reddened, but her candid blue eyes were clear.

"Shame on you, Tommy, I'm only his chambermaid."

"I saw him buss you."

"The master's young," she said indulgently; "young gentlemen are bound to kiss a wench once in a while, if she's underfoot."

My fretfulness was wearing off. I was too tired and too thankful that Susan had come to me at all to argue further. I shut my eyes.

"Don't go," I begged.

I must have fallen asleep almost immediately. When I awoke it was dusk. Susan was on the floor beside me, holding my hand. Too exhausted to move or even to speak I lay quiet. Presently, unaware that I was awake, Susan spoke to my mother.

"I must go."

"Aye."

Susan was troubled.

"I'll come back if I can."

45

"Aye."

"But he'll be angry when he finds out that I've come even once. He's afraid of poor people's sicknesses."

My mother spoke in the flat voice of one broken alike to hopelessness and heartlessness.

"Tommy'll die soon," she said.

The hand holding mine tightened convulsively.

"No," Susan protested, "he's not that bad."

"He's too bad to starve."

"Starve!"

"Aye, Kate did. It's not with us like it is at the squire's house."

For what seemed to me a long time there was silence. I was too tired to speak or even to care much, but I felt that my life hung in the balance. Susan let go of my hand, and I seemed to smell the grave's mold; she spoke fiercely and death receded.

"I'll come back," she said. "I won't let Tommy die."

She kept her promise. She came back with a cart and a husky boy. They took me to Denham, the home of Master John himself, or to call him properly, Squire John Denham. There I was installed in a snug room that was blessed with sunshine, fresh air and a clean bed.

Susan, having performed the miracle of fetching me from Plymouth mews to Denham, was seemingly content to rest on her achievement. True, at first not a day passed without my seeing her; but her visits were generally hasty; a cheerful word, a pat of the pillow, a light kiss and she was gone. If she did stay longer she grew uneasy, afraid of the squire's displeasure. For a time I fretted over this; but I soon ceased to care how long Susan stayed or if she came at all; for Polly Bragg was appointed my nurse.

Polly's new rôle was not of her own seeking but because the squire did not want Susan near me. As a consequence, when she first appeared at my bedside she was sullen. But the mood soon passed. Indeed it was impossible for her to sulk for long if a man was nearby, even one such as I then was; for it was her nature to engage men in combat—love or hate, it made little difference, and in fact with her the two were not always far apart. So within a week or two after her first appearance in my room Polly and I were embarked upon the love that was to steer its troubled and at times fantastic course through so many years.

In its beginnings, our feeling for one another was neither one of passion nor romance. In fact our emotions were most roused when we quarreled. We were hardly more than children and if I had been well we might have romped together in the fields or stables; but bedridden as I was we were denied this normal outlet for the restlessness that the first faint stirrings of desire were arousing in us.

Thus most of our quarrels were trivial, the squabbles of children who had nothing better to do; but one starting no more ominously than many others had a bitter end for me.

### 2.

As I have already observed, after Polly took charge of me my interest in Susan waned. Nonetheless, I was not too blind to see that my sister acted strangely. For one thing she came to see me less and less frequently; for another, when she did come she was generally accompanied by one or the other of the servants, whose manner towards her was a mixture of resentment and respect. Only Polly had no fear of her. She disliked Susan and despite the fact that the latter was invariably gentle with her, as indeed she was with everyone, she took no pains to conceal it. It was this hostility that led to the scene that opened my eyes not only to Susan's shame, which I already more than half suspected, but also to Polly's ruthlessness.

Polly was sitting on the foot of my bed, railing at me because I failed to gain strength more rapidly, when Susan, accompanied by Jane Bragg, came into the room. Jane was carrying a dish of early strawberries sprinkled sparsely with real sugar. Susan took the dish and brought it to me. She spoke eagerly.

"See, Tommy, I got you real sugar. It came all the way from some place called Barbadoes."

Barbadoes! The treasure trove of the west. I thought of the dry Tortugas and pirate gold.

"Are you sure it was Barbadoes?" I asked anxiously.

She was so proud of her delicacy that she forgot caution.

"John told me so himself," she said, and added proudly, "John and I eat sugar every day."

Polly pounced instantly.

"See, Mamma, how silly you were to make me promise not to tell Tommy about her! She's proud of being the squire's doxy."

I had just snatched the dish of strawberries from Susan's hands, but at Polly's words I lost interest in them, and even their precious cargo of sugar from Barbadoes. Vaguely conscious of a disaster I could not altogether define, I looked uncomfortably from a stricken Susan to a frightened but sullenly defiant Polly.

Jane Bragg recovered first. Doting mother that she was, and half afraid of her daughter to boot, she berated her shrilly.

"For shame, to talk of Miss Susan so, good as she's been to you too." Then she betrayed the cause of her unusual vigor. "And don't forget that instead of being like an angel itself to you she might have you thrown out and me along with you. Now tell Miss Susan you're sorry, and I hope, knowing as she does that you're a fool, she'll forgive you."

Jane looked expectantly at her daughter, but Polly, her mouth fixed firmly, shook her head.

"I'm not sorry," she muttered rebelliously.

As Jane lifted her hand to strike Polly, Susan intervened.

"Leave her be," she said, her voice trembling.

"But I won't have her talking so," protested Jane.

Susan threw out her hands helplessly.

"Why not?" Her scant self-control gave way. "It's true, and I'm not ashamed either. I love him, I love him."

With that half truth, for she did love him, she stumbled out of the room. Jane Bragg followed her, but not until she had delivered a final admonition.

"God help you and me both if she tells the squire how you talked," she cried.

"Pooh!" retorted Polly contemptuously, "Susan's too soft to tell."

During the whole of the stormy scene Polly had not moved

48

from the foot of my bed. Now, her mother gone, she sat there, sullen eyes staring boldly into mine, daring me to come to my sister's defense. But I was too stunned to answer their challenge. No doubt I was even stupider than need be. I should have known well enough why a young squire picks a fisherman's daughter as his chambermaid. And in a sense I had known, but to know and to admit knowledge are two different things, and this was my sister and more mother than sister. My mind was adjusting itself slowly. Finding that I was not going to blame her Polly relaxed. She was even magnanimous.

"Maybe I oughtn't have said it," she admitted.

"Maybe not."

"Well, I did though." She slid off the bed. "Give me some strawberries."

"How do you know?" I demanded.

"I never tasted sugar."

"How do you know—about Susan?"

Polly tossed her head impatiently.

"Everyone but you does. Ever since she came we've all thought so, but until lately we couldn't be sure. Now, though, the squire's no more than in the house when he sends for her."

"I don't believe it," I declared.

Polly was amiable.

"Then don't fool." She kissed me playfully. "Now let's eat strawberries."

My protest had been but a gesture. I knew the thing was true. Susan was the squire's fancy woman. For a fleeting second I saw Evalyn, bedraggled and limp, in the arms of the bailiff, her hair moving gently in the wind. I shuddered at the memory, but this was even worse. I had never loved Evalyn, never really cared what she did with her body. I had even taken pride in her success as a bawd, and in petty ways had profited from it. But Susan was different. I shoved Polly away. More from surprise than anything else she fell back.

"Get me Susan," I demanded.

She laughed wickedly.

"I daren't. She might be with her John."

My nerves snapped.

"Damn you," I screamed. With all the strength I could summon I threw the dish—strawberries, precious sugar and all—at her. It missed her but hit a table nearby. The saucer broke. A fragment of flying china cut Polly's cheek. It was not deep but it drew blood. Polly laughed.

"You're mad," she purred, as she leaned over me, "because your sister's the squire's mis'."

Blood was dripping on the bed linen. Paying no heed Polly clambered up beside me. As she talked she ate the berries which were strewn over the bed.

"I don't see why you're mad," she said.

"She's not your sister," I retorted sullenly.

"If she was I'd tell her a few things. Why, she's as sweet as this sugar and hasn't any more sense than you have. Lets herself be stuck in the country, still wearing servant's clothes and except when he's with her still doing servant's work. He won't treat me that way."

This took time for me to understand; when I did I was incredulous.

"You," I scoffed. "Who'd want you?"

"The squire, when I'm a little older." She said it as indifferently as if she were talking about next day's breakfast. "Only I won't be as easy as Susan. I'll have more than strawberries, I can tell you. He'll buy me new dresses and sugar plums every day before he so much as kisses me."

The thought of the squire kissing Polly revived my anger, which had temporarily given way to astonishment.

"He'd better not kiss you," I declared fiercely.

Polly's eyes were wide.

"Why not?" she asked.

"Because you're going to marry me."

I was surprised to hear myself say such a thing. Not so Polly.

"When I'm ready I'll marry you," she agreed.

"Then stay away from the squire."

We were off on another quarrel. By evening I was exhausted. I hated the young squire, hated Susan who had given herself to

50

him, and if I loved or hated Polly Bragg I didn't know. That night I dreamed that I was chasing Susan, Polly and the squire over acres and acres of strawberries big as gourds. Near-by was a mountain of West Indian sugar; my mouth watered for it but I could not stop long enough for even the smallest taste. My limbs grew heavier and heavier; finally I dropped exhausted. Then they turned on me. Sitting in a row on my chest those three dangled the berries above me, but if I tried to take one they popped it into their own mouths. Tiring of this sport they turned to love-making. The squire kissed one girl then the other. I struggled to get up but their weight was too much for me. With a terrific effort I finally roused myself from my nightmare. I was wringing wet from perspiration. A cool hand was on my forehead. Susan was murmuring soothingly.

"There, Tommy, don't fret. It's all right."

"Get away," I shrieked, "get back to him, where you came from."

"Please, Tommy, you mustn't get so excited. You're sick."

With an effort I sat up. Susan was leaning over me. I hit her as hard as I could. Delirium made me strong. With a little moan she slipped to the floor. The last thing I remembered was looking at her still body and laughing. She had hastened to me from her bed, but she was not in her petticoat, as an honest wench would have been; instead she wore a nightgown. I had heard of such things in jail. Some of the women there had boasted of having them and it was said that ladies wore them but Susan was not a lady.

That was the beginning of my relapse. For weeks only thirteen-year-old Polly Bragg's determination that death itself should not take from her what she had marked for her own kept me alive. In the end she won. As the summer faded my strength returned. By fall I could sit up.

On the surface things seemed as before my second illness, but in reality this was not true. Since my childhood Susan had been the source of all those things that men, if they be infants or patriarchs, require of women: admiration, care, encouragement, affection; now, I found that though I still cherished Susan, Polly

51

had supplanted her as the axis around which my life rotated. Thus I had passed another of life's milestones; and, as if sensing this, there was a new constraint in Susan's attitude toward me when she came for an occasional visit, and a surer air of proprietorship about Polly.

During my second convalescence I learned to read. Like so many things of profound importance this was accidental. I was propped up in bed. Susan had just looked in. She had stood in the doorway for a moment and spoken but a brief, shy word of encouragement; but even this had been enough to send Polly away from my bedside to the window, where she stood looking sulkily out. After Susan was gone she remained in a bad humor. I tried to rally her but it was in vain. At length I found out the reason.

"Did you see her dress?" Polly demanded indignantly.

I shook my head. How should I know what Susan wore? Had she appeared before me naked I suppose I would have been startled, but otherwise Susan was merely my sister who undoubtedly wore clothes as other women did.

"A new dress," stormed Polly, her eyes filled with tears of vexation, "and not of stuff like servants wear, but real silk. It ought to be mine. It was so pretty."

I had become resigned to Polly's resolution to supplant Susan in the squire's affections. This had been the easier because I was sure that she could not do it. So now I laughed.

"Squire will buy you a bib and tucker," I teased.

Polly glared at me for a moment; then, with one of her sudden changes of mood, she laughed wickedly.

"When I was a child I spoke as a child, I understood as a child; but when I became a man I put aside childish things."

She was only teasing but she spoke with an intensity that sobered me.

"What's that?" I asked.

"The Scripture, stupid," she replied airily.

"What do you know of the Scripture?"

"Lots."

She turned from the window, then in a rapid sing-song voice

deluged me with verse after verse from the Bible. I can recall but little of it, nor does it matter. Only at the end she dropped her teasing, or seemed to. Darting to my bed she took my hand and with her voice charged with new meaning spoke softly, her tongue caressing each word.

*"Let him kiss me with the kisses of his mouth: for thy love is better than wine.*

*Because of the savor of thy good ointments thy name is as ointment poured forth, therefore do the virgins love thee."*

Without pausing, without, I am sure, knowing all that it meant, yet sensing its full-blooded ardor, Polly finished the Song of Songs:

*"Make haste, my beloved, and be thou like to a roe or to a young hart upon the mountains of spices."*

When the last line ceased to pulse through my brain I was dumb. I had never been so moved by words; and I had never wanted Polly in quite the warm disquieting way that I wanted her at that moment.

"Where," I finally managed to gasp, "did you learn that?"

"I read it in the Bible."

Wonder was piling upon wonder.

"You read?"

"Yes, I learned how ever so long ago."

"But why?"

Even Polly could be smug.

"The old squire taught me himself, before he died. Mamma begged him to. She said I was to be a lady."

Polly reading! Polly a lady! Like the women of the gentry.

"Why would the old squire bother to teach you to read?" I asked doubtfully.

Polly shook her head.

"He always liked me. Once, I remember, he said that the damned Puritans couldn't let a man do ought to a wench that God had made her for, so he might as well teach me to read."

I was jealous that Polly could do what I could not; and vaguely uneasy at the thought that she could enter a world that remained locked to me. It crossed my mind that the young squire could read.

"Teach me," I demanded.

At first she demurred. The truth is, that although proud of her learning, Polly was never fond of books. I doubt if as a woman she ever opened one except at my behest. However, after much pleading on my part she consented to be my teacher. That very afternoon she fetched a large Bible. Polly was methodical. She opened the book at the first page. Laboriously she spelled out for me the first words.

*"In the beginning God created the heaven and the earth."*

And thus, like God himself, Polly Bragg created a new world.

By All Saints' Day I was well and needed only to regain my strength. I began to walk around the room a little; soon I was able to go out doors. In the stables I struck up a friendship with the head groom. One day when I was talking to him Jane Bragg came to me.

"Your sister wants to talk to you," she said.

I was glad to hear this. Improved health had brought with it a kindlier temper. Moreover, as I grew used to the idea of Susan's position I became more or less reconciled. After all, the squire was of the gentry. They used all of us as they saw fit. Susan's lot was far happier than Evalyn's had been, or for that matter than that of my overworked mother, who was, so far as I knew, a woman of strict virtue. So though I still resented my sister's whoredom I accepted and grew used to it.

"Where is she?" I asked.

Jane Bragg had been dispatched on a diplomatic mission. She was not to be balked of her negotiations by too easy a triumph.

"She's afraid you won't see her."

This evidence of Susan's gentle timidity tempered my pleasure.

"She can come to my room when she pleases," I said stiffly.

"She's afraid of Polly."

I knew that this was true, but hearing it said merely irritated me further.

"Why should the master's mis' be afraid of a thirteen-year-old servant girl?" I sneered.

Polly's mother's gesture was one of bewilderment rather than pride.

"Everyone's afraid of Polly," she said with conviction.

"I'm not."

Jane looked at me.

"I'm thinking you'd better be—most of all," she said grimly. "Come now, quit acting the fool. I'll take you to your sister."

Susan was waiting in a small sitting room. After the first greetings we were silent. I was embarrassed, while Susan apparently found it difficult to say whatever it was that she had summoned me to hear. At length she broke the awkward silence.

"I hope you don't think too bad of me, Tommy."

"No matter what I think," I muttered.

Susan was too honest and too simple to permit false pride to stand in the way of an understanding.

"I did it for you, Tommy," she pleaded.

"No," I declared roughly; "if you wish to be the squire's woman it's no affair of mine, but don't go laying the blame on me."

"It's true, Tommy, before God."

"I saw him hugging you in the woods a long time ago."

Susan pondered this before replying. When she did answer she talked to herself as much as to me.

"Yes, I saw him first years ago. For a long time we met in a little clearing in the wood. That was the happiest time for me, and for a while it was enough for him. But then he wanted me to lie with him. I wouldn't do it. It wasn't that I didn't want to, but somehow I couldn't. We used to quarrel something fierce over it, but I held myself against him, and no matter how angry he was when he left me, he always sent word that I was to meet him again."

"Why did you consent?" I demanded. "You knew what it was he wanted."

"I love him. Maybe you will understand that some day. Then after Father was dead he brought me here as his servant. It was harder then, but I still didn't give in."

She paused and sighed. But if the sigh was of regret for her lost maidenhood, or of contentment with the joys of surrender, I could not for the life of me tell.

"Then you got sick. Mother said you'd die if you stayed in Plymouth, so I asked John to let me bring you here. He wouldn't let me at first, he's so scared of sick folk. But when I told him that he could have me if he would save you from dying he gave in."

"You shouldn't have done it," I declared uneasily; "I'd rather have died."

I knew this was a lie, but false as the words were they touched Susan. Tears came into her eyes as she attempted to speak gaily.

"Pooh, Tommy, you mustn't say such things. I was but a silly frightened girl and now I'm glad. I love John and I'm happy in being his. Only I don't want that you should hold it against me."

I surrendered, but not graciously.

"All right. It's naught to me and it would have happened anyway."

It was enough for Susan. With a glad cry she threw herself on me. In a second we were blubbering in each other's arms. When we were calm again Susan spoke with more assurance.

"I knew you'd understand," she cried. "Now I can tell him you'll do it?"

"What?"

"Why, John will let you stay here. Not in the house, of course, but in the stables. The groom has told him that you are a likely lad and he needs a boy."

At first I would not consent, but Susan overwhelmed me. She reminded me that at Denham there was no hunger, nor would I have to seek shelter from wintery winds in a miserable hovel in Plymouth mews. Nor did she fail to point out slyly that Polly Bragg would be sorely disappointed if I left.

I consented to accept the squire's offer.

The next day I began my career as a stableboy. I moved from the manor house to the stables, where I lived in a cubby-hole above the harness room. I learned to care for the horses, and during the harvest I gave a hand in the fields. It was not a hard existence, nor did I dislike it, but the hatred that had flourished in my breast until it was far too vigorous to wither under the first smile that a gentleman deigned to cast upon me, and my determination to go to the New World were more than enough to prevent my accepting it as my final lot in life. To be a groom at Denham was well enough for the winter months when few ships sailed, but spring would come and I would go to Plymouth and from there find my way to America.

Despite such heroic resolutions I stayed at Denham for more than five years.

# IV

THE FIRST year passed, a quiet one at Denham. But the winds of chance were blowing strange things to England's shores, and perhaps the strangest of these was the Young King who "came home" in May of 1660.

To a stableboy buried in the country it might seem of little importance whether his sovereign wore his hair in long curls and swore "odd's fish," or clipped his head and intoned Scripture through his nose, but nonetheless, when Charles II landed at Dover Beach piping a new tune, such creatures as Tom Bone, his sister Susan, and Polly Bragg trod new measures.

For although at first it was so gradual that I was not aware of it, Denham changed with the times. Squire John, our master, was not without virtue, but he was weak and shallow with no ambition greater than that of following the fashion of the moment. So Susan, whose gentleness and devotion to her lover made her his slave, became a human weathercock, her estate indicating which way the wind blew with the English gentry. When she first went to Denham Cromwell was alive. In those days the squire was a sober young man who attended church, lived frugally, drank sparingly and swore not at all. If he had designs on his chambermaid his attempts to put them into execution were furtive, and when Susan resisted, his fears of exposure were doubtlessly a greater protection to her virtue than her own gentle remonstrances.

Then Cromwell died. Squire John bought a wig (a modest one to be sure, for it was not yet quite certain which way England would finally turn), swore upon occasion, grew tipsy now and

58

then, openly flaunted Susan (who, thanks to my illness he now possessed) before the servants, and I have no doubt boasted of what a devil of a fellow he was before other blades of his acquaintance.

Charles landed in England. He brought with him foreign ways, foreign oaths, foreign women. The squire's wigs grew more numerous, their tresses were longer and more elaborately curled; his oaths grew rounder, more full-bodied. Occasionally he was heard to utter "odd's fish." Susan must now play the part of mistress to a man of fashion. She was no longer permitted to make even a pretense of serving. Instead, decked out in the gowns and furbelows of a lady, she was installed in apartments of her own. There she sat, idle, lonely and none too happy, awaiting her lover's pleasure.

She was given her own servant, too. Polly was appointed her maid. Greatly entertained by this twist of fortune I teased Polly, but if she was chagrined she did not show it. She even joined in my laughter at her own expense, swore that her mistress was kind and proudly exhibited the ribbons, laces and old clothes that Susan gave her.

I, myself, seldom saw my sister. Occasionally she came to the stables, but the squire did not like this nor did I. There was a constraint between us. Susan still feared my disapproval, while I, despite angry self-assurances to the contrary, felt a little in awe of this elegantly dressed girl who called my master "John," and had made of Polly Bragg a demure handmaiden.

The pendulum swung further. From Whitehall sensuous tides flowed stronger. All over England country gentlemen were lodging their mistresses in town, ostentatiously exhibiting them at every opportunity. Our squire was not to be left behind; Susan must go to Plymouth to live in fashion. There, fittingly bedizened, she could be exhibited before a larger and more admiring audience than the manor afforded.

And indeed at this time Susan was a creature of whom her master could well be proud. Just turned twenty, her small well-proportioned body was fully developed. Her mouth was generous, her blue eyes serene, and they dwelt on her lover so tenderly that the squire could rest assured that every witness would know how completely he possessed this luscious morsel of womanhood.

Susan did not want to go to town, but she had no choice. She came to the stables to tell me good-by.

"Maybe John will bring me here sometimes," she said wistfully, "or maybe you'll come to see me in town."

"Might," I answered ungraciously, "but I'm thinking of leaving myself."

"Don't, Tommy," she begged. "It's a good place you've got. And," she added, "Polly will be so lonesome if you and Jane are both gone."

That Jane Bragg was going was news to me.

"What's she leaving for?" I asked.

"She's to go with me."

"Then you aren't taking Polly?"

Susan blushed at her own magnificence.

"John says Polly is too little. I'm to have Jane as my housekeeper and another girl or two from town."

"You're getting too big for your boots," I grunted. But my thoughts were not on what I said. If Polly was to remain at Denham perhaps my half-formed plans to leave were hasty. It was late summer. I could probably not get to America this year anyway. I would stay awhile longer.

Two years slipped by. Life was peaceful at Denham. Our quiet routine was disturbed only when the squire, who spent most of his time in town, made one of his infrequent appearances with a gay crowd of friends who came to the country for a few days of riding, gambling and drinking. Since Denham did not bring Susan with him on such occasions, and I seldom went into Plymouth, my sister faded further and further into the background of my life. And Polly Bragg's shadow was lengthening. We became accepted sweethearts. I regarded her as my own. Some day we would be married, and I would take her to America, where together we would find all those adventures which I had so often conjured up out of poverty, loneliness and helplessness. For her part Polly

60

caressed me when in the mood, teased me if it suited her humor and entered into my dreams with unflagging zeal. So, lulled into a sense of security, it did not occur to me that this girl, sixteen now, old enough for marriage or love, might have ambitions and plans of her own. In the autumn of 1663 my complacence was shaken.

The head groom was a lazy easy-going fellow who paid little attention to me so long as I did my work and a fair share of his. Taking advantage of his good nature and the squire's absence, Polly and I frequently rode. This was a new sport to me, but Polly had been wheedling the stablemen into letting her use the horses since she was a child. A born horsewoman, she took ditch and hedge with a cold recklessness that brought my heart to my mouth. Occasionally she was thrown or went down with her mount, but she always came up laughing or swearing (depending upon how badly she had been hurt), but determined to conquer the obstacle that had brought her to grief. Unlike me, who viewed a horse as a convenient and, if sanely handled, safe means of getting from one place to another, Polly regarded riding as a sport in which she could pit her skill and her mount's brute strength against snares laid by fate or the devil. Frequently when I could or would not go with her, she rode by herself.

One such day the squire returned unexpectedly to Denham. It was mid-morning. Seeing him riding up the lane I ran to meet him, as was my duty, in order to take the horse. I hoped that Polly would not choose this moment to come riding into sight, and thus expose her use of the master's horses. But Polly would not be Polly if she failed to find trouble wherever it was brewing. The squire had not more than dismounted when she hove into view in a distant field, galloping hell-for-leather toward a high fence. The squire and I both held our breath until she had cleared the hazard. Then he turned to me.

"Who's yonder?" he demanded.

"I don't know, sir," I lied.

He frowned.

"A trespasser. Give me your hand, I'll look into it."

"Don't bother yourself, sir. I'll do it," I volunteered.

"Your hand, fellow!" he ordered curtly.

I stooped dutifully, clasping my hands so he could put his foot into them. Heaving up, I half carried, half tossed my master into the saddle. Of all my duties as stable boy this was the one that I most disliked—making myself a human mounting block for the fine gentleman to step on. But this time I was too worried to be resentful. Polly was on the squire's best hunter. With sinking heart I saw him pull his horse around and canter off toward the far field.

Polly saw him coming. She waved gaily, then, she told me later, recognizing him, she tried to run away. The squire accepted the challenge. It was an exciting chase. Polly's hunter was more powerful, but the squire's mount was faster. Finally, her first impulsive fear having subsided, Polly headed toward the stables. Across the fields she came, clearing the hedge and into the meadow. The squire, who by this time must have recognized her, followed more cautiously. Polly rode straight to where I stood.

"Scold me for taking the horse," she gasped as she drew up beside me.

My mind did not work quickly enough. Before I had grasped Polly's generous intention the squire drew up beside us. As he did so Polly spoke to me in mock anger.

"What if I did take out the horse when you weren't about? It's not yours, it's the master's and he doesn't care if I ride his horses." She turned to the squire appealingly. "Do you, Master John?"

The squire found it difficult to determine whether or not he should be angry. The exhilarating dash through the morning air had undoubtedly cooled his first wrath; moreover, he was a skilled horseman, capable of appreciating Polly's mad riding. I saw him looking at her appraisingly. Perhaps he was really seeing her for the first time. She was a small disheveled elf sitting astride the huge hunter. Her eyes were defiant, but as if to belie their fearlessness, her large mouth was tremulous. She was undoubtedly an appealing figure. Her cause was further helped by the fact that as they faced one another, each astride a horse, the distance between a country gentleman and one of his servants diminished. Sensing this as I stood below them I felt a tinge of jealousy.

"Please, master," Polly begged.

The squire made up his mind. He laughed.

"You ride damned well," he said.

Polly almost seemed to curtsey from the animal's back.

"You're kind, master," she simpered.

"Where did you learn?"

"Here at Denham, sir."

The squire laughed again.

"On my horses, I suppose."

Dismounting, he threw me his bridle.

"Rub both animals down well," he ordered, "and after this let the girl ride when she wishes. Only," he added severely as he turned to Polly, "not on my hunter. Odd's fish, the way you ride you might break your neck, or a devilish sight worse, the horse's."

With that he left us. Polly remained astride the horse, her thoughts seemingly far away.

"Get down," I said.

Wrenching her attention back to the present she grinned at me.

"My stirrup, sirrah," she ordered haughtily.

Though relieved that we had not gotten into trouble I was uneasy at the scene that I had just witnessed. Polly's obvious satisfaction and her teasing increased this feeling. I had seen Polly dismount unaided a hundred times.

"Fall off," I grunted, "and be quick. I must rub him before he cools."

Laughing, she slipped to the ground.

"Fool," she gurgled, "didn't you hear Master John say I was to ride whenever I wanted?"

"Then ride and be damned," I retorted, "but he said naught of your using my back."

"He will, though, Tom Bone, he will," she cooed as she turned toward the house.

A few weeks later the seeds that accident and Polly's shrewd wit had planted began to bear fruit. The squire and a dozen of his friends arrived at Denham in mid-week. By Saturday they had tired of eating, gaming, and even drinking. The master sent for Polly. One of the guests, it appeared, fancied his horse Clansman's speed and his own skill as a rider. Growing tired of his boasting, and recalling Polly Bragg, our own master had asserted that he had a servant lass, who, mounted upon his own horse Snowman, could beat the braggart in a race. Argument followed, a sizable wager was made and Polly summoned. She consented to ride. The race was arranged for the following day.

As soon as she was away from the gentlemen, Polly came running to the stables. She was aglow with excitement. I did not like her news but could find no just cause for complaint; nor for that matter would it have mattered a curse to Polly, Squire Denham, or his friends if I had.

"Mind Snowman," Polly begged. "See that he's well fed and rested, because I'm going to win if I have to carry the horse in."

"Likely you will," I said disagreeably; "Snowman's a sweet enough little beast and fast, but Clansman's said to be the fastest animal in the county."

"Just the same we'll beat him," declared Polly doggedly.

The dawn was crisp. It promised just such a day as keen sportsmen delighted in. I fed Snowman and saw to it that his white coat was spotless. Then I set about the weary business of waiting until high noon, when the race was to be run. All morning I expected Polly to appear at the stables. It was inconceivable that she should not come to see her horse, give me a hundred contradictory orders, turn the stables upside down. But she did not come.

Toward noon the gentlemen began to drift toward the stables. Still Polly had not appeared. I saddled Clansman. He was a large deep-chested beast with good legs and strong hindquarters. He was as black as Snowman was white. I looked doubtfully at Snowman; he was so much smaller, though at Denham we fancied his speed. My heart sank. It was almost noon. Saddling Snowman

I led the two animals out. By this time the full company had gathered. The young men were soon clustered around the two horses, pointing out their faults and virtues, wagering with one another on the outcome. Squire Shelton, Polly's adversary, was favored, but Polly had her supporters. Noon came and still no sight of Polly. The young men grew restless. Shelton turned to chaffing his host.

"I say, Jack, has your amazon grown coy? I warn you, I'll claim the wager."

"She'll be here," replied Denham; but he cast anxious glances at the manor.

"Turned chicken-hearted, I warrant," someone declared.

"If she's run away we'll hold you for our losses, Jack," warned one of those who had put his money on Snowman.

The squire turned to me.

"Go fetch her," he ordered.

Before I had time to move a loud cheer went up from the assembled crowd. Polly in white hose and white silk doublet, booted and spurred, had appeared as if from nowhere. Where she had gotten the stuff heaven alone knows, but undoubtedly she had spent the morning contriving her costume. Almost before I could catch my breath she had vaulted into the saddle. There she sat smiling gaily down on the young men.

Squire Shelton swept her a courtly bow.

"I vow, ma'am, I'm vanquished before the race is run."

Polly dropped her eyes. Shelton turned to our squire.

"We wagered fifty pounds last night, Jack. Isn't it so?"

Denham nodded.

"I'll make it a hundred," suggested Shelton boldly, "against the girl."

I had not taken my eyes off Polly. At Shelton's words her figure stiffened, the eyes which had dropped so modestly lifted. In them, as they swept Shelton, was shrewd calculation. But only I saw this. The others, as they closed about the two young squires, were shouting and laughing, Denham with the others.

"Hell and·damnation, Dick, I don't own the wench; besides, she's too young."

65

Polly jerked sharply at Snowman's bit. As she intended the horse reared. All eyes turned on her.

"Take the wager, Master John," she begged. "I'll beat him."

He answered indulgently.

"You're a good lass, Polly, but what if you lose? Would you go with him?"

Polly never appeared more innocent.

"Oh, yes, sir, and I'd be very useful, sir, I'm sure. I can sweep and scour hearths and make beds and empty slops and—"

She was interrupted by a gale of merriment. She paused as if bewildered, then appealed to the squire. "Have I said something wrong, sir?"

"Nay, I vow you're priceless," gasped Denham. "And now, Dick, would you still wager a hundred pounds?"

"I'll make it a hundred and twenty-five," declared Shelton unabashed.

"A sporting offer."

"Will you sell me a share in your wager?"

"Accept, accept."

"It will make good sport."

Despite this chorus of approval Denham still hesitated. He was looking at Polly. Finally he shrugged.

"Done, Dick," he cried.

So it was that Polly Bragg was wagered against one hundred and twenty-five pounds. It was a good price; better than that demanded by most of the elegant ladies that I have known, but at the time I had no idea of the current prices of female flesh, nor could I have gained comfort from it if I had. Bursting with anger and hardly aware of what I was doing, I shoved through the ring of gentlemen to Snowman's side.

"You shan't do it, Polly," I whispered harshly.

Her mouth grew hard.

"But I think the girth's tight enough," she said loudly.

Before I could reply she slipped to the ground. Standing beside me she pretended to test the girth.

"Be still," she whispered fiercely, "or I'll hate you. I'll never

66

speak to you again." She straightened up as she said in a louder tone, "Help me, Tom?"

I hesitated, half in a mind to argue further, in no mind at all to help her on the horse. The squire barked irritably.

"Did you hear her, fellow? Be quick. Help her onto the horse."

Automatically I moved to obey. As Polly put her little foot between my two hands and placed her hand lightly on my shoulder, her eyes, smiling into mine, were dancing.

"I told you you'd be serving me to get on horses," she whispered.

Straightening up viciously I heaved her so hard that I almost threw her over Snowman's back.

Meanwhile Shelton had already mounted.

"Ready, sweet?" he called to Polly.

"I fear a poor girl like me will have little chance against such a fine gentleman," replied Polly meekly. "But I must do my best for Master John."

Someone shouted impatiently, "A truce to talk! Race."

They walked their horses to the starting point.

The course which had been agreed upon formed a rough oval, beginning and ending near the stables. It was a hard run, well over a mile in length with jumps over fences and the stream. The riders pulled their horses up. They sat immobile for a moment, as if frozen on their mounts. Only Shelton's eyes moved as they swept greedily over Polly's small body, sheathed snugly in its white trappings. Polly's eyes were fixed straight ahead, but her lips trembled provocatively.

Then they were off. The gentlemen were laughing and shouting. Despite the fact that most of them had wagered against her they were cheering for Polly. They were gallant, and besides they were reasonably sure that the girl would be beaten. A hundred yards or so from its start the course carried the riders out of sight. At this point, Clansman, ridden hard by Shelton, had a slight lead. After they were gone, for me at least, interminable seconds dragged into endless minutes. During the brief time that the race lasted I was in a hell of jealousy. The realization that Polly, whom I had been pleased to regard as a child, was a desirable woman in the eyes of others, brought me face to face with my own hunger for her. I felt miserably certain that she would lose the race. I knew that if she did that she would go with Shelton; and I knew that despite her assumed innocence that she was fully aware of what it was that the squire wanted of her. What I did not know, and it tortured me most of all, was if she wanted to win or lose. As I thought of her deliberately losing, something in my stomach seemed to turn over like butter in a churn; my hands, limp at my side, trembled. Just when I felt as if I could stand it no longer, Clansman shot into view. On he rushed, five yards, ten, before Snowman appeared. I groaned. But it was not quite the end. The greater weight of his rider was telling on Clansman. As they battled up the meadow the space between the two horses diminished. Snowman's nose almost touched Clansman's rump. I wondered why Polly was holding a course so close to her rival. The meadow was wide, there was plenty of room for both horses. Shelton was riding heavily. Up came his riding crop and down on Clansman's flank. He was merciless, his arm working like a flail. The horse responded gallantly, but could not shake off the white shadow that clung to its side. Polly, riding lightly, far forward on her horse, was leaning over its neck. She almost seemed to whisper in Snowman's ear.

Everyone was shouting. In the desire to win, gallantry was forgotten. "Clansman! Come, Clansman!" "Snowman! Ride, Polly! Ride! Bring her in, little witch!" "Clansman!" "Use the lash, Polly." "Clansman wins! Clansman wins! Clansman wins!"

I think that I alone was silent. My mouth was so dry that I doubt if I could have made a sound had I tried. My heart was pounding with the hoofs of the approaching horses. Polly was trying. I knew that now. But I knew, too, even though Snowman had crept up inch by inch until his nose was at Clansman's neck, that it was too late for him to win. They were almost to the finish.

And then, when it was too late, when she was as good as beaten, Polly raised her riding crop for the first time. A sob gathered in my throat, but it died from very despair. Why had she waited so long? I wanted to look away, but could not. Polly, straining far forward, cut down with all her might. The lash snapped viciously,

68

not on Snowman, but across Clansman's nose. The great beast swerved and reared violently, almost throwing its startled, cursing rider. Snowman sped over the finish line.

At Polly's trick the spectators' shouts had died in a gasp. Shelton, after quieting his horse, threw himself from its back. He strode to Polly, who still sat astride the trembling Snowman.

"You little bitch," he said from between clenched teeth.

Polly did not answer. Her face was expressionless.

"You did it deliberately, damn you."

She was still silent.

He raised his arm threateningly, his own crop still in his hand. "Answer me, trollop. You did it deliberately."

"Oh, yes, sir," said Polly, sounding like an obedient child. "I hit him on purpose."

Denham had joined them. He looked worried. He shook his head disapprovingly.

"Damn it, Polly. Why did you do such a thing?" he asked.

Her eyes grew big, her mouth trembled.

"Why, master, I wanted to win so I could stay here at Denham where you have been so kind to me."

She was not a child now, but a girl turning into a woman. Jealousy took possession of me again. The squire softened.

"But if you foul, you forfeit, Polly," he said gently. "So you see you must go with him after all."

"And the first thing I'll do is beat some manners into you," promised Shelton, his voice heavy with satisfaction.

Polly was unperturbed.

"I beat him," she declared, "so I won't go with him."

"But you cheated," protested Denham weakly, "a gentleman doesn't do such a thing."

"I wouldn't know what gentlemen do. I'm only a servant girl. I try to win any way I can."

Someone in the background laughed. The atmosphere cleared a trifle. In the end Polly stayed at Denham. She was stubborn, and as someone pointed out, the estate of an English gentleman was not a slave market where a girl could be sold or passed from hand to hand against her will. Denham paid a hundred and twenty-five pounds in lieu of Polly, and even Shelton's good humor was restored.

The matter settled, Polly slipped from her horse and after making an elaborate leg, which seemed proper enough, dressed as she was like a boy, accompanied me to the stables.

I was relieved but angry.

"I'm amazed you didn't let him win," I grumbled, as I rubbed the animals down.

"Why, Tommy?"

"You're so anxious to be a gentleman's doxy."

Her eyes grew round.

"Me?"

"What else?" I sneered. "When you were still little more than a baby I found you in a lane, running after your Master John."

"I remember," Polly admitted.

"And since I've been here, you've told me yourself that you'll have him, despite the devil."

Polly agreed again.

"And yet," I wound up furiously, "you act a damned innocent when I say you aim at being his whore."

She shook her head.

"That's Susan. I'm going to be his wife."

Had Polly informed me that she proposed being John Denham's sister I would have been no less amazed. For some moments I stared at her speechlessly, wondering if this was mere simplicity or ambition to the point of madness. Then jealousy and anger resumed possession of me.

"But you're going to marry me," I shouted.

She nodded soberly and I began to fancy myself in the grip of a nightmare.

"We can't both have you, lawfully."

To this she merely shrugged.

It was fantastic. This bastard daughter of a scullery maid calmly declaring she would be mistress of the manor and the wife of a stableboy besides. Fantastic and laughable, yet as I looked at her I was unable to laugh. My own desire for her was too strong.

70

Besides, the events of the last hour had shown me clearly the lengths to which Polly would go, the risks she would take. I was silent. Polly, wise beyond her years, smiled and came to me. She ran her fingers through my hair.

"Turn around," she said.

Grudgingly I straightened up from my task and faced her. Putting her arms around my neck she yoked me with her full weight, pulling me down toward her. I saw her small heart-shaped face; her gray eyes stared mistily into mine, her tongue caressed my lips lightly for a moment, then lingeringly. It was then I tasted her heavy red mouth. For the first time Polly gave me the kiss of a woman. When we drew apart we were both breathless.

"I'd rather it was you than any of them, Tommy." Her voice trembled.

Intoxicated by such an admission I spoke boldly.

"I'll have you myself," I declared.

"Of course."

I misunderstood. My heart beating wildly, my knees almost knocking together, I reached out for her. She almost yielded before pushing me away. It was a gentle push that sprang from fright rather than disinclination. Through bitter, parched, aching years I was to curse myself for submitting to it, but then it was too late. I stepped back obediently.

"I love you, Polly," I said awkwardly. I had never said such a thing before.

She replied soberly.

"I know, Tommy, and some day you'll have me."

Her mood changed. She almost danced as she moved away from me. Her voice, as well as her words, was mocking, as she chanted tavern doggerel:

> *"Wise maids don't bed*
> *With men they'd wed."*

She was gone. I realized that despite her kiss she had made no promises to relinquish her designs regarding the squire. I felt uneasy, certain that there would be a sequel to the day's events, and cursed heartily the ill luck that had brought the master to Denham the morning that Polly was riding his best hunter.

## 3.

My fears were well-founded. After the day of the race, whenever the squire and his companions came to Denham they sooner or later called for Polly. The young men treated her like a pet kitten, caressing and teasing her by turns. She submitted with an air of childish innocence, but I doubt if she ever let them entirely forget that she was a woman. Although this was far from agreeable to me I could do nothing. In fitful spells Polly exerted all her energy to conciliate me, but I knew that if, despite her efforts, I persisted in protesting against her conduct I would end by losing her altogether and I was afraid to force such an alternative. Besides, so far as I knew, Polly was not actually harmed by the squire and his friends. So I waited uneasily for something, I did not know what, to happen.

In mid-February the squire brought an unusually large party to Denham. As always when gentlemen were at the manor house I was worried. The second night after their arrival I was prowling around the grounds trying to find Polly. At length, sneaking into the garden, I approached the house itself. I heard laughter and singing from the direction of the dining hall. Creeping to an open window I cautiously raised my head above the ledge and looked in. My caution was needless. There was little chance that anyone would see me.

The gentlemen had finished dining. They were deep in their cups. Bottles—empty, half full and as yet uncorked—littered the table. At one end of the room a half dozen or so of the merrymakers were singing in drunken harmony:

> *"Back and side go bare, go bare,*
> *And foot and hand go cold,*
> *But belly, God send thee good ale enough,*
> *Whether it be new or old."*

Beyond the singers another group was gambling. In its center sat the squire. On his knee perched Polly Bragg. She had on an elaborate, slightly soiled gown that I recognized as one that Susan had given her. She wore a livid yellow ribbon in her hair, her cheeks were rouged, her large mouth was painted red as May cherries. On her chin was a heart-shaped patch. Doubtlessly, to these young dandies accustomed to the courtesans of Plymouth and even London, Polly was a figure of fun; but I could see no cause for merriment. I knew that Polly herself was in earnest. One of her thin arms was around the squire's neck; in one hand she held a pair of dice.

"Throw them, Pol," urged the squire.

With a giggle Polly complied.

"Bravo, Pol! bravo! you've won again." The squire gave her a squeeze and a kiss.

"I vow, I do protest," lisped an effeminate-looking dandy, "damme, she's a witch." He thrust his glass at her. "Here, pretty Pol, a drink for a kiss; mayhap some of your devilish luck lingers on your lips."

Obediently Polly took the proffered glass and drained it. As she lifted her face to pay she swayed slightly. Her eyes were bright, her mouth slack. I knew that she was drunk. Too sick for anger I turned away.

> *"Back and side go bare, go bare,*
> *Both foot and hand go cold,"*

The roisterers' song rang through my ears. It followed me through the gardens and floated aimlessly through my head long after I had returned to my hole over the stables.

But I was haunted by more than a sound that night. The ghost of my murdered father, the shades of my two dead sisters—one starved, the other a suicide—Old Jenny's charred bones, all called to me—not for pity, but for vengeance.

My hatred for the gentry flamed anew. Who were these fine gentlemen that they could take a man's father, sisters, sweetheart as it pleased them? I swore again that I would be even with them. But I could do nothing so long as I remained a stableboy. I got

73

up from my pile of straw and gathered together my few belongings. It did not take long. I was soon out of the stable and in the lane. After a last look at that part of the manor house where I knew Polly customarily slept, I turned my back on Denham and on Polly Bragg.

With heavy heart but resolute determination I turned toward Plymouth. The dawn was just beginning to break. A week later I was on a fishing vessel bound for America.

# V

## I.

WHEN I WAS young it was the custom among far-seeing ship captains of the West Country to take each year a few green men or boys to the fishing banks off Newfoundland. This practice insured a plentiful supply of sailors and fishermen, which in turn meant not only that there would be no difficulty in getting hands, but also that wages could be kept so low that the ship owner might rest assured that he would be able to pocket the major share of the profits gained from the fisheries.

Three days after I fled Denham for Plymouth I was signed as a green boy on a fishing vessel bound for Newfoundland. A few days later I was at sea. From the first hour I was happy. The work was arduous but I was young and strong, accustomed to hardship and to any task that came my way. I was fortunate, too, in escaping the brutality so commonly encountered by lads first going to sea. Our captain, Peter Couch, was more merchant than seaman, and cared little for the discipline of the ship, being far more interested in the number of quintals of cod that he might bring home than in all the traditions of the sea combined. Only once on the whole voyage did he speak to, or so far as I know, even notice me. On that occasion I had just clambered down from the rigging.

"God grant that ye'll make a better fisherman than you do a sailor," he grunted as I reached the deck. That was the greatest cruelty I ever suffered from Captain Peter Couch.

The crew was composed of such men as I had known all my life at Saltash and Plymouth—that is, ordinary English sailors.

75

They were rough men who spoke only when something needed to be said, unless they were drunk, when they boasted of their adventures so noisily that I often thought they were avenging themselves for the silence that was so often imposed upon them by the overwhelming vastness of the sea. They showed me what I must do, cuffed me if need be, all without emotion or interest. Occasionally they played rough pranks on the greenhorns, but these were never deliberately cruel. For the most part I was left alone.

The ship itself, the *Cape Race,* was an ordinary fishing vessel: broad-beamed, low in the waist but high forward and aft. Like all its kind it was awkward in the wind, but sailed well enough when going free. She was of eighty tons' weight and carried forty-odd men and eight boats. It would be hard to imagine a more prosaic vehicle for an enchanted journey, yet to me it was a veritable wishing boat. It was carrying me into new worlds and unknown adventure.

My tasks and my preoccupation with the future kept me so busy that I had no time to waste on thoughts of the past. Thus it is no wonder that with the canvas booming above my head, the waves beating against the vessel's sides and the clean salt breeze washing me that memories of Denham faded. As the weeks passed, even the image of Polly Bragg weaving drunkenly on the knee of the squire became dimmer and dimmer, until it finally disappeared altogether. Thus the ghost was laid, and, for the time being, I was no longer haunted.

I made one friend during the voyage. We were almost three weeks out. It was twilight. Temporarily idle, I stood in the waist of the ship watching the water. In a curious inverted way the ocean gave me confidence. In the face of its immensity I felt all men—lord, gentleman or fisher lad—must be equal, if only equally small. A voice broke into my reverie.

"I've waited three weeks for you to remember me, Tom Bone."

Turning, I recognized a fisherman who called himself Bill Smith. During the past few weeks I had noticed him looking at me curiously, a grin twitching the corners of his generous mouth. My attention thus caught I had fancied he looked familiar, but try as I would I could not recall when or where I had seen him.

My failure had been the more annoying because Smith should not have been difficult to remember. In unimportant but nonetheless definite ways he was unlike the other members of the crew. When sober he laughed boisterously and told the tallest of tales, but with drink he turned mute and sat brooding sullenly. At such times he was unapproachable; only his eyes were exposed to the curious. They were naked from pain, as if he saw something far away and yet too close. Drunk or sober he dropped no word of his past, and this was the stranger because he was ordinarily not taciturn, as are most seamen on a voyage, but talked as if for the pleasure of talking and the entertainment he got from the sound of his own voice and the conceits of his own mind. It reminded me of the way the gentlemen who came to Denham talked. And he swore like a gentleman, emotionally and for effect; a fisherman swears as he speaks, impassively and generally without rancor. These things, as well as the nagging of my memory, had aroused my curiosity regarding Smith, so when I turned and saw him grinning down at me I was more than slightly interested.

"I've thought I knew you," I said.

"The Red Indian," he suggested.

I knew the tavern, but I still could not remember Bill Smith. I had seen many sailors there and said so. Smith sighed dolorously.

"I'd 'a' sworn you'd remember me. So much for man's opinion of his own importance."

"I saw so many," I repeated apologetically.

"Aye, but this was a special night. I'd wager it was the first time you were ever drunk."

Then as his laugh boomed out I remembered. I saw him, not standing at the rail of the *Cape Race* but indistinctly, as through a fog of strong drink. He was my companion of that Christmas Eve when I had last seen Evalyn alive.

"And if I'm not even more mistaken," he was continuing, "when I left, you were in a fair way to lie with your first woman. Tell me, did the slut give you good sport?"

"She was all right," I muttered, ashamed of the truth and unwilling to have him believe that I had failed with a girl.

77

"I'll warrant," he roared. "And how did a boy like you get from a corner of the Red Indian to the decks of the *Cape Race?*"

I had not talked much to anyone for weeks. With the excuse Smith had given me I was soon babbling as fast as my tongue would move. I told of Denham, my sister Susan, the squire and even of Polly Bragg. When at length I had talked myself out, my new friend nodded.

"They are a bad lot, these gentlemen—and women, too. A man, unless he's a gentleman, may be harmless, but women, whether of gentle or common birth, are all alike. They are weak and that's why a strong man's at their mercy. You're wise to flee, Tom, before one of them has so entwined herself about you that to cut her out of your life you must cut out your very heart, or what she's left you of it."

As he spoke he forgot himself and I knew why, despite his seaman's clothes, coarse talk and booming laugh, he had seemed different from the others.

"You're one of them yourself," I blurted out.

"What's that? One of what?"

"One of them—a gentleman."

He did not reply for a moment. When he did he spoke gravely. "There was a time when I called myself a gentleman, but now I am Bill Smith. Shall we remember that? The rest is a secret between us."

"I hate all gentlemen," I muttered.

"You may be right in that, but it's Bill Smith, the fisherman, not another man who died somewhere in the past back there in England, who asks you to keep his secret." I still hesitated; he went on in a lighter vein. "Come, be reasonable. Because you hate Denham you must not condemn a whole class, including those who have foresworn it."

"Denham's not the worst," I retorted. "There are those like Edward Cousin."

Smith's arm shot out, his strong fingers gripped me as in a vise. "What do you know of Edward Cousin?" he demanded.

"I know he's the devil," I stammered, frightened at the sudden change in my companion.

"When did you last see him? Where is he?"

"You're hurting me."

His grip relaxed slowly.

"I'm sorry. Now tell me quickly."

I told my story. By the time I had finished he had regained his composure.

"Your tale isn't a pretty one. But never mind, some day we'll find Cousin, and when we do—" His voice trailed into nothing. When he resumed, it was to change the subject. "And now what do you say? Shall we be friends?"

I grasped his outstretched hand.

After weeks of fair sailing land was sighted. It was mid-afternoon; the fogs through which we had been running for the past few days had lifted. I was busy on deck when the words I had so looked forward to hearing came from aloft.

"Land ahoy."

A sailor near me grunted; another raised his head briefly. Leaving my work I ran to the ship's rail. At first I could see nothing but presently a dark line emerged against the horizon. I was looking at America.

My ecstasy was dispelled by a cuff accompanied by an order to get back to work. The fog soon closed in again, so it was the next morning before I got my first good look at the New World. It was unbelievable. As I stared I seemed to hear my father's voice, "Cold and white and green." The water of the harbor where we had anchored during the night was a black green, while huge green cedars marched toward the edges of the cliffs, which in most places fell sheer to the water. On the mountains beyond snow gleamed under a bright sun.

We were in Conception Bay. I learned later that it was one of the island's largest harbors and that twenty or twenty-five years ago a settlement had been there; but on that morning when I first saw it, harbor and shore were empty save for a few fishing vessels in the bay and half a hundred or so men standing in small groups on the beach.

The sight of these vessels and men angered our captain. Cursing furiously he called his officers to his cabin.

"Why does he care?" I asked Bill Smith. "There's plenty of room in the harbor."

"In the harbor, but the beach is not so big and the captain knows that the best of the stages, splitting tables, flakes and all the rest will be taken."

It was a meaningless jargon to me. My face must have betrayed my bewilderment. Bill laughed.

"You, a fisherman's son, and never heard of flake or splitting table," he jeered.

"There's lots I never heard. My father did not like talking of the Banks. I think most of the fishermen try to forget them when they're home."

"And they're right. But you'll soon learn that there is more to fishing than throwing a hook into the water. But look, the council of war is over."

As Smith spoke the officers came out of the captain's cabin. The mate left the others and came toward us. As he passed he ordered us to accompany him. A few minutes later a boat was put overboard. Besides the mate, there were six seamen in it. I pulled an oar, doing it awkwardly, but no one seemed to notice. The men's attention was on the beach, toward which they cast quick glances over their shoulders.

When we reached shore I could see that each of the small knots of men I had observed from the ship was centered around a cluster of wooden tables and long troughs. The group to which our mate led us was the smallest in sight, four men in all, apparently ordinary fisherman. As we faced them they regarded us stolidly. Three of them had stout clubs in their hands, another held one of the large chunks of lead used by the fishermen as weights for their lines.

"Who is your master?" demanded our leader sharply.

"Captain Robert Hare, *Bristol Maid*."

"Where is he?"

The other—it was the fellow with the weight—muttered some unintelligible reply. The mate turned toward the harbor and after a careful scrutiny of the ships there spoke with a new satisfaction.

"I know the *Bristol Maid*. She's not there."

"She's on the Banks," the fisherman growled.

"You're lying, it's too early. The cod won't be in." Our leader advanced a step, the rest of us closing in with him. "You're lying," he repeated. "Where is the *Bristol Maid?*"

The answer was reluctant. "She's not come yet."

"So you've been here all winter, and your captain's from the West?" the mate purred. "Haven't you heard that settlers aren't liked in the west of England?"

"We're not settlers. We only watched the stages for the winter." The fellow broke into startling fury. "And, by God, I'd hang before I'd do it again. Alone here, just the four of us. Never seeing another human, only a savage once in a while. Alone here with ice and snow and wind. A man goes crazy."

"Interesting," murmured our mate, "but you see these stages that you so kindly cared for belong to Captain Peter Couch, master of the *Cape Race*, out of Plymouth. He built them last year. We'll take them now."

"Like hell you will. Not after we watched 'em through the bloody winter." He raised his voice and cried, "They're trying to steal our stage."

Our leader raised his hand. At the signal we attacked. Plunging in with the others I dodged a club and struck out. My fist crashed into someone's face. I heard a shout from behind. As I swung about something hit me. When I opened my eyes I found myself stretched out on one of the wooden tables. A stranger was leaning over me. As I started to sit up a bucket of the coldest water I had ever felt was splashed in my face.

"There you are, boy. Lie still and you'll be all right," a man grunted, and turned away.

Despite his advice I sat up and looked around. A few feet away was Bill Smith. He grinned encouragement.

"Steady, Tom. Battle's over and you're still alive," he called cheerfully.

I saw that two husky fishermen were holding him. As he spoke one of these nodded agreement.

"That's bein' sensible," he said and loosened his hold.

As I looked further I saw that all of our men were captive. They were bruised and battered and apparently, like Bill, fully reconciled to defeat. Only the mate was unhurt, his clothes still immaculate. I was puzzled by this until I remembered that he was an officer and as such would give orders for the fishermen to crack one another's skulls, but could not be expected to participate in the ensuing brawl. Strangely enough, although the only one of our party unhurt, he alone appeared to be angry.

"What the devil does this mean?" he shouted furiously at the men crowding around us.

An old man stepped forward. He spoke quietly, but with an air of authority.

"I was watching, mister. Your men struck first."

"What if they did?" the mate retorted hotly; "these stages were built by Captain Couch last year. We were but taking possession of his rightful property."

"Have you ever been on the Banks before?" asked the old man.

"What does it matter if I have or haven't?"

"If you haven't there's some excuse for your ignorance of the customs here."

"I acted under orders of my captain."

The other spoke gravely.

"I know Peter Couch. It's like him to give orders to someone else when there's a fight in the offing. He knows that when stages are deserted in the autumn they belong to the first comer who claims them."

"But these fellows stayed all winter," countered the mate, "and though I may not have been on the Banks before, I come from the West Country and I know how our people feel toward settlers."

The old man's face clouded as he agreed with quiet vehemence: "Damn settlers and sacks; between them they ruin honest fishing captains."

"Then why do you help them against us?"

"We have no proper law on the Banks, except maybe at St. John's, so for common protection those who have stages bind themselves against any newcomer who tries to take them. Peter Couch knows this, so when you go back, mister, tell him that if he would stop at Conception Bay he is welcome so long as he regards the rules of the Banks, but he's not to send more men to start quarrels among us."

The mate hesitated, unwilling to admit defeat, but he had no choice.

"I'll deliver the message," he agreed sullenly.

At a nod from the old man we were released. I half expected the fight to begin again, and was ready, for my head throbbed damnably, and the only relief I could think of was to inflict a like injury on someone else. But my companions felt otherwise. As they prepared to return to the boat they talked amiably enough with their late antagonists, exchanging greetings, asking questions, cursing cheerfully over the blows so recently received. But the mate remained disgruntled. Assembling us as quickly as he could he gave orders for our return to the *Cape Race*.

The captain had been able to see enough from the security of his own deck to know what had occurred. When the mate delivered his message Peter Couch turned red with rage.

"Who in Hell's name dares tell me the rules of the Banks?" he spluttered.

"I don't know, sir," confessed the mate.

"Captain William Hyde out of Dartmouth, sir," one of the men volunteered. "He was here last year."

"Hyde, eh." Couch growled, "The old fool should have been dead years ago. He thinks with his rules and customs of the Banks that he's a damned fishing admiral of a hundred years back. But I'll show him, God damn him. I'll show him that he can't govern Peter Couch."

The mate, who was young and still angry, agreed eagerly. "Aye, sir, with the whole crew we'll show them who rules Conception Bay."

Couch looked at his officer with evident distaste.

"So you'd have another fight, would you, mister? And lose half a dozen men through injury, or even get one or two killed?

And how many quintal of fish would that cost us? Had you thought of that, mister?"

The mate had difficulty in keeping abreast his captain's seeming change of mood.

"I understood you to say, sir," he said stiffly, "that this Hyde was not to be permitted to bully us."

The captain resumed his bellicose tone. "I can come to Conception Bay if I'll behave like a good lad, can I? Does this mighty Hyde think then that there is no fit bay for a fishing vessel save Conception? We'll show him. At dawn we sail."

With this bold defiance our gallant captain turned on his heel and made his way to his cabin to gloat, no doubt, over his victory. The mate stared after him open-mouthed. Bill Smith laughed. The rest of the men turned to their tasks, seemingly not caring if they remained at Conception Bay or went elsewhere, or if they fought or fished.

## 2.

That night Bill Smith made clear much that had puzzled me on the beach during the afternoon.

"Your father must have been taciturn indeed," he said when I asked him to explain. "I thought every boy in southwestern England who lived near the sea knew the history of the fishing banks. Why, when I was a boy, though I never expected to see the New World, much less come here as a fisherman, I listened thirstily to the romantic stories of the Grand Banks and its fishermen."

"No doubt it seemed romantic to one living in a manor, or some like place," I replied with one of the rare references to his gentle birth that I permitted myself; "I doubt if it was so romantic to the men themselves. Certainly it was no romance this afternoon. So tell me what right we had to fight for those stages and they to herd together to protect them. Who are settlers and what are sacks that will ruin western fishing captains? Why did those men stay all winter, and what authority does Captain Hyde have?"

"Hold on," cried Bill laughingly; "God, boy, give me mercy.

84

In one breath you've demanded the history of Newfoundland."
He paused, then went on more soberly. "The story of Newfoundland and its waters is the story of fish. Each year the squid come
to the banks off these shores and the cod follow the squid; fishermen follow the cod, though why squid, cod or man should want to
frolic in such damned inhospitable waters as these, with their hunks
of ice big as mountains, the devil only knows. But they do and
have done so for nigh two hundred years now. In the early days
when the English first started coming here England was so busy
changing its religion, much as Henry VIII changed his wives,
that she had no time to establish government or give protection
to the men on the far-away fishing banks. So, left alone, the fishermen established a rough sort of government of their own. The
captains of the first three vessels to arrive in a harbor became, for
that season, fishing admirals, and it was their duty to maintain
order and to act as judges when there was trouble."

"What sort of trouble?" I interrupted.

"Oh, fights among the men; for you will find that after you've
worked from before dawn to dusk you're allowed to get drunk
and quarrel with your shipmates, or if you are in luck with men
from another ship; but more often the admirals were called upon
to decide on possession of the best fishing stages."

"Stages," I exclaimed impatiently. "What are these stages for
which we try to nearly kill each other?"

"You'll find out from experience soon enough. For the present
it's enough to tell you that they're where the fish are dried, cleaned
and cured. You see, to get the best price the fish must not only
reach the markets early, but they must also be well cured. If
they are not dried and salted properly they rot, and rotten fish
must be sold at low prices to street vendors who sell to poor
people, or to the planters on the sugar plantations who feed them
to their negurs. So a convenient place to put up your drying tables
and troughs, close to the water's edge and exposed to the full sunlight, is almost as important as a place on the Banks where the
catch is heavy.

"The first who came took their choice of stages, and if they
were lucky enough to find the tables and all the rest still standing

from last year they got those, too. Any late comers who tried to take them were dealt with by the fishing admirals."

I was beginning to understand the brawl of the afternoon.

"So our captain tried to steal someone else's stage, and Old Hyde, the fishing admiral of that harbor, prevented?" I asked.

"Well, yes, something like that, but there's something to be said for Captain Couch. There haven't been any fishing admirals for I don't know how many years and that stage was ours last year. Besides, in the old days no one lived on the island all winter. In fact, settlers would not have been tolerated. They were, and still are, hated by the captains because they take possession of the best stages before the ships from England can get here."

"But those fellows we fought this afternoon weren't settlers," I protested.

"Not exactly," Smith agreed. "That's probably why the others on the beach helped them, but they had stayed all winter, reserving a stage."

### 3.

Toward evening of the next day we entered a cove. It was small, with only a narrow strip of beach, but it satisfied Captain Couch, so we dropped anchor and prepared to establish ourselves in this nameless harbor. The following morning we set to work. During the next few days I learned that fishermen, Newfoundland fishermen at least, had also to be woodsmen and carpenters. Trees were cut down, stripped and split. Out of the lumber we built the flues, splitting tables, flakes and stages used for curing the fish. When we had finished, the cod had not yet come to the Banks so we had little to do. During one of these leisurely days Bill Smith and I climbed from the cove to the cliffs that towered over us.

"Look," Bill said.

Before me lay the sea. It was no longer cold and green but sparkling blue in the bright sun. On either side and behind us stretched green-clad mountains crowned with snow. The land seemed as vast as the sea itself. A deep sense of fulfillment settled upon me. This, with its great distances and its raw might, was the New World. Here there was room for a poor man, while a rich one would find no humble fellow at his beck to pull a forelock as he jumped to do his bidding. Instead the winds of the trees would sigh and the waves of the sea would dance in glee at the presumption of a strutting turkey cock who dared venture into a young fresh world with no gift save the title "gentleman." I tried to tell Bill Smith something of what I felt.

"There's equality here of a kind," he agreed, "but it's the equality of common hardship and suffering. It's a stern land, and I think it's more apt to make the gentleman into something less than he was than to exalt the humble. There's a gruesome story in the West Country that a company of Englishmen, wrecked on these shores without food or weapons, turned cannibal and ate one another before the last of them were picked up. Some were gentlemen, I suppose, and some of humble birth, but when they were dead and devoured and what was left of them passed through a man's bowels to fertilize a spot of this new world, I suppose they were equal."

"You can't frighten me," I boasted. "It may be a harsh land but I'm here and I intend to stay."

"Stay," Bill echoed in surprise.

"Of course. You don't think I'm going back to England, do you? England's behind me—somewhere in the mists, swallowed by the ocean for all I care."

Bill spoke thoughtfully. "Yes, England's somewhere yonder in the mists, but she's not through with you, Tom. She holds you as firmly here as she held you at Denham. You're free up here for a few hours, but when you go back to the cove you're a fisherman again, belonging to Peter Couch all summer and when the summer's gone he'll take you back to England. There he'll keep two-thirds of the profit from the sale of the fish you caught. The other third will go to you so you can live until spring when he's ready to use you again."

"I won't go back," I cried. "When fall comes I'll go to New England."

"How? You are on an island, and even if you could find your way to the mainland you would face hundreds of miles of waste, not to mention wild animals and savage men."

87

"Ships come from New England. I've heard the men talk abou.
them."

"Yes, they come to carry on an illegal trade with us, but it's
doubtful if one will visit so small a cove, and even if it did it
would do you no good. You're Captain Couch's man and for the
New Englander to steal you would be like stealing another's
property."

"I've heard of men who were stolen, though."

"The New Englanders smuggle a man away now and then, but
only if he can pay or if he will sign indenture papers. If a ship
should come you might escape that way."

"I won't do that," I declared; "I've had enough of service.
The New World's a free land and in it I intend to be free."

"Well, then," said Bill dryly, "all you must do is wait for a
miracle; meantime we'd best get back to the cove, for Captain
Peter Couch may have work for us two free men to do."

A few days later the fishing began in earnest and I had little
time to worry about my future. We went out in the boats early
in the morning, five men to a boat. Though in the sea fisheries
the French used nets, we English in the shore fishery used large
hooks and lines weighted with heavy lumps of lead. The fishing
day was about ten hours long, unless the men had the good fortune to fill their boat in a shorter time. During the remainder of
the daylight hours—and Newfoundland, like England, has long
summer evenings—the fish were cut, cleaned and put on the drying tables for the sun to cure. The dry fish was taken from the
tables, salted, and packed in barrels which were stowed in the ship's
hold. When the day's work was done, or rather when it was dark
—the work was never done—the men could, as Bill had said, get
drunk. Bill himself did so frequently, but after a few attempts I
discovered that although my head was strong enough my belly
was weak and that the hours of the next day spent in a small boat
with my stomach tossing more than the water around me far out-
weighed the short periods of exhilaration derived from rum. Bill
jeered at my weakness, declaring I must overcome it before too
many years passed as only the young could afford the luxury of a

88

queasy stomach, but despite such japing I held to my resolution to drink moderately.

One evening in the middle of July when we returned to our cove we found a strange ship anchored there. It turned out to be a New Englander come to trade. That night a brisk business was carried on between the visitor and our people. I found that even Peter Couch was not above turning a profit from smuggling. With a couple of companions I was sent to the hold, where stowed away in a corner we found a quantity of goods of a kind not commonly needed on a fishing voyage. West England cordage, cloth caps and hats were carried to the deck and loaded on the small boats which were bound for the New England vessel. These came back laden with oil, wine and other produce from Spain and Portugal, whence the trader had just come. Meanwhile our fishermen, like their captain, were doing business. Whoever could scrape up enough money was buying rum, raw first-run stuff, but cheap, costing less than a shilling a gallon.

As I worked and watched I felt a thrill of anticipation. I saw in the New England vessel a bridge upon which to cross to my promised land. I determined to be on it when it headed south, and during a moment's respite from work I confided my resolution to Bill Smith.

"How will you do it?" he asked.

I had to confess that I had no ideas.

"Well, you had best get one, for these traders do not waste time. They will finish their business tonight and tomorrow be on their way."

Thus prodded I drew aside a lad from the foreign ship, who had come to help unload a boatload of stuff.

"Where are you from?" I asked him.

"Out of Providence."

I had no time for diplomacy. "Will your captain take me there?" I demanded bluntly.

The boy showed no surprise but he was cautious. "Maybe; he takes a man from the Banks now and then."

"Could I talk to him?"

"I reckon, but not tonight. He's with your captain."

"But I must leave for the day's fishing before dawn," I exclaimed in dismay.

"We'll be gone before you're back."

"The devil with fishing then," I declared recklessly. "I'll see your captain tomorrow."

So it was arranged that the lad should bring the captain to a cave I had discovered, about halfway up the cove.

"Are you sure he'll come?" I asked anxiously, as I tried in vain to picture a ship's captain sneaking out to meet a common fisherman, and a mere boy to boot.

"He generally goes where he smells a profit."

This reply did not offer unadulterated comfort, for I could offer little profit, but I had to be content with it. As I finished my work I wondered how I could avoid going out in the boat next day. I thought of feigning illness, but Captain Couch was not one to permit a man to miss a day's catch because he had a pain, and besides, I was afraid that with the strange ship in the harbor he would suspect my real motive. Finally, after I had finished with my work on the *Cape Race* I found Bill Smith and appealed to him for help. At first he tried to dissuade me.

"It's no use; the New Englander won't take you. You have nothing to offer."

"If I can only see him I'll persuade him," I insisted.

"You can see him easily enough, but I warn you you'll be disappointed."

"How can I see him?" I demanded, disregarding the warnings.

"Hide out tonight. Take a blanket and sleep in your cave. If you aren't here in the morning you can't leave with us."

"But what will the captain say?"

"Maybe he won't know. I'll try to get the men of our boat to take it out without saying anything, but even if he finds out, what difference? The boats must go with or without Tom Bone. By the time they return you'll be gone. Of course, if you prove to be wrong you'll have to take your punishment, but young cocks must learn their lesson."

I tried to tell Bill good-by but he only laughed at me.

"We'll sail the seven seas together yet, lad," was all he'd say.

So I took a blanket and sneaked to my cave. I did not sleep much that night. Despite the assurances to the contrary I was afraid the captain would not come. If he did I was hopeful of success. The necessity of my getting to America was so urgent to me that I did not doubt that it would move others.

Daylight finally came. I watched the boats leave the harbor. As they disappeared from view I felt as though I had been relieved of a great burden. I knew that a few men would be left ashore to work at the stages and guard our property from the New Englanders, but Captain Couch was gone and no hue and cry had been raised over my absence. But as time passed I grew uneasy. I had forgotten to bring food with me, so hunger was added to feverish impatience. I watched the sun anxiously. I was determined that if the New England captain did not come to me by noon I would go in search of him, even if by doing so I risked being caught by our own men on the beach. Such a risk was not necessary. While the sun was still well in the east, two figures detached themselves from one of the groups on the beach and came up the cove.

When the New England captain—for it was he—and my companion of the previous night finally reached me my hopes rose to new heights. For Captain Warren was a gentle-looking man with a kindly smile and merry blue eyes.

"You want to go to New England?" he asked abruptly.

"Yes, sir."

"How much money have you?"

"None, but—"

"I thought not, but no harm done by asking; and payment at the beginning of a transaction is a good thing; yet you look strong and no doubt are a willing worker. Times are hard in the colonies just now, but I'll guarantee that I can find a master for you."

"But—"

"Don't waste time, lad. I've done these things before. Listen sharp. I sail in about three hours. By that time I'll expect you to be aboard—without my knowledge, you understand. Tell the first of my men you see that you're a stowaway, he'll know what to do. When we're safely out to sea you can sign the papers."

91

"But, sir," I protested, "I don't want to be a bond servant."

"Not want to be a bond servant!" He burst out laughing. "I suppose not, but how then do you propose to pay your passage?"

"I'll work when I get to New England and pay you. Please, sir, help me. My whole life I've wanted to go to the colonies and what I ask can't mean much to you."

"It means a great deal to me. I live by my trade with the English fishing captains. Should I, then, gain a reputation for kidnaping their men for a lazy boy unwilling to pay for what he's wanted all his life? But since you're so anxious, I'll strike a bargain, though I'm a soft-hearted fool for doing it. I'll take you if you'll sign for three years' indenture instead of the usual five."

I shook my head despondently. "I can't forfeit my freedom, sir."

"Freedom," he snorted. "Do you think you'd be free if I landed you penniless in Providence? You'd be the slave of the first man who'd feed you and give you shelter. Money, or better still, land, makes you free. But I see you're stubborn, or too indolent to do ought but whine, so I'll waste no more time on you."

He turned on his heel and walked away. When he was gone I gave myself up to despair. I threw myself on the ground where I lay staring disconsolately into the bright summer sky. In its depths I could see my life unfolding before me. Each spring I would come to the Banks, each winter return to Plymouth. There, for a few months I would loaf on the waterfront, getting drunk and swapping lies with others of my kind. After another year or two I might marry Polly Bragg and live with her in a small over-crowded cottage. Each year she would bear me a child and each year she would grow scrawnier from too much work; her eyes would grow dull, her mouth slack, her skin wrinkled; her shoulders would droop under burdens too heavy for her to bear. As I conjured up this portrait as the years would draw it, I jumped to my feet. Shaking my fist at the blue sky I swore that I would not have it so. In my fury I called on Satan to help me as God was surely on the side of the gentlemen.

Exhausted by my emotion I sank back on the ground. As I lay there a plan came to me. Scrambling up I scanned the mouth of the cove. Our men were cleaning fish at one of the flues on the far side; some of the New Englanders were on the beach, but most of them had apparently gone aboard their ship.

I left my shelter and made my way toward the beach as carefully as I could. So far as I could tell no one paid any attention to me. At the water's edge I hid myself behind a large rock. Stripping, I made my clothes into a bundle which I tied together with my leather belt. After strapping this on my back I plunged into the water. It was cold, but I had swum in it a few times during the past few months and knew what to expect. I swam cautiously, keeping an eye on the corner of the cove where our own men were working. When I got to the New England ship I swam around it until its bulk was between me and the shore, then I called softly for help. After two or three calls a sailor stuck his head over the side. Without asking questions he disappeared and a moment later he threw me a rope.

"I'm a stowaway," I said breathlessly as I clambered up the rope to the deck.

Without speaking he led me to the hold. "Stay here until you're sent for," he said shortly, and left me.

The hold was only about half full of goods. Fearing that despite my care I might have been seen from the shore, I hid as best I could behind some barrels of salted fish. I was at once frightened and exalted. I felt sure that the New England captain would be angry, but once under way he would hardly take me back. It followed that in the end he must take me to Providence. There I had no doubt, despite his croakings, I could make my way. I'd be free, too, I thought with satisfaction.

The hold was dark. Time passed slowly. I grew impatient at what seemed an interminable delay in getting under way. But after a time my nervousness gave way to exhaustion. I had scarcely slept the night before and the morning had been one of strain. My eyes grew heavy and the last thing I remembered was thinking that when I woke I would be on my way to New England.

Someone was shaking me. A voice bawled that I was to wake up. My mind cleared rapidly. I recognized the sailor leaning above me as the one who had helped me aboard. Light streamed down the hatch and the ship was moving. I had escaped.

"Captain wants to see you," the fellow was saying. "Move lively."

Pulling on my breeches which were still wet, and grabbing the rest of my clothes, I followed my guide. Upon reaching deck I was dismayed to see that we were still in sight of shore. I reassured myself, however, with the thought that it was not likely that the ship's course would be changed to land a stowaway. The captain was waiting for me in his cabin. He nodded pleasantly.

"I thought you might change your mind." He pointed at the table in front of him. "There are the papers. You'll see that I'm a man of my word. It's only three years of service that I'm requiring of you."

I looked at the document on the table. I had prepared myself for anger, even severe punishment, but it had not occurred to me that the New Englander would interpret my presence aboard his ship as willingness to meet his terms.

The captain misunderstood my silence. "You can't read, I suppose, but don't fear. I'm an honest man. Any man in my crew will vouch for it. The papers provide for three years, no more."

I screwed up my courage.

"I can read but I can't sign."

"A cross will do."

"I don't mean that, sir. I mean I won't sign."

"Won't sign?" His kindly expression did not change.

"I can't, sir. I want to go to New England so that I can be free."

"Still that. So I am to take you to New England out of the kindness of my heart, just so you can be free."

"But I'll work, sir, and pay you back. Before God I will."

"Listen, lad, once for all. If you sign this paper of indenture I can sell you for three years' labor. If I have luck I'll get enough to pay the usual price for fetching an English fisherman from the Banks. That's my offer and it's a fair one. Your way isn't fair. Supposing you're honest, which I have no way of knowing, when you earn it I get my money. That is I get it if you find work and if there is anything left after you've spent what's necessary to live

94

on. I know New England and I know there's little chance of that. You babble about your freedom. You can have it if you'll work for it. If not, I have no further use for you and you must leave my ship."

As he spoke I knew that what he said was but common sense, yet, as I looked at the contract I felt as a prisoner who sees the scaffold which he must soon mount. I shook my head.

"I won't sign. Even if you send me back."

"Send you back?"

"How else am I to leave your ship?"

The round, rosy man before me was imperturbable. His eyes were still friendly, his manner bland as ever. "As you got on, no doubt, over the side."

I realized that he meant it. I must sign or swim back or drown. Through the porthole I saw the shore. It seemed a long way off. Panic seized me. I must get overboard quickly.

"Let me go," I cried. "Let me out of here."

"Take him out." The captain's voice was still quiet and friendly. As I hurried for the door he added, "You're a fool, lad, but you've got courage. If you ever come to Providence look for Captain Warren."

A moment later I plunged off the side of the vessel. Coming to the surface I struggled for a few seconds to find my bearings. When I had done so the shore line seemed horribly far away. As I swam I remembered tales the men told of the early days in the fisheries. How the ships would slip from their ports in January and race for the Banks in order to be first in the coves, so the captain might be fishing admiral and get the best stages. If two or more vessels arrived together, and the mists of late winter held them out of the coves, seamen, bribed by promises of large rewards, would plunge into the icy water and race for shore to stake their ship's claim. If three or four went from a ship one might get there. I told myself that I was strong as those men who had lived a hundred years ago, and the water I was in must be almost warm compared to that of late winter. Then my thoughts wandered. I wondered if my father had ever been in this cove, what Polly would think if she knew that off the edge of the New

95

World about which we had made so many plans, I was swimming for my life. Gradually my mind, like my body, grew numb from cold and I ceased to think at all. My arms and legs moved without conscious effort; my eyes remained fixed on the shore line, which grew dimmer and dimmer, as if a curtain of ice separated it from the sea in which I was struggling.

My feet, which had been sinking lower and lower, struck something. I roused myself from the lethargy into which I had been sinking enough to lift them. I was dully resentful that here was some new obstacle to my painful efforts to keep afloat. Despite my efforts, my feet kept dragging. Finally as I was on the verge of surrendering to the sea, it penetrated my sluggish mind that I was touching bottom. With a final effort I stumbled ashore. As I sank to the ground I was not thankful for life, only for the sand, hot from the August sun, in which I sprawled. I rolled over in it, so that every part of my body could take comfort.

For a long time I lay there, too exhausted to feel disappointment at my failure. Occasionally I rolled to a dry place. I was finally aroused by one of our men who had noticed me. He was prodding me with his foot, demanding what the Hell I was doing there, sleeping in the mid-afternoon sun. I was still too weary to do ought but tell the truth.

"He made me jump overboard and swim ashore," I explained drowsily.

"Who did?"

"Captain of the *Dolphin*. I wouldn't sign indenture papers."

The fellow was an old fisherman who knew the ways of the Banks.

"So he kidnaped and then tried to drown you. Well, it's luck you're alive."

He left me. Gradually I realized that unknowingly he had offered me a reprieve from Captain Couch's wrath. I had not run away. I had been kidnaped. Such was the story I told the Captain that night, sticking mainly to the truth, only changing it regarding the manner of my coming on the *Dolphin*, which I explained by saying I had been carried on by force the night before. The captain knew that the so-called kidnaping of Newfoundland fishermen by the New Englanders was generally carried out with the consent of the former, and clearly doubted my word. Yet I was here and had evidently been almost drowned, so he could do little but grumble and curse Captain Warren as a thieving pirate.

But though I escaped the captain's wrath, Bill Smith, when I told him my story, took me to task.

"The captain was right, Tom. You had no right to ask him to take you for nothing. He earns a living just as you do. You would do well to remember that you must be willing to pay for what you want, or shrewd enough to take it without paying. You were neither in this case, but only a silly boy expecting a thing for no better reason than that you wanted it."

"But how am I to get to the colonies?" I asked petulantly.

"Since you will not indenture yourself, you must pay passage."

"But I can never get so much money."

For a long time Bill did not reply, and indeed, I thought dejectedly, what could he say? As he and Captain Warren pointed out, I would not pay with the one coin I had—my freedom—and I possessed no other. I sank further and further into gloom. Finally Bill spoke.

"I've toyed with an idea of late, Tom; but because you're young and no doubt anxious to get to a place where you can have some fun, I have not mentioned it."

"Fun!" I laughed bitterly. "People such as I are not supposed to have fun. We only work so our betters can amuse themselves."

"Good," said Bill quietly; "if you feel that way, perhaps you will be willing to stay here in Newfoundland with me through the winter."

Newfoundland—through the winter! I thought of the men at Conception Bay, how they had spoken of their winter on the Island, and how they had looked as they spoke of it. I thought of the vast forest behind me, of the desolate sea, dark green when it was sunless, before me. And England, which I had sworn I never wanted to see again, suddenly seemed good, with its warm taverns filled with jolly company. I pictured myself in such a tavern, spending my money, lying about my adventures, getting drunk with no thought of the day to come. And I thought of Polly Bragg. With money I could have Polly too; if not, there were other women.

Bill Smith guessed what was in my mind.

"Maybe you don't hate England as much as you thought you did, and maybe you don't hate Polly after all," he said.

"Didn't I try to get to New England so I would never have to see either again?"

"Then it must be as the captain said. You won't pay the price for what you want."

"But I don't see how staying here all winter will get me to the colonies."

"If you go back to England your wages from the year's catch will be spent by spring. Then you must come back here for another season, spend the money you get in order to live through another winter, and so it will go until you die. But if you stay here in the winter you'll spend nothing, and at the end of next year's season, when you get to England, you'll have two years' pay coming—enough to step from the *Cape Race* to a ship bound for the colonies."

I realized that there was sense in what he said; the idea fascinated and yet frightened me. I raised objections. How could we stay through the winter? What assurance did I have that Peter Couch would pay me my two years' share? If he did, what if I still did not have enough to go to America?

As I raised each obstacle Bill demolished it. After his experience at Conception Bay the captain would be glad to have us stay and keep his stages at no cost but that of provisioning us through the winter.

As for being cheated, Peter Couch was a close man but an honest one—all Plymouth knew that; I would get my pay. And it would be enough for my passage back to the colonies. If not, Bill promised to give me his own two years' earnings, or as much of them as I needed.

But when at length my objections were beaten down and I asked Bill why he himself wanted to stay, he shook his head and smiled wryly.

"It's a hard question you ask, Tom. Perhaps I'm growing tired of masquerading as Bill Smith, and would like to be myself for a few months, with none but you to see me; or maybe it's because there are things can happen to a man that makes the solitude of a frozen wilderness seem kind."

"What of Cousin?" It was the first time I had mentioned him since that day on the ship. "You won't find him in Newfoundland, in mid-winter."

"Nor in the England of Charles II, so Cousin must wait. Some day I'll find him. Meanwhile I must be patient, and I find patience easier here, with the forests, and the mountains and the sea."

In the end I agreed to stay, and as Bill Smith had predicted, he had no trouble persuading Captain Couch to leave us. He even agreed to increase our share of the next season's profits if the stages were preserved and in good condition when he returned.

## 4.

The *Cape Race* left Newfoundland in late August. It was mid-May when she returned. Bill Smith and I lived alone in the tiny cove for eight and a half months. During that time we saw no other human save half a dozen red Indians who visited us one day in early spring. Bill was able to talk to one of them in French. He learned that they were Micmacs from Acadia, who had come to Newfoundland the summer before with the French. Thus we learned for the first time that the French had established a permanent settlement on Placentia Bay. Bill said this was information of great political importance, but in the winter of 1665 I found many things more interesting than high politics. Bill and I cut down trees and built a solid cabin; we trapped and hunted for food. In short, I got my first lessons in pioneering; and I often thought how queer it was that I should have as my teacher an English gentleman. When I told Bill this, he disagreed.

"Gentlemen, as we call them, should do things better. They're trained to leadership and to use their heads as well as their hands. They may—in fact they generally do—either abuse or neglect

99

their powers of leadership, but mark this, Tom, even in your fine New World, until such a time as the base-born can educate themselves and gain sufficient material possessions to be their own masters, they will be forced to turn to the gentlemen for leaders in times of need."

"But why?" I protested. "What can gentlemen do that I cannot?"

"He's learned the habit of commanding rather than obeying, of leading instead of following. There are other things, too, though less important."

Not long after this conversation Bill began to give me lessons in writing. Using his finger or the sharp end of a stick, he made letters for me in the snow. From the first I was fascinated. It gave me a sense of power that I could not explain to see letters of my own making. For hours, day after day, I practiced. First I merely made letters, then words, then whole sentences. I drove my teacher into an amused frenzy by my demands for new words and how to spell old ones. But by spring I could form letters better than he could, and spell almost as well.

One day in late spring I was on the beach by myself. Near the water's edge the snow had been washed away. I was idly tracing words in the wet sand. Presently I wrote "Dear Polly." I looked at it and continued. When I was done, I had written my first letter. It was undoubtedly a poor thing, lame and stilted, but no artist ever toiled over his masterpiece more painstakingly. I still remember how my pulse beat and I grew weak as I scratched with my sharp stick the word "love." I was overwhelmed with an almost intolerable desire to be back in England. I felt I could not stand the months that must pass before I could see a woman again. No, not a woman, Polly Bragg. Polly, on my knee as I had last seen her on the squire's, her arm around my neck, her eyes bright, her large mouth soft, half open and free to any man who wanted it. I cursed her, and called for her, and rolled in the sand.

After the *Cape Race* came time passed quickly, for she brought with her long days of exhausting work. I was generally too busy or too tired to think of Polly, but nonetheless, the winter had left its mark on me. I was still determined to spend my life in

America, but I no longer wanted to go directly to New England. First I must return to Denham where I would compel Polly to marry me without further nonsense. I did not intend to come to the New World again without a woman, and to me "woman" meant Polly Bragg.

The fishing was good that summer. We filled our hold and set sail for England in mid-August. In late September we reached Plymouth.

# VI

As WE approached England the thought of home and a snug corner in a tavern dissipated the cold magic of the fishing banks. Thus when we came within sight of Plymouth we were a boisterous lot. Then a strange thing happened. It was as though a ghost had boarded the ship. No one saw it, yet all knew it was there. Here and there a man still gave tongue to the pleasures that awaited him on land, but even as he talked his eyes wandered nervously, while his listeners, scanning the placid waters of the harbor, scarcely heard him. For the harbor was nearly empty of ships and the wharves beyond were deserted.

"War," I suggested to Bill who was standing by me at the ship's rail, but he shook his head.

"If it was war a convoy would have been sent to the Banks to escort the fishing vessels home."

We were silent until the ship cast anchor. It seemed a long time before a port official clambered aboard. The captain met him as he came over the side.

"What's wrong?" he shouted.

The fellow only stared from eyes heavy-laden with fear.

"What's wrong?" the captain repeated impatiently. "Where are the ships?"

"The plague," the official gasped in what might have been a whisper had panic not forbidden such reticence. "The plague. All England's in its grip. The worst in living memory. Men even say it's the Black Death come again."

Plague or no plague, Captain Peter Couch sold his fish and paid his crew. The men divided one-third of the profits of the voyage; Bill and I received an added sum for guarding the stages during the winter.

I no sooner had my money than I headed for Denham. A strange girl opened the door. She said Polly was no longer there but lived in town where she served the master's mis'.

For a moment I considered the girl. She was trim enough, with a prettier face than Polly's, and I knew, as men do know those things, that she was willing. But I decided against it. Only Polly could slake my eighteen months' thirst.

As I hurried back to Plymouth my disappointment gave way to satisfaction. If Polly was Susan's servant it followed that she had failed in her designs upon the squire. In such a case she would doubtless welcome heartily a man with two years' pay in his pouch. The thought of Polly, humble and striving to please me, was like fire in my blood. Unconsciously I increased my pace until I was almost running. Thus bloated from self-esteem that sprang from the possession of a little silver, I forgot what I should have remembered about Polly Bragg. I even forgot the plague.

Plymouth reminded me. Fearfully I hastened through almost deserted streets to the house where Susan was lodged. At last I stood before its heavy door. Just beyond was Polly. Then I saw the wisp of straw: since the Black Death the symbol of a plague-stricken house. I fought back panic. Perhaps the wind had blown the straw there. I forced myself to examine the door and found what I had known I would find. The lock was on the outside of the door—outside, where any rogue who would might lift it and enter, but the house was safe—from men. Meantime, those within were locked in until the malady ran its course and the victim died, or in rare cases recovered.

I stared at the lock. It was ready to my hand. Beyond it was Polly. I turned and ran. I did not stop until I reached the wharves. The water, at least, might be clean.

I spent the following hours in an agony of indecision, for although my fear of the plague did not lessen, after the first surge of panic had subsided I was tormented by the thought that it might be Polly herself who was stricken. In the end anxiety triumphed over fear and I returned to the house. The wisp of straw was still there. The lock was still on the outside of the door. I made my way to the back where I shouted as loudly as I could until a shutter was thrown open. The face in the window was drawn and pale. The large eyes stared down at me blankly.

"Susan," I cried.

Slow-dawning recognition brought her features to life. "Tommy," she gasped, but even as she spoke the spark of life grew dull again. "Go away," she said in a flat voice. "Go away or you'll die."

To ask was pure physical pain but I had to know.

"Who?" I groaned.

Susan only looked at me.

"Who?" I shouted wildly. "Answer me, damn you. Tell me if it's Polly."

She shook her head. "It's John."

I had heard of gentlefolk dying from plague, but without reflection had rejected such talk as foolish. Experience had taught me that only the poor suffer. Hunger, cold, hardship were for them alone. Why then should God not reserve for them the most dreadful of his diseases? But here was proof that I had been wrong. Or perhaps I had been right about God, but it was the devil who sent the plague, and he, at least, is no respecter of rank. I laughed. I could not help it. I lost all control of myself. I sat down, then lay flat on my back, from where I hurled salvo after salvo of thunderous mirth at the Providence that had been so japed by Satan.

My vehemence stirred Susan out of her lethargy.

"What is it?" she cried.

"The squire," I gasped. "He was always so afraid of poor peoples' sickness."

"Maybe you'll think it even funnier that your Polly's his nurse,"

Susan snapped. "No one else goes near him. They're shut up together, just the two of them."

I thought this over and decided it was a lie. Susan would not permit another to tend her precious John. When I told her so a spasm of pain distorted her tired face.

"I wish it was me," she cried. "But if I did, who would look after my babies?"

"Babies," I repeated fatuously. "In there? But whose?"

"Mine, goose." Susan laughed, and I did not know if she flushed from shame or pride. "And of course they are here. At least one is, he's over a year old—the other's on the way."

I understood Susan's conduct, but not Polly's. Nor could my sister enlighten me. She only knew that when the squire was stricken all the servants save Polly had fled. She had gone to the sick man and after a prolonged talk had emerged only to order that food and water be left outside the bedroom door. Susan thought some kind of bargain had been made.

"What bargain?" I demanded.

"I don't know, and—oh! Tommy, I'm afraid. Lately he's been looking at her, like he used to at me—before he took me."

"Has he only looked?" I interrupted harshly.

"I think so, but after this—" She paused and her voice went flat. "But it doesn't matter any more. He'll die. Likely they'll both die."

"Likely," I agreed miserably, "but tell Polly I've come back for her—to wed her."

I could do nothing more until the squire recovered or Polly died.

### 3.

I spent the following days in a nightmare of apprehension. Each morning I hastened to Susan's window certain that I would be told that Polly was ill. But Satan had other plans for Polly Bragg and she remained healthy. During these days Bill Smith was my only companion. But Bill was worn and preoccupied. He said little and drank steadily, growing more and more morose as he sank deeper into drunkenness. Then without warning he disappeared.

A few days later he walked into my lodgings. Under his arm he carried a large package wrapped in heavy linen.

"I've brought you something." He undid his package and revealed a round dozen books. "Read them, and God grant you more joy in them than I've had. They are my parting gift."

"Are you going away?"

"For a long time." He smiled. "As a matter of fact Bill Smith is about to die."

"Die?" I gasped.

Bill nodded solemnly. "And a strange death for a man. He'll die giving birth to a pirate."

For an instant I thought he was drunk again, but as I looked at him I knew he was not. He was haggard and seething from some inner excitement, but he was sober and sane. And after all, I reflected, a man who would turn from gentleman into fisherman might well change from fisherman to pirate. And for that matter a pirate's life would be far better than one spent on the Banks off Newfoundland or in the plague-stricken mews of Plymouth.

"I'll go with you," I declared.

He gripped my hand. "I'd like nothing better, Tom, but there are some things a man must do alone. If I fail though, perhaps some day you will carry on. I've found Edward Cousin, or at least his trail. He's engaged in the slave trade between Africa and the West Indies."

At Edward Cousin's name my impulsive desire to turn pirate dissolved, for to tell the truth I was not anxious to cross his path. Any man of courage will fight the devil if he must, but one with money in his pouch and a heavy-mouthed girl almost within reach does not search him out. I tried to cover my retreat.

"But why turn pirate?" I asked. "Can't you go to the Indies and wait for him?"

"I could. But pirates are outside the law"—the evil in Bill Smith's voice matched Cousin's own—"and when I find Edward Cousin I want to be outside the law."

He dropped my hand and went toward the door. At that moment, sure that I would never see him again, I felt that I was deserting him.

"If you fail," I cried, "I'll find him."

Bill paused. "If that should happen," he said slowly, "tell him before you kill him that the maimed spirit of a woman who was called Prudence will be able to sleep in peace after he's dead."

"A woman called Prudence," I repeated dutifully.

"Yes. Though when Edward Cousin knew her she was scarcely a woman at all, but rather a child. She was my wife. She died three days ago."

I was lonely after Bill left England. At first I sought companionship in the few public houses that were open, but because of the plague the company in such places was so scant, and the fear hanging over them so heavy, that a few such visits convinced me that they offered no solace for my low spirits. In desperation I turned to Bill's books. Reading grimly, determined to forget the outside world, I soon became fascinated. True, there was a great deal that I did not understand, but even so, the magic woven of words held me under its spell. So the days passed, unsubstantial shadows, made up in part of half-comprehended ideas gleaned from books, and the rest of anxiety for Polly.

A day finally came when Susan told me that Denham was out of danger and that I could see Polly the next afternoon.

"See her," I shouted. "I'll do more than see her. I'll marry her."

Susan smiled happily. "That's right, Tommy. Do it and take her far away."

"To America," I promised.

I was busy the rest of the day. By good luck I had heard only recently of a ship bound for Virginia. I arranged passage with its master for myself and my wife. I found it cheaper than I had expected, for with the plague in England and low prices for tobacco in Virginia trade was slack.

"Plenty of room," the master assured me gloomily. "A light cargo and a few poor devils who have indentured themselves in return for passage."

When I was done with the ship's master I collected the gear

that I needed. Evening was falling when I made my final purchase, a thin band of gold. Bill had told me of these rings that gentlemen give their wives to wear on their fingers as a token of marriage, so with the money saved from the passage I bought one, resolved to show Polly that even though she had missed her squire, she had found a man who could give her the baubles that she so greatly valued. With the ring safely in my pouch I was done with my preparations. I had only to wait until the next day.

I slept badly that night and spent the following morning wandering aimlessly along the wharves. The sun was scarcely overhead before I burst into Susan's house.

I was too late. During the morning Polly Bragg had wed John Denham.

That was the end of the story that a hysterical and nearly prostrate Susan told me. Its beginnings went back to a time shortly after my own flight from England when Polly, who was bored with Denham, fled to Susan in Plymouth and begged a place in her household there. For the first few months she was docile and unobtrusive, and the squire seemed unaware of her existence. But Susan was bearing her first child, and as the months passed and she grew too heavy to furnish him sport, or even please his eye, Denham had grown restive, and Polly was there. It was nothing serious, or at least so Susan thought, a fleeting caress on his part, a pert word on hers, but this had been enough to frighten Susan who upbraided Polly. Polly denied everything.

The child was born and for a time things were better, but with the coming of winter another crisis had arisen. I was the unconscious cause. Upon coming to town Polly learned I had gone to Newfoundland. During the spring and summer, ignorant of the cause of my flight, she had awaited confidently the return of the fishing fleet. But when the *Cape Race* came home and the men told her I had stayed in the New World she had concluded that I had abandoned her, and, whatever her previous intentions regarding her master had been, from that day she turned grimly to the task of ensnaring him.

So the winter and summer passed and autumn came and was

almost gone. Then the plague came. When the squire fell ill the servants fled, and even Susan, pregnant again, afraid for her babies, refused to go near the sick man. It was then that Polly Bragg came to his rescue.

That had been the situation when I arrived in England, and so far as Susan knew it had remained so until that very morning when a triumphant Polly had brought her patient from the sick room to announce that she was leading him to the altar. For that, it appeared, was to be the consequence of the conversation between Polly and the squire. Seizing her opportunity the girl had driven a hard bargain. She would defy death to do its worst to herself or the squire, if on the day the latter arose from his sickbed he would make her his wife. Ill and frightened, Denham had agreed. That morning Polly had dragged him off to seal the bargain.

I was stunned by Susan's story. Polly was mine, not the squire's.

"And didn't it make any difference," I asked bleakly, "when you told her I'd come home to marry her?"

Then I heard the comedy's last bitter jest. Unaware of the bargain between the squire and his nurse, and afraid that if Polly learned I had come home she would abandon her patient, Susan had not told her of my return. I cursed Susan, but as I did so my hopes revived. Perhaps Polly had determined to marry the squire only after she became convinced that I had forgotten her.

If this were true there was a bare possibility that I could find them before they were married and dissuade Polly. Susan did not share my hopes.

"Polly won't let anything delay her," she assured me dismally. "She'll have John while he's still too weak to resist. I heard her say that they would take a carriage to Denham."

"Then I'll follow them to Denham," I declared.

"What good will it do, even if you get there before they're married," Susan sighed. "Polly won't give up being a squire's lady just to go into the American wilderness with you."

"If I find them she will," I retorted fiercely.

"Well, we needn't quarrel about that. They're wed by now."

"Then I'll take a widow to America."

I said it impulsively, but once said I knew it was true. If John Denham had married Polly I would kill him.

It was late afternoon when I left Plymouth and twilight when I passed through Saltash. Nothing there had changed. Women and old men sat in the doorways of the cottages, children rolled in the dust that still held the lingering warmth of the autumn sun. I passed the cottage where I was born. Another fisherman's family lived there. A squalling baby was being comforted by a child not much older than itself. A flood of memories washed over me. When they had ebbed I had forgiven Susan for her misguided deceit, and my hatred for Denham had increased until killing him, which I had first thought of only as a last desperate measure, was desirable in itself. During the rest of the way to Denham I plotted murder.

Nevertheless, when I had entered the squire's grounds I grew fearful. I had once witnessed a hanging. The scene came back to me vividly. I sat down under a bush. Should I give up my design of violence and merely plead my cause? But did I have a cause? If they were already married Polly would belong to Denham. The thought was unbearable, and jealousy rescued courage as my resolution hardened.

I went on. Soon the house came into sight. It was dark. My heart sank. What if they had not come to Denham after all, or had come and gone? But with the plague abroad where else could they go? The dining room was on the other side of the house. It was probable that they would be there, at least the squire, who, I recalled, often stayed at the table drinking long after the meal was finished. So slipping into the garden from which I had stumbled that night two years ago, when I had last seen Denham, I made my way around the house. Light shone from the dining room, and as I had expected on an autumn night, a window was open. I peeped in. Only a few candles lit the long room. At first I could see no one, but as my eyes became accustomed to the light, I discerned dimly through the shadows at the far end of the table a figure, head fallen forward resting on outflung arms.

The squire alone and drunk, I thought exultantly. I crawled into the window. The figure did not move. Halfway down the

110

room I realized it was that of a woman. For an instant I thought it was Polly, but while I still stood, undecided, she lifted her head. It was Jane Bragg. She looked at me dully. Her eyes were red, her face tear-stained.

"Who are you?" she demanded in a thick voice. She was drunk.

"Where's Polly?" I demanded sharply.

"She's gone."

I staved off panic. "Where's the squire?"

"Gone. She wouldn't stay here only long enough to get some things. She dragged him off to London. He was half dead with fright, but she told him a man couldn't be taken twice with plague."

"But she hasn't had it," I interrupted. "Surely she wouldn't go there where it's worst of all. They've only gone to Plymouth."

"London. We warned her, Squire and I, but Polly was not afraid. So she had her way and by now they're bound for London."

As Jane talked a note of pride crept into her voice, but then remembrance pierced her drunken stupor.

"God help me!" Her voice rose to a shriek. "They've gone." Her head fell on her outstretched arms. "Christ forgive me," she moaned. "Christ forgive me."

I hastened to her and shook her until she raised her head. Recognition flickered in her dull face. "Tom Bone," she mumbled.

"Never mind," I growled. "When did they go?"

"This afternoon. God forgive me for being such a coward. God forgive me and God forgive my poor Polly."

My despair found a victim. "Your poor Polly," I sneered. "And why your poor Polly? She's got her squire. He's even wed her. And no doubt you're glad as she. It's not every scullery maid's bastard that does so well. You probably planned it since the day she was born."

For a moment Jane Bragg stared at me in sheer horror, then she broke into a crazed laugh.

"God, what a joke! Planned it since the day she was born— and they brother and sister." I stared at her, unable to speak. She caught her breath in a great sob and continued brokenly. "Hear that, Tom Bone. I've never told a living soul till now. The old squire, the young squire's father, was my Pol's father too, and now they're wed and it's their bridal night."

I did not believe it. It was a drunken fantasy conjured up from gin and excitement. I recalled the rumors I had heard as a child. I remembered that Polly herself had told me that the old squire had always been fond of her. If the village knew of it, and the squire himself took no pains to hide his affection, the young squire was sure to have heard of it, and Polly too. And why should it have been kept a secret? It was no extraordinary thing for a serving wench to bear her master's child.

I told Jane Bragg all these things, but she brushed them aside.

"It was just before the wars broke out," she explained, "and the Round Heads with their pious faces and their mean ways were already in control hereabouts. The master, who was tight-fisted, said if they found out about his sin, as they'd call it, they would use it as an excuse to fine him, or even take some of Denham for themselves. So he wouldn't let me tell who Pol's father was."

"But people did know. I heard it myself."

"They guessed but they didn't know, and none dared say it to the young squire."

"But surely you must have told Polly," I insisted desperately. "You wouldn't have kept from her the knowledge that her father belonged to the gentry. You'd have been too proud of it."

"I had to. The old man died while Cromwell still ruled England, and on his deathbed he made me swear an oath I wouldn't tell. It was an awful oath that would damn my soul to break."

"So you damned your daughter's," I cried.

"How could I know this would happen? She was only your sister's serving girl when I was sent back here from Plymouth, and I didn't hear of her again till they came today. Then I kept putting off telling them."

"You knew they were going away."

"I didn't really believe she could persuade him. I was in the kitchen when John—he's the stableboy—came in and said they were gone. Then it was too late."

As Jane babbled drunkenly a scene I had witnessed a few years before rose before me. One day while wandering in the streets I had become aware of an unfamiliar noise. It was a roar, low and angry and cruel, as if it came from the throats of beasts rather than men. Hastening in the direction from which it came I ran into a street crowded with men and women. A cart was going by. In it was a man, but I scarcely saw him, for tied to the cart's tail, barefoot and stripped to the waist, was a girl. Behind her walked a hulking brute with a whip. He lashed her mercilessly. As she stumbled along, blind from blood that flowed from a gash on her forehead and tears that streamed from her eyes, I thought how pretty she might have been. Almost as pretty as Polly.

Most of the people were only shouting coarse insults, but some were throwing stones. As I looked one struck the girl. I was so close that I could hear the thud as it sank into her flesh. The girl's body recoiled, she stumbled as if about to fall, but as she started to sink, the whip coiled around her naked waist and brought her moaning upright. She staggered on.

"What have they done?"

The woman I asked was decently dressed and looked respectable. But as she turned reluctantly to answer me I saw that her eyes were heavy with hate. Her mouth worked convulsively. She had a stone in her hand.

"They're brother and sister," she said.

I still felt sorry for the girl.

"Why do they torture only the woman? The man is equally guilty."

The woman licked her lips.

"He's to hang," she said with satisfaction. "But she is only to be whipped through the streets to the place of execution, where she must watch her brother swing alone for what they did together. After that she will go free—unless we kill the nasty thing first."

She turned away from me and hurled her stone.

As I recalled the scene I fancied that I could see Polly Bragg at the cart's tail. Her cheeks were streaked with tears, her body was lacerated by the lash and bruised by stones. She stumbled toward me, her face twisted and ugly from weeping.

113

The fantasy faded. I was in the dining room at Denham again. The unlovely creature before me was not Pol but her mother, Jane Bragg, who had struggled to her feet and was lurching toward me. For what I then did I can only plead that my provocation was great. I was desperate over losing Polly, and horror-stricken at the thought of her fate if her mother's tale became generally known. So as the drunken woman clutched at me I struck her. I did it in a fit of fury rather than with conscious intent to injure her, but I struck hard. She spun half around, staggered and fell. After that she was still.

I stared down at her. Blood trickled from a gash in her forehead. It ran down the side of her face and stained the heavy rug upon which she lay. I tore a piece from the cloth that covered the table and dabbled at the wound. The blood ceased to flow, but it seemed to me that the body under my hands grew cold. I believed that she was dying. Panic seized me. I fled from Denham.

I crept back to Plymouth through little-used country lanes. Safe at my lodging I took stock of my position. I felt no remorse. With her mother alive Polly was in constant peril of the cart's tail. True, Jane Bragg had kept her secret through the years; but in that revealing second during which I had realized what I must do I had seen clearly that the past was no guarantee for the future. Jane Bragg was not strong enough to bear alone the weight of her daughter's sin. The very fact that she had spoken to me was proof of Polly's danger. No, even though I believed that I had killed Jane Bragg, I was not sorry.

Although her mother was not on my conscience Polly was. I struggled with her problem until far into the morning. In the end I resigned her to whatever destiny fate and her own ambition might ordain. Now that I had removed the danger of discovery and punishment she might well pass the rest of her life as a squire's lady. As to her sin, that was in God's hands, not mine. So I put aside my first impulse to pursue her to London, and once again resolved to thrust all thoughts of Polly Bragg from my life.

I turned my thoughts to my own future. I believed myself a murderer, and the morning's thin sunlight was heavy enough to cast the shadow of the gallows. I must leave England. The ship was ready to go, arrangements with the captain were already made. I need only explain that my wife had lost her courage and would not venture into the wilderness. Such things happened. Only the strong went to America.

There were still a few hours to pass before the ship sailed. I decided to tell Susan good-by. She had not slept. Despite her dismal certainty to the contrary she had sat up all night hoping that I might succeed, and her John would return.

Afraid to admit that I had been to Denham I could not even tell the truth, so I pretended that after leaving her the preceding evening common sense had prevailed over anger, and I had gone home to make preparations for leaving England.

Susan burst into tears and begged that I, at least, should not desert her. I had been so concerned with my own problems that Susan's plight had not occurred to me. What would she do now that her lover had abandoned her? With a child, and another on the way, no man would be likely to want her for a wife. Anger more intense than that of the previous day took possession of me. By what right had the Squire of Denham ruined my sister's life? She should have married a countryman or even a fisherman, and borne him a child each year. I could see her standing in the midst of her brood, tired and disheveled, worked too hard and not always well treated, but nonetheless happy. Instead (for hoping forlornly that her lover might return the poor creature had decked herself out as he liked best to see her) she sat before me, a mock figure of fashion. Her hair was piled high, elaborately curled and powdered, her cheeks were heavily rouged, her small hands, clutching convulsively, were white and smooth from lack of work. The cruel egotistic waste of the gentry! Here was a woman who could help a man live an honest life, who could live one herself, but instead she sat rouged and powdered, decked out in silk and velvet, idle until such time as her master grew ruttish.

And now another Susan shoved herself into my seething brain— the little girl who had loved and taken care of me. I swore wrath-fully that I would save what was left of her life. Denham might desert her but she would not starve or go into the streets. Polly was gone; Susan would go with me to America.

But Susan would not. She refused flatly. As long as John Denham lived she would wait for him in England. When he brought his bride back from London, she would go to Polly and plead to be taken into the household if only as her meanest servant. I could not shake Susan's resolution. I begged, I threatened. I cursed her and in my rage I even wept over her. It was useless. In the end, exhausted and beaten, but determined that if Susan must go to John Denham or his wife as a suppliant she should at least be free from all necessity save that forced on her by her own folly, I took the precious leather pouch from my belt.

"Take it," I said gruffly as I tossed into her lap the profits of two summers and a winter in Newfoundland. "With that, if you come to your senses, or Pol has you thrown out as she probably will, you can find an honest man for a husband. See you choose better than the last time."

Without waiting to witness her tears of gratitude I hastened away. I was afraid I might change my mind. As I left the house I reflected angrily that I had turned murderer for love of Polly, and forfeited my freedom out of pity for Susan. I cursed all women.

I told the ship master that I had lost all my money gambling. He consented to take me aboard as cargo, but as times were hard in Virginia and the planters could ill afford more workers, I was forced to sign for seven years' service.

# Book Two

# VII

## I.

THE ILL treatment of blacks at the hands of certain captains engaged in the slave trade is well known, yet the negurs of Africa suffer no more during the Middle Passage itself than many Englishmen who cross the Atlantic as indentured servants. Insufficient food—and much of that rotten—overcrowding, disease and brutal treatment sometimes result in the loss of half the human cargo. But in 1665 the plague in England and tobacco at half-penny a pound in Virginia were enough to prevent overcrowding of vessels engaged in the American trade. In the case of the *Hampden* the cargo consisted mostly of farm implements and household furniture. There were only a few humans on its bills of lading.

The voyage was uneventful. Perhaps because there was plenty of living space we escaped disease, and our captain was shrewd enough to see that our rations were sufficient to bring us to the market in good condition. So when the *Hampden* cast anchor off Jamestown I took my physical welfare as an omen of the future and looked hopefully at the shore line of Virginia. It was the first of January, and I assured myself that the old miseries were gone with the old year.

The captain, after telling us that he hoped the news that he had indentured servants on board would bring buyers to the ship, turned to the business of unloading the cargo.

After what seemed a long wait a skiff drew alongside our vessel. Its two occupants were much alike. Each was tanned by the sun, with rough hands and weather-beaten faces. Each wore good but plain clothes. "Not like the gentlemen who visited Denham," I told myself with satisfaction.

After they had come over the ship's side I could hear one of them speaking.

"It's an outrage to have bound them for seven years," he was saying to the captain. "Five's customary and it's enough."

The captain smiled frostily. "The price is the same for seven as it used to be for five, Mr. Lester. If you wish to change the papers to read for the shorter term you may."

"Don't do it, Lester," the second planter interposed. "It would only cause dissatisfaction among the others."

The one they called Lester sighed.

"I'm afraid I don't need your argument to persuade me, Eaton. Times such as these are too hard to permit generosity."

As he spoke he was scanning us closely, and presently he motioned me to step forward. He looked at me more closely and prodded me impersonally as if I'd been an animal.

"Six pounds?" he asked the captain.

"Right. Sterling."

"And no hidden clauses in the papers providing special privileges or treatment?"

"Treatment according to your own laws."

The money changed hands, and I was James Lester's bound servant. We were rowed to the south side of the river where a black waited with horses.

"Can you ride?" my master asked.

"I served as stableboy once."

When we had mounted I waited for him to ride ahead, but he motioned me to his side.

"I like to talk to a man once in a while," he said simply, and my resentment at service dropped clean away. As I drew abreast him I even lifted my hand from the reins and pulled at my forelock.

"Don't do that," Lester ordered sharply. I must have looked startled for he continued more quietly, "This isn't England. We're all men here." A cloud crossed his face. "Except the negurs."

I, who had lived so long in England, found this hard to believe. "No masters and servants?" I gasped foolishly.

"Nonsense. Of course there are masters and servants. There always will be. You're my servant, and you'll find me a hard master if you shirk. But it's the work of your muscles that you owe me, not the abasement of your manhood, for when your term is up you'll be a free man and a landholder. Then where's the difference between us?"

I listened and was rich in contentment. All those days when I had dreamed on Plymouth's wharves were vindicated. And now I had entered the land of Canaan. But Lester's next words reminded me that even Canaan is not Paradise.

"Of course," he said, "there are some who do not feel as I do." He smiled wryly. "My wife is among them. But don't let that discourage you. There's too much land for them in the New World. So much it will swallow them—for who will be a servant when he can own land of his own? Europe and the past belong to them, but America and the future are ours. And now enough of this. Tell me of yourself, and particularly what you can do."

I told him as much of my story as I thought needful. When I was done he said bluntly that he was disappointed. He needed not a fisherman but a farmer who could care for four acres of maize and a thousand tobacco plants.

"I can learn," I assured him.

"No doubt, but it will take time, and as you have not been in a hot country before I shall not be able to work you in the fields this summer. Men die if they work too hard before they grow used to our climate."

He talked on in an easy rambling fashion, telling me of the country and its people. It was twilight when he pulled his horse to a stop and flung out his arm.

"Sidney Hall," he said.

"Sidney Hall," I repeated blankly.

"The house is behind those trees." He laughed tolerantly. "My wife christened it. Her name was Sidney. She's proud of her gentle blood."

When we came within view of the house I knew why its master had laughed. Sidney Hall was a two-story frame house some forty feet long and half as wide. It was painted white and glistened clean in the winter sunshine. At each end was a brick chimney. In England it would belong to a gentleman of modest means.

My master led me to the rear of the house. Here there were a cluster of out-buildings. I recognized stable, barn and henhouse. The others, I learned later, were cabins for the servants, sheds for drying tobacco, summerhouse, dairy and kitchen. This latter was built separately so that the rest of the house might escape the odors as well as the insects and dogs that are an inseparable part of a Virginia kitchen.

Lester dismounted and bade me follow him. We entered one of the cabins. There was one room. It was about twelve feet square with no floor other than hard packed dirt. The walls were painted white, the windows were of glass. The furniture consisted of two rough-hewn bedsteads, one chair, and one chest. One of the beds was bare, the other was littered with an assortment of hides and skins. My master pointed to the latter.

"That's Abel's. I'll find something for you. One day you'll kill a bear, then the skin will make you comfortable. The chair and chest are Abel's, too. You can make your own. Now settle yourself. I'll send for you later."

He was gone and I was alone in a rude shack with a dirt floor and bare walls. But I was satisfied, for through the windows I could see the fields. Except for patches of snow they were earth-brown and ugly in their nakedness, but they were American fields, and beyond them lay millions of acres of untilled land. Some of it was mine.

The negur who had ridden with us from Jamestown came in. He tossed his bundle at my feet. "Master said to fetch it to you."

I picked it up and sat down to examine the contents. There were two blankets and a bolster for my bed, and some clothing. This last consisted of a canvas suit, three pairs of stockings, two of woolen drawers, three handkerchiefs and a cap.

"Master says you'll have a wool suit and shoes later, and a rug if you want it."

I knew all this was provided for by the terms of my indenture, nevertheless I was grateful.

"That's good of him," I said.

"Master's always good."

"What's your name?"

"Abel. I live here."

Perhaps to prove his ownership he sat on the one chair in the room. Now that I knew I was to live with him I looked at Abel with more interest. He grinned.

"We will be friends."

"Yes," I replied.

That settled, he grew expansive.

"I don't belong to master. I'm missy's slave." He spoke proudly. "Eve and I are the only negurs at Sidney. We're house negurs. I don't work in the fields like you white servants."

"Who's Eve?" I asked.

He burst out laughing.

"Eve is Abel's mammy. You'll go to Hell for sure if you don't know that."

"Your mammy?"

"Sure and Miss Eliz'beth's, but different. She nursed us at the same time. Now she's Miss Betty's nurse, only Miss Betty's too big to need one."

I found all this confusing.

"Who are Miss Eliz'beth and Miss Betty?"

His soft brown eyes grew wide with surprise.

"You don't know who they are?"

"I just got here."

"Miss Eliz'beth is married to master. Miss Betty's their child." The enlightenment of so much ignorance exhausted the son of Eve. He yawned. "I'm going to sleep now."

Without troubling to move from his chair to the bed he shut his eyes. As I stared at him he began to snore. Going to sleep was one of Abel's sure gifts.

In the year 1666 Virginia was divided into two political factions. The north side of the James River was dominated by the plantations of the Cavaliers, who regarded themselves as the heirs of the Old World aristocratic tradition. These men and their followers supported the harsh rule of Governor Berkeley and were deaf to the rising tide of complaints from the small farmers, most of whom were former indentured servants. These self-styled aristocrats also professed deep devotion to the Anglican Church and the privileges of the crown.

On the south side of the river were the Puritans. They too were Anglican and they accepted the Stuart restoration, but they held firmly to the right of men to run their own business, free of interference from priest or government clerk. Some of them, such as Captain Willoughby or Richard Bennett, were as rich and powerful as their neighbors across the river, but their wealth did not make them forget their principles.

My master, James Lester, though not of the front rank, was prominent among the Puritans. His plantation, Sidney, lay above Jamestown, on the south side of the river. It covered about ten thousand acres, a large holding for those days, but much of it was not tilled. Some of the land was already worn out, but the greater part had not yet been cleared. That which was cultivated was mostly in tobacco. In addition a considerable amount of maize was grown and some wheat. Near the house was the vegetable garden. Peas, beans, turnips, radishes, onions, potatoes, cabbages, cauliflowers, carrots, parsnips and lettuce grew almost without care. Pumpkins and squash were raised in the fields with the maize. In the barns were horses, well cared for, while hogs and cattle were turned into the woods where they ran wild, feeding on wild grass, leaves, pine mast and acorns. It seemed impossible that man could want in such a country, yet I was to find that even the wealthiest were facing ruin.

When I came to Sidney there were, besides Abel and Eve, eighteen male servants and five female. This was a large number even for an estate of such size, but James Lester had no sons to help him and his wife Elizabeth was prevented by habit and health from assuming responsibilities. All the servants were indentured and looked forward eagerly to their day of freedom. They were treated well at Sidney, but the men longed for land, the women for husbands.

One of the servants came to me the day after my arrival at Sidney.

"Master sent me," he said. "Can you handle an ax?"

Assured that I could, he led me across the bare winter fields and into the woods beyond. There nine or ten fellows were already at work.

"This lad's Tom Bone," my companion said. "He's new. Jock, give him a hand if he needs it. I've work elsewhere."

The man called Jock leaned on the mattock with which he had been grubbing at the heavy undergrowth which covered the ground. The chance to rest was seemingly welcome, for he talked to me at some length about the work. A new field for the coming spring planting was being cleared. Most of the men were cleaning out the heavy undergrowth or rooting up stumps, but a couple on the edge of the clearing were chopping down trees. As we talked a tree fell. The fellow who had cut it down turned in our direction.

"Split 'er?" he asked.

My companion, who seemed to be in charge of the group, grunted affirmatively, and glad of a further excuse to talk instead of work, explained that as the land was cleared it was fenced. The trunks were stripped, cut into lengths of ten or twelve feet and split. The fence was built by laying the rails on one another, zigzagging each new section. It was called a worm fence, and I have never seen any other kind in Virginia. Having exhausted his explanations my instructor regretfully decided that we must go to work. He bade me make use of an ax I had been given and returned to his mattock.

Determined to prove myself a strong and willing worker, I approached a large tree that stood in the middle of the clearing. In my ignorance I supposed the giant had been passed over because no one possessed the courage to attack it. I set to work bravely and for a few minutes the chips flew. When I stopped to rest I turned to see if my industry was meeting with the approval which I believed it merited. To my surprise all the others were leaning on their tools, grinning broadly.

"What's funny?" I asked.

Jock pointed to a wide bare strip which encircled the trunk of the tree. "Belted," he said and explained that the big trees were not chopped down. Instead, a deep-bitten circle was cut into them and they were left to die. Crestfallen I turned to smaller game on the edge of the clearing.

Accustomed though I was to hard work I was exhausted when I got back to my cabin that night. Abel was already there. When I threw myself on the bed without speaking he yawned comfortably.

"I haven't done much today," he declared. "House negurs don't have much to do." I was too tired to retort and as he continued was glad of my forbearance. "So I suppose I might just as well get us something to eat."

As Abel prepared a large dish of fat bacon and hominy he talked. Although only half listening I learned that on some plantations the servants ate with the master, and so it had been at Sidney until Lester's marriage. The new mistress had put an end to it, and, in Abel's opinion, quite rightly. Now the occupants of each cabin prepared their own food, drawing what they needed from the master's stores without check or question as to where it went. Meat every day, not three times a week, and all the corn meal and hominy a man could eat. In Abel's case this was a great deal.

After I had eaten I felt better. I even rallied sufficiently to challenge Abel's superior status. "After seven years I'll be free," I told him, "but you'll still be a slave."

"That's right," he agreed amiably. "When you've worked in the woods and fields seven years you can work the same way for yourself, only harder. I'll still be at Sidney, eating plenty, sleeping plenty and not having much work to do." As if to prove his point he went to sleep. Abel's going to sleep resembled the falling of tropical night. It was sudden and complete.

The weeks that followed fell into the pattern of that first day.

I learned that in Virginia the winter's work was to clear new land for the spring tobacco planting. The soil wore out rapidly, and although tired fields are sometimes used for other crops, King Tobacco demands fresh rich food. If it does not get it a poor leaf results; and in 1666 even first class produce was fetching only a half-penny a pound. So I grubbed, cut down trees, split rails and built worm fences.

During those first months I seldom saw my master and did not even catch a glimpse of his family, but I learned a great deal from Abel who never tired of talking about them. One night I made a breath-taking discovery.

"He's a mighty good man," Abel was saying of Lester, "but he isn't an aristocrat like Miss Eliz'beth."

Lying on my couch I argued lazily. "All the aristocrats are not on the north side of the James. Look at Nathaniel Bacon for instance, he's on our side of the river."

"He's a gentleman."

"So's our master."

Abel sniffed.

"He's a mighty good man but no more a gentleman than you."

"Thank you. But I'm only a bound servant."

"That's what I mean. So was he when he came to Virginia."

For a moment I did not realize the full import of what Abel had said. When it dawned upon me I jumped from my bed, the day's weariness forgotten. Ten thousand acres of land, a solid house such as Sidney Hall, a score of servants, yes, and a wife from among the aristocrats north of the river. "Say that again," I demanded, clutching Abel's arm.

"Say what?"

"That the master was a servant."

"Sure he was. The same as you. But don't mind that, he's a good man, and rich, or Miss Eliz'beth wouldn't have married him."

I laughed exultantly.

"I won't mind it. I promise you. So he was a bound servant, and he got rich, yes, and, by God, he bought your aristocratic Miss Eliz'beth the same as he might a brood mare."

From that night my ambition had new spurs. I had dreamed of America since boyhood but Lester's example put flesh and bones on fantasy and made my wildest humors but common sense.

I pumped Abel dry of all he knew about Lester's early days, which was not very much. Eve had passed on to her son the contempt of her mistress' family for James Lester's common birth. Abel reproduced this much for me. He could do little more. I resolved to talk to Lester himself. At length I found an opportunity to do so.

It was late winter, tobacco-planting time. A plot of newly cleared ground had been selected and carefully fenced. The stumps had been taken out and the earth sifted until not even the smallest root remained. After the seed had been sown and covered, a thin cloth was spread over the ground.

As I worked I felt a curious excitement. I had been in Virginia only a little more than two months, but I already knew that my present and my future depended on tobacco. The whole plantation of Virginia lived on it: if tobacco failed Virginia failed. So when the tiny seeds were safe in the earth, protected from insects and the tame and wild beasts of farm and forest, with the warm sun caressing its bed, I lingered after the others were gone.

"It makes a man feel like praying, doesn't it?"

It was Lester, himself, come to see if the planting was finished. Anxious that the master should not think me lazy I tried to explain to him the mood that had kept me there. He nodded sympathetically.

"It's been many years since I planted my first tobacco, and I still want to say a prayer when the seed goes into the ground. Many years," he repeated slowly. "I was young then, like you are now, looking at a tobacco bed for the first time."

I clutched at his words.

"Like me, sir?"

"Much like you."

My heart was beating hard. I was frightened at my own boldness.

"An indentured servant?"

128

"Why, yes. It's well known that I came as a bound boy. I hope you're not ashamed to work for so humble a man."

"Ashamed," I cried, "I'm proud. I'm going to be like you. I only wanted to be certain that it was true that Sidney belongs to a man who once had no better chance than I have now."

"It's true, and now you'd best get back to work. Work built Sidney, not dreams."

I started to obey but was scarcely ten yards away when he called me back. Hoisting himself onto the top rail of the fence he bade me join him. He was silent for a while and when he did speak it was in a far-away voice.

"Maybe I was wrong," he said. "The years are long and a man forgets. Perhaps dreams did go into the building of Sidney. But be that as it may I wouldn't like to discourage a lad like you, who stands where I stood a quarter of a century ago."

So sitting on a Virginia worm fence I heard James Lester's story. He had been born of yeoman stock near Norwich in East Anglia. His childhood was spent on his father's small freehold, where with the rest of his family he had fought against want. It had been a hard battle, and when a slump in the wool trade, upon which so much of East England depends, occurred, it was hopeless. So when a neighboring Puritan squire, disgusted with the falling revenues from his land and the ecclesiastical policy of the Archbishop Laud, determined to risk his fortunes in Virginia, James Lester bound himself for five years' service and accompanied him.

Land at that time was cheap and tobacco sold at two shillings a pound. Lester's master prospered, and he himself worked with a single aim: to be ready to meet the day when he should have land of his own. In this he succeeded so well that when he became a landholder no one could coax more tobacco or maize from the earth than he.

He took land just above Jamestown, and denying himself every luxury but ambition, worked harder than any servant or slave. After a few years he sold his plantation and moved up the river to the present site of Sidney. Luck was with him. Because of the civil wars in England the Dutch took over a large part of the

Virginia trade, and as a consequence tobacco which had by this time dropped from two shillings to two pence a pound went up a penny.

Before a decade had passed Lester owned ten thousand acres of land and ten servants. He was liked by his fellow planters who elected him to the House of Burgesses, where his position brought him in touch with the self-styled aristocracy who lived on the north side of the James River. Then, at the age of forty-two, he married one of their daughters, Elizabeth Sidney by name. She was eighteen years old, and her family, despite its gentle blood, or possibly because of it, had failed to prosper, so that the only dower she brought her husband was Eve, her old negro nurse, and the latter's son, Abel. It was for her that Sidney Hall had been built.

Up to this point my master's tale had been told vigorously, but as he brought it to an end he grew listless.

"I bought a couple more serving wenches for the house," he said, "and because it shamed my wife that I should work in the fields 'like any common fellow,' as she put it, I quit. No, I haven't had my hands what you'd call deep down in the dirt for fifteen years, and for ten, I haven't even talked—as I'm talking to you —to a man who has. Not since the terms of service of the boys who were with me when I married expired. I never got to what you'd call knowing the new ones." He smiled wryly. "So, Tom Bone, you see it can be done. A penniless bound boy can become such a gentleman that he can't soil himself with the dirt he loves, or be friends with men like himself. There's your goal, boy. You can reach it, but only if you always hold in mind that it's getting there alone that counts, not what you've found when you arrive."

# VIII

## I.

Months passed. Because it was my first year in Virginia I did little work in the fields after it turned hot, but helped Abel and the females about the house. Naturally I grew to know more about the household at Sidney Hall. Our mistress, Elizabeth Lester, was still a young woman. She was tall with blue eyes, fair skin and light brown hair. A biggish nose jutted incongruously over a small prim mouth. Pretending to a languor, which I believe she thought gentle, she shunned even the supervision of our daily work. Old Eve, the negress, ran the house. In doing so she quarreled boisterously but good naturedly with the white girls under her direction. One such quarrel gave me food for thought.

For shirking her work one of the wenches, Alice, had been cuffed by the negress. A raucous exchange of abuse had followed during which the girl taunted the old negress with being nothing but a slave.

"Born a slave," agreed Eve, "an' I'll die one. But if I can beat some sense in that head of yours, you might die a lady—the Lord help the gentry."

It was evident that the girl had never aspired to so much, for she rejected such an idea scornfully, but Eve persisted.

"Does seem like the good God wouldn't permit, but I've seen uglier gals, and with no more sense than you, marry rich planters and be ladies, or at least what passed for them. Women are still scarce in Virginia so a man weds what he'd not look at somewhere else."

Stung, Alice now embraced the idea she had lately rejected.

"What do you know about white men?" she jeered. "I'll marry a rich one just like you say and be a lady. And then I'll come back here to visit the mistress. We'll sit in the parlor and drink tea, and when you stoop to wrap a rug around my feet I'll kick your black buttocks for you, I will."

"Don't you fill up that hollow head of yours with fool ideas like that," Eve warned. "Even if some planter did marry you, mistress wouldn't have nothing to do with you. She's a real aristocrat and can smell trash no matter what kind of wrappin' it's got around it. Why," she sniffed in conclusion, "she's just as apt to allow Miss Betty to marry Tom Bone here, as let you sit in her parlor drinking tea."

"She married the master," retorted the girl, "so why shouldn't Miss Betty marry Tom?"

The bickering went on but I no longer listened. I had left England swearing that I was through with women, and at Sidney Hall I had been too busy to think of them, but the wrangling of the two women had brought the matter before me in a new light. A man who planned to be a successful planter needed a wife to help him and to give him children who in turn could help him. This was another of the miracles of America. A child was not just another mouth to feed. It was a pair of strong hands to wield an ax, or skilled fingers to guide a needle. The more strong children a man had the broader would be his tilled fields, brown in the winter, but green with tobacco and maize in the summer, and yellow with ripe corn, pumpkins and squash in the fall. So in this primitive world a woman became an earth goddess again, symbol of fertility. I knew that someday I must have a wife.

Despite Alice's chatter I dismissed Mistress Betty with scarcely a thought. She was twelve or thirteen, almost old enough for marriage, while I still had years of labor to serve before I was even a free man. Besides, though Betty was quiet and pleasant, I wanted no aristocrat for a wife. What I would need was a strong woman, used to work and able and willing to bear me a child each year. I looked at Alice. Her coarse red hair was coiled carelessly around her head. Wisps of it hung over her face where it paled against her ruddy cheeks. Her eyes were brown, her mouth full and her chin long. But I was less interested in her head and face than in the broad thighs and strong legs that I could see limned behind the thin skirt, which, damp with sweat, clung to her body.

That evening I went to Alice's cabin, and during the following months I saw her as often as my work permitted. It was a strange courtship, for although I spent many evenings walking with her in the soft Virginia moonlight, or sprawled on the ground with her hard hand responding to my gentle squeezing, I never once spoke of love, or for that matter, had a single tender thought for her. Instead I unfolded my plans for the future without bothering to find out if she understood and approved her rôle in it. It was no wonder then that I was annoyed when in the autumn she greeted my proposal of marriage with a burst of laughter.

"Lord, Tom," she shouted, "I been wonderin' all summer what it was you was after."

"Now that you know," I retorted, "what do you say?"

She said no. In the first place it seemed that I did not love her, and this great, red-haired, big-boned creature's head was fairly bursting with romantic nonsense. Besides indentured servants could not marry, and although her service would be up in two years, I was bound for well over six, and with men throughout the colony wanting wives she would be a fool to wait for me.

So like a new-born infant that emits one feeble wail and dies, my courtship ended. Nevertheless the necessity of marriage was now deeply rooted in my consciousness, and every girl I saw, instead of being a reflection of the faithlessness that was Polly Bragg, was now a creature of blood and bone—and a possible wife. Briefly, for the first time in my life woman meant something other than Polly Bragg.

Meanwhile, during the long summer days and nights, so hot that men said they could hear the maize growing in the fields, the largest tobacco crop that America had ever produced was ripening. Almost everyone at Sidney responded to nature's generosity with a pleasant glow of well being. Only our master did not seem to share in the general elation. One evening I learned why. He was standing in front of a drying shed where I had been working.

"Never such a crop, sir," I ventured.

He laughed sourly.

"Our Master in heaven has smiled. Now we only have to beg the favor of our earthly lords."

"Is anything wrong?" I asked.

"Everything's wrong," he answered vehemently. "The cost of the things that we must buy is greater each year, and taxes grow heavier, but the price of tobacco goes down. In my own time I have seen the Virginia planters transformed from independence to frightened beggary. Men who once had confidence in themselves and their future now whine for the mercy of an English merchant or the favor of a colonial politician. Tobacco sold for two shillings a pound when I came to Virginia, now it's half-penny, and with this year's crop much of it will go for a farthing, some will not sell at all."

Moved by Lester's intensity I forgot that I was only a helpless servant. "We won't bear it," I cried. "Surely there is something we can do."

His voice had a cold edge. "Aye, there's something to be done, and some day we'll do it. There's trouble coming in Virginia and maybe not so far off. Mark that, Tom, and remember it. There are limits beyond which men won't be pushed. We'll take a chance with the cold and the heat and the floods and the droughts. They come from God, and He has a way of evening things up if a man will be patient and keep working. We'll even risk our lives as we push further and further into the wilderness, and in the end we'll triumph over the savages. But it's price that ruins us. Prices set by men in England who sprawl in country houses and around council tables, while they prattle about trade balances, or bray indignantly at the disloyalty of the colonists. Statesmen they call themselves and yet there's not a man among them with sense enough to see that loyalty cannot be wrung from slaves; for, mark you, we are slaves. Slaves to their damned navigation acts, as surely as the blacks here in Virginia are slaves of their owners."

He walked away quickly, and I went back to work; but I remembered what he said.

134

The autumn and winter passed quietly at Sidney. Even the news that England and Holland were once more at war brought only a pious hope that it would cause a rise in the price of tobacco. But with spring came disaster, the first of a series that before it was done threatened ruin to Virginia and launched me on an undreamed-of tide of fortune.

The great hail storm came in April. Never before or since have I seen such hail. Driven by a high wind chunks as big as hens' eggs pelted the countryside. The tobacco was not yet far enough along to be seriously damaged, and the maize was just being planted, but cattle and hogs were killed by the hundred, and the mast which ordinarily served as food for stock was largely destroyed.

I was planting maize in a field by the woods when the storm broke. My companions dashed for their cabins, but I did not go with them. It was neither duty nor industry that kept me. I was playing a game. I remember it yet. I was trying to reach the end of a row with both my supply of maize and pumpkin seed exhausted. When the storm broke I had only a few more hills to plant and the seed was about gone. In sight of victory I refused to flee. I clung to my resolution, but by the time I was done the hail stones had grown so large that I gave up hope of reaching the shelter of my cabin and made for the wood.

Under the trees it was not so bad. I hugged the bole of a large oak and waited. I do not know if it was the smell of the ice-laden air, the unearthly appearance of a copper-colored universe slopping over with glittering white pellets, or the rattling and creaking of the forest, but as the minutes passed a strange mood crept over me. I was no longer afraid of being hurt, or concerned over the damage that I knew was being wrought. Instead, I was gripped by a spirit of fierce exultation. I felt in every fiber of my being that I was a part of this angry, crashing world at whose very center I fancied myself to be. It was for this that I had abandoned England. I laughed wildly until the sound of my voice pierced through the thunder of the storm itself.

This humor of mine would not be important had it not given significance and omen in my own mind to the incident which followed. Under the strange spell that gripped me I moved away from my protecting oak and wandered deeper into the wood. I do not know how long I had walked when I heard someone calling me. "Tom Bone." It was faint but clear. "Tom Bone." It was closer and then not ten feet away huddled by a fallen tree was Miss Betty. She was a pitiful figure. The brown curls, wired to stand out from the small face, were drooping forlornly against her cheeks, while the straight bangs across her forehead were straight indeed, each hair a string dangling lifelessly where the wind had tossed it. Her clothes were in equal disarray. The long full skirt was wet and muddy, the sleeves of fine linen were torn, and even the chemise had an ugly rent where, no doubt, the fingers of some low-hanging branch had caught it. But her feet were strangest of all. One shoe was heavy with mud, while the other was nowhere in sight, though a small foot protruded from under the soiled skirt, stocking torn, and, as I could see, with the flesh bruised.

Her story was brief. She had come to the woods to pick flowers. Abel had accompanied her but urged by a whim she slipped away from him, so when the storm broke she was alone. She ran for home, caught her foot in a wild grape vine and turned her ankle. After that she crept under the fallen tree and waited for the help which she knew must sooner or later arrive. Now she wanted to be taken home. When I explained that this was impossible, made unreasonable by pain I suppose, she insisted. Angered by her stubbornness I picked her up roughly. She cried out in pain.

"Does it hurt?" I asked none too sympathetically.

"Of course, you fool. Can't you be careful?"

Offended, I carried her in silence to a sheltered place at the edge of the woods, where even she could see that we could go no farther. I made her as comfortable as I could and turned away, reflecting as I did so that Miss Betty was as spoiled and useless as her mother. I was wrong.

"I'm sorry." She thus put aside her discomfort in order to make amends for her small discourtesy, but I was too churlish to accept her generosity.

"No need to be," I muttered. "I'm only a servant."

"Father says such things don't matter."

"And what does your mother say?"

Her eyes opened wide in surprise.

"Mother's an aristocrat."

"So it's only right that she should have bad manners."

My sarcasm was wasted. "Yes," Betty agreed solemnly. "Toward servants and slaves, that is, and common people."

"And you?" I asked curiously. "Do you agree with your father or your mother?"

Her answer was so long in coming that I thought she might be offended, but she was only considering the matter. When she finally replied her voice was flat.

"Mother says I'm an aristocrat like her. Only I'm not to marry beneath me."

"Does your father know she says that?"

"Of course. Sometimes I'm not sure he really agrees, but she always has her way. Even about Christopher."

I asked who Christopher was.

"Christopher Carr from across the river. I'm to marry him."

"Do you want to?"

"They're aristocrats."

"But do you want to marry him?"

"I'd rather marry you."

If the storm's largest hail stone had hit me squarely on the head I could not have been more befuddled or bereft of my senses. Kitchen tales of women of quality falling in love with their servants floated through my bemused mind. I remembered as from a great distance Alice's saying that I might well marry Miss Betty since the master had married her mother. I even recalled with some satisfaction that Polly Bragg was the wife of Denham. So at the first test my carefully nurtured contempt for the gentry dissolved before the dizzying prospect of owning one of them.

"You're in love with me?" I asked fatuously, even taking a step toward her. Her round eyes grew rounder.

"Of course not. But you're bound like father was, and I like father best." She grew confidential. "You see, I want to be like him. Not being a boy, it's hard. But marrying someone like him comes close to it." She sighed. "I suppose it's what Mother calls my common blood."

Her friendly candor dissipated my illusions. I felt as great a fool as I was, and only by physical effort did I keep myself from deserting her forthwith, and hiding myself and my folly in the forest. I doubt if I ever felt myself so much a servant to anyone as I did at that moment to twelve-year-old Elizabeth Lester. Nevertheless, when an hour or so later I carried her to the house, I could not but fancy myself holding her in my arms under other circumstances; and as her slight body pressed against me, I was moved as no woman but Polly Bragg had hitherto moved me. She was not much more than a child and it was mostly in my mind, but it made an impression that never quite left me. We were halfway to the house when I remembered there was something I must find out. "Do you like him?" I asked.

"Who?"

"Christopher Carr."

"Oh, yes, I like him. He's very nice."

She moved restlessly, shifting her position as she tried to ease the pain in her ankle. Finally tightening the ring of her arms around my neck she settled herself more firmly in my arms. "He's not as strong as you are, though," she said comfortably, just as the anxious people from the house came running toward us.

During the following days we worked hard to retrieve what we could from the damage done by the storm, and consequently I had little time to reflect on my recent adventure. Nonetheless I was not permitted to forget it, for Abel insisted that I had "saved" his mistress and so, as a hero, was entitled to every scrap of information that could be gleaned from the bedside of the heroine.

As the days went by Abel's reports were always the same, until at length they grew tiresome. That the ankle had been twisted badly and the sprain was severe I did not doubt, but after all the girl was well cared for and in no danger. One night, being unusually tired and out of humor, I told Abel as much, and added that I should like nothing better than to lie in bed for a few weeks.

He shook his head in solemn dissent.

"You'd get powerful tired laying there in bed doing nothing."

"I could read."

"Miss Betty can't," he chuckled unbelievingly, "and I doubt if you can either, Tom Bone."

Stung by his doubt I hauled my bundle of books from under the bed where I had stored it. As I dumped the books out, Abel's eyes bulged.

"Lord God," he muttered, "books."

I opened the Bible and read. When I grew tired, Abel, fascinated by the full phrases, pleaded for more. I refused and shoved the package back under the bed thinking that it would again rest there undisturbed, collecting dust. But I had not counted on Abel. Each night he begged me to read to him, and his pleasure was so great that I seldom refused. I tried a number of the books, but though he listened patiently to the others, in the end he always demanded the Bible. The Psalms especially pleased him, and I read them until he knew many from memory and would mutter them to himself, swaying back and forth to the rhythm of his own voice as he did so.

Eventually Abel spread the astounding news that Tom Bone could read, and that he even owned books, more books than Abel had fingers on both hands. As a result James Lester visited us. It was evening and I was reading.

"That's an unusual talent for the son of a fisherman," Lester said when I was done. "And it's even more remarkable that you should own books. May I see them?"

I assured him that I meant no harm in reading and never looked at a book during the day when I was supposed to work.

"Of course not," he agreed amiably, and came to the purpose of his visit. He wanted me to teach his daughter to read. He himself read and wrote only enough to manage his business affairs, and I gathered from half-guarded statements that despite her gentility his wife knew even less. But from his youth he had had the unlettered man's respect for learning, and upon hearing Abel's report of my talents, he had determined that I should continue

139

to work in the fields in the morning, but that the afternoons should be devoted to tutoring the invalid.

Miss Betty was propped in bed when I entered her room the next day. She greeted me eagerly and it was evident that she approved her father's plan. I had brought only the Bible with me, which so disappointed her that I returned to my cabin and fetched my whole store of books. Not until I had described the contents of each one were we permitted to start work. So began the first of many long hot summer afternoons spent with Betty. I was not a skilled teacher and knew of no better means of instruction than to repeat each word until my pupil knew it, but Betty was eager and apt, and with nothing else to occupy her mind made rapid progress.

Even after Betty was able to get out of bed the lessons continued. It was pleasanter after that, for when the heat became unbearable in the house, we sought relief in the orchard or in the woods beyond the fields. Nor did we always work. Although she was quick, Betty tired easily, and never an afternoon passed during which she did not at some time or other put her book aside and ask me to talk to her. And this solemn blue-eyed child was such an eager listener that it was not long before she knew more of my history than anyone alive, save myself. But yet there was one great gap in her knowledge: Betty Lester knew nothing of Polly Bragg.

One afternoon in early June we were under a giant apple tree. Betty was propped against the tree's trunk, I sprawled comfortably at her feet. We had been reading *The Compleat Angler*, but, Betty growing tired of it, we talked. I told her about my sister Evalyn.

"Poor Evalyn," she said pityingly, when I was done. "Why do such things have to happen, Tom?"

"Because people are poor."

She assented to this and even seemed to find comfort in it. "I don't suppose they mind so much," she said.

"Why not?"

"Why? Why, they just wouldn't. Not like gentlefolk, that is."

I remembered Evalyn's pinched dead face. I heard the consta-

140

ble's rough voice, "Just another whore drowned herself," and my animosity toward the gentry, long dormant, quickened to sudden life and erupted with uncontrolled violence. I seized Betty's injured foot and twisted it viciously. She cried sharply and fell sidewise. My anger evaporated. I was ashamed and afraid. Although I knew that she had fainted, I sat there helplessly, too paralyzed by horror to make an effort to revive her. After a few minutes she opened her eyes. We stared at one another.

"Why did you do it?" she asked.

"To hurt you," I muttered sullenly.

"But why?"

"Everyone has always been kind to you. I wanted you to know brutality."

"Like your sister did?"

"Something like that."

"You'd better take me to the house now."

So for the second time I carried her home. As we approached the house my thoughts turned fearfully on my own position. When my conduct became known I expected no mercy, and admitted to myself that I deserved none.

Eve came rushing to meet us. I waited for Betty's denunciation but none came.

"I tripped again," she said in a tired, flat voice. "Now you take me, Eve."

So Betty saved me, but she did not let me off entirely unscathed. As Eve took her from my arms she said slowly:

"I've been thinking, Tom. Maybe gentlefolk don't feel more pain than other people after all. Maybe it's just that they bear it better. They don't want to hurt others because of it, like your kind of people do."

I slunk back to my cabin. My remorse and shame increased as the afternoon passed, nor did it diminish during the night, or the next morning as I labored in the fields. By afternoon I was in an agony of uncertainty. Abel had told me that Miss Betty's ankle was injured as badly as before, and that she would be in bed for weeks. I felt I could not bear the shame of facing her, nor was I at all certain that she would consent to see me. Yet I had no excuse for not going to the house as usual. So I was fumbling with my books, trying to summon enough courage to go, when James Lester entered the cabin.

"I was just coming, sir," I said nervously.

"You won't be wanted."

I put my books away.

"How is she, sir?"

"She doesn't want to see you again."

I had no answer.

"What happened?"

"Didn't she tell you, sir?"

"Why does my daughter refuse to see you?"

I had never seen James Lester so angry. His voice was low, too low, and he stood there quietly, too quietly. He was like a spring too tightly coiled. In a panic of apprehension I considered repeating Betty's explanation to Eve, but in the end, chiefly because I was afraid to do otherwise, I told the truth. To my amazement he seemed relieved.

"Is that all?" he demanded.

"It was enough, sir."

My reply was ill chosen.

"Enough! Damn you. Enough!"

His eyes blazed and he took a step toward me. I thought that the storm was about to break, but more than any man I've ever known, James Lester was his own master. The fist he had clenched relaxed. He spoke in his normal voice.

"You had some excuse for anger, but none for such brutality toward a harmless child who was only repeating foolishness that she has heard. So in the future, since your manners are those of a field hand, the field is where you will spend your time."

He stopped, waiting it seemed for me to speak, but I was too ashamed to do ought but stand with my head hanging, like a recently thrashed cur. Rightly interpreting my silence as agreement with his view, Lester delivered his final warning.

"I don't treat humans as animals, Bone, so if you continue to act as a beast I'll sell you for the remainder of your term of service. And I'll find a master who does not share my scruples."

142

As he went toward the door my eyes fell on the books that I had been gathering together when he entered. Mustering all my courage, I spoke.

"Please, sir. I won't be wanting my books. Maybe Miss Betty—while she's there in bed, because of what I did—maybe she would like them."

After a moment's hesitation he picked up the books.

"I'll ask her," he grunted.

When he reached the door he turned. "Betty says she tripped. Only the three of us know the truth. It had best remain so."

## 3.

For over a month I worked in the fields. It was hot, even for mid-July in Virginia. The nights were worse than the days. Following Abel's example, I gave up trying to sleep on my bed and moved my straw mattress to the floor. I even tried to leave my cabin and sleep under the trees, but although it was cooler there, the insects, especially the mosquitoes, drove me back to the cabin.

As I worked in sun-drenched fields, or tossed restlessly in the stifling cabin, I thought of Betty. While in the fields I sometimes grew angry as I pictured her with Abel or one of the maids fanning her and giving her cool drinks. But at night, knowing the manor to be almost as hot as my cabin, I thought of her with pity, and remorse added to my discomfort.

During all these days I saw no members of the master's family. Abel reported from time to time on the invalid's progress, but, although he had no idea of the extent of my culpability, he blamed me for carelessness, and sensed that my banishment to the fields was a punishment. Once I asked him if Miss Betty ever mentioned me.

"Why would she talk about field trash?" he sniffed contemptuously.

After that I asked no question, but waited for such information as he might volunteer.

Squire Lester had said that our Master in heaven was kind, and that it only remained for the lords of trade in London to follow His example; but when in late August a fearful hurricane struck us, adding further losses to the damage inflicted by the spring hailstorm, it seemed that God Himself had turned His back on the plantation of Virginia.

Among the victims of the hurricane was the mistress of Sidney. She was returning from a visit across the river when the wind struck, and both she and old Eve, who accompanied her, were killed by a falling tree.

These were the first deaths that had taken place at Sidney, but Elizabeth Lester herself had chosen the site for what she proudly believed would one day be the ancestral burying grounds. She had even marked the place where each member of her family was to lie.

Submitting at her death as he had done during her life to his wife's pretensions, the master gave Elizabeth Lester a funeral as nearly resembling that of an English gentlewoman as he could manage. The servants were summoned to the funeral where we stood a respectful distance from the family. Lester and his daughter stood at the side of the grave. It was the first time I had seen the latter since I had hurt her. She was on crutches and looked pale and in pain. The grief I felt that day was for her.

The services had been read, the rough-hewn oak coffin was lowered into the ground, and the neighbors, who had come to pay their respects, were returning to the house. Only Lester and the servants remained. He spoke to them briefly.

"None of you will work today, except what's needful with the animals. Deport yourselves soberly. Abel, you and Bone stay here to fill the grave. The rest may go."

The others straggled off. Abel and I waited as Lester went back to the open grave of his wife. He stooped and picked up a handful of dirt. Stirred by a morbid interest, I was watching every move, and so observed that the many years James Lester had lived as a gentleman had not taught his fingers to forget their yeoman's love of the soil. While he held the dirt, his fingers probed it as if to feel the riches that they knew were stored there, and when they finally relinquished it to the grave it was reluctantly, as if knowing that it was too rich to waste on the dead.

144

"Good-by," Lester whispered and we heard the dirt falling like rain on the coffin. Then he motioned for us. He watched while we filled the grave.

"She wanted lilac and honeysuckle on it," he said when we were done.

"Yes, sir." Abel spoke in a husky voice.

He had not cared for Miss Elizabeth as he did for Betty, but he had been her negur, and like most members of his race he was sentimental. Moreover, he was deeply grieved at the death of Eve, who had been buried the day before. So his voice shook and his eyes filled with tears. As Lester looked at him his own somber expression was lightened by kindness.

"I shouldn't have asked you to stay, Abel. In my own sorrow I forgot that your loss is as great as mine."

Abel shook his head vigorously.

"She was my mistress," he said.

Lester's eyes strayed back to the grave.

"When the season's right, put in the lilacs and honeysuckle." He smiled sadly. "When it's my time, I'd rather have maize and tobacco, with great golden pumpkins at my feet, but I'll be here next to her, so put flowers over me, too, when you plant me beside her. Plant myrtle. It will look up worshipfully at the lilacs and honeysuckle. She would like that."

So he mocked her a little, but there were tenderness and understanding in his face, and as he walked away I wondered what it was that could so bind a man to a woman.

# IX

THE HURRICANE changed life at Sidney. Lester was no longer an old-world country gentleman. He was a Virginia farmer and his servants were his fellow workers in the fields. Once more his fingers reached deep into the dirt, laying enchantment upon seed and soil so that they yielded more to him than to other men.

Betty took over the duties of managing the house, and struggled valiantly to take the place of both her mother and Eve. But in the end it was my life that was changed most by Elizabeth Lester's death. I do not remember the date, but it was sometime in early fall that Lester came to our cabin.

"You two will move to the house," he said.

Our faces must have reflected our amazement, for he laughed and explained.

"You'll be a house negur for sure, Abel, as you always wanted to be. Help Miss Betty. Ease her burdens as Eve did for her mother. She has courage and determination, but too little strength." He turned to me. "Can I trust you?" he asked gravely.

"Yes, sir."

"Then take up your reading again. She's lonely and needs company and a little pleasure. See to it this time that you bring her only pleasure."

He spoke the last quietly, but I knew that it was a warning.

"Will she see me, sir?"

"Yes. If she'll give you her trust and liking again remains to be seen."

So Abel and I moved into the manor house and a new life be-

146

gan. Betty did not mention the incident in the woods, but, though it was autumn and forest and field were at their loveliest, neither did she suggest that we go out of doors. For my part, although I wanted to tell her I was ashamed, and beg her forgiveness, I was unable to muster the courage.

Winter came. The work in the fields was done, and the clearing and fencing of more and ever more land commenced. But I spent the greater part of my time in the house. Betty could read as well as I by this time, but we continued to pore over my books together; and during days when he could not work in the earth (for he never cared for the forest—it was only cultivated land that he loved) James Lester spent many hours with us. One day he learned that I could write. This delighted him, for he hated the simple accounts of the plantation. He taught me the ciphering that I needed to know and turned the books over to me.

Thus, as the months passed, a curious change was wrought at Sidney Hall. I, the servant, gradually assumed the management of the plantation. I supervised the packing and sale of the tobacco, bought whatever was needful, paid the bills and kept the accounts. James Lester returned to the soil. He had the pent-up love of fifteen years to pour into it, and he did not stint in his giving. In the beginning he directed me, but soon confined his aid to those occasions when I consulted him, and finally there came a time when he would scarcely answer direct appeals.

"I grow the stuff, Tom," he would growl impatiently, "you sell it."

Even in winter, when he worked but little, it was not much better. He was kind and would talk by the hour of his plans for the summer's work, but he was not really with us. Like the brown fields outside, he rested, waiting for the return of the growing season.

However I was not without help. Betty Lester was only twelve when, at her mother's death, she took charge of Sidney Hall, but she had her mother's conception of authority and her father's determination to get a task done, so I soon learned to take my problems to her rather than Lester. Problems were plentiful, for the late sixties were bitter years in Virginia. Tobacco prices were ruinous to the planter, but the cost of goods from England went higher and higher, and the taxes levied by Governor Berkeley mounted each year, although none could see what he and his council of bootlicks were doing with the money.

So no matter how much Lester produced, and I doubt if there was a man in Virginia who farmed so well, there was never enough to keep my books from reflecting an ever sorrier picture; and Betty and I spent many long evenings calculating every resource, and debating whether it would be better to take out our credit with the London merchants in tools or cloth. If Sidney survived those lean years, it was only because its master entered it clear of debt, and because after the death of Mistress Lester no attempt was made to imitate the life of the old-world gentry. Lester scarcely left the plantation, and though Betty, in response to urgent commands from her mother's folk across the river, visited them at infrequent intervals, she always returned sooner than she had planned, and with renewed zest for Sidney.

Thus five years went by. I was so content with my lot that one day, in 1671, I was moved to write to my sister Susan, in order that she might know I was prospering. It also crossed my mind that it was at least possible that Susan would pass the news on to Mistress John Denham.

I wrote, among other things:

"Here I am one of the family, and already I manage the plantation. The squire treats me as a son, and Betty, his daughter, is like my sister."

I also urged Susan to send me word of her own condition. All she needed to do, I assured her, was to find a ship bound for Jamestown. Anyone there would know of the plantation of Sidney.

I sent the letter by a sailor who volunteered to inquire after Susan, but as I never saw him again, or heard from my sister, I concluded he had failed in his mission.

I thought it a pity, for though I had boasted somewhat, my letter had been essentially truthful. In my own regard, at least, I had become one of the family; and I found it difficult to remember that in two years I would leave Sidney. That Betty should go away seemed even more unnatural. Consequently I could scarcely believe my ears when one evening at dinner she mentioned it.

"Grandmother says I am to marry this spring," she told her father.

I was so startled that I almost dropped my knife, but Lester did not even lift his eyes from his plate.

"Young Carr?"

"Of course." Her usually gentle voice was sharp. It was evident that she was piqued at his lack of interest, but Lester was unruffled.

"Your mother arranged it long ago," he said quietly, "and I gave my consent; but spring's too soon. I won't lose you yet. Tell them to wait a year. And then not spring. Winter, after the autumn work's done."

When he had finished his dinner he spoke again. "I'm not being selfish about your marriage, am I?" he asked her gently. "It's dull here, don't think I've never noticed it. A lass your age likes gaiety. But here there's only work, and no company save an aging father and the servants. Maybe you long to wed and go across the river where there's more pleasure."

"I want to stay here," Betty cried, bursting into tears.

There the matter seemed to rest, but Lester must have kept turning it over in his mind, for a few weeks later he again spoke of it. We were sitting in front of the fire.

"You like the lad?" he asked suddenly.

Betty, who had been talking to me, misunderstood.

"Tom and I are old friends," she said lightly, "of course I like him."

Lester frowned and spoke with slow emphasis. "I meant the lad across the river. The one you are to marry."

The blood rose in Betty's cheeks and her usually steady gaze faltered and fell before my own.

"Oh! Christopher? Yes, I like him."

It was little enough, but after that night I was no longer able to take Elizabeth Lester for granted, or regard her as a sister. I was not in love with her, but nevertheless, I was jealous; and I

149

resented the fact that this fellow Carr was to take her away from me. Moreover, knowing that she would be leaving soon, I realized that in reality it was not I, but this grave sixteen-year-old girl who guided the destiny of Sidney. Then the thought of marriage with Elizabeth Lester took possession of me. It was vain to remind myself that despite my master's kindness I was still nothing but a bound man with two years yet to serve. My newly born desire whispered that James Lester had been no better. I recalled that when it had first come to me that a man who would conquer the New World must have a woman to help him I had had better sense than to aspire to or even want Elizabeth Lester, and I repeated to myself a thousand times that she was not the sturdy creature to bear children and work by my side. But I raised these barriers only that I might demolish them. "What if Betty is frail," scoffed ambition, "children will still come to life in her womb, and as for work, she has something far more valuable than a strong back," and I saw stretching before me the fields of Sidney.

But more than an inner voice kept my new-found hopes burning. Sensitive as never before to all that Betty said or did, I could not help knowing that she looked upon me with more than a sister's fondness. I dared hope that she even loved me. Having thus taken root, the green shoots of ambition flourished until they had ripened into an obsession. I could think of nothing else. When I worked in the fields, I fancied that I owned them, and I could scarcely refrain from regarding my fellow servants as my bound men. When Lester spoke to me, I hardly attended his words, being so busy wondering what he would say should I suddenly demand his daughter; and I even caught myself gazing speculatively at Abel, wondering how I would feel when I owned, not only fields and woods, but also a human being. But the fires burned hottest when I was with Betty. The hours during which we labored over knotty problems of finance or supply, once calm, were now fraught with overtones too subtle to grasp, yet too tangible to be ignored. Betty scarcely made a gesture or uttered a word without my reading into them encouragement or rejection of the suit I dared not press. Nor in doing so was I entirely wrong, for as a woman will, Betty sensed the change in me and responded to it.

Thus before a word was spoken, a queer courtship was carried on between us, I trying to express my devotion without word or gesture improper for a servant, and she accepting my tribute without admitting its existence.

Such a situation could not endure indefinitely. One of us must break and it was I who did so. We were sitting on a bench going over the plantation accounts. Betty had just come out of doors where the November wind had blown her brown hair awry. As she bent over the books, I pressed a light kiss on her bowed head. Startled she raised her face toward mine. I was panic-stricken. I remembered that even the wench Alice had laughed at me when I proposed marriage.

"I'm sorry," I mumbled, and hung my head. I despised myself. Where now was my belief that I was the equal of the gentry? Merely touching one of their women threw me into a state of terror.

"Why are you sorry?" she asked tranquilly.

"Because I so forgot myself."

After that we faced one another silently while Elizabeth Lester fought and conquered her pride.

"I'm not sorry," she whispered at last.

When we were sensible again we agreed that I must tell her father immediately so that the arrangement with young Carr's family could be terminated. After that we would have to wait as patiently as we could until the remaining two years of my service had expired. Betty would be eighteen, an old maid she assured me laughingly, and in the same vein I vowed that I'd not run after a younger light-of-love.

I spoke to James Lester that night. He heard me through in silence, and summoned Betty. After hearing her, he said that he would think it over. Several days passed. For me it was a period of almost unbelievable suspense, but Betty was serene. When at last Lester brought the matter up, I felt like a prisoner awaiting the verdict of the jury. However, I soon learned that it was not I who stood before the bar. James Lester's whole interest was in his daughter.

"You still feel as you did?" he demanded.

When she replied vehemently, he smiled.

"Young," he murmured, "yet older than I had realized. Old enough to fall in love."

He arose from the chair in which he had been sitting and wandered around the room for some minutes. When he spoke again his voice was grave.

"Your Mother would have hated it."

I resented the fact that the dead should be consulted, but Betty only laughed.

"Would she approve the way you have lived during these last three years?" she demanded.

"That has nothing to do with it."

"But it has. When Mother was alive you allowed her to arrange your life. But you weren't happy. Child though I was, I could not help knowing it. Since she's gone you've been contented. Were she alive today perhaps I too would follow her wishes, but she's dead, so I will choose my own life, as you have, and be happy."

"No, I was not happy with her," he admitted, "and perhaps you who saw so much saw that she was not happy either. But do you know why, despite the fact that I loved her and denied her nothing, I could give her no joy in life with me? It was because I was born in a cottage. She could never forget that, or that my father and his father had sweat in the fields and meadows of Norfolk. That was why I gave up my work, the only thing I could do or wanted to do, and pretended to be the gentleman that God never intended I should be. But it was no use. My hands remained too rough to please her. And now you, her child, who have her blood in your veins would marry the son of a fisherman, with nothing to recommend him but the fact that as you've grown to womanhood there has been no other man near-by with whom you might fall in love."

Lester stopped, and if that moment I had been ordered to speak for myself I could only have stammered a lame apology for my presumption. But a woman's heart often finds tongue when a man's reason is mute. Betty was unabashed.

"I love Tom," she declared with spirit, "and that's all the

152

recommendation he needs for marrying me. As for blood, yours also runs in my veins."

She paused and looked fondly at us and laughed softly.

"More your blood than hers, I think. How else could I be so coarse as to love two such low-born creatures as you—and want to wed a mere bound servant?"

Lester surrendered.

"Very well. I'll cross the river and tell them." Then, as his world fell back into proper focus, he added, "I'll go when we've finished clearing the new north field."

He embraced her and left us. During the whole interview he had not so much as cast a glance at me, nor had I spoken. Thus heroically I won my bride.

A few days later, Lester, true to his promise, crossed the river. He returned grim and angry.

"You're free of them, Bet," he said. "I bought you off."

"Bought me?"

"Surely, my dear. You were not so vain as to believe that it was you that they wanted? No, indeed, it was Sidney. But fortunately the gentry will sell anything, including their women, so they sold you back to me, just as twenty-five years ago they sold me your mother."

"But why did you have to pay them?" Betty protested. "Couldn't you just say that I'd changed my mind?"

"You had nothing to do with it in the first place," he retorted. "It was your mother who pledged our word."

Betty sighed. "And since you're not like them, you keep your word. I hope the price wasn't too high."

"No price is too high to be free of them. Thank God, you had sense enough to prefer an honest lad like Tom, here."

It was the first time he had spoken approvingly of our marriage, but we now learned that he had thought of little else.

"You had best wed as soon as possible," he declared, and before we had absorbed the shock, he delivered another stunning blow. "And I'd advise you to go to Henrico County. The land there's good."

"Leave Sidney?" Betty gasped.

"Sidney's mine. Tom must clear and build up his own land."

He looked challengingly at us, but finding no more resistance than might be expected from dazed lack of comprehension, his mood softened. "Not that I won't miss you. But it's better that way."

He talked late into the night and the gist of what he said was that it was not good for young people in love to live close as we lived unwed. Moreover, since Betty had set her heart on me, I must get started on my own as soon as possible. Certainly he, Lester, would be a fool to hold his daughter's future husband as a servant. On the point of our leaving Sidney he was inflexible, although Betty protested that he needed us.

"I can make out," he assured her drily, "and in America it's new land that makes a man. You'll get Sidney when I'm dead, but meantime you must plant your feet deep into your own soil, instead of idling through the years on land someone else has cleared for you."

After some discussion, Betty and I decided to be married on Christmas day. This left only a few weeks for our preparations, weeks marked by short, busy days and long evenings. During the latter, Betty and I mingled plans for the future with lovers' kisses, bridling like any young animals about to mate. But to tell the truth, I was no more excited at the thought of having a wife than at the prospect of being free and a landowner; and although not unmoved by her nearness, neither was I racked by overwhelming desire.

One day my master came to me. In his hands were two pieces of paper. He handed me one of them. It made me a free man. As I read its stilted jargon the words dissolved into mist.

"A wedding present," Lester said jovially, trying to cover my unmanly emotion.

"You couldn't give me one more precious," I said.

"But I can." He gave me the second paper. It was a license authorizing the marriage of Elizabeth Lester and Thomas Bone.

Christmas came—my wedding day. Snowflakes drifted lazily from a sky of unbroken gray. Standing before an open window I remembered Newfoundland, and suddenly without warning my heart betrayed me. My body ached and the snowflakes, soft and wet as a woman's lips, whispered "Polly Bragg, Polly Bragg." Without knowing what I did, I replied "Polly," and the sound of my voice broke the spell.

Thus the mood passed as quickly as it had come, and if for a fleeting second during the wedding ceremony I fancied that I heard Polly's name, it was only the faint breath of the past, a cold wind whispering things over a grave. I closed my ears to it and repeated the marriage vows more fervently, knowing that I was unworthy of them.

2.

Six days after my marriage James Lester called me to him.

"You will be leaving tomorrow," he said.

"The gear's packed," I replied, "everything is in order."

He gave me five pounds.

"I hear there is a vessel at Jamestown with servants aboard. Ride down and buy a female for Betty."

"We have Abel," I protested.

"You will need him in the fields. Betty will want a woman in the house."

When I told Betty she was indignant at being pampered.

"I shall care for our home myself," she declared. "The new wench will work in the fields with you, so pick a strong one."

"In that case a man—"

Betty interrupted me, and I learned that when she considered the cause just, my wife of the honest blue eyes was quite capable of deceit. Her father, she pointed out, had said female, so to please him, female it must be; but where and how the woman worked was another matter, and one with which we need not trouble James Lester.

I reached Jamestown in good time. The ship was in the river. As I rowed toward it I recalled that day five years before when I stood in the place of the miserable creature whose services I was about to buy. For a moment I felt again the anxiety that had gripped me as James Lester and his companion came aboard the

*Hampden;* and I remembered that to those who are his bound servants a master can be almost as God Himself. I remembered, and smugly resolved to be kind to the woman who would soon be my indentured wench. Thus when I reached the ship I was fat with complacency. The captain met me at the rail. The women stood in a cluster at the bow.

"Four pounds—take your choice," the captain growled.

"I want a strong one for field work."

"Take your choice," he repeated.

It was then that I saw Polly Bragg. She was standing a little apart from the others, and when her eyes met mine she smiled. Her smile was confident, as if to say that she had always known that all she need do to summon me from the vastness of America was to appear at the mouth of one of its rivers. Nor did it occur to me that I had any choice but to take her.

"That one," I said to the captain.

"There's others stronger, younger, too," he ventured.

"She will do."

I gave him four pounds.

"Five years' service, my girl," he said to Pol as he handed me the papers that made her my servant.

I do not know why I spoke. Perhaps I had a vague idea that if she protested I would yet give her papers back to the captain. Perhaps I resented her quiet smile and wanted to plunge her into the whirl of uncertainty and confusion that I felt. In any event I warned her fairly.

"Five years' service," I repeated, "as a field hand on the edge of the wilderness, working with me and a negur slave. Will you like that?"

"I'm used to work," Pol said, and added demurely, "though to tell the truth I came to Virginia to find a husband."

The captain went ashore with us so we did not speak further until we were on the horses headed for Sidney.

"Did you know I was in Virginia?" I asked.

"Yes. Susan told me."

"So she got my letter."

"Yes."

"She never let me know."

"No matter. She told me and I am here."

This was the moment I had been dreading.

"But it does matter. You have come too late. I was married six days ago."

We rode in silence for some minutes. Finally Pol smiled wanly.

"Six days," she sighed, "and in England, so Susan said, you came less than six hours too late. It's a pity we always miss one another."

Such resignation to a situation which so disturbed me and clouded my future, making it uncertain as a woman's whim, angered me. Moreover, Pol spoke as though only a malevolent fate had kept us apart, when in reality the whole responsibility was hers. I recalled how she had schemed, even risked the plague, that she might marry Denham, and how I had tortured myself for her sake, missed her, ached for her, worried over her relationship to her husband being discovered, even murdered in my anxiety. And now, when I had only begun a new life in which she, or thoughts of her, had no part, she appeared, blaming destiny for her misfortune.

"But it's too late," I told myself. "The fine Lady Denham can work in the fields like the servant wench she is, and after five years find a new man to torture."

"It's your own fault," I said aloud. "Susan told me you had gone to marry the squire, and your mother swore to me that you had done so."

Pol did not defend herself. Instead she looked at me thoughtfully.

"So you talked to my mother," she said.

For the first time in years I recalled what it was to feel like a murderer.

"She said you had married the squire," I repeated uneasily.

"And it made you angry."

"Not angry, terribly frightened for you."

To my relief Pol reverted to the squire.

"I did marry John Denham," she said.

"If you are already wed, my having a wife can make no difference between us."

Pol shrugged. "Your wife is here, my husband in England—if he is my husband."

"What do you mean?"

"Can even the marriage banns make a woman the wife of her brother?"

"You found out!" I exclaimed involuntarily.

"You knew?"

"Not until too late to stop you from marrying him. I learned it after you had started for London."

"So it was you."

The winter sunlight was warm and the air still, but I felt a cold wind blowing from the past.

"It was an accident," I muttered. "I didn't mean to kill her."

"You didn't kill her. She died of the plague two months later."

"Didn't kill her," I repeated stupidly.

"No. But either the rum she had been drinking or the blow prevented her from remembering what happened. So we never knew."

"Thank God I didn't kill her."

"Thank God," Pol agreed soberly. "At least her blood does not flow between us."

Thus the guilt of murder which had lain so lightly upon me until Polly came, and then borne down so heavily, dissolved, and I was free to return to the problem of Polly herself.

"When did you learn you were brother and sister?" I asked.

She smiled bleakly at the anxiety in my voice.

"In time. I didn't lie with him."

She told me her story.

Polly and John Denham were married before noon. Polly had wished to go to London at once, but her husband had insisted that they must stop at Denham. There he got some money and a letter. They had left Plymouth before he read the letter. It was from his father, to be opened the day of his marriage. For the most part it was filled with the sort of sage advice that a man receives from his father, and having faithfully preserved, passes on unsullied by use to his son. But somewhere in its rambling contents was an admonition to care for the daughter of the servant Jane Bragg, for though fear of the Round Heads had made secrecy necessary, the girl was his sister.

Aghast, the new-wed couple hastened back to Denham where they found the bride's mother sprawled on the dining room floor with a cut in her head.

John Denham was so afraid of scandal that for several weeks they lived at Denham pretending to the servants that they were truly man and wife, but avoiding one another in private. When Denham finally screwed up his courage sufficiently to declare that his marriage must be annulled, Polly pointed out that it was too late to confess that they were brother and sister as the servants might swear that they had lived together, and there was no other ground for annulment.

More frightened than ever, Denham fled, leaving Polly undisputed mistress of the manor. He sent her money, but never saw her again. When any business had to be transacted he sent Susan, to whom he had returned. It is amazing that Denham endured such a situation for so long. But Denham was a coward paralyzed by fear. When he finally acted he chose a coward's way.

One night Polly was awakened by the sound of small stones rattling against her window. Looking out she saw Susan breathless from exertion and fright, but determined to save her precious John from committing a crime. For she had learned that he had hired bullies to murder his wife. They were coming that night. Polly must flee at once.

Polly was not a coward, but neither was she a fool. She realized that she could not seek protection from the authorities, because to reveal her secret was as dangerous to herself as to Denham. But if she did nothing she would be killed, so there was no other course but to follow Susan's advice. Besides, she had grown tired of her life. She had ease, even luxury, but it was dull and the novelty of being a lady had long since palled.

"Where shall I go?" she had asked Susan.

"Tom went to America when he learned you had run off with John."

This reply so astonished Polly that she momentarily forgot her peril, for she had never been told that I had returned to England after my two summers in Newfoundland. When Susan explained, Polly was swept by the same baffled rage that possessed me almost five years earlier.

"You're a fool, Susan," she had cried furiously. "If you had told me Tom was back I'd have gone to him the day he landed, plague or no."

"And John would have died," Susan had said simply. "But that's done with. Go to Tom now. I had a letter from him. He is near a place called Jamestown in the plantation of Virginia."

"How can I go? John's sent no money lately, and if I sold the plate that is here he could charge me with theft and be rid of me without resorting to murder."

"John never gives me money," Susan had confessed.

In the end Pol had unknowingly followed the pattern set by me. She left Denham and fled through dark lanes to Plymouth. There she found a ship bound for Virginia, and signing papers of indenture, came to America.

Polly had barely finished her story when we reached Sidney. Betty met us and scanned her new wench with critical eye.

"She's small," she said doubtfully, "and thin. Wasn't there a stronger one in the lot?"

Before I could reply, Polly sank almost to the ground in a deep obeisance. Her voice was so humble that I suspected mischief, but her words were as discreet as her bearing.

"I'm strong, ma'am, and I'll work hard. You and the master won't be sorry for having taken me."

Betty relented at once. "What is your name?" she asked.

"Pol, ma'am."

"Well, Pol, if you mean what you say, you'll get along well enough with us, and in five years there will be an end to service, and you'll be free to find a husband."

"Really, ma'am?"

"Indeed, yes. And there are good men in Virginia. Who knows. You might even find one like Tom here."

"Oh, ma'am," gurgled Polly ecstatically, "that's just what I'll do."

"Find the girl a place to sleep," I said hastily, and left them.

The next morning, accompanied by my wife, her negur slave Abel, and the indentured wench Polly Bragg, I started for the frontier.

# X

ONLY MY unslaked desire for Polly marred the first years on the frontier. I failed miserably in my brave resolution to regard her as nothing more than a bound wench, for it was beyond my strength to deny either my devotion or my passion. By mid-summer of the first year I had admitted defeat and determined to take my wife's servant as a mistress.

But I am ahead of my story.

In the winter and spring months Pol, Abel and I cut Hickorywood out of the wilderness. Betty chose the name.

"I've had enough of imitation English manors," she declared. "We'll have an American name."

After discarding a score or more suggestions she chose Hickorywood.

When we first landed from the shallop which had carried us up the James from Sidney I stood on the river's bank and was afraid. I knew that I was no farmer. I did not possess the magic by which James Lester compelled the earth to yield so abundantly. But Betty did not share my misgivings. Gently but firmly she took charge. At her command Abel and I made a shack of bark and branches. When that was done we cleared a seed bed for tobacco. Betty herself helped clean out the undergrowth, and Pol worked with such enthusiasm that I half jokingly commended her devotion. She laughed as she had laughed when teasing me at Denham.

"It's not for you I work. I like my mistress."

"You do, don't you?"

"More than I've ever liked any woman."

I pretended to be pleased, and in a way I was, but as Pol, who stood laughing at me, well knew, I was also puzzled and vexed.

I thought Polly should have been jealous of Betty and of her position as my wife. Apparently she was not. She was even cheerful.

"Don't you care?" I asked.

Pol understood.

"Of course I care, but that does not keep me from liking your wife."

I knew that Betty was fond of Pol, too. In fact, there were times when it seemed to me that the women were leagued together in a conspiracy to thwart my will. In many respects they understood one another far better than I understood either of them.

"It's all a mess," I told Pol emphatically. "What are we going to do?"

She swung her mattox fiercely.

"We shall work, Squire Bone, that Hickorywood may be a fitting seat for your children."

When the seed bed was prepared we turned our attention to a house. By spring we had finished it. True, Betty and I had only one room where we lived and ate and slept, but it was a beginning, and there was already, in addition, a half-story above us which was divided into equal parts, one for Abel, one for Pol.

"They can live there until we get the servants' quarters built," Betty explained.

But the servants' quarters were never built. There were always more important things to do. We broke the ground with hoes and planted the tobacco and maize under the trees of the forest. There was no time to cut these latter down, so we were content with ringing them. When this was done we built a kitchen, a dairy and barn. The servants' quarters should have followed, but Polly and Abel were satisfied with their loft, and it seemed a waste of time to add more buildings. Moreover, without putting our feelings into words, Betty and I had come to realize that the frontier permits little distinction between master and servant. When Polly, Abel and I came from the fields or woods where we had worked together all day, it would have been pretentious folly to dismiss them to servant quarters. So we sat down to our food together, and cared not a whit that such conduct would certainly be considered outrageous by the aristocratic Governor Berkeley in his mansion at Green Spring, or the shade of Elizabeth Lester, which for ought I knew might still be hovering over Sidney.

Thus we settled into a groove, and Hickorywood gradually emerged not only as a plantation but also as a manner of living. Abel, once so proud of being a house negur, throve on long days of back-breaking labor, while Polly hoed in the fields and hoisted logs for a worm fence. Betty assumed complete responsibility for the house, and did work herself that at Sidney she had only supervised. She was not strong and was often tired to the point of illness, but she scorned my occasional protests.

"When Hickorywood is a great plantation we'll have a hundred servants," she would say gaily. "I will be as elegant as you like, and so will Polly, for whom we'll find a rich husband. Abel can be a house negur again with a fine uniform, and you can go to Varina to race your own horses and wager on cock fights. Until then we must all work."

So, urged on by both Betty and Pol, I worked, and Hickorywood gradually emerged. It was the land of my own that I had so often dreamed of. It rescued me from the human masses that are treated as cattle, and gave me the freedom that only property can give a man. But it was not enough. I needed Polly Bragg.

Mid-summer came.

It was dusk. Betty, Abel, Polly and I had come fishing to try our luck with the trout which frequently rose to the bait late in the day. Betty soon grew tired and suggested going home, but Polly begged to be allowed to stay for another hour. When Betty granted her permission to do so, I declared that I too would remain.

Betty and Abel were hardly out of sight before a fish took my hook. When a brook trout runs downstream with his line, a man will even pause in the pursuit of a woman. For several minutes I did not care if Polly Bragg's eyes were soft or hard, whether her mouth cut a cupid's bow in her oval face, or slashed across it in an angry line. I did not care whether she lived at Hickorywood

164

or on the Spice Islands. When I had the fish safely in my hands I turned in triumph for approval. Polly was smiling; her eyes danced with excitement. I forgot the trout. As my hold relaxed it slipped from my hands and splashed into the stream. I hardly knew it.

"Clumsy," chided Polly.

I took her in my arms and covered her mouth with my own. I do not know how long we stood there, trying to gorge in minutes the lost nourishment of years. When I finally released her, Polly sank to the ground. She laughed nervously.

"You lost your fish."

"Damn the fish."

I sat beside her and put my hand on her breast.

"No," she said.

"Yes."

"Not now."

I thought she was relenting.

"When?"

"Some day, I suppose."

She said it reluctantly.

"Why must we wait?"

"Don't you see? It's not just that you're married. I wouldn't care for that. When you first told me, I even thought I would take you away from your wife, make you run away with me. But now I can't."

Frustration made me angry.

"You've turned very virtuous," I told her. "You were not so scrupulous when you threw yourself at every man who came to Denham."

Polly sighed and kissed me.

"See," she said, "I'm not so virtuous now. I've just given you all that any man in England ever had of me."

I was ashamed but I could not bear to surrender.

"But you admitted that some day—"

"I suppose so. We are man and woman, and I love you. An hour will come when we are alone as we are now, and I shall need you so badly that nothing else will matter. Then you'll have me as you want."

"But isn't this just such an hour?"

I spoke with all the earnestness that I could draw from my whole being. Polly scrambled to her feet.

"No," she said, "just now I want to catch a fish."

She put a fat worm on her hook. As she let the bait float toward a hole downstream, she grinned at me.

"Poor Tom, two fish in one day and they both got away."

I made a final effort.

"When?" I pleaded. "At least tell me when?"

"When my blood's turned to fire and my flesh to liquid because you're near me; or maybe when the full moon's high in the sky."

At that moment she caught a fish. She carefully removed it from the hook and put it into a basket.

"My fish don't get away," she boasted, and her eyes mocked me.

We went home, but though I had failed, the ice was broken. I had cast aside my own scruples and henceforward lost no opportunity to overcome Pol's. It seemed useless.

"My blood is still blood," she would tease. Or, "The moon's still in the first quarter."

But at times she grew serious.

"You know what I was at Denham," she said on one such occasion. "You yourself said that I threw myself at every man's head. And after you left I was worse—though I did cry every night for a week. Then I went to Plymouth to steal your sister's lover from her. I didn't have any excuse. I didn't love him as Susan did. I didn't even like him. I just wanted the things he could give me."

"What's that got to do with me?" I interrupted impatiently. "I'm not John Denham."

"But you are my master, and when I come to you, it will be as a servant girl, crawling into her master's bed. Isn't that what you accused me of wanting to be at Denham?"

"Yes. And it's a pity you've changed."

She ignored my churlishness.

"Don't be angry. In the end you'll have your way."

"Yes, I know. When a full moon's high in the sky."

The months passed. It was mid-summer of our second year at Hickorywood. Betty had gone to Sidney to bear her first child. Abel was down the river where he frequently went on business of his own. I knew that this business concerned the Indians who were almost always to be found near William Byrd's plantation trading post, but I did not dream that it would lead him to matrimony and the practice of the magic that he had learned from Old Eve.

It was evening; Polly and I were alone. We watched the twilight deepen into a purple haze. Minutes grew into hours. Night fell as we sat in companionable silence. I had been in the fields by myself all day. Abel had begged leave to start on his journey, and Polly had been busy with household tasks.

"I missed you today," I told her.

"I'm a good field hand," she said.

"I didn't mean that. I always miss you—even when you are with me. But today it was worse than usual."

"Look, Tom." Her voice was low, but it shook so that I glanced at her in quick alarm. Her face was suffused with color, her lips were trembling.

"Not at me, goose."

She pointed toward the sky. There, high in the heavens, a full moon rode. I took her hand and we went into the house.

When we sat in the doorway again I was bloated with self-satisfaction. "You won't sleep in your loft again," I told her complacently.

"Not until your wife comes back."

Her matter-of-fact reply emptied me like a wine cask when the bung's knocked out. Her ready acceptance of Betty's return nettled me.

"Don't you care that I have a wife?"

"Yes, I care. Sometimes so much that I hate both of you because you have one another, but it doesn't matter if I care or not, if I love or hate; what's done is done. You do have a wife, and maybe a baby by now. They'll be coming home in a few weeks and I'll go back to my loft."

There was no answer to this. Nevertheless, I did not propose to relinquish my newly acquired privileges. I told Polly so.

"Not when Betty is at Hickorywood," she said.

"Nonsense. What is the difference between then and now?"

"None, really. But somehow with just the two of us here it does not seem so mean."

Despite her brave words I did not believe Pol. I thought that having once given herself to me she would be unable to withdraw the gift. Consequently I was reasonably content until I remembered that her term of service would some day expire.

"What will you do when you are free?" I asked.

"Go away."

"You can't."

But it appeared that Polly could. Moreover, she intended to do so, and find a husband of her own.

"You will never love him," I told her morosely.

"No," she agreed, "but I shall make a good wife. And now, Tom Bone, I think you are wasting the little time that is ours."

I agreed with her. We went back into the house.

### 2.

Life at Hickorywood was not the same after Betty came back. She left us in the rôle of wife—she returned a mother. Jimmy was a healthy baby who slept and fed and gurgled and howled. Ordinary enough, I suppose, and yet he possessed powers that no wizard ever possessed. The transformation he worked in Betty was sometimes intangible but it was always perceptible.

That she should care for the child, nurse him, dandle him, croon over him, was in no way strange, and certainly I, who loved my small son, neither objected nor felt jealous. But the change in Betty went deeper than arousing a mother's love. It involved hereditary urges that a mere fisherman's son could not readily comprehend. I was raised as in a litter where, if possible, the progeny were kept alive until they could fend for themselves, and then pushed out to make room for others. But Betty was the daughter of Elizabeth Sidney, whose forbears had put pride in their name before immortality, and of James Lester of yeoman stock that loved and clung to the land that it might belong to their son's sons.

So to Elizabeth Bone, born Lester, the world had changed. Hickorywood was no longer an adventure, a game against chance and nature, a gesture of defiance of the pretensions of the aristocracy; it was an ancestral home, the future seat of James Bone, Esq. Life was not an idyl of love in the wilderness; it was the business of shaping destiny to the needs and ease of a child who must some day be a man. I was no longer a companion and lover, but rather a father—and the obligations of fatherhood transcended those of both husband and man.

In short, the birth of her child rendered Betty not only passionately maternal, but it also aroused in her a dormant atavism, and for the first time in her life the spirit of her mother, Elizabeth Sidney, surged within her. She was as serene as before and as gentle, and in all matters except the child, as simple and candid and wise. But she was not wise for Jimmy Bone. Love blinded her and made her a coward before the future, selfless devotion made her selfish.

But Betty's was not the only change at Hickorywood. Although Polly adhered to her resolution to be a loyal servant to her mistress, and nothing beyond a friend to her master, the hours during which she had belonged to me were not without their aftermath. I did not care for Betty less for having been Pol's lover, nor did I love Polly more, but I felt more strongly than ever that God had blundered—that Pol, not Betty, was my proper wife. And despite devotion to my son, even he, for whom Betty required that I henceforth live, was in a queer sense an alien—a creature belonging to this strange interlude that must sometime end in order that Polly and I might truly belong to one another.

So it was that even as Betty centered her life more and more in her family and its future, I grew increasingly restive, and as the months passed, more entangled in the web of conflicting emotions and loyalties. As Jimmy grew in being he tugged in one direction, as did Betty, while Pol, without effort on her part, or conscious will, pulled in another. I loved my son, cared deeply for my wife, and hungered for Polly Bragg. Confused and restless I waited and did nothing. The months passed.

"In less than two years I'll be free."

As she spoke Polly looked up from the seed bed from which she was digging young tobacco plants for Abel who was transplanting them. I knew she meant that in two years she would be gone. I was afraid. I could already feel the emptiness caused by her absence, and yet I knew that I could never be quit of her presence. I might go into the fields, but she would be there, and in the woods, and by the water. I felt sudden panic. No minute must be lost.

"Come." I motioned toward the forest which still pressed close to Hickorywood."

"I've work to do."

"Damn work."

She rose from the seed bed and after wiping her hands on her coarse skirt sat down on a near-by log. She stared at her feet which were bare because she liked to feel the fine sifted dirt of the seed beds between her toes.

"Well, master," she said demurely.

I knew that I would fail again, but my need for her was too great to leave room for reason.

"Well, I didn't order you to quit work that you might sit on a log and wiggle your toes. Come with me."

"What for?"

"You know."

She laughed indolently.

"You needed a field hand and paid four pounds for me, so I work or not as it pleases you, but I'll be your strumpet only when it pleases me. Now it doesn't."

"You don't love me," I declared.

"Don't make it harder," she begged.

I surrendered.

"Talk to me then."

170

"What about?"

"Anything."

She gestured in the direction of the field where Abel was working.

"What does he do when he goes down the river?"

"Sees the Indians that hang around Byrd's trading post."

"What for?"

"Business. He shoots a great many deer and we do not use all the hides. He gives these to the Indians who in turn trade them at the post for knives, blankets, iron kettles and such stuff."

"But what does Abel want with things of that kind?"

"He gives them to his squaw."

Polly so often left me speechless that I now enjoyed her amazement. Then I explained. What I had said was true. Abel was our best huntsman, so we often sent him into the forest. During his wanderings he had made friends with the savages, and taken one of their women as his wife. He had confided in me at the time and I had suggested that he bring the woman to Hickorywood, but he had refused. It seemed that a wife in the woods was all very well, but one in his loft was quite another matter. Even when he announced the birth of a son he was deaf to my renewed suggestion.

"Let them both stay where they belong," he said.

"But the boy's yours."

Abel sniffed.

"I've others. Some black, some red, some mixed."

After that I held my peace and until now had kept his secret. When I had done Polly thought a while.

"I suppose Abel could have learned his 'magic' from them," she said at last, and told her story.

For some time she had been puzzled by mysterious sounds which came from the other side of the partition that separated the two closets in the loft. Her curiosity was so aroused that at last she went to Abel's room. She opened the door softly. He was kneeling in the middle of the room, his back toward her. As she watched he rocked gently back and forth. After a moment's hesitation she entered. Abel faced her. The queer noise stopped.

"What are you doing?" Polly demanded.

He was visibly embarrassed. "Fooling with an old drum."

She looked at it. It was made of a deer hide stretched taut. She thumped it experimentally. The result was a dull, disappointing thud.

"That's not what I heard."

Abel leaned forward. One large hand, palm open, hovered over the drum. He swayed forward, half rubbing, half striking it. His mouth moved. A soft chant filled the room. Polly tried to make out the words, but if they had meaning it was in a strange tongue. "Gibberish of apes," she called it. Yet she was fascinated. She listened and grew uneasy.

"Stop it," she cried.

Abel straightened up.

"Really make it sing in woods," he boasted. "Just barely touch it here, so as not to bother them down below."

"Why do you do it?"

"Just something to play when I'm alone," he mumbled evasively.

Polly did not believe him, but it was evident that whatever his secret was he intended to keep it. She was about to leave him when she noticed that one of his hands was tightly clutched. She persuaded him to open it. On his palm lay a small ball of what appeared to be leaves, egg shells and hair. He insisted that it was only trash that he had picked up in the woods. Polly went back to her room.

The soft throbbing rhythm pulsed through her brain until she dropped to sleep.

"Some nonsense he's learned from the Indians," I said when her story was done.

"Maybe, but somehow I don't believe it is."

On the way to the house we picked up Abel. I asked him about the drum. He was embarrassed but unresentful. He was also stubborn.

"Just a drum I made," he insisted.

I was inclined to believe him, but nevertheless I related Polly's story to Betty. She alone had any real influence with Abel. I was his former fellow servitor, Polly was a bound girl, but Betty was an aristocrat, his beloved little mistress.

"Find out what he's doing," I suggested.

"I already know. He got it from Eve. She was brought to Virginia from the West Indies, where the negurs are very superstitious. When I was a child she used to rock back and forth and croon over me, as you describe Abel doing. The ball in his hand was a charm of some kind. They call it an obia."

"Witchcraft."

"Something of the sort. Voudou they call it."

Betty seemed unconcerned, but I was worried.

"You must make him give it up. It's dangerous."

"Surely you don't believe in it."

"There will be people who do." I was remembering Jenny, and how she had been burned for witchcraft.

Betty called Abel from the loft. He answered her readily.

"I'm papa," he explained. "I talk to the Indians through the mouth of the serpent. They believe it is strong medicine."

Betty dismissed him. When I reproached her for not learning more she answered indifferently. She thought it was harmless.

But Betty was wrong. Eve had engaged much more deeply in the magic practiced by the West Indian negurs than she suspected, and had imparted all her knowledge to her son. And unknown to Betty and me, Polly Bragg, whose curiosity and interest had been aroused, went to Abel's closet night after night until she won his confidence and pumped him dry. In doing this she was only amusing herself. Certainly she had no presentiment of the use she was to make of what she learned in the loft at Hickorywood.

## 3.

By dint of work and frugal living we at Hickorywood were holding our own. But these were hard times in Virginia. The price of tobacco was low and the maize and wheat crop was so short that the governor forbade the export of grain even though men were starving in Massachusetts Colony.

Only Sir William Berkeley, the Royal Governor, and his friends and henchmen prospered. They grew rich on land and the Indian trade, cheating white and red man alike. With their unsavory wealth they enlarged their plantations, built mansions, such as the Governor's own at Green Spring outside Jamestown, and bought more slaves. They were gradually establishing a gentry molded after that of England and, like the English gentry, they abused their power. They controlled the Council, and even the Burgesses, formerly the tongue of the people, was little more than creature to the Governor. Taxes on the small farmers were increased, but the rich exempted themselves. Privilege was creeping into the New World. Men grumbled, but the storm was only gathering and few heeded the clouds.

Spring and summer passed. The tobacco plants were cut, fastened to laths and hung on the barn rafters to dry. In the spring we would strip the leaves from their stalks, sort them, and pack them in hogsheads. But it was autumn now; there was maize to be cut, fences to be repaired and the winter clearing to be started. We also planned to add a new room to our house. We had entertained such hopes before, but this time they showed promise of realization because Abel had already cut the lumber—good boards split from eight-foot lengths of oak.

One evening in October Betty and I were sitting on a bench in front of the house talking about our plans for the new room. Polly leaned over a near-by flower bed pulling weeds.

"You might just as well build a servants' shack while you're at it," Betty said. "We'll need a new hand when Pol goes, and I think we ought to have a negur."

I knew that we would have to have someone to replace Pol, but it vexed me to hear Betty speaking of it so placidly.

"A good slave costs twenty pounds," I grunted.

"You got me for four," Polly called pertly from the flower bed.

"And I'll sell you for an impudent hussy to the first buyer who offers tuppence," Betty retorted.

She was only teasing, but I was miserable at the thought of losing Polly. Moreover, as was frequently the case, I was goaded into unreasonable resentment by the understanding and friendship that existed between these two women, both of whom I loved.

It stood like an insurmountable wall separating me from Pol. Without it I felt sure I might take her as I pleased. At the thought of this, desire and frustration possessed me. Both were so old that they should have been stale, yet they were so fresh that my heart pounded like that of a boy who feels the first overwhelming surge of lust. For a second I hated both these women, leagued together, as it were, to balk my manhood. I turned on Betty.

"Polly's a woman as good as you," I reminded her, "not a mare to be bought and sold."

Betty was unruffled.

"Hear him, Pol," she laughed. "He blames me. Tell us. Was it I who rode to Jamestown and bought you from the ship's master?"

Pol shook her head, and more sensitive than Betty to my moods, spoke foolishly.

"You're a fool, Tom," she said.

Her warning, indiscreet in itself, was too late.

"I had good cause to buy her," I cried recklessly.

Jimmy was playing in the yard. Betty rose and took him in her arms. She looked down into his laughing face, then brought him to me. When he was in my arms she spoke gravely.

"Yes," she said. "You knew one another in England; perhaps you loved one another."

My stupid rage ebbed like a racing tide. I was aghast. I saw us as Betty must see us: myself, with my child in my arms and my wife beside me—while not ten feet away, weeding furiously, was the woman I loved, who had been my mistress.

"It's true, isn't it?"

Betty was calm but inexorable.

Jimmy's small hand found and clutched mine. He laughed. My arm tightened around him. I prepared to lie, but Pol forestalled me.

"Part true," she said without looking up. "How did you find out?"

"I can't say exactly. The knowledge revealed itself gradually, like dawn on a summer's day when it is impossible to say at what minute the light comes. But I have known for a long time. It was little things: looks between you, secrets that I did not share; and you are so familiar with one another. Just now you called your master Tom, and a fool besides. That is over-familiar, even for the frontier; and it is strange that a husband should tell his wife that she is no better than her bound wench, even though it might be true."

Polly left the flower bed and sat at Betty's feet. I held Jimmy close and waited, feeling foolish and frightened and helpless. It was between them now—Polly and Betty. Pol started to speak. She was confessing.

"It was my fault," she said humbly. "Please don't blame Tom. When I saw him come aboard ship as we lay anchored there in the James I thought that Christ had at last taken pity and sent him to me. I begged him to buy me. He wouldn't at first. He said that being what I was, I wasn't fit to be your wench, but you know how soft-hearted he is. I reminded him of old times, and finally he gave in. He even promised he wouldn't tell you about me."

Polly paused.

"Go on," Betty commanded. "You need not be afraid."

"I'm not afraid," Pol sighed, "I'm ashamed. You see I didn't come to America of my own free will as Tom did. I was transported. They took me out of jail where I'd been sent from a brothel."

My whole body relaxed. I smiled down at Jimmy, whom I need not have held so tightly since I was not to lose him, and at Pol, whose ready wit had given me a reprieve from the decision which must some day be made. For a few months more I could have them both near me—and my son. But when I looked up I was less sure. Betty was looking keenly into Pol's meek, beseeching, upturned face.

"Is it true?" she asked. "Will you swear it?"

Neither Pol's eyes nor her voice wavered.

"I have been a whore," she said steadily. "I swear before God that I have been a whore."

"And it was that way you knew Tom?"

176

As she asked, Betty rose and took the child from my arms. My heart sank. It seemed that Pol had but tossed me out of the frying pan into the fire. But she was equal to the occasion. Brilliantly, and without hesitation, she fabricated deceit out of truth.

"Not the way you mean. I was a friend of his sister. You mustn't hold it against Tom, but she was a trollop like me."

"Evalyn," Betty murmured, and I thanked God that I had not been ashamed to tell her of my past and poor Evalyn's shame.

"Tom's told me about her," Betty continued thoughtfully. Then she made up her mind. She leaned over and placed a kind hand on Polly's forehead.

"I suppose you did it because you were so poor," she said gently.

Most people would have been content, but now that the crisis was past and she had won, the gamin that still lurked within the woman that was Polly Bragg emerged. She rejected Betty's commonplace excuse for her shame.

"Oh, no, it wasn't that," she cried, "my mother sold me. She was very beautiful. Rich men came to her. They gave her money and jewels and fought duels for her favors." (I thought of drab Jane Bragg and almost choked.) But Pol had only begun. "She was very wicked. She didn't love her children like other women. She had six babies, all girls, and she sold each one of them, as soon as they were old enough, to the mistress of a brothel. She was that greedy, and besides we were in the way. 'Gentlemen don't like to see their bastards underfoot,' she used to say."

Betty shivered.

"I never knew anyone so horrible," she gasped. "Did you know the creature, Tom?"

"A very wicked woman," I said solemnly, looking at Pol. "She was a liar, too. I especially remember that. And yet there was something gallant about her that made men offer their souls in exchange for her love."

Polly hastily resumed her story. Her voice was husky with emotion, but her smile was brave.

"I was twelve when she sold me. I ran away at first, but they always caught me and brought me back. It was awful. I remember one time when a sailor took me and—"

"Never mind telling us more," Betty interrupted. "All that's past. But there is just one thing that I don't understand. Why didn't you tell me?"

"I wasn't proud of it, and besides I thought to have a husband when my service was done. But now that you know—"

Her voice trailed off, and I realized with a start that this much was not play-acting. In saving me Pol had hurt, perhaps ruined, her chances for marriage. Despite myself I felt warm from exultation. No man would have her. She must stay with us now. My triumph was short-lived.

"Nonsense," Betty declared briskly. "It wasn't your fault."

"You mean you won't tell?"

"I mean I'll help you find the best husband on the James, and he won't be good enough for you," replied my amazing and utterly virtuous wife.

Polly was ashamed. To my amazement she seized Betty's hand and kissed it.

"You're good," she muttered, "and I have done things more shameful than I have told."

Betty looked at her with eyes full of pity.

"I'll put Jimmy to bed," she said. "You two take a walk."

It was her way of saying that she no longer suspected us. We did not speak until we reached the river. There I took Pol's hand.

"You did a brave thing," I said.

"Maybe. Maybe it was cowardly. Maybe we should have told the truth."

I looked at her and was not afraid any longer. If I had Polly Bragg beside me nothing else mattered, not even Betty and Jimmy.

"We still can if you wish," I said quietly. "I am ready."

She turned on me fiercely.

"You," she cried. "Do you think I did it for you? It's Betty I'm thinking of."

I was deflated and puzzled.

"But—but," I stammered, "do you care more for Betty than for me?"

Pol snatched her hand from mine.

"I love you," she said in a low angry voice, "though God alone

178

knows why I must love a fool; and at this moment I almost hate your wife. She is so good that she makes me ashamed. So good that there would be no happiness for me if I stole you from her. Make her wicked, make her cruel instead of kind, make her mean like we are. Do that and you can have me, and I'll show you if I love you."

She ran sobbing toward the house.

I followed slowly. When I arrived Pol was in her loft.

"You didn't seem to help her," Betty said mildly.

"No," I agreed.

"Well, she will feel better in the morning. But we must start looking for a good husband for her."

But Betty was spared that necessity.

## 4·

Early in November James Lester came to Hickorywood. As I showed him the plantation I was both proud and nervous. Both emotions were wasted. Lester was preoccupied. Finally I found out why.

"I've something to tell you, Tom," he said awkwardly when we were alone. "Betty, too, but the fact is, I'm rather afraid she won't like it, so I thought if I told you, and you told her—" He stopped in confusion, and I wondered what it was that could so unnerve James Lester.

"A man needs a wife," he finally stammered.

I burst into laughter.

"Of course you do, sir. Betty's mentioned it often. She'll be delighted. Who is the woman?"

"That's what I'm here to talk about. Women are scarce in Virginia. I could buy one of the gentry's ladies, I suppose, or a wench from a ship, but I want neither. I thought perhaps the girl you have here—"

"Polly," I gasped.

"Yes, Betty speaks well of the girl. And though I wouldn't need her in the fields I'd like a wife who knows what it is to be there." He grinned sheepishly. "And she's well made."

179

Yes, Pol was well made.

"You can't have her," I cried.

"Why not?" he asked.

Why not, indeed? Passion makes men mean as often as it ennobles them. It is selfish as well as generous. Why not? I lacked the courage to tell Lester the truth, so I resorted to a stratagem too contemptible for any emotion save love—too contemptible— and yet I did it.

"Because she's a whore," I told him, and repeated the tale Pol had spun for Betty.

"Poor girl," Lester sighed. "She deserves some good fortune. It will be a pleasure for me to teach her what a decent man's love is."

"You mean you would still marry her?"

"Certainly. She's still comely, and from what Betty says she's a good girl now, whatever she once was. Let me tell you, Tom, there's more than one lady swishing her silks in Virginia who was transported from England. Some for worse things than your Polly has done."

"What will Betty think?" I said weakly.

"You must explain to her as best you can. That's one reason I told you first."

As we walked back to the house, he explained his other motive in confiding in me, and doing so, he put the final touch to the comedy.

"I won't want her until the New Year. I just came to look at her. She's even prettier than I'd remembered. When I'm gone you must explain to the women."

"You mean I'm not only to break the news to Betty, but also to tell Polly you want to marry her?"

"Yes. If I spoke to her now it might make her a worse servant. I'll come for her early in January. You can tell her a few days before."

"What if she won't have you?"

"She'll have me," he said comfortably.

I knew he was right.

Just before he left us, James Lester gave me another shock.

180

"I wish you weren't on the frontier," he said.

"But it was you who sent us here."

"I couldn't know that there would be more trouble with the savages."

"I've heard of none."

"It's up in Stafford County, on the Maryland border. A farmer named Hen was killed last summer. Before he died he said the murderers were the Doegs from over the Potomac. His boy, who hid under the bed and escaped, said the same. Some of our men crossed into Maryland, and before they were done they shot not only a dozen or more Doegs, but a score of Susquehannocks as well. The Doegs are treacherous cowards, but the Susquehannocks were our friends. It's rumored they're on the warpath, and that Maryland and Virginia have sent armed bands against them. If that's true, the trouble may spread until the whole frontier's afire."

I did not believe it would be so serious. A local incident, more than likely, exaggerated by rumor. It had been thirty years since the last general uprising when Opechancanough had raided the frontier. I reminded Lester of this and added that we had had no trouble in Henrico County. The Indians were quiet, even friendly.

"I hope that you are right, but at the first sign of trouble send the women to Sidney. I marched with Berkeley in '44. I wouldn't want to see at Hickorywood some of the things I saw then."

"I didn't know you'd fought the Indians," I exclaimed.

"There are some things a man would rather forget, but I am remembering them now, and I repeat—get to Sidney if there's trouble."

He was in such deadly earnest that I gave him my solemn promise; but to tell the truth, my thoughts were much more on his matrimonial ventures than on the Indian peril. A few days later he left us. As the shallop disappeared, I reflected bitterly that the next time Lester left, Polly would be with him.

But I had not quite given up hope of frustrating my father-in-law's designs. Despite her gentleness, Betty had a strong will, and I believed it possible that she would oppose the marriage. It was all very well, I told myself, to foist a girl from a brothel on an unsuspecting neighbor, but to permit her to marry one's own father was another matter. So, as soon as Lester was gone, I broke the news.

Betty refused flatly to oppose her father's wishes. When I reminded her of Polly's past she was impatient.

"What would you have, Tom? My father's a full-grown man with a will of his own. You should know that. If he wants Pol, and she's willing, they will wed. What we can't help we must make the best of."

"She will be your stepmother," I reminded her. "Will you like that?"

Betty was puzzled. "I don't understand you," she said. "I thought you and Polly were old friends and that you were fond of her. You should be pleased that she's a chance to marry so well, and that we will still see her from time to time."

My jealousy had blinded me. Betty's words opened my eyes. If she married Lester there would still be opportunity for Polly and me to meet one another. Harboring thoughts that I did not yet confess to myself, I surrendered.

"Very well, but you'll have to tell her about it," I said.

"But I shan't. You are her oldest friend. Besides, if a woman's not to receive a proposal of marriage from her lover, she should at least have it from a man." Her usually grave mouth twitched. "Mind you be very romantic, as if you loved her yourself. I had to propose to you. You can now make amends when you speak to Polly."

"Stop it," I said harshly. "I'll do it, but there will be no romantic nonsense. Your father doesn't love her, and she will never love him."

"You can't tell. Perhaps they'll adore one another."

I only wanted to escape.

"I'll speak to her in January; until then, let's talk no more about it."

"Tell her now. Father freed you because you were to marry me. Can we do less for his future wife?"

"But we need her work."

"She'll work as hard as she ever did. But you and Abel must

add the new room immediately. It's not fitting that she should stay in the loft."

Polly was mending a fence. I told her of Lester's offer. As he had foreseen, she accepted it.

"I'd be a fool to hesitate," she said when I complained of her haste in making up her mind. "Any woman wants a husband, and here in America she can hardly live without one."

"You could stay here."

"I've told you why I can't."

"So you're determined to marry?"

"You know that, and since I am, it had better be James Lester. He's a good man, and besides, we'll be able to see one another."

"There is that," I conceded. "And I won't give you up for all you're being married."

"I intend to be a good wife."

That evening Betty insisted on a mild celebration. We toasted the betrothed pair in pohickory, and at Polly's suggestion Abel made an obia to bring her luck. Betty grew a little sentimental and kissed Polly and shed a tear or two. I've never known Polly to respond to affection from a woman, but that evening she did her best, and she had the grace to blush. Betty thought it was the approaching nuptials that made Pol's cheeks grow hot.

I contributed little to the merry-making, but since Pol knew why, and Betty thought she did, they ignored my churlishness. Finally I could stand it no longer. I left them and went for a walk. An autumn moon danced in the rippling river but I did not see its beauty, for I was remembering another July night when the moon had ridden high.

Under Betty's watchful eye Abel and I added the new room to our house, and Polly moved into it. Other than that there was no change at Hickorywood. Polly helped cut and shock the maize, and circled the trees or hacked at the heavy undergrowth with the same zeal as before. No, nothing had changed at Hickorywood— but the days passed.

True to his promise James Lester returned in January. He brought the rector and a marriage license with him. There was no nonsense about his courtship. He told Polly that he was gratified

183

that she had consented to marry him, to which she replied that she was honored and would strive to make him a good spouse.

Betty, Abel and I attended the wedding.

"Dearly beloved, we are gathered here together . . ." I heard the words and realized that here was no droning of meaningless ritual. The clergyman spoke to us, and to the man and woman before him. Their answers were quiet and firm. I listened, and under the spell of the service Polly drifted beyond my reach, further than she had been when the ocean lay between us, more inexorably than before I had ever held her in my arms. "Who giveth this woman to be married to this man?" I stepped forward and gave the bride away—gave away Polly Bragg. The ceremony went on. The ring was on Polly's finger. "Those whom God hath joined together let no man put asunder." The new-wed pair knelt to receive the final benediction. They rose. It was over. Polly Bragg was the wife of James Lester.

We left the house. It was a damp gray day. The winter air dissolved the prayer book's magic. I smiled woodenly, but under my breath I cursed the Church and its vows. Betty kissed the bride, while I gabbled to the groom about long years and much joy from his wife. Then Lester drew his daughter aside and Polly and I were face to face.

"Well, Pol. You're one of the gentry now," I said briskly.

"You always promised that I would be when we came to America," she replied evenly.

Before I could answer Lester rejoined us.

"Come, wife, we must be off," he cried jovially. "Kiss the bride, Tom. It's your privilege, and one that none but her husband shall enjoy after you."

While I hesitated Polly kissed me. She put a casual hand on my shoulder, raised herself on her toes, and lightly brushed my lips with her own.

"Bravo!" Lester applauded, "but I hope you'll have more warmth for your husband."

"No doubt you'll teach me, sir," Polly replied.

"That I will, and so as not to postpone the lesson too long, we must be off."

184

They joined the clergyman who was already in the shallop. The boat moved towards midstream.

"God be with you," Betty shouted. "Remember you're to return soon."

"When the maize is in," Lester called back.

I could stand it no longer. Leaving Betty on the river bank I rushed to the barn. There I seized an ax and made for the forest. Abel found me hours later, stretched on the ground, body and brain aching.

"You did a lot of chopping," he commented.

When I did not reply he sat down beside me. Finally he spoke again. "Maybe you better come to the house," he said; "Miss Betty might worry."

I lacked the spirit to resist. As we walked through the woods my companion talked guilelessly of the wedding and Polly's luck. "The obia I made her worked," he boasted. "I gave her another last night."

"Rubbish," I muttered.

"No, sir," he retorted indignantly. "It's real magic. It will make her husband dote on her and never look at another female."

"She doesn't need magic for that," I said morosely, but despite myself I was interested. I thought of the tales of black magic and witchcraft I had heard, and of the learned men who vouched for them. For an instant I saw Old Jenny at the stake, and for a fleeting second my mind dwelt on the holy wedding mass I had witnessed; but my need was too great: the emptiness within me was too vast to be long restrained by either fear or reverence. I was ready to sell my body to the flames and my soul to the devil if doing so would bring Polly back to me.

"Could you make me an obia?" I asked.

Abel snorted. "You don't need one. Miss Betty would never look at anyone else anyhow."

"I wasn't thinking of Miss Betty," I said recklessly.

His soft liquid eyes bored into mine.

"I reckon you don't need an obia for her either," he said, and added with some satisfaction, "But she's gone and magic's not going to bring her back."

185

## 5

As it turned out magic was not needed to bring Polly back. She and her husband were at Hickorywood less than two months later. Lester came to urge us to take shelter at Sidney.

"The savages killed thirty-six whites last month," he explained. "The trouble is spreading."

It was hard to abandon Hickorywood. We hesitated for over a week and finally compromised. Other planters along the river had heard the news, and a group were going to Jamestown to see what the Governor and his Council were doing to protect us. It was decided that I should accompany them, and that Lester and Polly would stay at Hickorywood with Betty until my return. There had been no trouble on the James, and we all agreed that danger was not imminent.

I had not been in Jamestown more than a few hours before my complacency was shaken. The village seethed with excitement. Men from the raided country were here, from Piscataway Creek and the upper Rappahannock. The wives and children of some of these were dead or, worse yet, captives of the savages. The families of others were huddled behind the hastily built palisades waiting for the help that was to come from Jamestown. These men spent the day urging the Governor and Council to action. In the evening they sat in one or the other of the half dozen houses that served as tavern or ordinary when the town was crowded, and got drunk. Then they talked. Their tale was always the same. Surprise. They had known there was trouble somewhere else, but not in their neighborhoods. They wept and cursed themselves for their lack of foresight. I listened and wanted to hasten back to Hickorywood, but my companions were of sterner stuff.

"We'll not go back until we have an army with us," they declared stubbornly.

But despite reason, pleas and threats the Governor would not send soldiers against the Indians.

"The forts are being strengthened," he said. "That is enough. Troops would only incite those savages who are still friendly."

Many men did not believe that the Governor was being candid.

They even said he was pleased that the frontiersmen were being massacred. For settlers damaged the fur trade, and Berkeley, they swore, preferred that Englishmen be murdered to the curtailment of the profits of himself and his henchmen.

At first I could not believe this, but as the days passed and news of fresh outrages reached us, and still nothing was done, I began to wonder, and gradually all my old distrust and dislike of the gentry which had been lulled to sleep by my own improved fortunes stirred within me.

"Damn them," I told myself. "It's as bad here as in England. Tortured flesh and ruined plantations are the price paid for the Governor's greed and his wife's luxury."

Nursing such sentiments it was natural that I should gravitate to that group who muttered that the people of Virginia should take matters into their own hands. We talked boldly and fiercely but we lacked a leader and were divided among ourselves. The majority were men embittered by personal loss, and these only required that they be led against the Indians. But a smaller group, including myself, felt that the savages were merely acting according to their nature, and the real authors of Virginia's woes were the aristocratic Governor and his privileged bloodsucking circle.

The bitterest among us was Joseph Trigg. He was also the most voluble and eloquent. With the aid of rum and grunts of approval from his companions he would unfold the history of Virginia's undoing.

"Taxes," he growled one night, "damned bloody taxes. Two shillings the hogshead on tobacco, a poll tax besides, then more taxes. Taxes to buy arms and ammunition for an army that's kept at home, taxes for forts that are never built and cannon that are never fired. Where do they go? I ask you—and you can't answer me. But I'll tell you. They go to line the coffers of His Excellency, our Governor, may he go to Hell. Two shillings on tobacco so that there may be seventy horses at Green Spring and fine wine in its cellars; taxes for forts that are never begun, but the outbuildings at Green Spring are built—barns, sheds, kitchens, servants' quarters. All of them well and solidly built, too, and filled with cattle, food, supplies, servants and slaves. Taxes for an army that is not permitted to protect wives, who work gaunt and bare-foot in the fields, from the savages. And why not? Why, it is so that the doting Governor's beautiful young wife can ride the two miles to Jamestown in an elegant carriage, and wear fine linen next to her soft, idle, white flesh; may she, too, go to Hell.

"Nor are the leeches that call themselves the Governor's Council any better. Two hundred and fifty pounds of tobacco a day they pay themselves for the labor of thinking up new taxes to levy on us—their milch cows—and they take a manservant and a house besides. The liquor they guzzle comes out of your pockets, too. But here is the best joke of all. Though taxing is their business, and God knows they are past masters of the art, they pay no taxes at all. They and the Governor have passed a marvelous law. It exempts them from all taxation—taxes are for common men, men like you.

"Well, they have finished me. When I was done paying taxes I hadn't enough left to pay the English factor, so my plantation was taken. They gave it to a kinsman of Lady Berkeley, a stripling fresh from England who had never worked in his life, but none-theless he must have a plantation and live like a gentleman, so they gave him mine. Mine, that I'd labored on for over twenty years, tearing it out of the forest that God Himself had planted there. But God was kinder than William Berkeley: He granted me the fruits of my toil. But maybe I ought not to complain, because the new owner was gracious. He let my wife stay as his house-keeper, so she's still at home; and my daughter was even more fortunate. She has been taken on as a servant wench at Green Spring itself. Think of it, boys, she can empty Lady Berkeley's chamber pot and maybe even catch a glimpse of His Excellency himself."

Trigg and I became fast friends, and as I listened to him my boyhood came to life again, vivid and real. My father was brutally murdered before my eyes, my sister starved to death and I could not help her; Evalyn killed herself. Susan was taken from me to be a rich man's strumpet; my mother was a drab, frightened drudge. I relived it all.

188

"I'm with you," I swore to Trigg. "I'd rather fight the Governor than the Indians."

So we talked, but we lacked a leader. Until one appeared we were harmless as bleating sheep, and shrewd, cynical William Berkeley knew it.

The days passed into weeks, and I remained in Jamestown. More settlers came with new tales of horror, but the very repetition of these made them so familiar that they grew less formidable. Then the blow fell, and like all fools who can only learn from experience I cursed my blindness when it was too late.

The messenger arrived at dusk. Still half-crazed from fear he told his news. The savages had slipped between Berkeley's silly forts and raided the plantations of Henrico and Charles counties. We bombarded the fellow with questions, but got little satisfaction. Some of the settlers had escaped, others were killed or captured. He had heard that Nathaniel Bacon the younger, who owned a station on the upper branch of the James, was hastening down the river resolved to get a commission to march against the savages. This last, however, was little consolation to those of us whose homes were in the stricken region.

I could find out nothing concerning Hickorywood. That night, despite Joseph Trigg's protests, I started up the river. I had to know.

Hickorywood was in ruins. The house was a charred skeleton, the barn and sheds gone. A frantic search of the wreckage revealed nothing.

I sank heavily upon the remains of what had once been an oak chest and surrendered to despair. The charred beams and scattered ashes of my home were less desolate than my thoughts. I harbored no hope more sanguine than that my wife and child had died painlessly. Somehow I felt less concern for Polly. She had always risen above her fortune, and I had no doubt she would do it even at death. But Betty, and most of all, Jimmy— In an effort to blind myself to the specters that assailed me I buried my face in my hands.

A hand stroked my head. I knew that Polly was beside me

but for the first time my heart failed to respond to her presence. There had been many times when I had sworn that if God would but give me Polly Bragg, I would never beg of Him another favor, but now in my need I found that she was not enough. The years of marriage had riveted me to my family as firmly as the years of love bound me to Polly.

"Tom."

Her voice pulled me out of the morass of despair in which I had been stumbling. This was Polly. She would know—whatever there was to be known. I looked up.

"Where are they?"

Her hand moved to my forehead and rested there, but beyond that she did not try to comfort me.

"Betty's a captive."

"And Jimmy?"

"Safe."

The weight that oppressed and almost smothered me lightened. The thought of Jimmy in the hands of the savages had been hardest of all to bear. He was so little. I sighed in relief, thanked God, and was stricken as I remembered Betty.

"Tell me," I said to Pol.

The attack had come in mid-afternoon when Lester and Abel were working in a distant field. The savages must have watched the men leave, because they approached the house confidently in a single body of half a dozen or so. Polly had seen them first. She had seized the gun which was kept loaded and ordered Betty to take the child and sneak out the back door. There was a good chance she could reach the woods, and Polly felt sure the men would come to her assistance when they heard the shots. The plan almost worked. The first shot had stopped the Indians. It should have given Betty time to escape, but Polly, glancing out the back window, saw her stumble, fall, attempt to get up, and sink back to the ground.

Polly paused in her story. She was looking at me curiously. I knew, without being told, what had occurred. I saw a girl, hardly more than a child, propped against a tree, and I heard her scream

190

as I brutally twisted her injured foot. I saw her sway and slip sidewise, unconscious.

"Her ankle," I said hoarsely.

Polly nodded.

"It might have happened anyway," she declared stoutly.

"Go on."

Polly had fired another shot. An Indian fell. The others stopped. A second later one of them made for the shelter of a near-by clump of trees; the others joined him. Polly knew she had gained a few minutes' grace but that was all, for when the attack was resumed the savages, their careless bravado dashed, would probably encircle the house, and discover the fugitives who thus far had been hidden from their view. Throwing aside the gun, Polly snatched and charged the pistol and ran to join Betty.

Betty's ankle was badly sprained. She tried to walk with Polly's aid, but it was no use. Polly was stunned and helpless before such disaster. Betty took command. She ordered Polly to take the child and get away.

"I tried to argue," Polly told me defensively, "but what was there to say? At any minute we might be discovered and killed or taken. Besides, she really wanted me to get Jimmy away. So I took him in my arms, and we left her lying there on the ground. She was smiling and telling Jimmy not to be afraid. I know what I did was right, and yet—" Her voice trailed off in self-reproach.

"You mustn't blame yourself," I said.

"I wouldn't," she answered slowly, "but for one thing. Before I left she begged for the pistol. I refused to give it to her."

"You might have let her have it," I said. "But it wouldn't have mattered. They would have gotten her, even though she killed one or two first."

"She didn't want it to shoot Indians with," Polly retorted somberly.

Up to this point, relief at my son's safety, interest in Polly's narrative, and sheer physical and mental exhaustion had somewhat deadened my emotions; but as the significance of Polly's words sank into my tired brain it quickened to life. Full realization of what had occurred dawned on me. It was like a mighty wave

191

crested with foaming horror. It washed over me and left me weak and terror-stricken. I recalled the poor haunted devils I had seen and heard in the ordinaries at Jamestown. I must be one of them now. I too must get drunk to rid myself of the picture of my wife helpless in the hands of the red beasts, unable even to take her own life. I hated Polly for having denied her that last poor privilege.

"I suppose you required the weapon yourself," I cried. "You were strong; you had two good legs and the forest for shelter, but you needed the pistol too!"

"It wasn't that," Polly said stonily.

"Then what was it?"

"It would have been as if I'd killed her myself."

"And why didn't you? That would have been kinder than to leave her for them to take."

Polly's calm broke into a thousand fragments. Her words blazed with angry passion.

"Because, you fool, I've been your mistress, and, God save me, I'm witling enough that it's likely I'll be again. If I had shot her, or even left her the gun with which to take her own life, would either of us ever have been sure why I did it? Could you have touched me again without wondering if I had killed out of kindness, or murdered the wife of my lover?"

I should have realized that Polly's ordeal had been a hundred times more severe than mine. It was she who had peered over a gun barrel as the savages approached. It was she who had hastened to the side of my injured wife, had fled into the forest with my son in her arms. But I was too immersed in my own feelings to consider hers.

"Do you think I'll ever want to touch you again?" I cried.

She turned abruptly and walked away. When she had disappeared into the woods my dejection grew blacker. Self-pity's fetid waters washed over me. After a long time Polly returned. She brought my son with her. With a shout he threw himself upon me, and for a few blessed breathless minutes we tussled in mock ferocity. Finally Jimmy's tiny fist buried itself in my hair. "Scalp," he shouted frantically.

I put him down and looked at Polly. She stared back.

"Where does he think his mother is?" I demanded.

"He knows, but he's still a baby."

"He knows?"

"I stopped at the edge of the woods to make sure what happened."

"And let him see?"

Her voice dripped disgust.

"I thought possibly you might return some day and wish to know the fate of your wife, and I was sure her father, my husband, would require that much of me. So I ran a small risk to your son's life, and my own, in order to know."

As Polly spoke I forgot Jimmy. When she had done, I brushed aside her contempt. I was back on the treadmill of my anxiety for Betty.

"What did you see?" I begged.

"Not much. I got to the woods before they found her. I even watched her crawl a few yards toward us. Then one of them came around the house. Betty lay still. I hoped for an instant that he might not see her, but he did, almost immediately. He started toward her. As he did so, I shot at him, but missed. I thought there was a bare chance that I might frighten them. They were frightened but not quite badly enough. The others came running around the house. They took Betty and fled. But they stopped long enough to set fire to the buildings."

"Did they—was Betty—?"

"They didn't hurt her. One of them picked her up and carried her away. That was all I saw."

Polly's voice, which had been kind as she spoke of Betty, hardened. "So your son escaped after all. I've kept him safe for you since. There's a shallop hidden about twenty yards south of the landing place. Take Jimmy and go to Sidney."

"What are you going to do?"

Polly was silent for some minutes. It was evident that she was weighing her reply. "I'm waiting for Abel," she said finally.

I had forgotten Abel and Lester too. I asked Polly where they were. Why they had not come when they heard the shots? It appeared that they had come, too late. After hearing his wife's story, Lester had bade her hide herself and the child in the woods, or if she could reach one, take shelter at some point where other settlers might be gathering. He himself had set off in immediate pursuit of the Indians. He had ordered Abel to accompany him, but despite threats and curses the negur would not go. When his former master was gone, he took charge.

"We'll go to my squaw's people," he said. "It's safe there."

The Indians were sullen but not unkind. Abel had not exaggerated his importance among them; his voudou had made him a great man. Nor, Polly discovered, had he deserted his "little mistress." He was merely intent on saving her in his own way. Having seen Polly and the child safely established he announced he would find the savages who had attacked Hickorywood.

"Why didn't you go with my husband?" Polly had asked.

"He won't find them. If he does they'll kill him."

"How can you do better?"

"One of the warriors here will go with me to trail them. When we catch up, I'll join them."

Polly knew that this was possible. Many braves from various tribes had joined the marauding Rappahannocks, and a few runaway slaves.

"What will you do then?" she asked.

Abel had grinned.

"Go on the warpath. Maybe help burn a few houses and kill a few whites. Somehow before I'm done I'll get Miss Betty free. You wait here."

Polly was still waiting. Every day she had come back to the ruins of Hickorywood to see if Lester had returned. So far there had been no sign of him. But she intended to wait until she had news, or until Abel came. Meantime she calmly suggested that I flee to Sidney.

"I'll wait with you," I growled.

"You can't. The Indians shelter me because Abel demanded it. But they are afraid of the Rappahannocks. They will not shelter a white man."

"Then I'll stay here."

194

"That's your affair, but what about Jimmy? Someone should take him down the river."

"You say he's safe with the Indians."

We argued further, but to no avail, so Polly took the child with her and went back into the woods. Left alone, I wandered over the plantation, seeing ghosts at every turn. When night came, indifferent to the consequences, I built a fire from charred boards that had once been part of my home and settled down before it. It gave out warmth but no comfort. "Abel's mad," I told myself broodingly. "He'll only succeed in losing his own life. And Lester is almost certainly already dead." That would leave Polly the mistress of Sidney. I had not thought of that. I looked at the dark ruin that had been Hickorywood and smiled mirthlessly. The wheel had taken another turn. Pol was up and I down. I remembered Elizabeth Lester and my amusement was real. Polly Bragg, bastard, serving girl, indentured servant, would reign in her place. "An improvement, too," I thought drowsily.

Someone was shaking me. I opened my eyes. A dark face was close to mine. It was Abel; Polly stood beside him, a new Polly. Her face and hands were nut-brown.

## 6.

Polly and I were deep in the forest. Less than a mile away lay the Indian encampment where Betty was held captive. She was alive and unharmed. That night we would attempt a rescue. Or rather Polly and Abel would; I was to have little part in it. The plan was theirs, and desperate and fantastic as it was, I could think of none better.

After leaving Polly, Abel had found the savages as he had promised, and had been accepted by them without suspicion. He had had no plans beyond that, other than to free Betty at the first opportunity. But he found to his dismay that there was little time. Often white women and children were held for months, enslaved, or even adopted into the tribe. But the Rappahannocks were in a wicked temper. They were determined that with the coming of the new moon they would torture their prisoner to

195

death. Abel possessed a shrewd mind and more than his share of cunning. He told the Indians that he was, or had been, Betty's slave, and swore that she was a fiend in woman's form who had cruelly mistreated him for the pleasure it gave her. Would they not give her to him that he might avenge himself according to his humor? His claims were recognized, but only to the extent of a promise that before she was permitted to die he might amuse himself by gouging out her eyes and tearing bits of skin from her bared back.

After suffering this rebuff, he racked his brain and wished that Polly, whose ready wit he respected, were there to help him. Then out of his longing for Polly's aid and his desperation, Abel conceived the first shadowy outline of the appalling scheme that we were here to carry out.

Upon the pretext that it was fitting that he have a few minutes of pleasure alone with his former mistress, he gained permission to see her. He unfolded as much of his plan as he had developed and assured her that in due time, with Polly's aid, he would contrive the remainder. At first Betty refused to sanction it, but finally faced, as I was later faced, with the barren fact that she had no alternative to offer, she surrendered herself into Abel's hands with the sole stipulation that Polly should place herself in such peril out of her own free will, or not at all. This satisfied Abel, who was confident that when it was needed, Polly's aid would be forthcoming; but meantime, the prelude to the melodrama that he was about to stage must be enacted without help; so after carefully instructing Betty in her rôle, he rejoined the savages. He turned braggart. He was a great medicine man, he boasted, who employed magic that came from islands far to the South. Grunting derisively, they demanded proof. He called for a cock and sacrificed it, voudou fashion. As he had foreseen, the red men were impressed by the mumbo jumbo but still skeptical. Anyone could kill a rooster. How were they to know if the "voice of the serpent" was indeed the august one of a powerful spirit, or merely the vainglorious squeaking of a braggart? Abel pretended to be outraged. He whipped himself into tumultuous fury.

"Bring a goat and the white woman," he screamed, "and I'll show you the power of the serpent."

The Indians were cautious. Before they would grant Abel's demands he had to promise that he would not harm their captive. She must be kept in prime condition for the sport that they themselves had planned, and which was now only a few days distant. However, once convinced that they would not be robbed of the pleasure of destroying their victim in their own way, they readily dragged her forth.

Abel had instructed Betty in her rôle. The opening scene was not difficult. The girl berated her former slave; she even struck him in the face. This seemed wholly natural to the Indians, for they were accustomed to the overbearing manners of the whites, whose arrogance frequently went unabated until the torture itself. Then, generally, though not always, it broke, and they whimpered like an Indian squaw. Moreover, Betty had shown fortitude. Since her capture she had neither complained nor begged for mercy. The savages valued such stoicism, and savored no pastime quite so keenly as that of breaking the body and shattering the spirit of an enemy who possessed it. In Betty's case they looked forward to a long and diverting evening. Consequently when she abused the big negur, they grunted approval and waited with interest to see if he really possessed magic strong enough to subdue her without violating his promise to do her no physical harm.

Abel had the goat brought in. Betty no sooner saw it than she screamed, and despite her ankle, tried to run. She was seized before she could fall.

"She's afraid," Abel explained complacently. "She knows my magic's powerful. When she owned me no goat was allowed on the plantation. I found one in the woods once, but they caught me before I could make medicine. She had me whipped till I almost died."

While he talked, Betty shrieked alternate imprecations and prayers. She even made a futile lunge at the goat, whose bleating added to the confusion. Abel now came forward with a hunting knife. He slit the animal's throat with one deft stroke. As the blood spurted out he caught a quantity of it in a gourd which he held ready. He turned toward Betty. Redoubling her screams, she tried to knock the gourd from his hands. He ordered the guards to pinion her arms to her sides. When she was helpless, he dipped his finger in the goat's blood, and with it drew cabalistic symbols across the girl's forehead. This done, he commanded that she be thrown on the ground. Kneeling beside her, he placed an obia on her body. Then rocking back and forth he chanted strange incantations that originated in the jungles of Africa. Betty, who had strained and writhed when first thrown down, gradually grew quiet. Abel rose and stepped back a few paces.

"Let her go," he told the Indians who had been holding her. "She'll be good now. Won't you, wench?"

"Yes, master."

She spoke so clearly that those of the spectators who knew only a little English could not fail to understand, and there was such humility in her voice that the ones who did not grasp the words themselves could yet feel their implications. But Abel was taking no chances.

"Whose a slave now?" he jeered.

She clung to simple, easily comprehended phrases.

"Me, white woman, black god's slave."

"Show them."

At his command she crawled to him and flung her arms around his legs. He left her there long enough for the Indians to appreciate fully the sight of a white woman groveling at the feet of a black. Then he spurned her contemptuously with his foot, and ordered that she be taken away.

After she was gone he explained to the savages that she would remain subject to his will three or four days. At the end of that time the spell would wear off.

"Weak magic," he acknowledged airily. "Not like the goat without horns. That magic makes any white woman, or man either, a slave forever. All you have to do is just look 'em in the eye."

When asked why one possessed of such powers had remained in bondage, he readily admitted that since he had been brought to Virginia he had been unable to find an opportunity to sacrifice the

198

goat without horns—until now. He cast a meaningful crafty glance at Betty who was seated on a log not far off. After suitable reluctance, he explained what he meant. The savages were shocked. They were not cannibals. Abel tempted them, embroidering his arguments with fanciful tales of occasions when he had participated in such rites while still in the islands to the South. He frankly admitted that a white child would be preferable, but the girl would serve. Nor if they were squeamish was it absolutely necessary to eat the flesh: a sip of the blood would be sufficient. He finally won them over, and having done so, he came to the most delicate stage of his undertaking. He confessed that he could not perform the ceremony himself. He was a "papa" and spoke through the mouth of the serpent and could command minor magic; but only a priestess goddess could perform the rite of the goat without horns. Fortunately he knew where such a priestess was. He could fetch her in four days.

After much talk and considerable tobacco had been wasted, the Indians decided that Abel should go for the priestess. But they warned him that the new moon was only five days distant, and if he failed to return by that time they would carry out their original program.

Before Abel left he reported his progress to Betty, and gave her a hunting knife.

"If I'm not back use this," he advised her grimly. "Better that way."

Two days later he got back to the village where he had left Polly. She assented to his plan and threw herself into mastering it and elaborating its details.

"But why must I stain myself brown?" she asked.

"You're going to be a mulatto. Indians would be suspicious of a white woman."

So she rubbed the juices that he brought from the forest into her face and hands. It was not enough for Abel.

"All over," he ordered. "Priestess goddess don't wear many clothes."

"How do you know? It's all a fraud anyway. You never saw a priestess goddess."

Abel grinned.

"Maybe not. But you got to look the way the Indians will believe a priestess goddess ought to look. That can't be like every brown wench they ever saw."

Polly submitted and Abel was satisfied. He decided, however, to take some of the juice with him in case it should wear off during the return trip through the forest.

But one problem remained unsolved. Even if Abel's incredible scheme worked, Betty could not be out of the Indians' sight for more than a few hours without arousing their suspicion. Injured as she was, how could she get to Hickorywood and the hidden shallop before they recaptured her? Abel confessed that he had failed to find a satisfactory answer to this puzzle.

"She'll just have to hide till they're tired hunting," he told Polly doubtfully.

"They'll find her, and you know it."

He ruefully admitted that they probably would.

Polly considered the matter.

"We'll make a litter and carry her," she finally decided. "A long enough start will give her a chance."

"Who'll carry her? You can't do it alone, and I got to stay in camp to keep them from following you."

"Tom is here."

So they had come to Hickorywood and aroused me out of a sound sleep—and now we were two days in the forest, and less than a mile from the place where Betty was held captive. Dusk was falling. Abel had gone to the encampment to set the stage for the coming of the priestess. Polly was asleep. For over an hour I had been watching her. Her eyelids flickered, her eyes opened. She rubbed them and sat up.

"It must be near time to cozen the vermin," she said as she glanced at the sky.

Jaunty as her words were I was not deceived. Polly knew that she might soon be dead.

"Why do you do it?" I asked abruptly. "Betty's nothing to you; you were only her servant."

"Abel is only her slave, but he's with her."

200

"That's different."

Polly picked some wildflowers that were growing within reach. She put them in her hair.

"They seem fitting for a goddess," she said.

"But you haven't yet told me why you are playing goddess."

"Why shouldn't I? I've been chambermaid, indentured servant, and wife to two squires. Why not goddess?"

"Stop it," I cried. "In another hour you may be going to your death. I must know why."

"She's a white woman. Isn't that enough?"

"No."

"Very well. She is also your wife."

"So if anything happens to you, it is because of me."

"Not you alone—us."

"And I must hide in the bushes and wait while a woman that I love is out there."

Polly was picking flowers again. She did not look up.

"There will be two women out there," she reminded me.

I knew that she was remembering how I had sworn that I never wanted to touch her again.

"Forgive me," I said.

"That's easy enough. But which one of us do you love?"

It was a woman's question and one which Polly had every right to ask. Yet how could I answer it? Love is such an easy word to say, and yet it means so many things. It means to cherish and protect; it means to pursue and to elude; it means to abase and to serve; it means to master and yet adore. I believe that to a woman it means above all else to cleave to, but, to a man, that may be the least of its meanings. So I searched vainly for an answer to Polly's question, for there are times when the falsehoods that rise so glibly to the tongue cannot be uttered. This was such a time. Polly was very near. I wanted her and I knew that I had only to reach out my hand; but Betty was facing unspeakable torment. She needed me and I could not help her.

"God save me! I love you both."

Polly laughed shortly.

"I suppose I must be content with that. I'll recall it when I have the knife at her throat. And now I must bedeck myself as Abel's priestess goddess."

"You look like a bird of paradise with half its feathers plucked," I told her when she had made herself ready.

She shivered.

"Never mind what I look like. Give me my cloak."

But even after the cloak was around her she continued to shake.

"Cold?" I asked.

"Frightened."

I took her hand. We did not talk. We were waiting for the signal. At last it came, the low throb of a drum. Abel had not boasted in vain in his attic at Hickorywood. In the forest he could truly make the "ole drum" sing. We stood up.

"Got everything?" Polly asked.

I picked up the rude litter, my gun and pack.

"I guess so."

"Let's go."

Darkness had fallen while we waited. We crept forward cautiously. After a few minutes I saw a dull glow in the sky. It was the reflection of a fire. I had known it would be there, but nevertheless I shuddered. What if Abel had failed and Betty was now standing in the center of a circle of burning faggots which were being pushed ever nearer. Unconsciously I quickened my pace. Presently I could see the firelight flickering through the trees. Polly caught my arm.

"This is as far as you had better come," she whispered.

"But how can Betty walk so far?"

"She'll have to, or die."

She pulled the cloak off her naked shoulders and handed it to me. The light of the new moon trickled through the trees. Polly's face was drawn. I drew her into my arms. Her body strained against mine. For a moment at least my doubts as to the nature of love were dispelled.

"I love only you," I whispered.

She pushed me away.

"You'll be free to choose when I've brought her back to you."

The drum, which had never been stilled, throbbed with a new

urgency. It was the call for the priestess. Polly left me. When she was safely beyond hearing, I followed. I had had enough of obedience. If I could not aid the others, I would at least watch over them. If the affair miscarried, I was determined to die rather than slink back to safety alone. I reached the edge of the clearing and took shelter behind a bush.

The savages formed an unsealed oval around a large fire. In its open end squatted Abel. Polly stood in front of him. He gave the drum a final blow and prostrated himself before her. Betty emerged from somewhere in the shadows. An Indian was on either side of her, but I was relieved to see that though limping, she walked by herself. When they reached her, Polly dismissed the guards with a peremptory gesture. Abel rose and forced Betty to her hands and knees. She crouched there docilely on all fours, like some soft white animal. Abel threw a garland over her head. The goat without horns was ready for the sacrifice.

Abel resumed his drum-beating. Polly writhed and twisted to its rhythms in a dance of her own improvisation. Meantime a goat was brought. Abel slaughtered the animal as before, but this time it was Polly who wrote in blood across Betty's forehead. When she had finished this, Abel handed her the knife. She pressed it against Betty's throat. Then something went awry. The knife somehow twisted. Fresh blood, her own, covered Polly's finger. The discomfited goddess turned furiously on her unfortunate assistant and let loose a flood of abuse. Abel cowered in seeming terror. As for me, in spite of my almost unbearable anxiety, I grinned. No Indian would comprehend the words; to him they might sound as Polly intended they should: like the jargon of a priestess from the southern islands; but to me they were as familiar as my boyhood, for the goddess was lashing her acolyte with the tongue of an English fishwife who pours forth her wrath on an erring husband or a successful rival. The homely billingsgate warmed my heart. Bless Pol! That was the world we belonged in, she and I. We should have stayed there instead of trying to play gentlefolk in this accursed American wilderness. But I had little time for homesickness. Abel, in apparent obedience to some command from his mistress, had turned and begun to harangue the Indians. Polly wheeled back on Betty, spit in her submissively upturned face, and jerked her to her feet. The crisis had arrived. The two women started to walk out of the circle.

I watched them as long as I dared, then hastened back to where Polly had left me. I could hear them coming. Polly, partially to reassure the savages that their victim was not far away, partially to warn me to be prepared, continued her noisy tirade. When they reached me I had the cloaks ready, the pack was slung over my shoulder and my gun was at hand. But we could not yet go. Unless Abel succeeded flight was useless. So we stood waiting, Polly grasping the hunting knife, I with my gun ready. Time was interminable and motionless. At last the drum sounded. Abel had won. Polly sobbed and sank to the ground. She had fainted. Paralyzed by this new catastrophe, I stared at Betty.

"She'll have to be carried," she said.

I looked at the litter doubtfully.

"One can't—your ankle—"

"The litter idea was never any good," Betty cut in. "You can't carry such a thing through the forest. Take her in your arms."

I picked Polly up.

"But you?"

Betty grimaced.

"I'll manage to walk until she comes to."

Betty tried bravely but as she limped beside me I realized with a sinking heart that our pace was hopelessly slow. Even after Pol had returned to consciousness we made but poor time, and after a few hours I despaired of our escape. However, it was Betty who first dared voice the dread that oppressed us all.

"They'll overtake us," she whispered.

Neither Polly nor I wasted breath in denying what we knew to be true.

"Without me you could escape," Betty groaned after a few more minutes.

"Yes," Polly answered. "We could."

"Put me down, Tom."

I plodded on.

"Put her down."

At Polly's command I stopped in sheer amazement.

"You've got to rest anyhow," she said calmly. When we were all seated she continued. "We may as well settle this. They are almost sure to catch us. What are we going to do?"

I had no better plan than to stumble on, hoping against hope, praying for a miracle.

"It's folly," Betty protested. "There's no need for all of us to die."

"I think there is."

As Polly hurled her challenge, she looked at me and smiled. Her eyes were mocking. Would I desert Betty? If so, would I leave her the means of self-destruction? Or kill her myself? I had it in my power. It would be easy; it would be sensible. It might even be kind. One sharp thrust—she need not even know it was coming—and my wife would be dead, out of danger, out of pain, out of being. Polly and I could hasten through the forest, safe and together. For she would go with me. Her eyes told me that even while they mocked me. But she knew that I would refuse, as she had refused at Hickorywood.

"Pol's right," I said gruffly as I picked Betty up, "we'll die together, or all live."

"It's fortunate to have a choice," Polly said. I knew that she was reminding me that with the child to save, her choice had been more difficult.

Betty's arm tightened around my neck.

"Perhaps it is right that Tom should stay with me," she said gravely, "he is my husband. But you, Polly, have already done far more than we have a right to ask, or can ever repay. Don't put us further in your debt. Save yourself."

Thus with unconscious cruelty Betty asserted that I belonged to her, and attempted to separate Polly from us by a wall built of the words that had been read out of a prayer book. Polly brushed it aside.

"Stop bleating such nonsense," she commanded airily, "or I'll turn you into my little white goat again."

I felt Betty shudder.

"That was hideous, even to pretend," she said.

205

Polly did not reply. Perhaps she too was remembering, because when she spoke again she had discarded her banter.

"If they come, Tom, don't waste time fighting."

I knew what she meant. Resistance would only result in capture. And no second fantasy out of the West Indian jungles would invade the American forest. But there would be time for two thrusts. One for Betty, one for myself. Polly had her own knife.

I trudged on praying for courage. And my prayer was answered, for presently I realized that courage was not a matter of fortitude in dying; it lay rather in daring to live. I told myself that there must be a way to escape the savages. Soon it came to me that there was a way, though it was dangerous.

When we came to a place that suited my purpose I put Betty down.

"We'll wait here," I said.

Pol was incredulous.

"You've given up?" she asked.

"It's no use to run."

"What else can we do?"

"Fight."

My scheme was to ambush the savages. Both women agreed that it was our only chance to live. While I was still explaining my plan of action Abel appeared. He was dismayed at our being no farther. The Indians, he said, were not over an hour behind him.

"Then we have an hour," Betty said. "Tell us what happened after we left you."

"As we go," Abel said.

I told him our decision.

I do not know if he agreed to its wisdom, but he accepted our judgment. With a shrug he told his story.

As Polly strode out of the circle with Betty in her wake, Abel had warned the Indians not to interfere with or pursue them. To do either would be to court a horrible unnamed fate. Having thus gained their attention he held it by explaining that the sacrificial knife had turned in the priestess' hand because he, the acolyte, had blundered in the preliminary rites. The only remedy was for the priestess to take the victim to a secluded spot where she would purify her. There must be no witnesses. One pair of prying eyes would destroy the magic, in which case all present would fall under the curse of the serpent.

This subterfuge had kept the warriors quiet for over two hours while Abel alternately beat his drum and harangued them. At the end of that time, sensing by their restlessness that the game was near its end, he played his last card. He was attacked by violent spasms which culminated in his slumping to the ground where he lay in an apparent trance. The natives crowded around him, but for some minutes he resisted their ministrations and even a few lusty kicks. At last he stirred uneasily and regained consciousness. He told them that the serpent had spoken to him. The priestess' work was done. The white goat without horns was at last ready for the sacrifice. He was to fetch them, but he must go alone.

There was some opposition to this, but in the end the natives' fear of the serpent's wrath prevailed. But he was warned to return soon, or they would come after him.

Abel was satisfied. A lead of an hour or so was all that he required for himself, and he had sadly miscalculated our speed.

When we had heard Abel's story I disposed my small force.

We backtracked a hundred yards or so, in order that the Indians might not become suspicious through losing our trail. Then we divided our small supply of arms. Betty took a carbine, with which she was an excellent shot; Pol a pistol and a knife. Abel and I had only our long knives.

"You mustn't warn them by shooting too soon," I cautioned the women. "Wait until Abel and I attack."

"But then we might shoot you," Betty objected.

"We must risk that. Our only hope is surprise. If you shoot they will scatter, and we are lost."

Abel agreed.

When we were hidden in a thicket I finally voiced my doubts.

"Have we a chance?" I asked Abel.

"They won't send many after a negur and a couple of women," he replied.

"But I was a priestess," Pol protested from her nearby thicket. "I let you dress me up like a heathen whore just to impress them."

Abel laughed softly.

"Once those devils decide they've been fooled they won't be impressed," he said.

"So I might be the white goat myself next time?" Pol asked.

"I guess they're through with goats. If you get caught you'll be just another white woman tied to a stake."

That sobered us. We waited in silence until the savages came. There were ten of them moving rapidly and almost soundlessly in single file. Abel and I let them pass until the last two were abreast us. As I leaped I heard the guns crack, and above that, a savage war whoop. This last came not from the savages, but from Abel—and to my astonishment Pol echoed it.

"Now where the devil did she learn that," I wondered. Then I forgot everything as my knife bit into an Indian's back.

Females, simpering and languishing, sometimes ask me how it feels to be in a fight with your life the stake. For me, at least, an adequate answer is impossible, though I think I once made a clever Frenchwoman understand by comparing hand-to-hand knife fighting with something she herself knew.

"It's like love," I told her. "You lose yourself. For the moment the world stands still and nothing exists but you and your antagonist. Every muscle quivers. Then it is over. The world comes slowly back into focus—and you are languid from fulfillment. Unless of course you are wounded."

The Frenchwoman laughed.

"In love one is not wounded," she said.

"You have been fortunate."

"Not at all. But I am a shrewd warrior."

That day in the forest we too were shrewd warriors. None of us was more than scratched. Abel alone killed three Indians; I knifed two. Betty and Pol shot four, and Pol leaped from her hiding place to sink her knife into the back of the last one as he tried to flee.

When it was over I looked at my companions. Abel's thick lips were parted in a smile, his gentle eyes rested contentedly on the dead bodies. It was difficult to believe that he was the shouting bloodthirsty giant of a few minutes ago. Pol's eyes still sparkled. She looked at me and grinned. She touched a corpse with her foot.

"Goat without horns," she said.

I looked at Betty. Her lips were moving, and I knew that she was praying—thanking God for her deliverance, the stern Puritan God of battles.

For two days we waited uneasily at Hickorywood while friendly natives sought in vain for some trace of James Lester. Either he was dead, or, giving up the search for his daughter, he had preceded us down the river. The third alternative—that he had been captured—haunted me, as I have no doubt it did the others. But no one voiced it. On the evening of the second day the report came that the Rappahannocks were again in the vicinity. Afraid to delay longer we fled down the river.

Betty sat in the rear of the boat. She looked fondly at Jimmy who was on her lap. Then her face clouded.

"We're penniless," she sighed, and I knew that she was thinking of her son.

"We're still alive," Pol reminded her.

"*We* are, yes."

Polly flushed.

"I am not unmindful of your loss," she said stiffly.

"Yours, surely, as well as mine. He was your husband."

The strain was having its effect on both women. I was afraid that they might quarrel. I tried to speak cheerfully.

"Maybe he is already at Sidney."

It was thin comfort. I did not believe it myself. Neither did Abel.

"You should have let me stay to look for him," he told Betty. She shook her head.

"You risked your life and worse saving me."

"I am your slave," he said simply.

"No. You have earned your freedom."

We were all surprised, Abel most of all.

"What would I want to be free for?" he asked.

"To get land of your own, perhaps even slaves."

The big black laughed.

"And worry about caring for them? I'd rather be your house negur."

"I haven't any house," Betty reminded him.

"Come to Sidney," Polly intervened. "There you can be free and a house negur both." She looked at Betty. "You know he is yours when you want him."

"He is free. He can choose for himself," Betty replied.

Polly grinned at Abel.

"I'm not a lady," she admitted, "so maybe not fit to be waited on, but we could practice our war whoop some more and voudou."

"Don't mention voudou," Betty cried.

I knew that she was recalling her captivity. She had cried out at night, and even during the day there were times when her face was twisted by some memory.

"Tell us," I urged.

I had urged this before thinking it would relieve her, but she had always refused. Now to my surprise she spoke to Pol.

"To begin with I hated you for denying me that gun," she said.

"But you see I was right."

"I suppose you were, but I would not pass through those days again for life itself."

"Was it that bad?" I asked.

"I shan't ever again be afraid to die," she replied, "if it's in God's way, not the devil's."

She closed her eyes and, though the day was warm shivered. A shadow seemed to envelop her. She looked old.

"Must I see it forever?" she muttered.

"What?"

Her eyes opened so that horror might spill out of them.

"There was another captive," she whispered. "They tortured him. I was forced to watch. The fire that roasted him was slow, yet it was the only friend he had that night, because after a long time it killed him."

"Forget it," I urged.

She looked at me with pity.

210

"When he was dead they thrust his burnt flesh on me to eat."

"But they didn't scare you, Miss Betty," Abel broke in eagerly. "The heathens told me so themselves. Seemed like they were proud of you."

Betty smiled wanly.

"Despite their cunning they are easily deceived."

"Did you tell Abel about the man who was killed?" Polly asked suddenly.

"No. Why?"

"I thought maybe that was where he got the idea about the goat without horns."

"Lord, no," Abel chuckled. "Old Eve used to tell me about that. Really ate them on the islands, she said. While I was trying to think of a way to get Miss Betty free, I remembered a story about a papa who took the white goat away to purify her some more, and never came back. Most of the worshipers believed the serpent took them both, but Eve figured the papa wanted the girl himself; she was young, and tender for things besides eating."

"Why didn't you do that?" Polly asked.

"Do what?"

"Take Betty away to purify her, and never come back."

"I knew they'd catch us if somebody didn't stay, so I had to ask you to help."

"And you came," Betty said, choking. Her earlier vexation with Polly was entirely forgotten.

"It was my fault you were there," Polly began uneasily, but Betty interrupted.

"I had no claim on you, yet you and Abel risked your lives, and more, for me. I do not deserve such friends."

Polly was uncomfortable, but Abel visibly expanded under his mistress's praise. He also grew magnanimous.

"Tom helped too," he pointed out.

"Of course," Betty cried.

Polly grinned.

"He led the retreat," she said.

They all laughed at my discomfiture, and our talk turned to the future.

As we proceeded down the river we stopped frequently. We found the settlers everywhere in a state of fury. Their rage was divided about equally between Berkeley and the Indians. Their hopes were fixed on Nathaniel Bacon.

"He's already spoken for us in the Council," one small planter assured me.

"And demanded a commission to lead us against the Indians," added another.

"He has sworn to go without a commission if there are more raids," put in a third.

"We'll follow him, too," earnestly declared a big fellow who had been forced to flee his plantation. "We'll follow him into the wilderness or to Hell."

"Or Jamestown?"

"God bless Nathaniel Bacon for a hero."

"God damn William Berkeley for a coward."

"He's worse than a coward. It's his bloody avarice."

"The fur trade."

"He'd rather see us dead than forego profits."

"God damn Berkeley."

All along the river we heard such talk. The fires of revolt kindled by the red men were spreading to the white.

"They should not talk so of the Governor," Betty said uneasily.

I recalled Hickorywood. Five years' labor gone. My son alive only by the grace of God and the wits of two brave women. Where had Berkeley been when my wife lay helpless? Or when my house burned? I heard Abel's chant, and saw Polly writhing half-naked in a circle of savages, Betty crouched at her feet. Where had the Governor been that night? At Green Spring, no doubt, where he and his young wife dined pleasantly and supped wine through a long evening.

"God damn William Berkeley," I said.

Betty winced, not at the profanity, to which she was all too accustomed, but at the use to which I put it.

"The Governor is the King's person in America," she protested.

"Then God damn the King," I said light-heartedly.

"No, Tom."

I was surprised at her vehemence and told her so. She was Puritan, not a high church loyalist who lived on favors from the King or his Governor. She admitted that much freely but insisted that men could be bad, yet that which they represented noble.

"You sound like a Jesuit," I jeered.

"Then my father's one."

"Your father!"

"Ask him."

Polly and I exchanged a fleeting glance. Wherever we stopped we had inquired in vain after James Lester.

"Do you think he will be at Sidney?" I asked.

"I must believe it, until I know."

"It's no use," Polly said gently. "He's dead."

"If he is, though my obedience is still due the official, then I say with you, God damn William Berkeley."

As Betty spoke it, it was not an oath, but a prayer; and I did not envy the Governor his ease at Green Spring.

Lester was not at Sidney nor had anyone there had word of him. I went to Jamestown where I talked to men who had fled the upper reaches of the river. They had much to say but no word of James Lester. Heavy-hearted, for he had been good to me, I returned to Sidney.

"The damned gentry orphaned you as surely as they did me," I told my wife angrily. "Edward Cousin murdered my father, William Berkeley killed yours, though neither had the courage to do the deed himself."

Then, with Betty's and Pol's consent, I made a mound next to the grave of Elizabeth Lester. Abel and I planted myrtle on it, as he had asked, but in one respect I violated the dead man's wishes. At the foot of his grave I planted a pumpkin vine.

"Grow for him," I begged as I pressed the earth around it.

We stood for a moment by the grave that held no body, but which yet held as much of James Lester as the earth can ever hold of any man—that is, his memory. Betty wept softly. Pol was dry-eyed but grave—we all knew that he was dead.

213

"Sidney is yours now," Betty said to Pol when we were back in the house. "We are here on your sufferance."

"I couldn't do without you," Pol replied.

"Not now, perhaps. But when the troubles are past we shall return to Hickorywood."

"And leave me alone?"

"Rich widows, especially if they are young and pretty, are not long alone."

Pol laughed.

"I shan't hurry and I doubt if you can go back to Hickorywood soon, so let's not think of the future."

But I could not help thinking of it. I did not want to return to a Hickorywood where there would be no Polly Bragg, and even less did I want Pol to wed again.

When I told her this she sighed.

"Will you stay here as my overseer," she asked, "or must I return to Hickorywood as a servant?"

As the days passed we settled down at Sidney. Like all the rest of Virginia we were waiting to see what the Governor would do, but meantime we worked. The plantation had suffered during its master's absence. We set about putting things to right, and soon without conscious intention we fell back into the familiar pattern wrought at Hickorywood. Betty took charge of the house, Abel and I worked outside, as did Pol, despite Betty's protest that it did not become Sidney's mistress to labor as a field hand.

"I played at being mistress of a manor once before. It is dull business," Pol said.

Only two things disturbed our newly established routine. Virginia's troubled political pot finally boiled over, and Henry Gibson laid siege to Pol's heart.

Tired of waiting for the Governor's consent to fight, Nathaniel Bacon declared that he would defy the old man and march against the savages without a commission. He called upon all men of courage to gather at Jordan's Point on the south side of the James.

I did not heed the call.

"Someone must stay at home and watch Berkeley," I told Joseph

214

Trigg, who was on his way to Jordan's Point. "He is more ruth-less than the savages."

Trigg was satisfied with this excuse, as were Betty and Polly, but in my heart I knew that it represented only half my reluctance to leave Sidney. The truth was that during those days I thought more of Henry Gibson than of Governor Berkeley.

Henry Gibson was a newcomer from England who less than a year before had taken possession of North Bend, a plantation a few miles below Sidney. He had called on James Lester and his bride while the former was still alive. He told them that he was lonely, living as he did with only servants for company.

He was barely a man, and a spoiled, immature one at that. He reminded me of the young gallants who had come to Denham. The same oaths, the same empty chatter about horses, women and liquor. Even the same wigs. In short, he represented that which I had hated in England and which I held responsible for the pres-ent troubles in Virginia. My dislike of him was intensified by his obvious devotion to Pol and her placid acceptance of it. I protested against this latter.

"Only a lad's passion," Pol said.

"But he will ask you to marry him."

"He has already. I refused him."

"Then why in God's name do you still encourage him?"

"He amuses me."

"Are you sure that's all?"

She looked at me from under arched eyebrows.

"Thus far he has not been as demanding a suitor as you, though he did have marriage to offer," she said.

"Forgive me. And don't marry him," I begged.

Pol laughed a little sadly.

"Love is a gale, Tom. Not the hot breath of a playful puppy."

I was reassured, but I liked Henry Gibson no better than be-fore. Nor did he like me. So we bickered and jabbed at one an-other, but until late spring we avoided actual blows.

Meantime the political crisis heightened.

When Berkeley learned of Bacon's meeting at Jordan's Point he called for volunteers to aid him in putting down the rebellion, as

215

he termed it. About three hundred men answered the summons. They were the rich men of Virginia, owners of large plantations and many blacks; men of such great wealth that they were exempt from taxes and acquired new land without paying for it. They lived at a safe distance from the Indian raids. These men were indignant that mere farmers should have the impudence to defend their homes from the savages without Sir William Berkeley's approval. They seized sword, fusil and carbine and hastened to assist their patron.

William Berkeley was not a coward. In a cause near to his heart, such as hatred or the protection of privilege, he could act with decision and courage. He himself led his cohort of gentlemen to Jordan's Point. They arrived too late. Bacon had already gone. The Governor was in a fury. However, for the time being he could do nothing more effective than hasten to Bacon's plantation, Curles Neck, in order to gain what satisfaction he could from terrorizing Bacon's wife. After assuring the poor woman that her husband would be hanged he returned to Jordan's Point. There, with his gentlemen about him, he settled down to await Bacon's return, resolved to claim for the gibbet all who might escape death in the forest.

While he waited ominous rumors assaulted his aristocratic ears. It appeared that all the rogues had not accompanied Bacon. Small planters all over Virginia were caressing their carbines, grinding their hunting knives. They swore they would not permit Nathaniel Bacon to hang for the crime of shielding them from the red horror.

"May heaven blast them," the old man was reported to have roared. "This is what comes when the rabble are permitted to own their own land."

Presumably he stopped there and did not call God to account for having so mismanaged creation that a crude fellow of common blood is the equal of a man of birth if both are behind a gun.

But Berkeley did more than swear. He swallowed a portion of his pride and all but the choicest morsels of his vengeance, and proclaimed that, save for Bacon himself and a few of his leaders, all who had marched against the Indians were pardoned, provided of course that they return peaceably to their homes, and in the future render humble obedience to their gracious Lord Governor.

Strangely such magnanimity did not satisfy the commoners. Complaints that for years had been whispered were now shouted. Taxes, privileges, trade acts, corruption, all must be remedied. And they must have a leader who would protect the frontier. If William Berkeley refused to be such a leader, Nathaniel Bacon was at hand.

Perhaps Sir William remembered the King who more than thirty years before had sent him to Virginia: unfortunate Charles who had been forced to bend his royal neck to the executioner's ax because he had been too stubborn to bend it to the storms that blew from his subjects' will. Perhaps, because he was old and consumed with malice, he was already dead, except for hate, and gladly sacrificed his principles that he might be more certain to hang Bacon. Whatever the reason, he surrendered to the popular demands. He dismissed the Burgesses, who were his creatures, and called for a new election. He even made preparations to march against the Indians, though it is true that his choice of an enemy was the Pamunkey, who, except for a few renegades, were friendly, rather than the warlike Susquehannock who were still in force on the upper reaches of the river.

These Pamunkey had tried to avoid trouble by fleeing into the swamps. Berkeley ordered them back to their reservations. Their Queen refused to obey and the Governor prepared to use force, but at the last minute changed his mind. There was still unrest among the small planters. The levies might be needed to kill them. So the Indians were spared, and Berkeley resumed his vigil for Bacon until he was obliged to hasten to Jamestown in order to be sure that the new Burgesses, who were assembling, knew their duty and the limits to their authority.

Only a few days after the Governor left Jordan's Point, Bacon and the remnant of his army stumbled out of the wilderness. They were exhausted, half starved, and reduced in numbers. But they were victorious. Although the task was not completed the first step toward making the frontier safe had been taken. The savages had received a lesson that they would not soon forget. Those who at the risk of their lives had administered that lesson had a right to expect the gratitude of all Virginia. Instead they found their leader and any who might follow him branded a traitor. At least so the Governor said. But the people of Henrico County did not agree with Berkeley. They had elected Bacon as their representative in the House of Burgesses. So the issue was squarely drawn. Berkeley, though he knew Bacon had returned, waited in Jamestown. Bacon went to Curles Neck to rest. What would happen next? All Virginia waited with bated breath. The more anxious men grew, the shorter were their tempers. This was as true at Sidney as elsewhere.

I had been active in demanding reform. Gibson was one of the Governor's lackeys.

"There's not a fashionable wig in your General's whole damned army," he sneered one day.

"Wigs," I scoffed. "Some of the poor devils even lack scalps. But the Governor and his poltroons are still immaculate—and safe."

"Damn my liver, you're insolent," he shrieked, and slapped me smartly on the cheek.

I was dumbfounded. The whole affair was ludicrous, taken straight out of a book on conduct proper to a gentleman. Nevertheless it pleased me. Pol might yet change her mind and marry Gibson for no better reason than that he was handsome and underfoot. It would be as well to kill him. I had no doubt that I could. At Hickorywood Betty, Polly and I had spent hours shooting with old dueling pistols given me by Lester. As a result I was not only a dead shot but could load and fire very rapidly. I had also practiced some with sword and dagger, and though far from expert in this form of fighting I felt I could overmatch Gibson. As these thoughts flashed through my mind he was speaking.

"I shall be honored to give you satisfaction," he said pompously, "my second will—"

At this point Betty and Pol decided the nonsense had gone far enough. Betty begged me to remember that Gibson was only an unlicked cub, too young to be held responsible for his antics.

"He is not too young to come courting," I grumbled.

218

Polly flushed.

"Hold your tongue, Tom," she cried angrily.

She then devoted herself to Gibson. Before she was done I pitied him. He apologized to me and to the company and retired disconsolate and angry.

"You settled that," Betty declared admiringly after Gibson was gone, "but I am afraid you have lost a suitor."

"I doubt it. He will sulk a few days and return to me."

"Was it so that he could return that you prevented my fighting him?" I asked, still disgruntled at the lost opportunity.

"Perhaps—and the fact that he is Lady Berkeley's cousin and the Governor's ward. You might find killing Henry Gibson dangerous sport."

"The closer he is to Berkeley the better the sport," I retorted. "But why hasn't someone told me how important the young cock is?"

"Because you growl like a mad dog when anyone so much as mentions Henry," Pol replied.

The matter rested there for a few days, until, as Polly had predicted, Gibson returned. It was chiefly his heart that drew him to us, but he also had news for me.

"Your Nathaniel Bacon has proved himself a coward and a scoundrel," he declared triumphantly, and launched into his tale.

Bacon had at last come to Jamestown. Rejecting the offers of his army and the citizens of Henrico County to guard him, he had gone down the river with only a few companions. As they approached the capital they were greeted with cannon shots. They turned the sloop and fled up the river, but coming under the guns of an English ship were forced to surrender. As Bacon was carried back to Jamestown, a prisoner of the Governor, he could have expected no mercy. Yet, although his companions were put in irons to await trial, he himself, after a testy admonition to conduct himself as a gentleman hereafter, was paroled. A few days later the reason for this leniency became apparent. In return for a signed statement promising to abandon his efforts to aid the common men of Virginia, Bacon was forgiven. He was even restored to his place on the Council.

At first glance such conduct on the Governor's part seems to give the lie to the charges that he was harsh, but actually he had acted with his customary cunning. Nathaniel Bacon hanged would be a martyr. All Virginia might rise to avenge him. Nathaniel Bacon alive, seeming to bask in the Governor's favor, was a stench. It would be long before poor men would trust another popular leader.

So on the whole it seemed the troubles had not ended badly for Sir William. Privilege was once more firmly entrenched, the Indians had been taught a lesson without spending public money which could be put to better use by the Governor and his circle, and his enemy was under his thumb. True, there were the promises of reform that had been made when things looked so black, and the new Burgesses to be dealt with; but promises can be starved to death and men bribed or intimidated. At least this was Henry Gibson's view. He had recently been to Green Spring.

When Gibson had finished his tale I declared that I would go to Jamestown the next morning to learn the truth. The flickering hope that he had lied merely to plague me was extinguished by Gibson's prompt rejoinder that he had business at Green Spring and would ride to town with me.

I did not want his company, but his offer, coming as it did, could not be rejected. We started the next morning shortly after daybreak.

# XI

## I.

An old world clothes a man in false garb. Habits of thought, long since outworn, render him a dignity he does not possess or burden him with a contempt he does not merit. A new world strips him bare. In England Henry Gibson might have passed for a young blade whose wealth and position atoned for his bad manners; in America he was visible and naked, a bag of ill-smelling wind. By the time we reached Jamestown I disliked him even more heartily than before.

We covered mile after mile of clean woods and fields, and not one of them but was fouled by his passing. He regaled me with the gossip of his world. This lady had the pox, which was uncommon amusing, that one a new lover; a dashing gentleman had received a doublet straight from London, which he had traded to his neighbor for a comely and long-coveted negur wench. This last Henry considered bad taste.

"Though damn my eyes if I won't have one some day, just for the experience," he concluded judiciously.

"Part of a gentleman's training," I murmured.

Such sympathy encouraged him.

"Damn my teeth, yes. Matter of fact, there is one at Green Spring I already have an eye on."

"Is that your business today?"

Our little disagreement over politics was forgotten. We were two men of the world, gentlemen who understood one another. He gave me a sportive leer; his wink was lewd.

"I fancy I'll let that fruit ripen for a little. She's young yet. Besides, just now I've got something better there."

"A lady?"

He dismissed ladies with a sniff.

"Ladies will do when a man marries, but I don't care for them in sport. Too demanding, too languid. Love's an animal's game, so give me a good animal. The one I speak of is a wench in my cousin's service. Was a lady of sorts once, I'm told; her father owned property at least, but now she dances the tune I whistle, and that's a merry one, I can tell you."

He sniggered self-consciously.

The servant was the only one of his boasted conquests in which I believed. She would, I thought, mark the uttermost limits of his capacity. Only a stripling with little or no experience, or an old man groveling at youth's careless feet, would be as fatuous as he was before Polly. The girl at Green Spring was the only woman he had possessed, as Polly was the first lady to whom he had raised his eyes. Of course he thought her a lady. She was the mistress of Sidney.

I decided to amuse myself and at the same time make still more pricking the already thorny course of love. What would this arrogant youngster say if he discovered that his adored Mistress Lester was but recently my bound wench? I spoke to him in mock confidence.

"I would advise you to hide your dallying from Polly. She mightn't understand."

"Naturally," he agreed tolerantly, "you ain't fashionable at Sidney. After we are wed she will learn to know polite society and view such things in their proper light."

Words like these, hollow as they were, had sinew enough to stagger me. I controlled myself with difficulty.

"So you hope to marry her," I said casually.

He was so surprised, and where Polly was concerned so blind, that for a second he forgot his worldliness.

"Why, yes. If she will have me," he said.

I laughed indulgently. He recovered his pose and continued in his usual vein.

"Why, damn my soul, she's got a fine figure and owns Sidney. What more can a man want in a wife?"

"Nothing," I hastened to assure him. "I was just a little surprised to hear that you would marry her."

He was growing uneasy.

"Have you any objection?" he asked stiffly.

"By no means. On the contrary, I am pleased at her good fortune. She is a good girl."

"What in devil's name are you driving at?"

"Nothing, nothing at all. I am only surprised, as I've already said. It gives a man a turn to see a wench like Pol rise so sudden. First James Lester, now you."

"I don't like your talk," he growled.

"What's wrong with it?"

"You aren't respectful toward Mistress Lester."

"Respectful toward Pol?" I laughed again. "She's a worthy creature, and as you say, well shaped. You should see her in the tobacco field, by the way, when the sweat's molded her dress against her body. But respectful is a word that is hard for me to associate with Pol. Why, most of the time I still think of her as my bound wench."

"Bound wench!" he gasped.

"Yes. Don't say you didn't know."

"Damn and blast my soul if I did. Why didn't you tell me? Or why didn't she, the artful slut?" He swung around in his saddle until he faced me. "Your servant, was she? And what else?"

"You said a mile back that we weren't fashionable," I reminded him. He was not listening.

"I begged her the honor to be my wife," he broke out angrily. "Damn my liver, I got on my knees and pleaded with the trollop. Father's some gentleman's gardener, I suppose. Or worse."

"She's a bastard, I understand."

He spluttered furiously, damning himself from head to foot. I was pleased with my work. I knew that Pol could bring him to his knees again, puling whatever sentiment she required, but while out of her presence he would hate her. Pol, of course, might be angry, but she would forgive me. Her servitude was no secret. Neither she nor Lester had tried to conceal it.

The rest of the way to Jamestown Gibson sulked. He was still so angry when we arrived that he forgot his sole purpose in riding with me had been to gloat at my discomfiture upon proof of Bacon's treason. He bade me a surly farewell and rode off. As he disappeared I thought that his creature at Green Spring would endure that day whatever his vindictive spirit could devise. She would serve him as the waxen image of Polly Bragg. I sighed for the poor girl and almost repented my jest.

I rode down the Old Great Road into Back Street. Jamestown was quiet. There was none of the excitement that had prevailed when the "riffraff" had poured into town to beg to be allowed to fight the Indians. A stout middle-aged couple walked at the side of the road. I judged them to be a small farmer and his wife. Two gentlemen on horseback clattered by, splattering the pedestrians with mud and abuse. The farmer hunched his shoulders and trudged on. There could be no doubt of it. Good government had returned to Virginia.

I passed the State House. Inside the Burgesses might be assembled. At Varina Nathaniel Bacon had been chosen one of them. I remembered the scene—the excitement, the hopes, the prayers. A new day had seemed to be dawning. But now Bacon was not with the Burgesses. He sat at the council table with the Governor.

Beyond the State House was the church, beyond the church the main village. Here a number of houses served as taverns. I spent the day going from one to the other of these, drinking more than was my custom, listening to men talk. Gibson's account of Bacon's submission was true. He had omitted only one detail. The men who had been put in irons were later freed. However, the credit for their pardon did not belong to Bacon. The Governor had freed them at the request of a member of the Council.

Late in the afternoon I ran across Joseph Trigg. I insisted that we go to an ordinary. There over rum and water he delivered his views. He was saturnine as ever. Bacon's men were rightly served, he thought, for trusting a man of good birth. The more Trigg drank the bitterer he grew.

"I'll turn pirate," he said morosely. "The seas are yet free."

"Will you leave your wife and daughter?" I asked.

"My wife died while I was in the forest. My daughter is contented."

"Contented?"

"Strange to us who gave so much to be free of service, isn't it? But she is not to blame. Like you, Mary is still young enough to hope; and I will say for Lady Berkeley she's kind to her servants." His face clouded. "There's something else, too."

It was painful to listen.

"How are you going to join the pirates?" I asked hastily.

"There is a fellow here looking for a crew. I was at sea once. He promised to take me. You want to join us?"

"No."

"You might change your mind."

"If I do I'll look for you."

The talk shifted to less personal matters, where it drifted lazily. It must have been an hour or two later when Henry Gibson entered. He was accompanied by half a dozen youngsters of his ilk, all of them the worse for drink. Unobserved, for we sat in the corner of the badly lighted room, Trigg and I watched them. Presently they fell to tormenting Gibson.

"How goes your suit at Sidney?" one asked as he winked at his companions.

"Why do you keep her hid?" another demanded.

"I'll warrant he's jealous," cried a third.

Gibson was scowling. It was evident that the day had not improved his temper.

"Surely you didn't take me seriously," he sneered.

"Curse me, if she hasn't rejected him," bawled the one who had first spoken, "and now the villain would cheat us. Don't you recall, Henry, you wagered you would have the lady safely wedded by the end of summer?"

Gibson's laugh was uncertain.

"Damn my eyes, you heard me wrong. It was bedded I said."

This sally was greeted with such uproarious delight that he grew more cheerful and evidently decided that such an opportu-

225

nity to avenge himself upon Polly for having been so brazen as to permit a gentleman to make a fool of himself over her, was not to be lost.

"Aye, it was bedded, and that reminds me, bullies, it's time to settle the score, though damn my teeth if I am not half ashamed to accept a reward for such rare diversion."

He sniggered so fulsomely that even I who knew he was lying could almost taste of Polly's flesh. But he was too coarse to recognize the value of restraint. He elaborated each detail. He piled grossness upon indecency. To make real his vision of paradise he stripped Pol bare of every virtue, and in doing so exposed the obscenity of his own mind. For doubtless he had experienced in his fancy every act he now described. I could fairly see him tossing on his bed, his lips wet, his slack mouth drooling, as he conjured up the delights that Polly denied him. Now with an audience before which to parade his lickerish fancies, he grew drunk from his own lust. I have no doubt that before he had finished, he half believed that he was speaking the truth.

As I listened I did not at first feel any impulse to rush to the defense of Pol's good name. I was no gentleman, and the females in my life had been mere women, some good, some bad, but their virtue had never been matters of public concern. Moreover, if the blackening of Pol's reputation would prevent men from courting her I was willing that she should be fairly washed in scandal. Had I not, myself, told Lester that she came out of a brothel? So I listened and even derived a faint satisfaction that Pol was being served a dish of her own cooking. She should not have encouraged the young scoundrel.

But as the filth became more nauseous, rage dispelled my complacency. It was my Pol that this coxcomb was claiming as his own. Men would cast sly glances at her and fancy that they saw Henry Gibson in her arms. Gossip spreads quickly. In a few days the whole countryside would know that Mistress Lester had found solace for her husband's death. Suitors might be less anxious to marry her after hearing of Gibson's success, but there would be no lack of them to call upon her. The thought was intolerable.

I joined the circle around Gibson. They were so engrossed that no one heeded me until he himself, pausing to observe if his efforts were being properly received, saw me. He got unsteadily to his feet. Rising to meet him, I did not waste words but smashed with all my strength at his scurrilous mouth. He whimpered as he fell. His friends looked at me dully.

"Why the devil did you do that?" one finally stammered.

"I disliked his conversation," I replied, and returned to my seat.

"That wasn't a gentlemanly blow," chuckled Trigg. "You should have slapped him smartly with the open palm."

"The devil with my open palm," I growled before I grasped his meaning. The possibility had not occurred to me. I told Trigg so.

"Might be a good idea to consider it now," he said dryly.

Gibson was struggling to his feet. His mouth, still bleeding, hung open. Two teeth were gone. He reached for a glass of brandy.

"Damn my teeth," he muttered.

His companions tittered. This was too much for his vanity.

"Where is the damned bully," he bawled.

Someone pointed toward our corner. He lurched toward us.

"Doubtless you will give me satisfaction."

My anger had cooled. I remembered that both Pol and Betty had objected to my killing this young fool. I also remembered that he was the Governor's kinsman, and that I was a man who had applauded Nathaniel Bacon. I did not know what to say, so I said nothing. He translated my silence into fear, which it was, though not of him. He lifted his hand; I observed that the fist was properly unclenched.

"If you strike me I'll knock the rest of your teeth out," I warned.

"I would be happy to be spared the need if you will only set a time," he retorted smoothly.

"I won't fight you."

The book had not taught him how to deal with such an uncouth ruffian.

"Will nothing make you fight?" He was near to pleading.

"No."

The matter might have ended there, though probably I would

have had to swallow an insult or two, had Trigg not intervened.

"You had the way a few minutes ago," he suggested to Gibson.

"Keep out of this," I cautioned, but it was too late. Gibson's brain, addled by the drink and the blow I had given him, was thrown back into focus by the suggestion. He twisted his swollen lips into a sneer. He turned and faced the room.

"Damn my eyes," he cried. "It seems I have a rival at Sidney whose mistress appears to have been over-generous with her charms. This gentleman, too—"

"That's enough," I snapped. "I'll fight you."

His lies were bad enough; to have him stumble upon the truth was unbearable. Besides he was so damned persistent about being killed.

"Tomorrow?" he asked.

"I am a dead shot," I assured myself. "I am in no danger." But tomorrow was very close. I wanted to see Polly first.

"The day after," I said.

"Pistols at twenty paces."

"Forty."

"That is a long shot."

"It's still too close."

He called God to witness that he was doing his best to conduct matters in a seemly fashion. For the second time Trigg took a hand.

"I'm Mr. Bone's second," he announced. "Name one of your friends yonder and we can arrange the details."

Within a quarter of an hour Trigg and I were riding down Back Street. Much against his will I had insisted upon returning to Sidney, late though it was.

"I'll never get to sleep," he complained, dismal as Pitch and Tar Swamp which lay just beyond the road.

"Never mind that. What arrangements did you make?"

"Dawn, in a meadow on his place, five miles below Sidney."

"The devil! We get up before sunrise and go five miles to reach him. He will be fresh, with an extra hour's sleep."

"I know. I was overreached there. But I had to make concessions in order to name the distance."

"Forty paces?" I asked, feeling more cheerful.

"Fifteen."

"What?"

He said it again. "Fifteen."

"But a man can't miss at fifteen paces."

"Oh, I reckon he could if he was scared enough, but it's not likely, so you better shoot careful and first," he said soothingly. But I was not so easily reassured.

"Do you want me killed?" I complained.

"I want Henry Gibson killed."

The words were so charged with venom that I forgot my own troubles for a moment while I puzzled over Joseph Trigg. Why had he interfered when I tried to avoid the duel? Why had he forced himself on me as a second? Since I was to do the fighting I had a right to know.

"Why do you want Gibson killed?"

"He's the one who got my land."

"North Bend?"

"Yes. The Governor's wife wanted a plantation for her cousin. I was behind in my taxes so they took North Bend."

"He isn't to blame for that."

"Maybe not, but he took my daughter, too."

I remembered the girl at Green Spring that was to serve Gibson's purposes until the Negress was a little riper. I recalled his boast that she had once been a lady of a sort.

"The servant at Green Spring," I said involuntarily.

"So you knew."

"Not that she was your daughter."

"Well, you would have known that, too, had you gone to town oftener. He boasts of it in every ordinary in Jamestown. Talks of her as he talked of Mistress Lester."

"Why haven't you killed him yourself?"

"I started to when I first heard, but before I could find him Mary caught up with me. She made me promise not to do it."

"Such promises don't have to be kept."

"I've always spoiled her," he said inconsequently, and to my surprise added, "I'm a little afraid of Mary."

229

"So I must do your killing for you?"

"Looks like it." His voice was laden with so much regret that I laughed.

"All right, you old scoundrel. I'll do it."

## 2.

"So you've turned gentleman," commented Pol next day when I told her what had occurred. "Will you wear your hair in curls to your shoulders, or buy a wig?"

"But I couldn't let him bawl out to the world that you are my mistress."

"I suppose that by shooting him, or getting shot, you will convince the world that I am not?"

I withdrew to new positions.

"There is Trigg's daughter, too," I pointed out; but my strategic retreat was not a success.

"Heavens," Pol cried in disgust. "Are you going about the world killing every man who seduces a maid? Besides, if you told me the truth, she wasn't mentioned in the tavern, nor did you know that she was Trigg's daughter until after the quarrel."

"Anyhow, I promised Trigg I'd kill Henry Gibson."

"It's wicked folly, Tom."

I knew Pol was right. I had known it the night before as I rode home through the darkness; I had known it when I awakened that morning. But I had resolutely refused to acknowledge it, even to myself. Now Pol told me in hard clear words what I had been too cowardly to tell myself.

"There's death in it one way and ruin another," she said simply.

"What can I do?"

"What can you do with him fifteen paces away, a gun in his hand? Kill him and hasten back to us. God knows what after that."

I tried to comfort her but she shoved me away.

"Tell Betty," she said wearily. "Maybe she can make you see reason."

But Betty approved.

"Of course you could not permit him to say that you are Pol's lover," she cried indignantly. But she was less sympathetic regarding Trigg's daughter. "It seems to me Joseph Trigg could defend Mary's reputation himself," she said, and added coldly, "If it is worthy a defense."

"You talk as though you knew them," I cried in surprise.

"All my life."

"Tell me."

Somewhat reluctantly she complied.

"When my father came to Sidney he and Joseph Trigg were friends," she explained, "and when we were little, Mary and I played together. But my mother considered Trigg and his wife beneath her and wished to have nothing to do with them. In the end, as usual, she had her way. We ceased to see the Triggs and seldom mentioned them. I suppose that is why you never heard of them while you were at Sidney."

"But why didn't you resume your friendship after your mother's death?" I asked.

"By that time there were stories about Mary."

"What kind of stories?"

"Men. Of course, they may not have been true."

I should have abandoned Mary Trigg then and there, but despite her attempt to be just there was such disapproval in Betty's voice that it aroused in me a spirit of perversity.

"You don't disapprove of Pol for the men she's admitted having," I pointed out. "I think you should be equally kind to Trigg's poor daughter."

Betty's voice was cold as virtue.

"Pol was the victim of circumstance; Mary Trigg, if half what is said be true, flings herself at men. The cases are quite different."

I had learned long ago that when Betty said a thing was different it was useless to argue. It meant that she had reached certain conclusions through reasoning far too subtle for me to comprehend. Besides, in this case she was right. It was different. Polly's fancied sins were far away in time and place, Mary Trigg's only a few miles down the river. Pol's shame was softened by the glamour of a well-fabricated romance, Mary's stood ugly in the light of truth. I abandoned the Triggs and explained that when the fight was over I would be obliged to flee from Virginia.

"Nonsense," said Betty.

She knew about these affairs. She had learned as a child in the days when she visited her mother's kinsmen. Gentlemen seldom killed one another. That would make defending their precious honor too perilous. A flesh wound, or even a futile shot, was sufficient to right the worst wrongs. All that was necessary was that I refrain from exceeding these limits. I recalled the fifteen paces.

"What if Gibson doesn't play by your rules?" I asked doubtfully.

Betty echoed Trigg.

"Aim carefully and shoot first. Hit him in the arm."

"What if I miss?"

"Think of Jimmy and me and you won't miss."

She spoke so earnestly that I promised to follow her advice. When I told Pol she approved. I did not confide my change of plans to Joseph Trigg.

Trigg and I were silent next morning as we rode through the woods. I was preoccupied with my own thoughts. These were not cheerful. Betty's strategy, which had appeared sound enough in the snug security of Sidney, was less plausible when viewed in the gray half-light that precedes dawn. Perhaps I would be wiser to keep my word to Trigg. But that meant fleeing from Virginia. I could hear Polly's voice—"Must you always be running away?"

Henry Gibson, with a second and a surgeon, was already at the meeting place. This proved to be an abandoned tobacco field, clear of trees and therefore without shadows. At one end was an old tool shed, half in ruins and weathered until it was the color of the dull morning sky. Not far distant was a freshly scored target. It was evident that my opponent had not wasted the preceding day.

We met near the shed. The seconds conferred over the final details. I looked at Gibson. He was pallid. It came to me that despite his tavern truculence this was his first duel and that he was frightened. His first words confirmed it.

"D'you know that your damned second insisted on but fifteen paces?" he asked tersely.

Gibson's fright restored my confidence. My thoughts suddenly broke free from the weary circle that they had been traveling for the past twenty-four hours. I had an inspiration worthy of some of Pol's own, only mine was more sensible. Trigg had suggested that a nervous man might miss at fifteen paces, a badly frightened one almost certainly would. I replied sternly to Gibson's question.

"Do you know my second is the father of Mary Trigg at Green Spring?"

His mouth worked convulsively. He glanced nervously toward Trigg.

"What has that to do with us?" he muttered.

"It's why we are to fire from fifteen paces. He wants you dead."

"Dead—dead—but that's monstrous. Gentlemen, that is—a shot or two—for honor, you know—not kill—"

I was delighted at the success of my strategy. He was literally babbling at the first smell of death.

"Mistress Lester's honor," I reminded him gravely, "is surely more precious than a man's life."

As I mouthed this solemn nonsense the last vestige of the weight that had borne so heavily upon me lifted. I was light-hearted again and, in my new exuberance of spirit, light-headed. I grew so intoxicated with the comedy I played that I forgot death was the almost certain penalty if I had miscalculated in placing Henry Gibson in the rôle of buffoon. My only regret was that I lacked a proper audience. If only Polly could see and hear me strutting through my rôle. I recalled the mockery in her voice when she had accused me of turning gentleman. "Gentleman indeed," I told myself gleefully, "why, odd's fish, I'll yet wear my hair to my shoulders, monstrously curled." Meantime Gibson stared at me aghast; his mouth trembled like that of a child on the verge of tears. I fixed him with what I hoped was a ferocious glare.

"Damn my liver," I roared. "Up the river I killed two men for merely whispering that they had glimpsed her ankle."

It was absurd, but it was such stuff as filled his own head, and besides, he was too terror-stricken to reason. I know not to what

233

heights my fancy might have carried me had the seconds not called us.

The weapons were offered for our inspection. It had been agreed that we should each use his own, or, if either wished, one of his opponent's. Gibson's pair were beautiful, the latest product of the gunsmith's art. The sight of them steadied him.

"Interesting antiquities," he noted sarcastically, nodding toward mine.

"They shoot," I said, and picked one up. As I had done so often when matching skill with Bet and Pol at Hickorywood, I primed the pan, brought the cock up and back and fired. The target was a full forty paces distant. My bullet lodged just off center.

"This one shoots truer," I said carelessly as I picked up the second gun.

Even Trigg was impressed.

"And I insisted on fifteen paces," he said weakly.

We took up our positions, Gibson with his back to the weathered shed, I silhouetted more clearly against the sky. I recognized this paltry bit of strategy but did not think it of sufficient consequence to protest. Our arms were at our sides; the pistols were pointed harmlessly toward the earth. The signal was given. I loaded rapidly. When Gibson raised his eyes from the gun over which he had been fumbling he found himself staring at death just fifteen paces distant. His trigger finger tightened convulsively. He had not even aimed at me; the shot was wild. Now it was my turn. I lowered my gun, examined it carefully, raised it again. I pointed it at Gibson's head, his breast. He was trembling so violently that I doubted if he could stand much longer.

"Shoot," he screamed suddenly, and began to twist his head.

Instead I lowered the pistol.

"To give you time to pray before you die," I told him; then for the last time raised the weapon. Inch by inch it came up, past his feet, to his waist, to his belly, straight at his heart. His last scant remnant of courage fell away. With an agonized wail he started to run. But his miserable legs would not carry him. Before he had gone six feet he tottered and fell. He buried his face in

234

the ground, his hands clutched convulsively, his body racked by sobs.

His second started toward him.

"Wait," I called.

He stopped.

For five minutes or more we stood there, no one moving. Gibson grew quieter. Finally he lifted his head. His face was dirty and tear-stained. He was whimpering softly. I have never seen such a picture of cowardice. But that is not strange, for I have never known a poltroon to equal Henry Gibson.

"Admit that you lied in the tavern," I commanded.

He complied fulsomely, confessing that he had traduced Pol from sheer spite because she had rejected him. He admitted himself a liar, a vain braggart mean enough to ruin a woman's name for sport. He swore it all upon the salvation of his soul. When he had finished I asked the witnesses if they were satisfied as to Pol's virtue. They were. I gathered they were less content over their late principal. They were looking at him as if they saw him for the first time. But they could settle their scores later. I was not yet through with him.

"Mary Trigg," I said.

Without waiting for prompting he renewed his protestations. The tale was the same, only the heroine had changed. This did not suit me at all, nor, I believed, would it help Mary or satisfy Trigg. Marriage was required, that very day. Gibson balked. To my surprise, however, his friends sided with me. The surgeon was a kindly man who had known Trigg and his family in their better days. The other, a youngster not yet twenty, seemed to think it an excellent joke that Gibson, who had apparently made overmuch of his relationship to Berkeley, should take a servant for his wife. After considerable argument, capped by my threat to claim my unexpended shot, Gibson surrendered. He made one condition. All present must swear not to reveal what a craven he had proved himself on the field of honor.

"But what of Mistress Lester?" the surgeon protested. "If we remain silent, her name will not be cleared."

The door of the shed opened. Polly stepped out. Across her

arm rested a carbine. Her eyes sparkled with mischief; she was grinning broadly.

"My reputation is safe in such a champion," she said solemnly, and as she went on she even fetched a sigh. "Indeed, I am happy that this has not ended fatally as with those two poor creatures up the river, who only jested a little about my ankle. So by your leave we shall accept Henry's proposal to trade silence for Mistress Trigg's happiness, and, as the only woman present, I shall take charge of the wedding arrangements."

Of us all, only Joseph Trigg accepted Pol's sudden appearance calmly.

"You are a good woman, Mistress Lester," he said sincerely, "but your generosity is as vain as Tom's good intentions." He turned to me. "You should have killed him, lad, like I planned. He's yet too young to wed, and I leave you to judge if William Berkeley is likely to give his consent."

Once more Pol saved the day.

"Was too young, Joseph," she cried gaily. "He came of age five days ago." She looked down demurely. "He was kind enough to repeat his offer of marriage. I felt a poor fatherless thing like me would not so presume; but now he will have a woman worthy of him. Go to Green Spring immediately, Henry, to fetch your bride. And be sure to return, or I myself will see to publishing this morning's affair."

"And I'll kill you, promise or no promise," added Joseph Trigg.

"I'll get the rector," offered the surgeon. "He's a neighbor of mine."

The wedding was to take place at Sidney. Pol and I rode back to tell Betty and help prepare for the company.

"How the devil did you get in that shed?" I asked.

"I made Trigg tell me where the meeting was to take place and started an hour before you."

"Why?"

She rubbed the carbine.

"I always could shoot better than you."

That was boasting. I outshot her four times out of five, but I let it pass.

"You would have killed him?"

"Just in case of accident," she said lightly.

"Much good that would have done me," I grumbled, "the accident being my death."

But Pol's spirits were too high to be quenched by unpleasant possibilities of the past. She was fairly gurgling over my swaggering, bloodless victory. With a deft jerk of the reins she brought her horse close to mine, and leaned precariously over to brush my cheek with her lips.

"I love him," she warbled lightly to the woods. "I love him; and he is a fool I love."

I was feeling the effects of the morning's work. I remembered that Gibson's quaking hand might have accidentally leveled the pistol at me. I was afraid of what might have been and repentant of my own folly.

"You like me to be a fool," I complained, "and yet it's you who always pretend that I should be sensible."

"You should," she retorted promptly, "for you are a poor fisherman's son who came to the New World to make a fortune and be like the gentlemen you think you despise. Until you've done it you won't be happy."

This was a new Polly.

"And what about you, who, ever since you were a child, wanted the things that gentlemen could give you?" I asked.

She had turned serious as she spoke of me, but now she laughed again.

"Pooh! I got them, didn't I? and the gentlemen, too. At Denham—at Sidney. I know now that things you can touch only weigh you down—while it's the ones that you feel that give you wings. Besides, I don't need to long to be a lady, I already am one—half, anyway. I'm the beautiful bastard daughter of an English squire, and men shoot one another over my spotless virtue.

*"I love him, I love him,*
*And he's only a fool."*

The merrier she was the more melancholy it made me. Life lay in riding forever with this new Pol, more desirable even than the old. A mad romantic Pol—or was it a wise disillusioned Pol? I rode on, wondering and sighing. Life lay ahead, too. At Sidney.

Betty was delighted with the turn that events had taken, although she was still without enthusiasm for Mary Trigg and mildly resentful of the share Polly had played in the morning's adventure.

"You were scatterbrained, Pol," she said reprovingly. "Tom managed without you, and even if he had failed, you would not have improved matters by killing Henry. Besides, what do you think those gentlemen thought when they saw you there?"

"That I'd come to see my lover fight," responded Polly promptly, still lost in the insouciant mood of the ride home. "Does it matter?"

Betty sighed.

"You are a vexing creature. Naturally it matters if people say that my husband is your lover."

"I am scatterbrained," admitted Polly humbly. Thus she came back to reality.

The wedding was a complete success. The groom made the best of it, and the bride was radiant. She was a small creature of gold and white. Yellow hair and gold-flecked, yellow-brown eyes. Her skin was the whitest I have ever seen, and despite her service, still soft. Her nose was finely cut, her mouth small, her lips—the upper one short, which gave them the appearance of always being half open in invitation—were uncommonly red. She was perfectly proportioned from well-turned ankle to swelling bosom. As I looked at her I found it impossible to believe her the creature Betty had hinted at. I conceded a man or two might have taken advantage of her, but nothing worse.

Only when the church's insoluble magic had been woven, and I claimed my kiss, did I wonder a little. In some indescribable way the kiss was ardent. It was in no way unseemly, but it lingered on my lips like a pungent perfume that hangs too long in the air.

One morning a few weeks after the wedding Trigg brought startling news from North Bend. A messenger had just arrived

238

there summoning Gibson to Green Spring, where the Governor's supporters were gathering. For Nathaniel Bacon had slipped out of Jamestown on the pretext of visiting his sick wife, and was raising the country. The Capital was boiling with excitement. The Burgesses, torn by fear of the Governor on one hand and Bacon on the other, were in a state of panic. Berkeley himself was active. A palisade had been thrown up on the narrow neck of land that joined the town to the north bank of the river. The biggest guns the old brick fort boasted were removed and mounted to protect the new defenses. Trigg, himself, was on his way to Middle Plantation where Bacon had his headquarters. Would I join him?

Betty bitterly opposed my going.

"I like Berkeley no better than you do," she protested, "but he is the King's representative in Virginia."

"I remember when Oliver cut off the King's head," interrupted Trigg.

"And your Oliver's bones now lie in unhallowed ground and his naked skull has been exposed."

"But, Betty—" I protested.

"Remember your son," she interrupted. "If you care nothing for loyalty and right, remember your son."

She was so vehement that for the time being I surrendered, and Trigg departed alone muttering about females. All that summer while Virginia seethed with civil war I was a spectator. And I was angry with Betty, who had kept me from joining the fight against the aristocrats.

Trigg had been gone but a few hours when we had another visitor from North Bend. It was Mistress Mary Gibson. Her husband was already home, again quaking with fear, begging his recently despised wife for protection. Most of Berkeley's followers, Gibson among them, had deserted him. Sycophants and spoilsmen, they had scuttled before the harsh winds that were blowing from the frontier like birds driven before a gale. William Berkeley was no coward. Abandoned by those who had enriched themselves through his favor, he awaited his victorious enemy in lonely decency.

Such was Mary Gibson's report. She herself was going to Jamestown to greet the rebel army. She longed to see her father. Would I go with her? I said I would. I told my household that I was obliged to look after Trigg's daughter. The truth was I longed to be in at the kill.

"Remember you have promised not to join Bacon," Betty cautioned, as she kissed me good-by.

"And remember that little Mary only looks like an angel," contributed Pol.

I laughed at both of them.

We rode into Jamestown shortly before noon. Although Bacon and his men had not yet arrived, the half-built palisade across the neck was already abandoned; the guns were unmanned. As we passed the State House we could see men clustered in the windows. They were the Burgesses, awaiting the coming of Bacon in the humor of frightened apprentices who await the coming of a master whose work they have shirked. In another room, we were told, Berkeley sat with a handful of faithful councilors. Back Street itself was all but deserted. There were few pedestrians and no gentlemen on horseback to bespatter honest men with mud. Over the whole village hovered a cloud of anxious expectancy.

I took Mary to a tavern where we got such food as a flustered host could provide. He was fearful lest the town be looted. I made light of such a peril. There was nothing to loot. The State House, church, less than two score residences—that was Jamestown, capital of His Majesty's Plantation of Virginia.

"It's not much," conceded the landlord, "but all I have is here and I've heard it said that the rebels have sworn to pull down the town."

I laughed at him. While we were still talking a boy rushed in. "They're coming, Master," he cried, "I saw them at Sandy Bay."

This was our host's call to action. He ordered the windows barred and asked the guests to leave that the door might be barricaded. There would be no further hospitality until the day's events resolved themselves into some sort of pattern by which a canny man might cut his cloth.

As we walked back toward the State House I grumbled at being put out of the tavern. Mary disagreed with me. In her view our late host was quite right in preparing to defend himself against the approaching marauders.

I have always been a simpleton where a pretty face or well-made body is concerned, and Mary Trigg had both; consequently, although surprised at her vehemence, I was indulgent. She was still young, I told myself, and a fresh bride. Such a child could not be expected to understand politics. At some later date, when there was more time and her new lord's glamour had tarnished somewhat, I might instruct her. So I contented myself with reminding her that her father was one of the marauders. She pouted prettily, and explained that hard-bitten Joseph Trigg was a dear man, but foolish and easily deceived. Her absurdity made protecting her the more imperative. I drew her arm through mine and pulled her close to me.

"They shan't hurt you," I promised.

The arrival of Bacon and his men postponed further folly. Fears of pillage proved groundless. There was no looting, no disorder. No building was destroyed, or, save the fort, even occupied. The army halted on the green in front of the State House. Bacon demanded a commission as General of an army to be led against the Indians. Upon receiving this demand, Berkeley rushed to the green where he hurled into Bacon's teeth a charge of treason. The old man was brave and angry.

"Shoot me," he cried, "fore God, fair mark shoot."

Bacon was unmoved. He swore no harm would come to the Governor or any man; but he must have his commission. Sir William returned to the Council chamber still vowing he would not comply, but late in the afternoon, urged by both Council and Burgesses, he gave way. The commission was signed and sealed. Nathaniel Bacon was now lawfully General Bacon. Actually he was more than that—he was the ruler of Virginia.

We found Joseph Trigg. He had been detailed as one of a small force sent to guard the ferry, but growing weary he had left his post. For once his saturnine nature was sweetened with good will. Beyond a mild regret that Bacon had declined the Governor's invitation to shoot, he was content with the world.

"A commission is not the only thing the General came for,"

he informed us complacently. "More will follow. New men will govern, and some old ones will learn the feel of chains, if not hemp. Elections are to be free; public offices will belong to the people; taxes won't eat up a man's plantation. Best of all, the magpies that swarmed around Berkeley will have their gaudy feathers plucked, and those of us they robbed will get back our own. North Bend will soon be mine again."

Mary asked in a choked voice what was to become of Henry and herself.

"Maybe Henry can be hanged," Joseph suggested hopefully. Mary burst into tears and poor Trigg was lost. He promised that no harm should come to Henry, that he might continue to live at North Bend, where he would be called upon to do nothing more arduous than please his wife. Mary permitted herself to be comforted. She even grew magnanimous.

"Naturally, I'll be glad to see you recover North Bend," she said with a brave smile, "even if it does mean robbing poor Henry." Trigg choked on his ale. Before he had recovered, Mary hastened on. "Oh, I'm not blaming you, but you must admit that it is hard on Henry. It was not his fault that you couldn't pay your taxes."

"The vulture never kills its victims, it only picks the bones," growled Trigg.

She replied at a tangent.

"I suppose you will be going to fight the Indians."

He shrugged. "The savages haven't hurt me."

"But if Bacon restores North Bend to you, you can hardly desert him."

Trigg looked at his daughter searchingly. There were times when his fondness had difficulty reading her.

"I'm tough and I'll be back," he said at length. It was evident that his satisfaction with the world had fled.

Mary laughed indulgently.

"Of course you will, but before you go remember to get the General's promise that none of his bullies will molest Henry while you are gone."

"Hell," he snorted, "we're after men. Your husband has never been in danger, at least not since Tom here—" He stopped, confused. We had agreed not to tell Mary of the events which had led to her marriage, and we were sure that for reasons of his own Gibson had been equally discreet.

"Since Tom did what?" Mary asked.

"It was nothing," I assured her. "Your husband and I had a slight disagreement. It was settled satisfactorily."

"So that is why he won't go to Sidney. I supposed it was on account of Mistress Lester, who, as everyone knows, was so shameless in pursuing him."

It was my turn to choke with rage. Even to spare Mary's feelings I was unwilling that Polly's name should be dragged further through the sty of such a swine as Gibson. I decided that she must know the truth. But Trigg guessed my intention, and while I was still vainly searching for those impossible phrases that make pain palatable, he met the situation in his own way.

"Your husband is a damned cowardly liar and worse," he told her in cold measured words, "and Mistress Lester, being a woman of sense and not a scatterbrained child like you, perceived it. She was courteous to him, that was all. He rewarded her kindness with slander. Tom heard of it and chastised him so severely that I think his mouth is stopped. But if it is not, and yours as well, I shall not only withdraw from Gibson what small protection I might afford him, but will myself shoot him. Tell him so; and explain to him that I am no gentleman who plays with words idly, but a common man who keeps his promises."

Trigg left us a few minutes later. He pretended that duty beckoned him back to his post at the ferry, but I felt sure that this was only an excuse to leave us. He kissed his daughter fondly and assured her that so long as her husband behaved himself no harm would befall him.

Soon after he had gone Mary and I started home.

Now, as I recall our ride back to North Bend, I wonder that I could have been so dull as not to perceive Mary Trigg's true character. For she let her mask slip and yet I failed to see the face behind it. I can only excuse my stupidity on the grounds that I was blinded by the preconceived notion that Mary was the innocent victim of Gibson's lust. I had accepted her father's plea that there was much to be forgiven in her conduct at Green Spring, rather than my wife's harsher judgment that she had given way to the first man that reached for her. As a matter of fact neither was entirely right, but Betty came nearer the mark.

For well over an hour we rode in silence. I believed that Mary was smarting from the tongue-lashing delivered by her father. The longer I considered it the more unjust it seemed. Undoubtedly she had merely repeated what her husband told her.

"Don't take it so hard," I finally begged. "Your husband was drunk when he said it."

"Said what?" she asked absently.

"Why, about Pol—Mistress Lester," I stammered.

She wrested her thoughts from wherever they had been and looked at me with a certain amount of interest.

"You mean when you quarreled?"

"Yes."

"Why did you defend her?"

The question might have been innocent enough, yet I knew that it was not innocent at all. Though I did not at this time recognize it, there was an evil aura that enveloped Mary Trigg and everything she touched. Strange that anyone so small and dainty should make flesh so heavy and foul. For the only time in my life I was ashamed that I had possessed Polly Bragg. What difference, I asked myself guiltily, between the master of Hickorywood who tumbled his wife's servant and the young blade at Green Spring who dallied with his kinswoman's wenches? Somehow, as Mary's eyes mocked me and her twitching mouth whispered wordlessly that flesh is flesh and all of it hot for pleasure, there was no difference at all. Useless to urge that Polly and I had loved one another since we were children together in West England; that a malicious fortune had thwarted us until nature itself had intervened to require fulfillment of its claims. All my joy in Pol, save the pleasure that I had had from her body, faded into nothing, while that pleasure suddenly seemed so obscene and yet fierce that unconsciously I urged my horse at a quicker pace. Mary's low warm laugh brought me back to her side.

244

"You haven't answered my question."

"I could not sit by and see a lady defamed," I muttered.

"God forbid." She laughed again and changed the subject.

I learned of what she had been thinking. She was not so naïve regarding politics as I had suspected. She had evidently given them considerable thought. Bacon was in power, so one hastened to bow to his authority and seek favor from his friends, as she had done from her father. But did I not agree that the General was but a passing storm? Was she not right in regarding his followers as a renegade rabble? She had observed that I wisely held myself aloof from the movement.

I made light of her grave airs and bade her not worry her golden head about such weighty matters. She was a sweet child, but clearly unable to comprehend politics. Bacon would remain master of Virginia. There was no doubt about it. All the common men were back of him, and even a few gentlemen such as Lawrence, William Byrd, Drummond and James Crews. Moreover, those who held back would soon flock to his banner now that success roosted there. Finally, justice was on Bacon's side.

Mary Trigg was clever but far from infallible. She was visibly impressed by my confidence.

"What will happen to Berkeley?" she asked.

"Shipped back to England," I responded airily.

"On the day he is I shall go see Nathaniel Bacon."

"Why?"

"Why, to pay my respects, of course. But tell me, now that he has gained power will he risk his newly won position by going against the savages or stay sensibly at home?"

"He swore to fight the Indians. He will march as soon as he can equip his men."

"Then I don't suppose he will have time to redress all the grievances before he goes. Matters such as Father's affair, for instance." Suspicions began to stir faintly in my besotted brain, but she laid them, stillborn. "Poor Father. It seems a pity that he should have to wait."

"You can keep the plantation for him," I assured her.

"Naturally, but what if he should be killed?"

Her eyes misted at the very thought of such a tragedy, and the mask dropped back into place.

Betty and Pol received each in her own way my news of the day's work at Jamestown. Pol, insensible to politics where they did not immediately touch her, was pleased that the business was settled. But Betty was troubled.

"If the first adventurer that comes along can overthrow the authority of the Governor, where is there security for us or what we build for our children?" she asked.

"If the Governor rules justly he need not fear what you call adventurers," I answered sharply.

"Perhaps not, but nonetheless I don't think I care for your Nathaniel Bacon."

I did not argue the point further, but as the weeks passed, the tiny rift widened until it became a chasm great enough to alter the course of our lives.

I was wrong when I predicted that Bacon would march against the savages as soon as possible. He first turned to statecraft, and many of Joseph Trigg's prophecies were fulfilled. The Burgesses voted a series of long-needed reforms; taxes were lowered, special privileges were abolished, and if no heads actually fell, a number of the more vicious spoilsmen that had attached themselves to the Governor were forced out of public life.

At Sidney I greeted these reforms joyfully, Polly with indifference, and Betty, who approved the actions but disliked their source, with mixed emotions. Betty and I, after a further trial or two, learned not to discuss politics, but the cloud between us remained, and at Sidney, as in all Virginia, open strife was averted by the narrowest of margins. Even this was wiped out as the summer progressed.

In late June the Indians struck again, this time forty miles from Jamestown itself. Bacon, who had justified his defiance of Berkeley largely on the latter's unwillingness to suppress the savages, could not ignore the challenge. He left Jamestown for the counties where he raised troops and gathered supplies. Bacon was no sooner gone than Berkeley, who had submitted to the reforms sullenly, sprang into action. He declared Bacon a traitor and swore to protect the people of Virginia from the outrages and oppressions of the "usurper." Having thus justified himself, he rode into Gloucester County where he believed he had many supporters and called for volunteers. A few answered, but when they heard it was Bacon they were to fight, they turned their backs on the Governor and went home. It was reported that this so infuriated the old man that he fainted from rage. Soon after he fled across the Chesapeake to the Eastern Shore, leaving Bacon undisputed master of the rest of Virginia—with a master's responsibilities.

Bacon established headquarters at Middle Plantation and faced his dilemma. Should he march against the Indians, leaving the implacable Governor to stir up new trouble for him, or should he neglect the Indian peril and make war against Berkeley? Personal safety dictated the latter course, but it would leave the frontier victim to further horror, so Bacon decided against it. However, before trusting himself in the wilderness, he did what he could to secure his rear. One measure to this end was to summon the leading men of the colony to his headquarters in order, he said, to have the benefit of their counsel in the matters of state. In reality his purpose was to involve them in whatever treason he himself might be guilty of, thus binding them to his interest during his absence.

I was summoned with the others. This was due entirely to the influence of Joseph Trigg, who persisted in regarding me as a prospective comrade in exile should Bacon come to grief; but when the call came I did not know this and was insufferably proud that my merits entitled me to be numbered among such company.

Again Pol and Betty opposed my going. Pol mocked my pretensions.

"Look at you," she jeered, "strutting like a peacock with its tail spread because Nathaniel Bacon permits you to risk your neck for him. When you feel the hemp will you be happier for knowing that there will be gentlemen of high standing on the gibbet with you?"

"Women," I said, mustering the dignity proper to a man of influence, "do not understand politics."

247

"They understand men."

Betty's protest was far more serious and deep-rooted. Not only was she concerned over my safety, and with it her future and that of our child, but also her conscience was profoundly disturbed.

"It's wrong," she said; and I found that for all my years with her I had not fully comprehended the character of the quiet woman who was my wife. She possessed the Puritan conscience, and though it had been somewhat broadened and sweetened by a world of wider horizons than England offered, it was still the stiff-necked conscience that killed a king in the name of justice and put joy in the stocks for the sake of purity. Now, in the case of Betty, it had traveled the full circle and supported the principle of legitimate government, and was the more unyielding because her heart, always suspect, opposed it.

It's wrong, Betty's conscience said. "It's wrong," she repeated to me.

I urged in vain that, rebel or patriot, Nathaniel Bacon ruled Virginia, that his requests were commands. The time had come when men must choose; I must go to Middle Plantation or the Eastern Shore. It was Bacon or Berkeley.

"Better Berkeley," she said relentlessly.

I swore that I would only pay my respects to the General and come home. Surely no man could promise more fairly.

"It's wrong," she said.

When I pushed my skiff away from the wharf and headed upstream only Polly was there to wave farewell.

There were somewhere near a hundred planters at Middle Plantation, the greater part of them men of substance. All applauded Bacon's determination to wage vigorous war against the Indians, and most of them approved the violent means he had employed to get his commission. But sentiment was divided regarding the reforms he had forced through the Burgesses. A few disliked the measures themselves; others, like Betty, recoiled from usurpation of authority; and all of them with much to lose knew Berkeley to be both vindictive and greedy. Those who supported Bacon, commission or no, would face ruin if the Governor ever

248

found himself free to wreck vengeance on their persons and seize their property for himself and his friends.

Bacon called us together. He spoke with his customary vigor. He was leading men into the forest, he said, to face the cruelest enemy that had yet stained the pages of history. Those assembled would not share the perils of the campaign, but would remain at home, secure in person and property because others braved fever, torture and death. Could they then do less than swear to give the Governor no aid in his malicious intent to punish those who for the common good defied him? Unless they would take such an oath he, Bacon, refused to lead men into the wilderness only to bring them back to face alone the malice of Berkeley.

No one dissented. The clerk was set to work drawing up an oath. But Bacon was not yet done. He required that those present should also swear to resist troops of the King, himself, should such be sent to Virginia. The planters were unwilling to take such an oath. They said so in no uncertain terms. To refuse to aid the Governor was one thing, to aid Bacon against the King was another. The argument was bitter. The planters would not commit themselves to treason; Bacon declared flatly that in such case he would disband his army, throw up his commission and leave Virginia to the mercy of the savages and the protection of William Berkeley.

As was so often the case, the Governor himself proved Bacon's greatest source of strength. The old man's villainy gave constant meaning to the young one's recklessness. At the very moment when the discussion was hottest, when the deadlock seemed hopeless, a messenger arrived from the fort at Tindalls Point. He came to beg for immediate aid against the Indians. Unless help was forthcoming not only the fort must fall before the first attack, but all the women and children who had taken shelter there would be captured. Such news was incredible. The fort at Tindalls Point was the strongest in Virginia. No Indian force would dare assault it. To believe it could be taken was absurd.

"Not so," shouted the messenger. "For though the fort is still there its guts are gone. Yesterday the Governor came. He took away all our guns and ammunition. Carried them to the Eastern Shore."

249

The assembly was appalled. Nathaniel Bacon could have said nothing that would have buttressed his cause half so strongly as did Berkeley's action. There was no Indian menace on the Eastern Shore. It was the one place in Virginia safe from attack. Yet the guns had been taken there. There could be only one explanation. Women and children were to be left at the mercy of the savages, the plantation fortresses were to be abandoned, so that the hate of one old man could have its way. Nor could the assembled landholders regard themselves as disinterested spectators. If the government withdrew all protection, and at the same time Bacon dismissed his army as he threatened to do, they were as defenseless as the poor devils at Tindalls Point. After much muttering and swearing a group detached itself from the crowd and approached the General.

"Where's your damned paper?" one of them muttered.

The deadlock was shattered. One after another, all present signed. Among the last of the names to appear on the document was that of Tom Bone.

Betty looked at me out of angry eyes. She did not attempt to hide her contempt.

"I suppose you had to sign," she said.

"Of course. What else could I have done?"

"Stayed at home."

"But I couldn't. Bacon himself sent for me. The others who were summoned went, and all signed."

"Then you were in poor company," she retorted coldly. But as if repenting the bitterness of her words she threw her arms around me. "Promise you will give up following this Nathaniel Bacon," she cried. "Don't let him part us."

I was startled by her vehemence, and touched, but I refused to promise.

"I signed a compact back there," I said.

"Are your promises to me the only ones you can break?"

"Your demands are unreasonable."

"Bacon's are treason. It's wrong, I tell you, wrong."

The weeks slipped by. We quarreled, regretted it, agreed to

250

let the matter lie, quarreled again. During these days I often found myself recalling James Lester's reluctance in giving us permission to wed. Out of the wisdom of his own suffering, he had warned us that ours were two different worlds. Then we had been so sure of ourselves, but now, despite both our efforts to prevent it, the barrier between us was growing ever more formidable.

# XII

## I.

IT WAS early August when Bacon wrung from the wary planters their oath to support him. A few days later he plunged into the woods. He was gone until the middle of September. During this absence his suspicions of Berkeley were amply justified, for he was no sooner in the wilderness than the Governor, from his head-quarters at Arlington Plantation on the Eastern Shore, once more issued an urgent appeal for his supporters to rally to him. With Bacon safely beyond recall some responded. Most of these were rich planters, few in numbers, but carrying with them considerable wealth and some retainers.

A source of strength that ultimately proved to be of far greater value to Berkeley than any aid given him by his Virginia adherents was found in the loyalty of the masters of the English ships that came to Virginia during the months of turmoil. As Englishmen they naturally sympathized with the King's representative, and as beneficiaries of the trade laws they abhorred the colonial threats to repudiate these by violence. Consequently they sided with the Governor, and their assistance, reinforced by flagrant violations of the most solemn promises, enabled Berkeley to seize the small ships left by Bacon to guard the water routes, and emerge further dishonored, but master of the river and bay. This not only rendered his Eastern Shore retreat safe from enemy attack, but also gave him the means to launch his own offensive where and when he would.

Encouraged by this improvement of his fortunes, Sir William issued still another call for recruits. His appeal was typical of the cause and the man. He did not promise justice, or better government, or to redress the grievances of the people of Virginia, only further plunder for the privileged. Any man who joined Berkeley was promised exemption from all taxation and the prospect of seizing for himself the property of Bacon's supporters—the men who were even then staggering hungry and sick through the Great Dragon Swamp that the frontier might be free from fear. The Governor found men mean enough to respond to his call, not many, but enough to enable him to reoccupy Jamestown. This was September 7, 1676; a few days later Bacon came out of the wilderness, sick with fever, his forces decimated, but victorious and indomitable.

The news that he and his men had been proclaimed outlaws, that his fleet was lost, the capital in the hands of the enemy, did not daunt Nathaniel Bacon.

"Gentlemen and fellow soldiers," he cried, "I know you have the prayers and well wishes of all the people of Virginia."

With no promise of reward greater than that, he led his army towards Jamestown and the enemy. The army consisted of one hundred and thirty-six weary, half-starved men.

When word came to Sidney that Bacon was encamped a few miles from Jamestown, I resolved to join him. Twice already Nathaniel Bacon had led men to fight my fight, and twice I had remained behind. The first time it had been out of love for Pol, the second time I had heeded Betty's pleas. Women had made a weakling of me. Now, regardless of price, I must assert my manhood. Nor would I ever find a more worthy cause. This was no mere fight against Indians, but a challenge hurled at all I most despised, a defiance of the gentry itself—the gentry, whose pitiless selfishness had ruined my childhood in England and pursued me to America where, for its own profit, it had sacrificed Hickorywood to the savages.

I told Betty my decision.

She opposed it with all the vigor of her strong nature.

"Violence against the government is sinful," she said.

"Then I choose to do wrong."

Her voice was cold.

"But it is not your right to choose, for though you make the choice Jimmy and I must pay for it."

"I don't see why."

"When you side with violent, lawless rabble you brand yourself, and branding yourself you brand your son."

"You have changed since that day when you told your father you loved common men," I told her angrily. "You are half aristocrat and you are remembering it now; but those men you call a rabble are my people. I was born with their brand. Your people, your mother's people, have pursued and oppressed me. Now I mean to fight them—to kill them—to rob them—as they have killed those I loved—and robbed me."

I started to leave her.

"Don't go." She was pleading now. I stopped.

"I've not changed, Tom. I still despise the aristocrats with their foolish airs and their selfishness—their Henry Gibsons. If Bacon were in the right I would gladly bid you follow him. But he isn't. You are joining reckless, ruined men such as Joseph Trigg, who having failed would vent their bitterness on others. That isn't America. America is a place where men like you and my father are free, not to destroy what they envy, but to obtain a better life for themselves and their children."

I thought then and I am even surer today that she was wrong. True, she herself had not changed, but those privileges which she had so willingly abandoned, she wanted for her son, and to that end she was willing to reproduce in the New World the injustices and the inequalities of the Old.

I told her all this. It was useless. She was blinded by her love for Jimmy and her hatred of violence.

"Your Bacon will lose in the end," she insisted, "and you will be hanged as a traitor."

"I choose even that to living as Berkeley's serf."

We quarreled through the afternoon. Anger, bitterness, sorrow were alike futile. I refused to remain at home longer while men fought for me. Betty would not credit me with any motive nobler than hate.

"You have never recovered from the wrongs you suffered as a

254

child in England," she told me. "You still want to hurt people, as you hurt me years ago, merely because I had not suffered enough to please you. But you can't build your new world on hate. Remember that when you are pillaging with your Nathaniel Bacon."

Betty nursed her anger through the evening meal. When we had finished she took Jimmy to bed.

"We'll talk tomorrow," she told me; and I knew she would not rejoin us.

I turned to Polly for comfort. She laughed at me.

"Go on off to your wars, Tom. Betty will be here when you come back."

"But I want her to understand," I said.

"Well, she won't. Nor for that matter do I."

I was dumbfounded, and what little restraint I had clung to during the long afternoon slipped from me.

"I should have remembered you too are half gentry," I said angrily.

Then Pol and I quarreled.

"Damn you," I cried at last. "I'll go this very night, and the devil with all women."

Pol did not beg me to stay.

"I'll tell Betty," she said stonily.

I saddled my horse and rushed into the hot, heavy night in a mood of bitter madness.

It was late when I left Sidney. The road was lonely. Consequently when, a mile or so below North Bend, I saw a rider approaching I was surprised. My surprise increased when I drew close enough to see that it was a woman. As I passed she called my name. It was Mary Gibson.

She had been in Jamestown with her husband, who at the first change in the winds of chance had shifted his allegiance back to Berkeley. When word had come that Bacon was approaching, Mary started for North Bend. As her father's daughter she could protect the place from any of Bacon's men who might attempt to use her husband's defection from the General as an excuse to loot.

She urged me to stay the night at North Bend. She would be glad for a man's protection.

I was about to refuse when I remembered that neither Polly nor Betty liked Mistress Gibson. In a burst of spite I turned my horse toward North Bend. My ill humor melted under the warmth of Mary's gratitude. Once we were settled comfortably in her house it seemed but natural to unburden my soul. I doubt if Mary even heard half of what I said, but her small mouth puckered in ready sympathy, and her eyes were large with admiration. By the time she went to bed I was more than ever convinced that she was a sweet child whose only fault lay in too trusting a disposition. Here was I, for instance, alone with her. Another sort of fellow . . .

Next morning as I continued my journey towards Jamestown I was in a chastened mood; and I knew that Betty's suspicions of Mary were justified. The gossips had not exaggerated. I doubted if they had told even half the truth.

Mistress Gibson had come to me in the night. Flattered, I had taken her willingly enough, but before morning, though the sport was good, my self-esteem had been punctured. Mary Trigg was the only complete wanton I have ever known. Abel would have served her as well. I had happened along the road and Mary had picked me up in much the manner I had seen the fishermen of Plymouth take the trulls in the grog shop.

The knowledge was not soothing, and as I rode through the gray morning light I was ashamed. I was glad that I did not have to face Betty that day—or Pol either, though I assured myself that actually they were to blame.

A man's women should be meek and not bedevil him.

2.

When I reached the plantation opposite Sandy Bay where Bacon had established headquarters, his army, now increased to about three hundred men, was breaking camp. Joseph Trigg, whom I found without difficulty, explained.

"We're going to Jamestown."

He said it casually as if it were no more important than a visit

256

to a neighboring market town, yet I realized that those four words might spell treason. Although Betty had failed to shake my resolution to join Bacon, she had opened my eyes to the gravity of the step I was taking. Until now, although there had been a threat of force, and although the Governor had been defied, there had been no actual violence. But a clash at Jamestown meant civil war, small though the scale might be. We who followed Bacon were engaged in insurrection. Such men must succeed or face ruin.

"Or turn pirate," suggested Trigg when I told him what was in my mind.

"Do you still cling to that?" I asked.

"Yes, and what's more important, I know a pirate—Joshua Wren. Wren is a skunk, but he would take us."

"Not me. I have a wife and son."

"Well, keep it in mind."

When we arrived at the approaches to Jamestown we found that Berkeley had not been idle. The town lies on a peninsula in the James River and is connected with the shore by a narrow neck. We found this neck strongly defended. A new palisade had been built with three heavy guns guarding it. A small fleet hovered in the river ready to open fire if we came within range. Added to this we were outnumbered. The prospects for success were not bright. The position appeared impregnable to me, but Trigg was undismayed.

"You should have been in the Dragon Swamp," he said, "where there was nothing to fight save fever, insects, reptiles and hunger. Here we are well fed, and the enemy are clearly before us, not playing hide and seek through the whole damned American wilderness."

We reached Jamestown in the evening. The General took us within a few hundred feet of the palisades and ordered us to begin at once to erect breastworks. We worked most of the night and by morning had a rude sort of protection. Then, inasmuch as it seemed impossible that with superior numbers and equipment on his side the Governor would permit our little band to invest his capital, we sat back and waited for an attack. None came. Instead rumors began to spread. Where they originated no one knew, but all through the camp and up and down the breastwork it was whispered that Berkeley wished to treat with us. His terms were reported to be generous. At length Bacon took sufficient cognizance of these rumors to deride them. The Governor, he reminded us, had made promises before, only to break them. He was a dishonored old man who knew no integrity except that enforced by knife and carbine. When Bacon had spoken the muttering ceased.

My own day was enlivened by more than fighting and gossip. Polly Bragg came to the wars. Trigg found her and brought her to me. She was dressed in a leather jacket and shirt. She had cut her hair. A fusil lay lightly in the crook of her arm.

"She's joined the army," roared Trigg in delight.

I stared at her.

"I didn't know you were interested in politics," I finally said.

"I don't give a damn for your Bacon or Berkeley either," she replied calmly. "I told you yesterday that I agreed with Betty in thinking you should stay at home."

"Then why are you here?"

"She just likes a fight," Trigg chuckled.

"Go away," she told him, good-naturedly.

Trigg obeyed. When he was gone Pol turned to me gravely.

"I'm here because Betty has left you. Early this morning she took Jimmy and went to an uncle's across the river. She's done with you, Tom."

"But she can't do that," I protested, "just because I choose to follow Bacon."

"It wasn't that, though I suppose it does have something to do with it."

"I don't understand."

"She heard you ride away last night and followed. Before going she told me she could not bear to part with you in anger. It was late when she returned. She left Sidney early this morning. She didn't tell me why. Just said that if I saw you to tell you that she was gone and would not return."

"Was that all?"

"There's a little more. Some verses from the Bible. Something about green before the sun. She said you would know."

I did know.

*"He shall lean upon his house but it shall not stand: he shall hold it fast but it shall not endure.*

*"He is green before the sun, and his branches shooteth forth in his garden."*

Betty and I had learned the lines because we liked the sound of the words, although they had meant little to us. But now she recalled it and hurled it at me. But why? However my politics might offend her I had only acted in accordance with my convictions. Surely Betty was not justified in comparing me to the hypocrite in the Book of Job. I told Polly so.

"I don't know. She said if you had forgotten the verses I was to tell you that she could have tolerated your being an honest rebel, but that she would never forgive you for using your pretended principles as an excuse to abandon her, while you shamed yourself and your son."

"I still don't understand."

"Maybe this will help. As I rode down the river today I met Mistress Gibson. She looked like a well-cared-for white and yellow cat. Overfed and warm and sleek and lazy. She said she had given you shelter last night."

"But how would Betty know?"

Pol shrugged.

"Maybe she didn't. But I've been thinking. She was gone last night just about long enough to ride to North Bend and back. Say she rode down fast, came in sight of you just in time to see you with your Mary, and came back slowly, while she made up her mind."

I was certain that Polly had guessed the riddle. True, I had not heard hoof beats, but I had been fully occupied, first by my own thoughts—then Mistress Gibson. It could have happened, and nothing else explained Betty's action and her message to me. But like the hypocrite she accused me of being, I resented my wife's lack of faith.

259

"Suppose she did see me enter the lane to North Bend with Mary," I said. "It was late and Mistress Gibson offered me hospitality."

"Your Mary's hospitality is well known."

"Lying gossip."

Pol's gray eyes opened wide.

"Is it?"

If need be I can lie as well as any man, but not to Polly Bragg.

"No," I admitted.

After that we talked about Pol.

"I came as soon as Betty was gone," she said.

"Why?"

"When she left you because of things that did not concern me at all, she freed me."

"You mean . . . ?"

"I mean that there is no longer anything to keep us apart."

I still hesitated.

"Betty will get over this; she'll come back to me."

"You can ask her," Pol replied calmly, "but she won't come. If I wasn't sure of that I wouldn't be here."

"But—"

"It's no use, Tom. She won't forgive you."

"I don't see how you can be so sure. You are here—even though you did meet Mary and find out that I stayed with her."

Pol laughed.

"Your wife is a lady—a real one, I mean. She wouldn't demean herself by engaging in a rivalry with a nasty piece like Mistress Gibson. But I will. And you'll have no more Mary Triggs," she added grimly.

We were still talking when the first shots were fired. Polly grabbed her fusil, I my carbine. The ships had moved in to rake our flank while the forces behind the palisade blasted us from the front.

Neither did much harm, and we answered their fire so vigorously that the ships withdrew. That ended the battle for the day. No one appeared to notice Pol. A woman handling a gun was not an unusual sight to the frontiersmen of Virginia.

That evening Trigg and a young gentleman I knew only by the name of Ned joined Pol and me. We watched twilight slip behind the night and the stars come out. Trigg and Ned speculated on the next day's events. The boy was enthusiastic, the old man cautious.

"It's the devil," the latter grumbled. "We can't advance without cannon and if we go back we're beat without fighting."

"We've got cannon," Ned protested.

"We have them but they are of no use to us in the rear, and who's going to mount them on the outworks yonder while from not over three hundred feet away they pepper us with shot from behind their palisade?"

"The General will find a way," Ned said comfortably.

"Aye, that he will, I can tell it to you now." Trigg scrambled to his feet and grinned down on us sardonically. He spoke in a fair imitation of Bacon's voice. "Lads, before you are dishonored rogues, behind you are the prayers of the people of Virginia." He sat down again. "Then we go out and put up the guns while they shoot at us. The devil of it is, I've known a good many rogues who shoot damned straight, and so far as I've experienced a prayer never yet stopped a bullet."

But it was not Bacon who solved the problem of mounting the guns. It was Polly Bragg.

"I know how you could keep them from firing," she announced.

We all laughed, but unperturbed she unfolded her plan.

"As I rode down the river this morning I met your daughter, Mr. Trigg. She told me that her husband is with Berkeley in Jamestown. There must be many similar cases within a few miles of here. If I were Bacon I'd collect a dozen or so such women and invite them to sit atop the breastwork while the guns were brought up. Then if Berkeley's men shoot at you they risk killing their own women."

"You'd put Mary up there?" growled Trigg.

"I would. How about you, Tom?"

Polly was fairly purring, but Ned saved me the embarrassment of an answer.

"But a gentleman could not do that," he told Pol severely.

261

"Probably not," she conceded. "However, as I am no gentleman, but just a trollop who followed Tom Bone here to camp, I think it would be fun."

With that Pol lost interest in her scheme, which she later confessed was never intended for any purpose more serious than to bait me regarding Mistress Gibson. But Joseph Trigg was no gentleman either. Presently he left us. When he returned he was grinning broadly.

"The General thinks it is a good idea," he said.

"What is?"

"Putting their women on the breastwork." He rubbed his hands together. "I'm going to enjoy this more than I did killing Indians. Only I'm sorry that Lady Berkeley is with the Governor. I'd like to see her up there, carriage and all, dressed in her finest silks."

"How about Mary?" Pol asked.

Even this unconcealed dislike for his daughter did not dampen Trigg's high spirits.

"There will be enough without her," he said good-naturedly.

Ned had been listening in glum disapproval.

"But Bacon can't do that," he now cried. "He's a gentleman."

"That's what he said at first," Trigg retorted grimly, "and Lawrence and one or two of the others thought the same. But I had picked up some of the lads to take with me. *Their* wives had been captured by the Indians, who most likely tore their nails out and ripped their entrails out of their living bellies. It was William Berkeley's fault—his and his damned gentlemen yonder in the town. Besides, the women won't get hurt. The bastards inside will throw a hard-working frontier wife to the savages for the sake of a few pelts or use an honest servant wench for their pleasure, but they won't risk puncturing the useless skin of one of their own ladies."

"When is this outrage to take place?" Ned asked, unable to answer Trigg's logic, but clearly unconvinced by it.

"A few of us are going to round up the hostages early in the morning. As soon as we bring them in the show will start. I'm off to bed now to be fresh for the sport."

262

Going to bed consisted of rolling over and closing his eyes. He was soon sleeping peacefully as an infant, but more noisily.

"He's nice," Pol said. "How did he breed such a daughter?"

I was wise enough to change the subject.

The next morning when news of the scheme to use the women as a shield spread through the camp it was greeted with varied emotions. Most of the men approved, but some like Ned clung to the belief that war, at least between white men, should be conducted on a gentlemanly basis.

"One should win fairly," I heard a rosy-cheeked youngster declare vehemently.

A gnarled, tired-looking man with thin gray hair dissented.

"One should win," he said.

Polly, now that Trigg had made her malicious fancy real, was ardent in defending it and even urged its extension. She suggested that I point out to Bacon that we might cross the isthmus itself behind a curtain of silk-garbed ladies.

I refused. I was already concerned over Pol's activities. If the insurrection failed, the leaders faced almost certain execution, though, as even Berkeley was unlikely to hang three hundred men, there was a certain safety in obscurity. But I felt sure that no leniency would be extended to those responsible for placing the women in peril. So far the idea was being attributed to Trigg.

"Let him have the glory," I begged. "He wants to go pirating."

Somewhat reluctantly Pol agreed. Ned too, when I explained my fears to him, was compliant, and as I had no doubts of Trigg's willingness to assume full responsibility I breathed more easily, secure in the belief that Polly was safe. I could now enjoy the coming drama without too personal an interest in the cost. This complacency lasted until mid-morning, when Trigg's detachment returned with the women.

When word came that Trigg had come into sight, Pol and I went with the others to see the captives. By the time we reached a point of vantage, Bacon was greeting the ladies with elaborate courtesy. As we watched, Trigg said something to the General and

263

gestured toward one of the women who was concealed from my view.

"Must be a notable," I said to Pol, as I shifted my position that I might see better.

The woman was Betty. Spluttering from amazement I turned towards Pol. She was gone. Anger superseded surprise. I shouldered my way to where Trigg stood.

"What in God's name does this mean?" I cried. "Betty here, but your Mary, whose husband—"

He interrupted me before I could say more. His apologetic explanation was one to which I could not take exception. Betty had gone to the home of Ralph Sidney, whose large plantation was only a few miles above Jamestown. The fellow, a member of the Governor's intimate circle of favorites, was with his master in Jamestown, but he had left his wife at home. It was for just such women as this that Bacon's men had been sent. The place was one of the first visited. Trigg ordered the slave who met him at the door to tell his mistress to prepare for a journey. Presently Betty appeared demanding to know why her aunt was being abducted. Trigg, whose orders were to bring the women in without divulging the purpose, refused an explanation. So despite pleas and threats Betty insisted on accompanying them to Jamestown.

"The General won't put her on the breastwork," Trigg assured me uncomfortably, "but she's so damned stiff-necked you had better explain things to her yourself and get her home. Wait by the oak we slept under last night. I'll send her to you."

Polly was under the oak. When I told her the situation she prepared to leave. I protested that I needed her to help me persuade Betty.

"You're a fool," she said shortly. "Can't you see that although I was thinking of that hussy at North Bend, and even that not seriously, it was I who suggested fetching the women. It is my fault Betty is here."

"She doesn't know that," I pointed out.

Pol's defenses broke. Her body seemed to shrink, her mouth trembled, her skin was flushed, her long lashes beat in vain at

264

tears that crowded out of hot eyes. And Polly was not accustomed to shame. Its angry heat evaporated her patience.

"You're a cruel blind fool, Tom Bone," she cried in a voice that was fuller because it was low. "Why do you think I came slinking away the second I saw Betty unless it was to keep her from knowing I am here?"

"What difference does it make if she knows or not?"

"Betty knows that I am not interested in politics. I myself have told her a dozen times that I don't care two pence if Bacon or Berkeley rules Virginia. So if she sees me here she will know the truth: that I followed you like any trull who tramps behind an army."

"But why do you care? Last night you yourself told Trigg and Ned that you had followed me to camp."

"Trigg and Ned," she said contemptuously. "What do I care for them? It's your wife I'm speaking of."

"She's got to know some day."

While we argued Pol had been standing, poised for flight. Now she sat on the bole of the tree. Her voice was tired and quiet.

"Very well, I shall wait. I'll sit here while you tell her that I was your mistress at Hickorywood; that while she bore your child I crept into her place; tell her that on the night when she was surrounded by savages with only Abel to defend her, and his drum throbbing its call for help, we hesitated while you held me in your arms; tell her that the fields and woods of the frontier saw our love, that the river played music for it, that even her slave knew of it; tell her Trigg knows, and any of the three hundred men here who care to look; tell her the world knows, and that only she has been blind. When you are done, then we two—her husband and his mistress—will bid her go back to her uncle's home and await further friendly advice."

Overwhelmed by Polly's passionate eloquence I momentarily forgot time, place and circumstance.

"Have you always felt this way?" I asked.

"Ashamed before your wife? Yes. A man's mistress must, even if there is a little triumph in it too."

"Why didn't you tell me?"

"Would it have changed anything?"

"I suppose not."

"Then what was the use of my distressing you with my complaints?"

"But now?"

"Now it's as I told you last night—Betty has left you. But that does not mean that I have the courage to face her. If you are braver I'll sit here—with my eyes on the ground—and listen while you explain."

"But I can't do that."

She got to her feet.

"Then until Betty has gone I'll hide like the coward I am."

But she kissed me before she left.

"Remember that, while you talk to Betty," she said.

Betty came to me a few minutes after Pol had gone. She knew by this time the purpose for which the women had been brought to camp. She was not indignant. She appreciated Trigg's view. She herself had been a frontier wife, a captive.

"I told the ladies that this would not be a thousandth time so fearful as being carried away by the savages," she told me.

"I hope they felt encouraged," I answered politely.

Actually I did not give a damn how they felt, but I was shy and ill at ease with this young woman who had been my wife for over five years. If she was aware of this she gave no sign, but laughed pleasantly.

"I am afraid not. The poor things are so used to gentle treatment. But I am sure that when we are all out there I can help them keep their courage at a proper pitch."

"But you don't have to go with the others. I am going to take you home."

Her voice turned hard. Her eyes challenged me.

"My home is with my kinswoman. I shall go where she goes."

I argued in vain. She had chosen her way and would follow it without favor from the enemy. Nor would she discuss our personal affairs.

"You have made the choice. There is nothing to say," she declared.

266

Someone called out that the prisoners were being taken to the breastwork. Betty hastened away. I suppose I might have kept her by force, but such a thing did not occur to me. I could reason and plead, but I had no right to command. Besides I have never been adept at regulating the lives of others. I find my own affairs vexing enough. So I let her go, and cursed and followed her. A few minutes later, my heart in my throat, I watched what was surely as strange a sight as Jamestown ever witnessed.

Eight or ten women detached themselves from our forces and approached the barricade that served as a shield against assault from Berkeley. Beside each woman was a man. Most of the ladies walked stiffly, eyes fixed straight ahead, mouth drawn into a stern line, but two or three strolled easily, as to a ball, and chatted gaily with their escorts. Among these latter was Betty, who looked up at the tall yellow-haired youngster beside her and laughed. The boy was Ned. I felt a surge of anger and asked myself why the devil I had not had wit enough to accompany her myself.

But there was little time for such speculation. The breastwork was reached. It was awkward there, some of the ladies finding it difficult to get to the top. Betty was not among those. She and Ned sprang up lightly, and for a moment stood alone laughing down at the others and calling encouragement. It was at that moment that I knew I had lost my wife, and I never loved her more. Presently they were joined by others, but I hardly saw them as my eyes strained into the mid-day glare. The world had shrunk to the breadth of a single woman's figure.

Our guns were brought up. This was the crisis. If Berkeley was resolved to defend his position at any cost he would order his men to fire. For minutes there was hardly a sound save the grunting of the men at work. Then a shout sounded from behind the enemy's palisade, and men ran out in front of it, cheering and calling words of encouragement to their women. Their shout was answered by cries of mingled admiration and triumph from our side. We had won. Pol's scheme had worked.

I sighed as the world expanded to its proper breadth. I wanted to sit down.

Pol and Trigg were under the oak tree.

"They're safe," I told them.

Trigg laughed.

"I knew the damned gentlemen wouldn't touch their own useless women."

Pol slapped him. She put the whole weight of her arm behind the blow, and she had worked in the tobacco fields for four years. He staggered back, then came toward her with an oath. I watched without much interest, too drained of emotion to care what happened, or so I believed. Besides, Pol did not appear to need my protection. When Trigg reached her the fury that twisted her face caused him to abandon whatever punishment he had contemplated. He stood defenseless before the lash of her tongue. Her words rattled like hot musket fire.

"You sneer at them, and haven't the wit to see that you are only making something less of the rest of us," she stormed. "Yet you yourself might learn from these gentlemen how to care for a woman. Or are you content with your own way?"

He stood grinning foolishly as a man will when confronted with an angry woman. If she had stopped there Pol would have driven him from the field, but the shame and anger that she had been forced to digest that day were having their revenge. She retched bitterness as a drunkard vomits too rich a dinner. She wanted to hurt and shame someone, as she had been hurt and shamed. Trigg was at hand, so heedless of his fist that unclenched and clenched again, she plunged on.

"Have you protected them?" she sneered, mocking his rising anger. "You let the very gentlemen you laugh at take the home that you had provided for them. And the weakest of them took your wife as a servant and your daughter for a whore."

As Trigg caught hold of her, my indifference vanished. I sprang to my feet.

"Leave be," he warned me. "I won't hurt her."

He shook her. Not violently, but slowly and easily, as if savoring the power of his muscles. Her slight body swayed under his hand, but her eyes glared unafraid into his own. Finally he shoved her away from him.

268

"Whore yourself," he said. "Only last night I heard you panting under this very tree."

Her angry retort was checked in mid-air. The blood drained from her cheeks. "It's true," she said and walked away.

I hit Trigg. He sat down with a grunt.

"You choose the most damnably stubborn women," he said after a moment, and added, "I'm sorry, lad. Pol's a good girl, but she shouldn't speak so of my poor Mary."

I thought of his poor Mary as I had last seen her, and the resentment I'd felt at Pol's humiliation gave way to pity for the fatuous father.

"We're none of us over-lovely," I said wearily.

I did not see Betty again that day. When the guns were mounted the women were sent back to their homes. No escort was provided for the return, but of his own will Ned took Betty. When he was back in camp he came to tell me that she was safe and lingered to talk about her.

"She told me," he said awkwardly, "why she was with her aunt."

I was surprised. Betty was usually reticent with strangers. But Ned was a nice lad and obviously smitten by her; perhaps she had thawed under the clean bright warmth of his admiration. And she had employed the impression she made on him to good effect.

"I think she was right," he told me boldly.

"Possibly," I admitted.

"And maybe she's got the right of it about politics too."

"Then why are you here?"

"Because I believed in Bacon's reforms. I still do for that matter; but Mistress Bone has shown me that this is not the proper way to go about achieving them."

"You might try the powers of reason on the Governor."
He flushed.

"I know the obstacles as well as you; but this way is wrong. I am leaving camp tonight."

He said this last defiantly as if he expected me to protest, and was prepared to defend his decision. But I was in no mood for argument. I thanked him for his attentions to my wife and bade him good-by.

The next day we bombarded Jamestown. Not much damage was done, but the noise alone was sufficient to gain a victory over the poltroons under Berkeley. The Governor himself and a dozen or so loyal gentlemen would have resisted, but their courage was wasted. The several hundred soldiers huddled in the town had come to divide loot, not face guns. They would not fight. So Berkeley, cursing friends and foe alike, was forced to abandon his capital less than two weeks after he had entered it.

We burned Jamestown. Without control of the river it was impossible to hold, and the General and his advisers were determined that it should not be left as a rallying place for the enemy. Moreover, the town had come to symbolize Berkeley's oppression. As the flames shot into the sky the men of Bacon's army cheered. They thought that tyranny was burning. So the first English town in America was burned by Englishmen. The savages must have laughed.

While Jamestown burned Pol and I sat on the south side of the river. We watched the fire across the water. For a long time neither of us spoke. My mind churned wearily, monotonously, over the events of the past days. I asked myself questions that I had asked a hundred times already. But I found no new answers. I had lost Hickorywood, Betty, Jimmy. Perhaps I would never see my wife again or my son. Why? Surely not Mary Trigg. A man could lie with a trollop without losing his wife. Betty could not leave me, could not take Jimmy away for such a cause. I could force her to return to me. I could—but did I want to? Did I intend to?

Pol touched me.

"Never mind, Tom," she said softly.

"But I do mind."

"Then make her come back to you. You can do it, though it will be against her will."

"I have been thinking that."

"It is your choice." Her voice was quiet.

I looked at her woman's body and into her face. Her eyes, wide

270

and honest, looked back into mine. She made no gesture. She was playing no woman's tricks of coquetry. She was neither bold nor modest. But love was naked in her eyes. Its promise was on her mouth.

"The time has come when you must choose," was all she said.

I looked at her and knew that there were no more hard questions with which to torture myself. The rest must go. I drew her toward me.

"Tom," she sobbed.

So out of the strands of poverty and plenty, charity and greed, faith and betrayal, failure and success, my dream was finally woven into a web of reality. I was in America . . . free . . . with Polly Bragg close in my arms . . .

## 3.

Nathaniel Bacon captured Jamestown on September 20, 1676, thereby making himself master of the greater part of Virginia. Less than six weeks later he was dead. Fever killed him. He had contracted it in the Great Dragon Swamp during the Indian campaign, and the war against the Governor prevented him from receiving the care needful for recovery. So he died.

Richard Lawrence, his most devoted friend, buried him secretly so that his body should not suffer indignity from Berkeley's malice, in case the latter regained power. It pleases me to know that today his once vexed bones are at rest somewhere in the soil of Virginia, for whose liberties he died. Fate was less kind to many of his followers. Laurence Ingram was chosen to succeed Bacon as General of the people's army. No worse choice could have been made. He was a capable soldier, but lacked the heart and resolution to lead a dangerous cause. After a brief period of confusion, negotiation and desultory fighting he laid down his arms out of fear for his own neck, and persuaded most of his followers to do likewise. Although isolated groups resisted for a short time longer, Ingram's submission virtually ended the rebellion. By December Bacon's leading supporters had fled the colony or were prisoners of the Governor; in January Berkeley felt secure enough to proceed with the murder of his enemies. It was murder. The accused were given no trial worthy of the name. They were not permitted counsel, nor in some cases were they even allowed to speak in their own defense. It would have been a waste of time if they had been. The Governor required their blood to wash out his own shame as a man and incapacity as an official; his followers were hot after newly confiscated lands. That was reason enough to hang a free-born Englishman in the plantation of Virginia in January, 1677.

As Betty had foreseen, I shared in Bacon's disaster. I followed him until his death and then served under Ingram. But I was too stubborn and angry to participate in the latter's ignominious surrender. Instead I joined Richard Lawrence and a handful of his followers. We fought a number of skirmishes, but ours was a lost cause. After a few weeks Lawrence admitted it. But he would not surrender.

"I'll trust to the mercy of the savages rather than that of William Berkeley," he declared.

With most of what was left of his little band he fled west into the wilderness.

I did not accompany him. Instead, with Joseph Trigg, I crept to Sidney where we held a council of war with Polly, who had gone back there after the burning of Jamestown. All three of us opposed going with Lawrence. Beyond that there was no clear course. Trigg was all for piracy. Pol was indifferent.

"Just so we stay together," she told me.

I hesitated. Piracy offered an opportunity to continue to fight. That appealed to me. I was embittered and rebellious; I wanted revenge. But I was tired too, and it would be difficult to fit Pol into a life among pirates. But what was the alternative? Another colony where Pol and I might start anew? In such a case could I hope to do more than repeat the pattern that I wove with Betty? To be sure, there were differences. I loved Polly as I had not loved Betty, and she would not permit hard principles of politics and conduct to rise above her own heart. But these would be mere variations in the pattern, not departures from the old texture of life. Nothing else had changed. We would be caught in the same

272

relentless vice of greed and power that squeezed the hearts out of so many men in Virginia. Strong men, too. Strong as Trigg. Bacon's fight had been a good fight, but before victory could be achieved it must be fought again and again. Men of my generation had lighted the torch. That must suffice us even though it had been dashed from our hands.

Meantime nothing had changed. Tobacco was half-penny again; the trade laws were enforced. The gentlemen were still invincible. The dice they threw were weighted and they would play with no others. The priest and the philosopher were in their pay. No one else had the leisure to think. Until they did think they must bend their backs in servitude, for their minds were chained by lies.

"Human dignity," writes the philosopher, "dignity of the common man." "God loves the humble," intones the priest. "The Holy Mother cares for the down-trodden and the meek." Hollow words . . . lies . . . half truths. I claim no knowledge of God or His ways, but I do not believe He loves a willing serf. If He loves He must love a man who walks upright, free under the sun. Nor, I think, can even the gentle Virgin be fond of a cringing slave who snivels in gratitude while his betters cuff him and kick him through the gates of paradise. "Dignity of the common man." There is no such thing and cannot be until there is no "common" man but only men, and all men are common in their dignity.

"But what does all that matter?" I asked myself fiercely. "I shall still have Pol. With her in my arms can the King have more?"

Still I hesitated. I did not discount my passion for Polly Bragg nor my dependence upon her. She was a part of me, but I was thirty-two years old and had learned what I would not believe at twenty-two: that Polly alone was not the sole end of living. She could give me sustenance but not complete fulfillment. For that I must look elsewhere. But where? My boyhood dreams of America were dimmed, for the New World was already feeling the shackles of the Old.

"I will not wear those shackles," I promised myself, and bade Trigg get word to his pirate captain.

Trigg told Pol where to inquire for Captain Wren. Until she found him we would hide in the swamp.

We lay hidden for three months. Abel brought us food from time to time. In late April Pol came.

"We sail in a fortnight," she said.

"You found Wren?" Trigg asked.

"No," Pol replied, "but I've had word of him. He was hanged in Charles Town three weeks ago. Eight of his men swung with him."

We digested this. I had never seen Captain Wren, but nevertheless his shadow as he swung at a rope's end darkened my spirit. What if Polly had made contact with him six weeks before?

Trigg laughed weakly.

"I always said he was a skunk," he declared. "I'll wager you've found a better rogue for us to fight under."

His joviality was hollow. Pol brushed it aside.

"I've taken passage for us with an honest, God-fearing New Englander bound for Jamaica," she said dryly.

"In God's name, why?" Trigg gasped.

Pol threw out her hands in a gesture of impatience.

"You've got to get out of Virginia, and Captain Reap does not ask questions. If his passengers choose to come aboard quietly in the night, it is their affair. He will even send a skiff a few miles above Jamestown to pick you up."

"But Jamaica!"

"Why not? It's as good a place as any. We can join the buccaneers if you and Tom still want to be pirates."

"Are you sure your Captain Reap can be trusted?" I asked.

"We must risk that. He is a New Englander who does not approve of Berkeley or his ways. Moreover, he has a reputation for honesty, and he took my money."

"Where, by the way, did you get enough money?" I wanted to know.

"I sold my rights in Sidney to Betty," Pol replied. "Her kinsman loaned her the money. I sold cheaply."

"Well, you've thought of everything," Trigg said. "Jamaica it is."

274

He left us alone.

Later Pol stirred in my arms and laughed lazily.

"I almost forgot to tell you, Tom. You're dead."

"Dead?" I echoed.

"Yes. It must have been six weeks ago. You died in the swamp, poor fellow. Fever." She kissed me. Her lips were fierce with possession.

"Squire Bone's dead. You're mine now."

"You didn't have to kill me for that," I protested.

"It wasn't for you I did it or myself. It was for Betty."

"Maybe you'd better explain," I suggested.

"Betty and Ned. You remember Ned at Jamestown? He is her slave, and she's fond of him. He will be a good husband."

"So you told her I was dead that she might marry again," I said.

"Of course."

I considered the matter. Despite myself I was jealous. My wife possessed by another man. And Jimmy—that was the hardest of all. During the long days in the swamp I had thought of my son a great deal. He was part of my life, a part of me, and I was leaving him. That I did so of my own will made the act no easier. That I loved Polly more made me love my son no less. I had comforted myself with the thought that at least the child would not be hurt. He was too little to care or remember. And he would be safe with Betty—and happy. They adored one another. But now Ned.

"I suppose he will be good to Jimmy?" I asked.

"He is a kinder man than you."

"And does Betty really love him?"

Pol opened her eyes wide.

"Haunted?" she asked.

"A little," I admitted.

She considered this. "Betty's at Sidney again," she said at last. "I'm only a guest now, but I think I'll invite you to visit us. Trigg can come later."

"But if Betty believes I'm dead?"

"She won't see you."

275

"Is it safe to leave the swamp?"

"Safer than ghosts."

It did not make much sense to me, but I put myself in Pol's hands. We reached Sidney the next night. Pol took me to Abel's cabin.

"You'll be safe," she said.

For two days I stayed there, waiting, thinking, planning. Most of all I wondered what the future held. "For now we see through a glass darkly," I muttered to myself during those days. At other times I recalled the past, and found it little less inscrutable than the future. What did it all mean? Here I was spending my last days in Virginia very much as I had spent the first ones. I was penniless, living in the shack of a negur slave.

Pol came to me the second night. She led me toward the house.

"Quiet," she whispered.

I looked through a window. The room was soft in the candle-light. Betty was sitting on the same bench upon which she had sat with me through so many evenings. In my old place was Ned. They were talking. As I watched she reached out her hand and touched him. He seized it, bore it to his lips. She laughed as her fingers caressed his mouth. Presently they talked again. Betty's expression was placid. The storm that I had raised when I answered Bacon's call had passed. Her eyes, troubled during those last days when I lived with her, were serene. Her body was no longer tense, but relaxed and quiet.

"Are you still haunted?" Pol asked when we were back in the shack.

I answered truthfully that I was not. I was humbled but not haunted. My last ghost was laid.

A few days after I had looked at my wife for the last time Abel brought Trigg to the shack. The next evening at dusk we started down the river. True to his contract, Jonathan Reap himself picked us up. We reached his ship without incident.

"Just keep below decks and you'll be safe," he told us.

"I've heard Berkeley's jackals are still watching outgoing ships," Trigg objected.

276

The captain's eyes twinkled.

"Jonathan Reap," he said with unction, "is known as an honest man, praise be God. And I've told them I'd do nothing displeasing to the Lord."

Trigg was satisfied, but I was not. Pol had left Sidney the day before, after telling Betty she sailed to join a sister who, having been transported to Jamaica, had wed a rich planter. She was not aboard. I inquired after her.

"Your wife does not have to sail secretly," the captain replied. "She comes aboard as a passenger in the morning."

When Reap was gone Trigg looked at me quizzically.

"Hell, Tom, things happen to you," he chuckled. "Last week you learned you were dead. Tonight you've a new wife."

"Go to sleep," I advised him.

The next morning, as Reap had promised, Pol came aboard. To my surprise Abel was with her. He joined us below decks.

"I didn't think you would leave Miss Betty," I said to him reproachfully.

"She freed me," he reminded me.

"And you refused freedom."

"That's so," he admitted, "but ever since I was a little boy I've wanted to go to the islands Old Eve used to tell me about. I used to shirk my work thinking about them."

So black urchins in America longed for new worlds as did white ones in England. That was explicable. Yet Betty might need Abel's devotion. I told him so.

"She might need yours, too," he reminded me cheerfully. "But I guess she'll get along without either of us, now she's got Mr. Ned."

Before I could think of a reply Trigg intervened.

"I doubt if they like free negurs in Jamaica," he pointed out.

Abel laughed. "That's fine. Miss Betty, Miss Polly and I have been arguing about that for a long time. They say I'm free, but I don't want to be. It looks like I'm going to have my way."

Later, when the ship was well out of the river's mouth, we went on deck. I looked at the receding shore line. Virginia had been

277

kind to me. Most of her men and women were people of sturdy virtues, courageous, loyal. I had found goodness at Sidney and Hickorywood. My heart was heavy.

Presently Polly came. She took my hand. We turned our backs on Virginia's fading shores and looked at the sea's limitless horizon

# Book Three

Book Three

# XIII

## I.

THE "TOPPING MERCHANT" was a galley-built brig designed and built in New England. It had character and like a child it was in the image of its progenitors. It had speed, without the sacrifice of too much cargo space, which translated into human terms means as much caution as is consistent with large profits. Add to these qualities the will and capacity to fight and you have the *Topping Merchant*. And you have the owners and their like, too, and the Captain who sailed her, and his crew. The latter were New England men, tough sailors with little stomach for adventure, but more than willing to defend themselves and their property against any who attacked them. To them the Caribbean was no magic land of romance. It was a market for fish that stank so that it could not be sold elsewhere. The pirates were damned blackguards to be avoided when possible, fought when necessary and hanged when a just God willed. They would run rather than fight, but felt only contempt for a man who would allow his ship to be looted to save his skin.

Jonathan Reap was no such captain. He was a sober man with the Bible ever at hand and the Lord's name on his lips. His mouth was a hard straight line as the Puritan preacher willed it should be, but his blue eyes still held the twinkle that the elves of East Anglia's fens put there at his birth. And mouth and eye ever fought to control his wagging tongue. For he talked incessantly, though it was impossible to foretell if an admonition or an anecdote would be forthcoming. Some of this talk was useful, such as the recollections with which he regaled us one morning

281

after we had outrun a vessel that looked and acted suspiciously like a pirate.

"I've run from them and I've fought with them," he told us, "and at one or the other I've always bested the brutes with one exception."

He paused and fixed an anxious eye on Pol.

"Tell us about the exception," she begged obediently.

The Captain sighed and settled down to his tale.

"They boarded me that time and overcame me. Their Captain was put out because of the trouble I'd put him to, but being a gentleman with a sense of humor, he didn't kill me outright. Instead he ordered my masts cut down and stole my cargo and kidnaped my crew. I was left alone, Captain of a helpless hulk. But I was not quite so abandoned to fate as the rascal thought. I rigged a jury mast of sorts and that, with the aid of the Scriptures which I read for five days, kept me afloat. On the sixth day God took mercy on me. The ship broke up on a reef, but with the aid of an oar I found floating near me in the water I made shore, if bare rock and a strip of sand can be called shore. Most unpleasant place I've ever been, but even so the Lord was good, for I have no doubt I was more comfortable than Jonah was in the whale's belly. I lived there for twenty-one days. It was the rainy season and there were natural bowls in the rocks so I had plenty of water. The heat was the worst thing. That rock must have been the chimney of Hell. Heat spilled out of it and off of it in waves. I took to burrowing in the sand and burying myself like a hog buries himself in mud on a hot summer afternoon."

"Why didn't you get in the water?" I asked.

"I thought of that, but a couple of sharks seemed to have the same idea, so I gave it up. Besides after the first few days I was too weak to enjoy swimming. Then, too, while digging in the sand I found some sort of bug, sort of a sand spider I guess. Anyhow I ate them. That way I got bed and dinner at the same time."

Pol made a face.

"How could you eat them?" she protested.

"They weren't so bad, though a little crisp on the outside and mushy within for my taste. Salty, too. The sea water I suppose."

"Is that all you had to eat?"

"Well, I caught a fish one day, like I was taught in the fens in the old country. He came up to look at me, and I looked back without moving. After a while I put my hand out, an inch at a time. Finally I got it in the water where I tickled the creature's belly. Coming forward all the time, real slow, tickling all the time till I had my thumb in his gills and could jerk him out of the water."

Trigg chuckled.

"Been reading about Ananias in that book of yours?" he inquired.

I was afraid that Captain Reap would take offense, but his blue eyes twinkled and his grim mouth twitched.

"Well, you can learn a lot from Scripture," he declared, "and hunger teaches you patience. Anyhow I stayed alive until God directed Anthony More to find me. He saw what was left of my shirt, flapping atop the oar that I'd made into a flag staff when it had served my purpose as a life boat. So he sent out a small boat and picked me up. Sometimes it seems like the Lord works with curious instruments."

"Who is Anthony More?" I asked.

He looked at me in pity.

"If you stay in this part of the world you will learn that."

"Then why not tell me now?"

"Because I've too much work to do to entertain you all morning, and because to me he is an instrument of the Lord sent to remove me from that rock. I don't speak evil of the Lord's instruments."

"It was an awful experience," Pol told him.

He fixed her with blue eyes. His mouth was grim indeed.

"You may well say it, young lady. Twenty-six days altogether and not one of God's creatures to listen to me, and when they rescued me I was too weak to talk."

He pushed himself to his feet and walked away.

Another time he related the history of the buccaneers. We were nearing the end of our voyage. The Captain pointed towards the horizon.

283

"Tortuga's yonder," he said. "Thirty-five years ago when I first sailed these seas the buccaneers were thicker than ants on its shores. Most of them prefer Jamaica now, where they are safe from the Spaniards. A few like Anthony More are still at Tortuga though."

"So Anthony More is a buccaneer," I interrupted.

"He is an instrument of the Lord created especially to take Jonathan Reap off a hot rock in the Caribbean," retorted the Captain, his twinkling eyes fixed on me, "and the buccaneers are limbs of Satan, though there was a time when in their own way they worked diligently for righteousness. That was years ago when they confined themselves to robbing and killing Spaniards who are not loved by God, Whose kindness extends to sparrows and the beasts of the fields, but not to papists and Spaniards."

"Tell us more about these buccaneers," said Polly hurriedly. She grew restless when the Captain set a course toward the Lord and His ways. The Captain was not deceived.

"You would be better advised to listen to the words of God, mistress," he admonished her, "but woman is on earth to tempt man, and she has proved one of the most successful of her Creator's experiments; so like Father Adam I must fall victim to Eve's blandishments, and indulge my weakness, which is to talk too much. The first buccaneers, I have been told, were Frenchmen who were driven from Hispaniola by the Spanish. They fled to Tortuga and lived there for some twenty years hunting wild hogs, eating the flesh, using the skin for shoes and belts, soaking their shirts and pantaloons in the blood. But these first Frenchmen were papists, so naturally not the scourge of the Lord, and it was not until forty or fifty years ago, when a Huguenot stormed and took possession of the island, that the huntsmen took to the sea.

"They were pirates from the beginning. There is no hiding that fact, for they attacked merchant ships, which is a great sin in the eyes of God and Jonathan Reap; and they sacked cities, too, on the islands and even the Spanish Main. But only Spanish ships and Spanish towns, and I am sure that St. Peter, who observes and keeps an invoice of all such matters, has made proper note of that.

"At first these sea-going hog slayers were mostly French, but gradually the English and Dutch joined the game. It got so bad that at last the Spanish sent ships and troops from Hispaniola to clean out the nest. They succeeded temporarily. That was when the buccaneers shifted their headquarters to Jamaica.

"Jamaica was a poor place, Port Royal and Spanish Town being only a cluster of miserable houses. The English captured it when Cromwell, who is now with the Lord, sent a fleet against it. But having taken it they did nothing more until the buccaneers came. The Governor welcomed them, because they promised protection against possible attack by the Spaniards, and because they brought with them the goods and the wealth which they had stolen. Since then Jamaica has prospered until today Port Royal has more taverns than homes and more brothels than taverns; and there are times when there is more gold and treasure there than even taverns and brothels can absorb.

"There must be near two thousand English in Jamaica today, besides the negurs, mulattoes and a few Spanish. Plantations are growing up around Port Royal and Spanish Town. That is where my fish go. But times are changing. Jamaica grows respectable when Henry Morgan himself serves as deputy governor, and the Governor, Lord Carlisle, discourages attacks on the Dons.

"So what do the buccaneers do? They abandon the Lord's work, which any Christian can plainly see is to attack Spanish papists, and rob indiscriminately. I tell you even a God-fearing English protestant is no longer safe from them. Witness my sojourn on that rock off Tortuga."

"From which you were rescued by a buccaneer," I reminded him.

"By Anthony More," he amended. "He is one of the old-fashioned ones. He attacks only slavers and Spaniards, whom he hates, as Drake hated them, and Hawkins and Grenville. They were pirates, too, if robbing Spanish papists is piracy, which it clearly could not be, being the work of the Lord.

"But it is more than a mere change of government policy that

285

has ruined the buccaneers. The first ones were simple men, ignorant hunters who lived on wild hogs, and when they took to the sea they remained simple men, except that they changed from hogs to the Spaniards. True, they did not eat his flesh, but they have been known to tan his hide when he was over-reticent concerning the whereabouts of hidden treasure, and many a time they have bathed their shirts and their pantaloons in his blood.

"But as time passed and the fame of the buccaneers spread their nature changed. Gentlemen from all over Europe came to Port Royal—broken-down gentlemen, intent on mending their fortunes, officers who had been careless with company funds, men of fashion who fled the bailiff and debtors' jails, poets whose verse was less light than their fingers, barristers who knew only sufficient law to flee from it, even churchmen whose necks chafed under a clerical collar; these and many others came for their health, for adventure and a quick fortune. But they are a wicked lot. An Englishman is no safer from them than a heathen Spaniard, whom the Lord despises, for they bow down to graven images. No, there is no difference now in fact, as there never was in law: buccaneers are cursed, thieving pirates, except for a few who still follow the old ways, such as Anthony More."

But for all his knowledge of the Caribbean and its unsavory characters Captain Reap had never heard of Bill Smith.

"He came out ten years since, you say," he growled disapprovingly, "a gentleman, and Smith is not his real name. I know the breed. A thorough-going scoundrel no doubt, whom the Lord has forgotten and whom you would do well to likewise banish from memory. I never heard of him, but if he is not hanged or killed by this time—and ten years is a long life for such rogues—you will no doubt find him sooner or later in a tavern at Port Royal, gaming away his money, or wasting it to buy finery for some dark-skinned wench whom the Lord intended should be naked in the jungles of Africa."

Nor though equally voluble on the subject could Reap give me any news of Edward Cousin.

"I don't know slave traders," he snapped, and his eyes were hard as his mouth. "Damned canting hypocrites, who sell humans and whine it is the Lord's work because the poor devils are thus brought to Christ. God forbid that Jonathan Reap should say aught that is good of a Jesuit but even they have not sunk to such deceit. They, too, carry the gospel to the savage, but they do not accompany it with whip and shackle. No, I do not know your Edward Cousin, but if he is in the African trade I would even prefer your buccaneering friend Smith.

"I am afraid," he added severely, "that you have evil friends, unloved of the Lord."

He was somewhat mollified, however, when I assured him that Cousin was not a friend, but an enemy that I intended some day to kill.

The *Topping Merchant* reached Jamaica without mishap. Port Royal surpassed Captain Reap's picture of it. I have never known beauty and ugliness, luxury and squalor, to exist so close together. The natural grandeur of the sea and the mountains was in no sharper contrast to the squalor of the town than the magnificent adventurers, swaggering through taverns in all their finery, were to their less fortunate brothers, whose luck at sea or gaming had been poor. The condition of the women was one of even greater extremes. Few of them were white, but blacks and mulattoes were plentiful. If one of them caught the fancy of a man who was in funds, or who had recently helped loot a ship that carried such stuff as women fancy, she would be bedecked in finery that fashionable ladies of Europe might envy. I have seen black wenches in gowns of French silk trimmed in the laces of Valencia. Costumes sent to the wives of Spanish or French governors not infrequently graced the velvet body of mulatto or octoroon. Jewels, too, glittered on the creatures around their necks, on their arms, even their ankles. And how their barbaric spirits reveled in such finery. They preened themselves like peacocks as they strutted in the brothels before their less fortunate sisters, or went through the antics of a lady for the delectation of the magician who had so transformed them. But alas, their apotheosis was short lived. Their benefactors would snatch their finery away as suddenly as they had bestowed it to give it to a newer Venus, or buy rum, or to gamble it away. The next day the princess would be a beggar maid or worse, half naked in a few rags, already hungry, whining for a farthing, or likely as not under a table, a dark-skinned bitch, watching eagerly for a bone or a caress.

There was gentry of a sort in Jamaica: the civil officials, a handful of naval officers, a few merchants and the masters of the plantations. These folk kept largely to themselves, though the men might be met at the brothels and the women seen in the carriages as they rode along the rough roads.

I soon learned to recognize Henry Morgan, best known of the buccaneers. He was a gross man who dressed richly, wore his hair to his shoulders and affected fiercely curled mustaches. But all his grandeur, with the Sir which His Majesty had bestowed upon him to boot, could not hide the thick cruel lips and heavy jowls. Although a court of fops in London might fawn on him as they hailed him as the successor to Francis Drake, men in the dives of Port Royal knew him better. He was a resourceful leader—they admitted that. He had a shrewd brain, a ready wit, a heavy hand and a lion's courage. But for all that he was at bottom only an avaricious, tight-fisted Welsh peasant who cheated his friends as readily as he robbed his enemies, and stole the treasure that his men had bought with their blood. What I saw and heard of Henry Morgan did not arouse in me enthusiasm to follow in his footsteps. To tell the truth, as the weeks slipped by, whatever inclination I had felt for piracy evaporated.

We lived at an inn which had the single virtue of being less squalid than the others. All the arrangements for the future were left in Trigg's hands. From time to time he reported negotiations for our joining some ship or other, but they always broke down at the suggestion that Pol be taken aboard. A woman was bad luck.

"Leave her here," Trigg advised. "She will be safe with Abel while we are gone."

I would not do it. Polly and I had been thwarted too often to tempt fate further. We would stay together.

One day Trigg broke in upon us with tidings of success. A captain had been found who would accept us all. He was a Captain

Crewe who had studied sufficient theology at Geneva to convince himself that he was among the elect, and consequently beyond the tricks of evil fortune; and he had a woman of his own from whom he could not tear himself, so he would welcome Pol aboard.

To Trigg's amazement, and to tell the truth my own surprise, I refused to go. Trigg argued in vain. Finally he went, shaking his head over my vagaries, but swearing continued friendship.

When Trigg was gone, Polly and I faced the future. We had been idling for weeks. Now we held a council. I had nothing better to offer than a new start on the North American frontier, but Polly was against it.

"What else is there?" I asked.

"Remain here, but as an honest man rather than a pirate. I still have a little money left. Use it to buy the stuff the buccaneers bring in. You can turn a good profit by disposing of it to honest merchants, men like Jonathan Reap."

"The day of the buccaneer is about over," I pointed out.

"A few years are all we need. Then we will buy a plantation and become sugar planters."

"You have thought it all out?"

"Naturally."

I agreed to try Pol's scheme, but insisted upon one condition. We must be married.

"While you were gazing into the water and planning how we would grow rich I looked into the sky and thought of that," I told her wistfully.

Her lips brushed my hand.

"But each of us is married—to someone else," she said. "At least you are, and I too, I suppose, unless John Denham has persuaded the courts that I am dead."

But I had resolved to ignore that. The old life was over, this was a new one in a new world, one in which Polly Bragg must be my wife. I had lost my son. Pol must give me another. I explained all these things and more, although less would have been enough. Polly was not hard to persuade.

We were married in a chapel that faced the sea—nearly fifteen years to the day since I had first asked Pol to be my wife. Abel

289

was there and the rector's wife, who sniffed and vowed there had never been such a sweet pure wife.

## 2.

Polly's idea proved sound. As she had pointed out, the buccaneers came ashore eager to turn their loot into money. But as official zeal against piracy increased the merchants and planters grew more and more reluctant to deal directly with the robbers. This gave me my opportunity. The docks, the taverns and the brothels were my offices. I was always ready to chaffer with a man who needed a little silver. But I did not take advantage of my customers when they were drunk, and I kept my word once it was pledged. Thus, though I drove hard bargains, I gained among thieves a reputation for honesty, and as time passed men came to seek me out.

But though business prospered and I found my work interesting, my real life was in a small brightly painted house that stood just outside Port Royal. Polly was there. With Abel and a small negur lass that I bought her she played housewife and devoted spouse. Together we roamed the countryside and the seashore. And we spent many long happy days hunting for our sugar plantation; for Pol clung stubbornly to the idea that eventually we must become planters.

"It's safer than your illegal trade," she explained, "and besides you must be a landholder if you expect to be counted among the gentry."

I spent hours telling Pol that I despised the gentry and had no desire to be one of them. She listened patiently, but I did not convince her.

"I know what they've done to you," she would say sympathetically, "and I know how you feel. You want to hurt them. Very well. I'll even help you, but to do it you have to be one of them. You can't fight men who are on top of you."

"You calculate too much," I told her. "I just want to fight."

"Very well. You do the fighting and let me do the calculating." It was a sensible arrangement, and one which I was generally

290

content to follow, but there were times when I rebelled against being managed. On one such occasion, after a furious argument, I left home swearing that I would never return.

In a blind towering rage I went to a brothel, determined to take the first black wench who caught my fancy. But first I got drunk. By that time my anger had subsided, and I had relented sufficiently to consider going home again. But not until I had had a woman. I had just pulled a mestee onto my lap when Pol entered. Abel was with her. She carried a knife in one hand and a horsewhip in the other. She threatened to knife anyone who interfered with her. She used the whip on my wench. No one interfered—not with Abel standing in the doorway grinning, flexing his muscles. As for me, I was too amazed to move. Moreover, I was drunk, and more than half relieved. I had not really wanted the woman—I wanted no woman in those days but Polly.

When she was done Pol threw silver to the squealing frightened negress.

"Be quiet," she said. "There's more than you would have had from him." She suddenly grinned and a gamin's light sparkled in her eyes. "And it was worth more to me than it would have been to him. I had more fun."

Then she came to me. Instead of berating me as I expected, and which I was prepared to resist, she dropped onto my lap. Her arms wound around my neck. Her voice mimicked the wheedling tones of the tavern girls.

"Take me, master, instead of that baggage," she begged.

The whores and rogues around us laughed.

"For God's sake, come home," I muttered.

The next morning I protested that she had made me ridiculous. But Pol was unrepentant.

"Betty left you when you rushed away from her in a temper and fell straight in the arms of Mary Trigg. Isn't my way better than that?"

"Yes," I admitted.

"Then I'll horsewhip any trollop who looks at you."

Her words were grim but her eyes laughed and her voice was

tender. I forgave her, even though for months I was the victim of waterfront jibes.

But Polly did more than keep house, wander with me through the country and guard me with a jealous eye. For although I purchased my goods in the dives near the harbor, my customers frequently came to my home. There Polly helped me; and many a close-bargaining merchant paid a few pounds extra after a good dinner made better by the pleasure of Pol's company.

"I could buy cheaper from the rogues who steal it," one of my guests, a hard-bitten New Englander, once complained.

"But then you could not have dinners with me and tell me about your marvelous adventures," Pol told him.

The old fellow—he must have been seventy—snorted, but his weather-beaten face twisted into a wry grin.

"I'm just from the Guinea Coast and the Middle Passage, ma'am. I haven't talked to a white woman for months. Maybe you're right. Maybe you make it a pleasure to be cheated."

"Of course I do," Pol agreed.

I recall another occasion even more clearly. It is one of those quiet memories that serves as a milestone to the past. Our guest was a French trader. For him to be in Jamaica at all was a violation of the law, so I had driven an uncommon hard bargain.

"Do not think that I am such a fool as I appear," he implored in mock humility when the business was done and he lingered over a cold punch Pol had brought. "I consent to be robbed only for the pleasure of feasting my eyes on a beautiful woman. I drink madam's health."

I smiled at Pol over the rim of my glass, and as I looked at her I was like a blind man who sees for the first time: Polly *was* beautiful.

The child I had romped and quarreled with in the dust of Saltash, the girl who had played so cruelly with me at Denham, the maid I had taken at Hickorywood was now a woman. Her large mouth, still too heavy for the heart-shaped face, was rich in promise, and her eyes as they moved secretively under drooping lashes or opened wide in surprise were ever-changing pools of laughter and passion. But despite eyes and mouth Polly's beauty

292

was not the divine loveliness of face and form that stirs men's senses and makes them reverent slaves until they have had their way and learned that their goddess is after all only a creature of bone and muscle. Polly's was a more evasive charm, that of a gamin day in April, when wind, cloud, rain and sunshine combine to weave out of light and shadow shifting patterns of loveliness.

As I stared at her that evening she smiled and swayed slightly toward me. Her full body was that of a woman approaching the high morning of her womanhood. Her flesh was brown from the sun and firm from work. My hand trembled so that the punch splashed over the side of the glass. I could hardly wait until the Frenchman was gone. At last he left us. I took Pol in my arms.

"You *are* beautiful," I whispered.

She pressed against me.

"Beautiful for you," she said.

Three years after our arrival in Jamaica, Pol and I were still in our small house on the outskirts of Port Royal. Nevertheless I was a man of substance. Back of my house were well-built sheds that were fat with goods. I was well known; even government officials occasionally dealt with me. But though growing rich, I was not yet safe. A certain John Hendon, planter and member of the Governor's Council, explained it to me. He had just bought some goods, and was sipping a glass of French brandy that Pol had given him.

"Excellent stuff," he said. "A pity it has to be smuggled."

"But it doesn't have to be," Pol protested. "It can be bought from English merchants."

"At a price, yes. But it's too high."

"Then let them bring it down."

"They could, of course, and as a planter I favor that remedy, but the merchants have a different one."

"What is theirs?"

"Hang the buccaneers and, I regret to say, those who encourage them, such as your husband here."

"Then you'll have to hang me, too," Pol cried.

Hendon bowed.

"Preposterous, madam. You will make a charming widow, and on the Council we are gentlemen."

"He meant it," Pol said when Hendon was gone.

"Part of it at least," I replied shortly, recalling how he had eyed her.

"Then get out of it, Tom, while there is time. Buy a plantation."

I knew that Polly was right. But I could not bring myself to make the change. I said that I knew nothing about sugar, and that I despised the land-holding gentry too much to be one of them. But these were only excuses. The truth was that I had come to like the waterfront—its smells, its sounds, its sights, its people. Even its perils.

So, though Pol urged me, I postponed a decision. I was still hesitating when Trigg came back. That was in the fall of 1680, the first day of the rainy season.

I had just come home from the wharf. It was growing dark. Pol and I stood at a window watching the rain. After weeks of yellow sunshine and clear blue skies, the gusty, gray, wet evening was pleasant. It wrapped one as in soft wet wool, soothing tired nerves. Yet in a curious way it stirred the blood.

"It quiets and excites me at the same time," Pol said.

I put an arm around her and we stood staring into the semi-darkness. Three rain-drenched figures came into view.

"I hope they aren't coming to see you," Pol said.

"Not likely in such weather."

But I was wrong. They came to our door. Abel let them in. One of them was Trigg.

"Hide us," Trigg begged, after we had greeted him.

"Who from?"

"The officials."

"But why?"

"There's no time to explain. They're searching now."

"Take them to one of the sheds," I told Abel.

"Tom!"

Polly's voice was sharp. Abel paused.

"If they are found here, Tom, you know what it means."

"But Trigg's our friend," I protested.

294

"You know what it means," she repeated.

I did know. It meant ruin, maybe the gallows for me. For Pol it meant being left penniless and alone.

"Very well," I said. "It is your choice."

"Go somewhere else," she told Trigg.

He stared at her in bewilderment.

"But, lass—"

"Hurry," she interrupted.

Her face was white, her hands were clenched. She did not look at Trigg.

He hesitated for a moment, then spoke heavily.

"I don't blame you. It's comfortable here. You've got something to lose."

Pol did not reply.

"Good-by," Trigg said to me.

I could not trust myself to speak. He took my hand.

"Never mind, lad. We'll make out."

One of Trigg's companions laughed harshly.

When they were gone we went back to the window. Our late guests stood huddled in the rain.

"Why don't they do something?" Pol muttered.

"What can they do? They have no friends."

"Please, Tom. Don't hate me."

"I don't hate you."

For some minutes we just stood there at the window, and Trigg and his companions stood outside. It was evident from their gestures that they were arguing the advisability of making for the mountains.

"Why don't they do it?" Pol cried.

"Maroons."

She shuddered.

Another minute or two and she could stand it no longer.

"The damned fools," she said fiercely as she ran to the door. A moment later she led the three men toward the sheds.

"I knew you couldn't do it," I told her when she came in.

Her gray eyes were bleak as the skies and almost as wet.

"Maybe I've just gotten you hanged," she said.

295

"Where did you hide them?"

"There is no place where they can be hidden. You know that. They're out there sitting on a bale of goods. Our only hope is to prevent a search."

"But how?"

"Use our wits and anything else God's given us."

"Careful," I warned.

"Careful be damned. It's too late for that."

At that moment there was a loud knock at the door. While we waited I saw Pol prepare for battle. Her eyes, clouded from anger and fear, grew clear. Her body relaxed. She smiled. I too made my preparations. I charged a pair of pistols and laid them on a near-by table.

Abel announced our guest. It was Henry Morgan himself. My heart sank. Morgan was a hard shrewd man. Moreover, he was wet and visibly out of temper.

"I want information," he said.

Pol curtsied.

"Indeed, Sir Henry. But you are wet. A glass of brandy."

Morgan looked at her and frowned less ferociously. I recalled with a mixture of relief and uneasiness that the ex-buccaneer was reported to have two weaknesses: women and greed. The latter often prevented his gratifying his passion for the former. But if a woman could be had cheaply— Pol looked at him from under half-closed lashes. Her body swayed toward him.

"It would be kind of you, ma'am," muttered Morgan ungraciously.

Pol poured out the brandy with her own hand. Morgan drank it. After that he turned to business. He was looking for "three damned bloody pirates." One of them was Ralph Crewe himself, just returned from a three years' voyage. During that time he, Crewe, had not only reaped a rich harvest in the Caribbean, but he had also crossed the Isthmus into the South Seas, where he raided unprotected towns on the Spanish Main. As a consequence the Spanish government had protested so vigorously that instructions had been sent from London that if Crewe came within British jurisdiction he must be arrested at all cost. When news came that the pirate was in Port Royal Morgan himself had undertaken to capture him. He had flushed him right enough. Not an hour ago. Even taken a score of his men; but Crewe himself and two companions had escaped. Knowing that I dealt with such rogues Morgan had come to me.

"I haven't seen them," I said.

"I dare say you are telling the truth, but considering your business I am sure you will not protest if my men, who are outside, make a search."

Before I could answer Pol took command.

"Tom," she cried, "we did see them."

I stared at her. Had she changed her mind again? Was she going to betray Trigg? Not, I told myself, after undertaking to protect him. I edged toward the table where the pistols lay. Pol, as if divining my purpose, spoke more rapidly.

"Remember, it wasn't a quarter of an hour ago. We were watching the rain, when three men came up the street. Why, they even stopped outside our house and argued. One pointed toward the house, but the others seemed to disagree. In the end they went on. For the mountains I suppose."

"Pointed toward your house?" Morgan repeated suspiciously.

Pol was playing a dangerous game and she played it coolly.

"Why, yes. I suppose they thought of asking us to hide them. As you said, it's well known my husband deals with buccaneers."

Her candor was disarming. While Morgan considered this new information, she plunged on.

"But, Sir Henry, my husband does not do business with such men as Ralph Crewe."

"And why not?" growled Morgan.

"It is too dangerous," replied Polly bluntly. "But we waste time. I propose that you stay here with me, while Tom leads your men in pursuit of the pirates."

"I need no one to lead my men."

Pol laughed gaily.

"Sir Henry Morgan needs no defense," she told him, "but my husband knows the rogues' hide-outs. Meantime if they *should*

297

be foolish enough to sneak back here, I'll wager you and I could handle the three of them."

Morgan wavered.

"Why are you so anxious to help the authorities?"

"None need the favor of the law so much as those who flaunt it; and I would give a great deal for a protector such as Sir Henry Morgan."

As Pol said these last words there was such a bold invitation in her voice and glance that Morgan was taken aback. He looked at me in quick confusion, as though I had already discovered him in my wife's arms. For my part I was angry and dismayed. But I was still determined to see Pol's game unfold. She had said she would fight Morgan with her wits or any other gift God had given her. Well, God had given to her generously and she seemed to be in a profligate mood with His gifts. Perhaps, presently, she would even use her wits. I would wait a little.

When I said nothing Morgan's heavy lips curled in an ugly sneer. He thought he knew what I was. But he was a crafty Welshman who did not take unnecessary risks.

"Do you agree with your wife?" he asked.

"We need protection," I told him.

He turned his back on me. When he spoke to Pol he dropped all fencing. His voice and words were those of a man who chaffers with a trull over price.

"You understand, my wench, that I am not to be cozened."

Pol looked him full in the face and laughed brazenly.

"It's well known that Henry Morgan boards his prizes," she said, and turned to me. Her voice and manner were almost as contemptuous as Morgan's had been.

"Take Sir Henry's men, Tom, and search for the pirates. And be thorough. Don't be home before midnight."

So she meant to play her game through. I walked to the table and picked up one of the guns. Morgan's hand went to his sword in quick alarm.

"What the Hell's this," he roared.

"Surely you don't expect him to go after Ralph Crewe un-

298

armed," Pol said quickly. "Hurry now, Tom. Please, you must do as I say."

I had intended to kill Morgan, but something in Pol's voice stayed me. Possibly she did have some trick in mind. Ever since childhood her wits had been quicker than mine.

"You're an over-hasty bludgeon," she had chided once. "Won't you ever lean to parry before you thrust."

Was I over-hasty now? While I hesitated I chanced to catch a glimpse of Abel. He was standing just beyond a half-open door, a long knife in his hand. Doubtless he had been there ever since Morgan's arrival, waiting in case of need.

"I'll go," I told Pol.

Morgan grunted and dropped into a chair. As I left the room Pol was filling his glass. He made an obscene remark. Her laugh was warm.

I drew Abel away from the door.

"Keep an eye on them. If Morgan tries to take her kill him."

The big negur nodded.

"Even if she seems willing."

"Sure," Abel said, and returned to his post, apparently unmoved at the prospect of murdering the most famous and dangerous buccaneer of his day.

For hours I led the soldiers a wild goose chase through the dark soaking night. I got home just after midnight. Abel opened the door.

"Trouble?" I whispered.

He shook his head.

Pol and Morgan greeted me affably. Even the report of the failure of my mission seemed a cause of merriment rather than chagrin. Presently Morgan heaved himself from his chair. He bowed over Pol's outstretched hand.

"A remarkable evening, madam, a damned remarkable evening."

"You must honor us again."

"Devil take it, but I intend to."

He turned to me.

"And I've no doubt we'll understand one another, Bone," he said condescendingly.

299

"Well," I said to Pol when Morgan was gone, "how did you manage to keep away from him?"

"And how do you know I did manage?" she retorted contemptuously.

I was tired, cold and wet. For hours I had been tortured by the fear that Abel might fail. I was still puzzled by the turn events had taken—by Pol's game. In short I was in no mood to be baited.

"Because, damn you," I shouted, "if your whore's scheme had worked Abel's knife would now be sticking between Henry Morman's ribs."

I expected Pol to defend herself and was prepared to overwhelm her with words, or if need be with the beating that she deserved. To my amazement her coldness vanished.

"You told Abel to watch us?" she asked slowly.

"Yes. To keep you from turning slut," I shouted.

She came to me.

"I thought— I thought—"

"You thought I'd save my skin by turning cuckold."

"Forgive me."

She was begging, but I would not be so easily appeased.

"Oh, I can forgive you that," I told her. "God knows that between you and Morgan I cut a sorry figure, but what I find it hard to understand or forgive is your willingness."

"Willingness?"

"To give yourself to him."

"Not willing, Tom. Before God not willing."

"Ready, then."

"Yes, I was ready. And do you find that so hard to understand and forgive?"

"Yes."

"Then you're a blind fool who cannot understand love. To keep Morgan from finding Trigg and the other pirates, and seeing you hang, I'd be not only Morgan's whore, as you call it, but that of every man in Jamaica."

I resisted my impulse to take her in my arms.

"And yet you were angry at me for seeming to fall in with your plans."

300

"Of course. It's one thing for me to be willing for your sake. It's another for you to permit it. I did despise you for that."

I resisted my impulse no longer; but when I had kissed Pol, she asked a question.

"And what did you tell Abel to do to *me* after he had killed Morgan?" she asked.

"Nothing."

"Don't you care then about virtue in your wife?"

I kissed her again.

"You have much beside virtue," I told her.

But Pol was serious.

"Wouldn't it have mattered?" she persisted.

"God, yes, but we belong to one another, Pol. Things can matter, but not enough to separate us."

She sighed happily.

"I was sure of it, Tom. That is why I was willing to do it."

That reminded me that I still did not know what had occurred while I was gone.

"How the devil did you satisfy Morgan?" I asked.

"I found something he wanted more than he wanted me."

"Tell me about it."

"For all his title and high office Henry Morgan is but a greedy, thieving Welsh thief. When you were gone I played for time, and in doing so asked how such a great man came to be out on a stormy night. He admitted, even boasted, that he had taken charge because he had information that Crewe had cached his treasure somewhere on the north of the Island. Morgan intended to know where. He knew ways to make men talk. Crewe would be glad to tell his secret in return for a quick death. Then he, Sir Henry, would have the treasure.

"Before Morgan started to talk I had no plan other than the hateful one that you suspected. But the man's greed was so evident that I saw another way. I hinted that you might be able to locate Crewe, and that together we might make a nice profit. He demurred at first, not out of honesty but because he thought to have all the treasure himself. In the end I convinced him that he could only reach Crewe through us. So we formed a partnership. You had best get Crewe in now so I can explain to him, too."

Crewe readily admitted his identity, and Pol explained the agreement reached with Morgan. Crewe was to reveal where the treasure lay. I would fetch and sell it, and Sir Henry would see to it that the officials were blind. For this Sir Henry was to take half the profits. Pol stipulated we must have half the remainder. What was left would belong to the pirates. Crewe cursed prodigiously, but in the end he agreed. His surrender was made more palatable by my promise to cheat Morgan in the final settlement. To my amazement Pol protested against this. It was when we were finally alone.

"Morgan's dangerous," she said. "Don't try to cheat him. Our share's enough without that."

"It's not more money I want. I'm getting even for the way he looked at you. And that reminds me: I still don't know how you put him off. I doubt if Henry Morgan is the man to let go one thing merely because he grasps at another."

"He hasn't exactly let go. He's just waiting. He believes that since we are partners there will be plenty of time."

"Did you give him reason to believe it?"

"I suppose so."

"But, damn it, Pol, Abel or I can't always be at hand."

"Of course you can't, and that's why you've got to get out of this business with the pirates. Deal with Crewe. I can put Morgan off that long. Then buy a plantation and we'll be gentry and laugh at a man like Henry Morgan. But while we are outside the law we are at his mercy. Both of us."

That is why I finally quit acting as a broker of pirate loot and became a West Indian planter. And if I never became quite the sort of gentleman Bill Smith was, neither was I so great a scoundrel as William Berkeley or such a villain as Edward Cousin. As for Polly, no lady in Jamaica possessed half her graces.

## 3.

The business with Crewe proved almost fantastically profitable. When it was finished I found myself a very rich man. And for a little time I was heady with success.

"It's nonsense to quit trade," I complained to Pol. "Give me another year or two, and I'll cover you with jewels."

"Another year or two of such business and I shan't need jewels from you. I shall have already had them from such men as Morgan," she reminded me.

My bubble burst.

"Get your plantation," I said. "But I warn you, I am a man of business not a farmer. I'll be no good as a planter."

"You don't have to be. Trigg will manage the place for us."

"Trigg?"

"Yes. He has had enough of the sea. He wants to live with us."

"You're a scheming witch. But what am _I_ to do in this new life?"

"Just be a gentleman."

"Good. I'll fight cocks and keep a negur wench."

"I'll risk even that."

We called the plantation Saltash. It was beyond Port Royal in the direction of Spanish Town. Trigg bought cattle and slaves and hired an overseer who knew both blacks and sugar. Pol supervised the building of our house and laid out gardens.

The house glistened white against the blue sky. Around it ran a veranda supported by wrought iron pillars that were shipped from England. The windows were large, with glass panes and shutters of bamboo to close against sun or rain. Within were floors and woodwork of mahogany, curtains of brocade and satin, covered furniture from France. House negurs, under Abel's stern supervision, moved about silently. Other blacks worked in Pol's gardens, where flowers grew in profusion and even trees and bushes burst into blossom.

In the midst of it all Pol moved, gay and contented. She savored to its full every hour of ease and luxury. But she never took it quite seriously. Nor would the gamin give way entirely before the lady. This worried Abel. Occasionally he even ventured a remonstrance.

"You're a lady, Miss Polly," he would remind her.

"Am I, Abel? Do you remember when we hoed corn together at Hickorywood, and you called me Pol?" she was apt to retort.

"Sure," Abel would admit.

"What makes a lady?" she asked him once.

He thought it over.

"White skin, land and negurs, I guess," he said finally, "and maybe feeling better than other people."

"Well, I can manage the first three, but I'm not so sure about the last. You see, I don't feel superior. Not any more, at least, as I did when I was a princess."

"You, a princess?" Abel stammered.

"Yes, back in England, where I lived in the kitchen. I was sure of it. A princess under an evil spell. Of course, other people treated me as Jane Bragg's bastard, but I knew better. I was very superior in those days."

Abel shook his head.

"I don't know about princesses, but you ought to act more like a lady," he told her.

"I'll try, Abel, for your sake," she promised.

But the gentry of Port Royal and the surrounding country did not share Abel's qualms. Saltash was a rich plantation, Pol a gay, gracious hostess. They accepted her hospitality and asked no questions.

Only one misfortune marred our happiness. During the second year at Saltash Pol announced she would bear a child. It was born dead, murdered by a drunken, incompetent butcher from Hanover, who styled himself physician. For a while we despaired of Pol's life, too. But she fought gallantly and recovered. She asked for her child. I had been by her bedside for three days; I was tired and dull. I could think of no way to spare her. I told her the bald truth. Her eyes filled with tears.

"I'll have others," she said.

"A dozen," I promised as cheerfully as I could; but I did not mean it. I was frightened. Pol was enough. I did not want to risk losing her.

When Pol was up again she hid whatever sorrow she felt. Life at Saltash was resumed on the old level, and I was contented again, and, with Pol safe beside me, secure.

Yes, I was contented. Why not? I was rich. I had a home and men and women to serve me. I had Pol. And yet there were moments of nostalgia when I wondered if the quest was more gratifying than the grail. Polly Bragg, the lean hard field hand at Hickorywood was less lovely and far less compliant than the ripe, luxurious woman who was my wife at Saltash. Saltash itself surpassed the most extravagant dreams of my boyhood—but what was I to do for dreams? Sometimes I wondered if a soul, freshly out of purgatory, might not look at the limpid peace of paradise and sigh because there was naught beyond the throne of God. Such moods were infrequent. When they came I spent days in the haunts of the buccaneers. I no longer did business there but I found peace.

I heard strange tales too. Stories of the maroons. These were the former slaves of the Spaniards that had fled Jamaica when the English approached, leaving their negurs to escape to the mountains of the interior. There they lived by hunting, fishing the streams and occasionally stealing. They reverted to the savagery of Africa, to which they added the vices and the cunning that they had learned from the white man. They practiced their magic unmolested by Christianity, until it grew rank as the tropics in which it throve.

One night I heard a man mutter hoarsely, "The goat without horns." I saw Betty again crouched at Pol's feet, saw the knife glitter in Pol's hand, heard the throb of Abel's drum, and shuddered. But while my fears were for the past there were many in Jamaica who shuddered as they looked into the future, or even into the present. People mysteriously disappeared from time to time, especially black children from outlying plantations. The drums would be heard from the mountains, slaves would huddle together, sheep helpless before the wolf; white men moved in grim-lipped groups. During my years at Port Royal I met no one who had witnessed anything with his own eyes, but when the wind blew from the mountains I heard the moaning of drums.

However, most of the talk on the waterfront concerned not the land but the sea. Valor and villainy were regarded with equal respect, and a good liar was as amusing as an honest man. The past was glorious, the future golden and the present could always be softened in a mist of alcohol.

But there was one cloud that marred this sunshine of careless villainy. Men from the slavers became more numerous each year. They were taciturn and sullen. They did not boast of what they had seen and done. When they were drunk they whispered through tight lips. They had money, but they smelled black. The buccaneers did not like them, quarreled with them, insulted them, but still their shadow grew larger, heavier. It darkened the land and the sea, from the Guinea Coast to the Islands of the Caribbean. As time passed I grew to feel that buccaneer and slave trader, as they brawled in the dives of Port Royal, struggled for the soul of the Indies. A fantastic idea, but I could not rid myself of it. The buccaneers were a cruel vicious lot, robbers and murderers, but in their way they represented a world of men who were free, masters of their own damned souls. The slave trade meant bondage. Bondage of the black to the land, but bondage of the land to the black, too, and bondage of the white to fear of the men he had made into cattle—fear that was in his eyes when the music of the maroons spilled out of the mountains.

Just as my fancy saw buccaneers and slavers struggle for supremacy, so two names emerged as symbols of the two camps. Names of men who though yet alive had already grown into figures of legend. Names about which clung tales by the hundred, tales shouted in defiance, or muttered fearfully as furtive glances darted into the shadows.

One of these names was Anthony More, the last of the true buccaneers, the heir to the sea dogs of Elizabeth. The Spanish tried to dislodge him from Tortuga. He outfought and outthought them. When they believed that he must flee, he attacked, when they fortified themselves against assault he struck elsewhere. He robbed them and taunted them, and when English officials

306

looked down long noses, disapproving and disavowing, he laughed at them, too.

But Anthony More did not always laugh. He fought another foe with greater vigor than he did the Spaniard. This was the slaver. Nor in this case did he confine himself to the Dons. Even the English were included. I know. As I listened to the stories of buccaneer and pirate I could almost fancy that there were two Anthony Mores. The buccaneers' More was a figure out of by-gone days of chivalry. He played the game of war with the punctilious Don, punctiliously. He was generous in victory, un-resentful of reverses, gallant at all times. But the slavers saw another man—cold, ruthless, ferocious; not a man at all but a devil, they swore, as they whispered dark tales of things that occurred on Anthony More's ships and in his island fastness.

"He will ruin the trade," I heard a furtive-eyed Portugee whimper; but a sharp-nosed New Englander was more hopeful.

"Not while Edward Cousin lives," he declared stoutly.

Edward Cousin was the most powerful figure in the growing slave trade just as Anthony More towered over his brothers in that last twilight of the buccaneers. I first heard Cousin's name in a brothel. A mulatto wench begged for a copper. I had none but shoved an untouched glass of French brandy at her. She shook her head.

"He says I mustn't."

"Who is he?" I asked indifferently.

"Master Cousin."

My heart stood still as my brain traveled backward into time. An English girl at Plymouth, a half-cast in Jamaica. I did not need to hear her story. I did not want to.

"Come with me," I said, and took her to Saltash.

"She is Evalyn," Polly exclaimed when I told her. We called her that and took her into our service.

When I next heard Cousin's name it was in fulsome praise. A minister spoke it. He was a poor creature, in a state of con-stantly bubbling flatulence that, defying nature, found relief through his mouth. He mistook the foul gas for eloquence. He was a louse who hid himself in the oily creases of the rich. He could not distinguish them from God. We were in the Governor's mansion. I had condemned the slave trade.

"There are abuses," he admitted, "but when carried on by godly men the heathen are brought to God."

"Good men," I ventured, "but scarcely what you call godly."

"Aye, godly men, like Edward Cousin. You have heard of him?"

I admitted that I had.

"Then you know that the Lord has smiled upon him, made him rich through His many favors."

"We were talking about the slave trade."

"To be sure, and fortunate is the son of Ham who falls to Cousin's lot, for he shows them the way to the Lord. I am told that His words are made known on the slave ship itself, and that God is the first civilized word that the heathen learn."

He closed his eyes.

"I can see it," he murmured. "The black children learning their first lesson, taking the first halting step toward the heavenly throne."

I could see it, too. The poor creatures, frightened, hungry, thirsty, chained flank to flank in the dark noisome hold, moving restlessly, gibbering "God . . . God." Maybe they thought it meant water, or light or mercy. Maybe they thought it meant Edward Cousin.

"Can't you see it yourself?" the priest urged.

"Clearly," I assured him.

"But even that is only a beginning. I myself was a witness one day when he brought a cargo in. There was a girl among them, young, not over twelve. But when she was brought to sale she had more to recommend her than youth, and a body that promised years of useful work. She had a soul."

"Well, well," I said. "Indeed."

"I saw it myself. She dropped to her knees, there in the marketplace before us all, clasped her hands and lifted her eyes to heaven. 'God, master, forgive my sins,' she prayed, and she repeated 'sin . . . sin . . . sin.'

"I am told, although I confess I have not had the honor of

308

an invitation there, that the negurs on Cousin's own plantation receive strict moral instructions, and gather together daily to sing hymns to the glory of God."

I made inquiries after Cousin. He owned a plantation near Spanish Town, but no one had been there. In fact it was said that he himself was seldom at home, since he spent most of his time in the trade, commanding his own ship, carefully selecting his own cargo, fighting Spaniard or buccaneer if they crossed his path.

Time passed. I heard more of Cousin, more of Anthony More. In company with the waterfront of Port Royal I waited for the day that the two should meet. My personal resentment toward Cousin diminished, seemed unimportant. He must be spared for Anthony More.

Five years went by at Saltash—quiet years, years without a history, years of happiness. The half-starved waif of the Plymouth docks grew to be a rich man. Saltash was as fine a plantation as any in Jamaica. "Squire" Bone men called me. This never ceased to amuse Pol, who was not impressed by my mounting dignity. But Pol was never impressed by anyone. When Henry Morgan, who insisted upon regarding himself our patron, renewed his offer to take her to bed she only giggled.

"You should have seen him," she told me gleefully. "He puffed and snorted and bullied and begged. And I laughed the merrier. I can afford to now, Tom. We are safe from such creatures."

Despite Pol's pleasure in Morgan's discomfiture I was angry. She protested that my choler was unjust.

"We move in polite circles now," she declared solemnly. "We must learn new ways. Really I am flattered. Practically all the leading men of Port Royal have honored me with similar proposals."

"I trust you always laugh," I told her.

She dropped her banter.

"I stood against you for two years when I loved you," she said. "Do you think I am likely to succumb to such as these?"

I kissed her and begged her forgiveness. After that we laughed together at her admirers. So when she announced that she was

309

going to have another child, unlike many gentlemen in similar circumstances I did not ask myself who its father might be. But if I was not concerned over the child's parentage, I was anxious about Polly herself. I did not propose to see her butchered again, and there was no physician but the Hanoverian in Port Royal. When I expressed my fears Polly laughed.

"The negurs are good midwives," she assured me.

I was not comforted. I resolved to take her to Havana. She refused to go at first and finally consented only on condition that we leave at once, although it was months before she expected the child.

"If I go, it must be while I can still have a holiday," she declared. "Havana is very gay. We shall have fun together. It will be our honeymoon."

"With a baby in your belly," I teased.

"What's unusual about that?"

She persuaded me. We entrusted Saltash to Trigg. With Abel and the wench Evalyn, whom Pol had adopted as her tiring-maid, we sailed for Havana. It was September, 1685. I had been happy for eight years.

# XIV

Two DAYS out of Jamaica we were caught in a hurricane. These sudden tropical storms are the terror of the Caribbean. They rise without warning and blow with inconceivable fury. Our ship fought back but in a few hours it was a battered, helpless hulk. When the skies finally cleared she was sinking. The Captain ordered us into small boats. I was with Pol, Abel, Evalyn and two seamen.

We had no food and only a little water. At the end of three days we were exhausted. The sailors had already given up hope when we sighted a sail. Long before the ship was close enough to see us we wore ourselves out with frantic, futile signaling and shouting. Fortunately her course carried her straight to us. As we were taken aboard I observed her colors. Blood red. She was a pirate.

After we were fed we were taken to the pirate Captain. I told him who I was and assured him that I could pay ample ransom for myself and companions. He had only to fix the sum.

"I've heard of you," he admitted.

"You will take us to Port Royal?"

"I will take you to Tortuga. Anthony More will decide."

"Anthony More!" I exclaimed.

He jerked his head toward the flag that I had briefly noted as we came aboard.

"Don't you know his colors?"

I looked again and saw what I had missed before. A small white fish was in one corner of the red banner. I recalled that I had heard that he had adopted such a device.

"He is not content with the blood rag of the others," a slaver had taunted. "He must have his own quarterings."

I could not move the Captain from his resolution to take us to his leader. In fact my effort to do so was only half-hearted. I was curious to see the great Anthony More, and I felt sure that he would not harm us. He made war only on Spaniards and slavers. We would be delayed, but that was of small importance. Pol had wanted a holiday; we were having one with unexpected variations. On the whole I was not displeased. I longed to see Anthony More.

Late one afternoon a ship was sighted. "A slaver," the lookout shouted as we drew closer. "One of Cousin's," he added a moment later.

I could see that the vessel was larger than ours. We would be outgunned and outmanned. Yet they were trying to escape. True, merchantmen did generally flee from pirates, but I had heard such tales of Cousin that I was surprised. I said so to the Captain. He flicked a glance toward the white fish that fluttered above us.

"Cousin's vessels always run from that."

"Why?"

"No one save Cousin knows, unless More does. But what am I to do with you? We put prisoners in chains during a fight, but you are not exactly a captive. Will you fight with us?"

"Do you think Cousin himself might be on that ship?"

"It's possible."

"Then give me weapons."

"And your negur?"

I summoned Abel and asked him if he wanted to fight. He did.

A few minutes later the Captain ordered the men to their stations. They moved quickly and with good discipline, but once there they twisted and muttered, impatient for the battle to begin, and yet nervous as any man is when death is near. The gun crews, action being closer at hand, were taut. The guns had been moved into place, their noses stuck through the gun ports. The sponges were wet, matches were ready to be blown to a white heat. Only the Captain's signal to fire was wanting. He stood silent, mouth closed grimly. Gray smoke erupted from the side of the slaver. A dull boom echoed across the water. Our ship shook. The slaver had fired first. For long minutes we could do nothing but wait, absorbing their fire, and watching with anxious eye the gradually narrowing strip of water that lay between us.

Finally the command came.

"Fire," the Captain ordered.

It helped our spirits, but did little damage to the enemy. It was evident that our only hope lay in boarding. The men themselves sensed this, though the gun crews did their best to anticipate the moment when the decisive action would begin.

At last we were alongside. Grappling irons locked the two vessels in a death grip. We were firing with small arms now. I saw men stationed in their rigging suddenly sway and fall, limp, awkward as rag dolls. I heard the thud of bodies against wood and knew that behind me our own men were likewise falling.

The moment came to board. The waist of the slaver was a few feet above us. At her rail crowded the defenders, grim and determined. Our Captain reached up, grasped the rail of the enemy ship with one hand, swung his cutlass as he pulled himself up, and disappeared. Could I follow him? While I still stood, irresolute, a great black arm circled my waist and lifted me. I never knew how I crossed the rail, but Abel and I stood side by side on the enemy's deck. It was all fight and blood after that. My cutlass swung, a man fell. I heard a low growl of triumph and knew that it came from my own throat. Abel was still beside me. A man stood on the quarterdeck directing the fight. I did not have time to look at him closely, but if Cousin was on the ship he would be there. We cut our way toward him but when we reached the quarterdeck he was gone. For the first time since Abel had thrown me into the fight I paused for breath and glanced around. As I looked at the main deck a few feet beneath me my heart sank. Only Abel and I still held our weapons; the others, overwhelmed by numbers, had given up. The Captain lay dead on the deck. A heavy-jowled brute came toward me. He summoned us to surrender. Instead we threw ourselves into their midst. This time I led the way. As I cut and slashed I heard a blood-curdling cry behind me. Even in the midst of hopeless battle I grinned. It was Abel, shouting the war cry of the Susquehannocks. We fought

313

with the desperation of the doomed, but it could not last. They were on every side, on our backs, under our feet. They beat me down; Abel lasted but a few minutes longer.

They bound us, kicked us and left us lying on deck while they boarded our ship. Presently the thing I longed for, yet dreaded, occurred. Polly was dragged aboard. She broke from her unwary captors and threw herself on me. They tore her away.

The goods from the pirate ship were brought aboard, the shattered vessel itself cast adrift. When the deck of the slaver was cleared, and its wounded cared for, the prisoners were assembled. There were not more than a score of us who were able to stand. With Polly and the wench Evalyn, we were herded to the quarterdeck. The man I had seen fleetingly during the fight awaited us there. It was Edward Cousin. He scarcely looked at us.

". . . thanks be to God Which giveth the victory," he cried in fierce exultation. The magic had not left his voice.

The mate, a broad-shouldered giant, who had led the fight, approached Cousin. As he did so he seemed to shrink in size.

"The prisoners—" he began.

"Hang them."

"Of course, sir, but—"

Cousin turned on him ferociously.

"The wicked shall be turned into Hell," he shouted.

"There are two blacks and a white woman," the mate explained, frightened but dogged.

"Let me see them."

Pol, Abel and Evalyn were shoved roughly forward. Abel was bound, the two women free. Cousin looked at them.

Evalyn could hardly stand from fear, but if Cousin recognized her he gave no sign.

"The negurs will bring a good price; put them under the hatches with the others."

Before anyone moved Pol stepped boldly forward. She pleaded valiantly. She told the truth, that we had been wrecked, that I was an honest merchant, a respected planter; surely a godly man could not hang me, rob me of my negurs.

"What is your name?" Cousin asked.

"Mistress Bone. My husband is Thomas Bone. We are of Port Royal. Perhaps you have heard of us."

"I have heard the name," he admitted, and added after a moment's thought, "Thomas Bone, step forward."

I obeyed. He looked at me for a long time.

"I have seen you before," he declared uncertainly.

Pol answered for me.

"In Port Royal, no doubt."

"No, no, before that. But it does not matter. Did these rogues of Anthony More force you to fight with them?"

Once more Polly intervened before I could speak.

"They did," she cried, "and the negur, too."

"I saw them," Cousin growled. "They accepted the obligation with enthusiasm. No ten men did the harm wrought by those two."

"They were told that I would be killed if they faltered."

Pol was winning. But I was possessed by a madness. Hate surged over me, stronger than the desire to live, stronger even than love; for a few fatal seconds I cared for neither my own fate nor Pol's. I would not live by Edward Cousin's grace. I would not give him the triumph of granting me life.

"I fought because I wanted to," I shouted.

Cousin looked at me. For a moment I thought he might even smile. He was almost happy.

"Hang him with the others," he ordered.

Polly was not defeated, even by my treason. She flung herself at Cousin's feet.

"All the paths of the Lord are mercy," she cried desperately.

Cousin looked down at her. Gradually his expression changed, and as it did so the madness drained from me; my bravado subsided. Fear, which the imminence of death had not aroused, overwhelmed me.

"No, Pol," I cried. "Let him be. For the love of God let him be. I'd rather hang."

Neither Pol nor Cousin heeded me. Theirs was the duel; I was a helpless bystander. As Cousin stared his eyes came to life, as I had seen them come to life once before. She looked back

315

boldly for a moment, then her lashes drooped slowly, she hung her head. She was at his feet, wholly submissive.

"There may be good in her," he muttered.

"Help me," she pleaded softly, "I need a man close to God to lead me to truth."

His voice rang strong again in feverish esctasy.

". . . joy shall be in heaven over one sinner that repenteth," he cried.

"And my husband?"

"You are shorthanded, let him work with the crew," he said to the mate. "But watch him. If he threatens trouble kill him."

He lifted Polly to her feet.

"Come," he said.

He made toward the cabin. She followed humbly in his wake. My despair was bottomless. I had seen Evalyn follow him thus. But Polly was not Evalyn. As she reached the door she flung me a slender strand of hope to which to cling during the days that followed. She turned. She was grinning roguishly. She blew me a kiss.

For a week I saw neither Polly nor Cousin. I was a haunted man during those seven interminable days. When Pol emerged would she be like the others, used, beaten, cast off, empty of everything but a hideous sense of sin? I was terrified, afraid to live because I might see her so, unable to die until I knew. I tried to reach the cabin but it was guarded night and day. When I approached it I was dragged away.

On the seventh day I was working on deck. My spirits were even lower than usual by reason of a brief ray of hope which had been extinguished. Hours before, the lookout had sighted a sail. I had permitted myself to hope she might be a pirate who would attack us. But as we drew closer to her it became evident she was a derelict. I was gazing at her dismally, wondering what dark fate had overtaken her, when a fellow near by grabbed me by the arm.

"Your wife," he said gruffly.

Pol and Cousin were coming out of the cabin. Pol came first. I knew at once that Cousin's work of salvation had gone awry. The others had left him in somber shapeless rags that befitted a

316

broken drab, henceforward dedicated to hungry penitence. Pol was magnificently garbed. Her dress was of silver cloth, cut so low that the large diamond pendant that hung around her neck nestled between half-bared breasts. Jewels glittered in her hair; on her feet were shoes adorned by golden buckles. She carried her head high; she walked with proud easy grace; her eyes as they met mine were not haunted by the consciousness of sin, but regarded me steadily. On her lips a smile lingered, although it was no longer roguish, but faraway, sad.

I looked at Cousin. He walked behind her. His gait was unsteady; he drew a shaking hand across a taut, haggard face. His mouth twitched. He glared hungrily at Polly. With a shock I realized that it was Cousin who was haunted, haunted by unslaked desire that would never leave him in peace. When he spoke his usually resonant voice was rough from rage.

"Take her," he cried, his voice breaking, "she is Jezebel. She is an instrument of the devil. Take her out of my sight."

The mate started toward her. Pol waited quietly, while Cousin groaned in agony. Suddenly the mate stood still, as if frozen to the deck. Every man within view stopped in the middle of his work to stare at the quarterdeck, unabashed and, for the moment, unafraid. Their grim master was on his knees before his prisoner.

"No, no," he babbled. "You must not leave me. Repent. It is not too late, repent."

I think Edward Cousin could have resisted anger; I know he was immune to tears. Polly merely laughed at him.

"Get up," she said lightly. "You look foolish on your knees."

He clutched her around her waist.

"Repent," he repeated, "I can lead you through the gates of Heaven itself."

"In that case I prefer to go to Hell," she said pleasantly. "Come, you promised to speed me on the way."

Cousin scrambled to his feet. His features were distorted by rage and humiliation. His body twisted, racked by thwarted lust.

"Have your way," he screamed, "but I'll send a broken body to the devil!"

As I leaped two men caught me. They held me fast through the

317

horror that followed. They keelhauled Polly. They stripped her of her finery and tied the ropes around her. I watched, helpless, terror-stricken. Polly was less afraid than I. I do not say that she was not afraid. Her face was colorless, her unruly limbs shook; but at the last when she stood bound and naked, defenseless against a fiend's malice, facing an ordeal that few of the hardiest seamen survive, she looked at Cousin and laughed.

But her last look was for me.

"Come after me, Tom," she said steadily.

So she commanded me to die with her.

"I'll come," I promised.

My captors led me to where they were lowering her. Her white body slipped into the water and was gone. It was my turn now. I must follow her. But first there was work to do.

Cousin still stood on the quarterdeck. His thick lips were parted, saliva drooled from his mouth. He was panting like a man overcome with desire. The men started to lead me aft where they would soon haul up Polly's bruised dead body. I did not intend to wait until then. The men who held me were vicious beasts, hardened by the most brutal business the world has known, but even they were shaken. Their grip relaxed. I broke away from them and sped to the quarterdeck. Cousin fell before my first blow like a tree uprooted by a hurricane. I stamped into his heavy, helpless face. As they overpowered me I kicked again. I felt his bones smash under the weight of my foot. By the time they dragged me away his face was a bloody mass of broken flesh. It flashed through my mind that at least he would not gloat over Polly's dead body. But I was not content. As my fist crashed into Cousin's face I realized that it would not be enough. I must break my promise to Polly, or at least postpone its redemption. I could not join her yet. I still had work to do. Not now, perhaps, for I was helpless, but hatred knows patience that puts the most constant love to shame. It has strength, too. Three men did not suffice to hold me. I broke way from them easily and was over the rail. The water closed over me and I swam.

318

# XV

WHEN I DOVE overboard I had no plan beyond escape. As I swam away I heard men shout, but no one bothered to lower a boat in pursuit, or to shoot at me. Undoubtedly they were sure that if the sharks permitted I would drown.

But if I drowned I could not destroy Edward Cousin. I remembered the derelict. It was farther away than I had thought but not too far away. I headed for it. I must have swum for hours. My head grew light, my feet heavy; only hate kept me afloat. When I reached the hulk I almost gave up hope. I could see no way to get aboard. Drearily I swam around it. A rope dangled over one side. I grasped it and hung there. I did not thank God; I shook my fist in the direction of Cousin's ship and prayed to the devil not to abandon me.

Somehow I pulled myself to the deck where I dropped, drained of strength and courage. During the hours in the water I had fought Cousin. Every minute I stayed afloat was in defiance of him. Safe on the deck I could no longer postpone my grief. Polly was dead. I had abandoned her there in the clear green water. I wept for her, and out of pity for myself. I cried myself to sleep.

I awoke slowly. Every bone in my body ached, my mouth was parched, my skin dry. "Pol," I muttered, thinking to feel her cool body next to me. She was not there. I opened my eyes. The sun beat down on an empty, desolate deck. Awareness crept like a black fog into my consciousness. I shut my eyes, only to see Polly sinking in the water. I wondered dully if they had hurt her unbearably. Perhaps she died quickly. I opened my eyes and struggled to my feet. I was weak and dizzy. I searched the ship. She was a total wreck, looted of everything of value except food and water. As long as she held together I would live.

I lived for weeks on that disabled hulk. Each day I sat hour after hour scanning the horizon for the land that I was sure would appear. I was not impatient. As the days passed I felt neither disappointment nor fear. Time died with Polly and our child. I could afford to wait.

Drifting with the aimless winds I brooded over the past. Gradually bitterness devoured all that had once seemed good in it. Kindness, generosity, decency—and I had experienced all of them —were forgotten. I remembered only injustice, cruelty, greed, deceit. Love had bade me die when I leapt over the ship's side, hate forbade it. I had obeyed hate's command, henceforth I was its slave. I would live for it, on it. When I finally saw land, purple on the horizon, my long vigil with hate had made of me a creature as evil as Edward Cousin himself.

I was reluctant to leave the wreck. Its broken twisted hulk was at one with my own desolation. While I hesitated a boat put out from shore and headed toward me. The occupants were buccaneers come to investigate. They were amazed to find a man aboard the hulk, and well they might be. I was a picture of ruin. I had not washed in weeks. My clothes were filthy, ragged, infested with vermin. My face was covered with a heavy unkempt beard, my long hair was matted and dirty. When they questioned me I replied sullenly. They concluded that I was mad, and perhaps they were not entirely wrong; certainly for many months I hovered precariously between madness and sanity. When they ordered me to accompany them to shore I obeyed indifferently.

I asked the name of the island.

"Tortuga."

My hate-laden turgid mind stirred. Tortuga . . . Anthony More . . . slavers . . . More attacked slavers, perhaps he too hated Edward Cousin . . .

"I want to see Anthony More," I told them.

"You will, when he returns."

We entered a cove. A ketch was at anchor; a number of canoes such as the Caribs make of hollow tree trunks, and often used by buccaneers, were drawn up on the beach. On the shore the trees came almost to the water's edge, under these were rude huts where the pirates lived with their women. It was the sort of community that is established at pirate rendezvous, exists until the place is abandoned, and disappears into the jungle.

The women were a motley lot. There were a few prisoners, being held for ransom, but most of them were there from choice, and fit companions to the men, English, French, Spanish, Carib, negur, half-caste, wife, mistress, prostitute. They worked for their men, brawled with them, bore them children, were jealous of them, unfaithful to them. They visited and quarreled among themselves, paraded their stolen finery before their less fortunate sisters, fought unscrupulously for male favor.

I was assigned an empty cabin. For weeks I lived there alone. At first a few careless attempts at kindness were made but I rebuffed these so sullenly that they ceased. I was waiting as I had waited on the wreck. Sooner or later Anthony More would return. When he did there would be time for action. Meantime I planned unpleasantness for Cousin.

I was given fresh clothing which I wore because it was more comfortable than the old. Because I enjoyed swimming I was in the water each day, and grew clean again. Otherwise I did not alter in any particular from the creature taken from the derelict. I let my beard grow. This changed my whole appearance. I was pleased. Tom Bone was dead, he had disappeared into the sea with Polly Bragg. It was a stranger that I saw reflected in the water. A stranger in the prime of life, a trifle under medium height, broad of shoulder, hard-muscled, strong and agile, and, above a magnificent body, a face thin and drawn, with fierce eyes, grim mouth, and a full beard, heavy, unkempt and streaked with gray.

There were days when I could no longer bear the ever changing monotony of the sea. It was too clear, too green, too blue. It had devoured Polly; it waited imaptiently for me. It moaned a funeral dirge, whispered an invitation, shrieked that I must fulfill my vow. When I could no longer bear it I ran away.

321

In the forest of the island's interior a few wild pigs still roamed. Men who have hunted both tell me that they are as dangerous as the wild boars of Europe. I killed them with a long heavy-bladed knife, much used among the buccaneers. The pirates did not at first believe this, but it was true. I stalked the animals with the skill acquired in the Virginia forests, and plunged the knife into them as they charged. As I felt the relentless plunging blade bite through heavy flesh, and saw the blood spurt, I was possessed by a fierce exultation. For a few seconds the beast was Edward Cousin, and indeed in my fancy there was an actual physical resemblance: the same cruel eyes and fierce mouth, the same grossness, the same brutal power. One day I carried one of the animals home on my back. I threw it before my cabin. Men exclaimed in surprise. After that they believed me, but were more certain than before that I was mad. No man in his senses would attack the beasts with only a knife. Few could carry one of the pigs unaided.

One day in mid-autumn while in the forest I unexpectedly encountered a man whom I recognized as one of the pirates at the camp. As I passed him he caught my arm.

"Go another way," he advised shortly.

"Why?"

"Luke Watling and Arsène Roach are yonder. They killed poor Tim Shea."

"Why?"

"Tim and I came on them by accident. They've got a woman there. I got away but they killed Tim."

What had occurred was clear. Contrary to the fantastic yarns told by people who know nothing about the matter, pirates treat women captives with consideration. There are plenty of females in port to be had cheaply; a captive is a commodity, part of the profits of the trade; to damage such goods is poor business. Naturally there are numerous exceptions, but generally the rule holds. Nowhere was it observed more strictly than among Anthony More's men.

But apparently Luke Watling and Arsène Roach had violated it. I knew Watling. He was a gentleman from London; Watling was not his name. He was a languid mocking rogue, with a reputa-

322

tion for reckless daring. I had never heard of Arsène Roach. But whoever he was, he and Watling had been found with one of the captive women and had not hesitated to kill rather than risk exposure.

I thanked the fellow for his warning and continued on my way. I was not interested. The woman was of no concern to me. She must be willing enough or she would not accompany the scoundrels into the forest. If she was not, it mattered little. Females had been raped before. The damage was not irreparable. I was not interested, but neither did I propose to turn from the trail that I was following.

A few minutes later I came into the glade where they were. I crossed it slowly, keeping a cautious eye on the group as I approached. I knew at once that the girl was as yet unharmed and that I had erred in presuming that she was a willing victim. She could not be so arrogant had the men satisfied themselves upon her; they would not have tied her feet together had she been compliant. She sat on a fallen log, her blazing eyes fixed on her captors. She was barefoot, her dress was of some cheap coarse material and fitted her badly. Obviously she was not a lady; ransom money would be paltry. Perhaps that was why Watling and his companion dared risk using her.

On the edge of the glade, only a yard or two from safety, lay a dead man, poor Tim, no doubt. He had been shot as he ran for safety. The two pirates squatted not five feet from the trail. Arsène Roach picked up his carbine which lay at hand. I saw him glance at Watling, saw Watling nod. He loaded it with casual deliberation. I did not quicken my pace. By the time I was a yard or two from him I realized that he intended to let me pass and shoot me in the back. Watling spoke to me languidly. As I answered I sprang. My knife went clean through Arsène Roach's neck. I withdrew the knife and faced Luke Watling.

He was smiling lazily.

"Sit down," he said. His hand was near his sheathed knife.

I had heard of Luke Watling's skill with a knife and I saw no sense in fighting uselessly. I sheathed my own weapon and

323

squatted beside him. He picked up something from beside the dead man. It was a pair of dice.

"We were about to game for her," he said pleasantly, nodding at the girl.

"She's yours now without the trouble," I grunted ungraciously.

"In good time I'll have her," he agreed, "but about you?" He stopped and stared at me questioningly. I did not reply. After a moment he continued. "We had to kill Tim. Tim talked too much."

"Is she worth killing a man for?" I asked.

Watling looked at the girl long and critically before he answered judiciously.

"That is as may be. Judging from appearances I would say yes. Of course the poor creature's at a disadvantage now, concealed by that sack thing she calls her gown; but yesterday poor Arsène here, whom you so unceremoniously killed, and I came upon her bathing. I vow she has a shape like Venus. From that moment we were as men enchanted. She has spirit, too. You can see it now in her eyes. She's frightened, but she's angry, too. That's all to the good; a spiritless creature gives no sport in the taming. Yes, she looks a good gamble, but you can never tell from the husk. The Lord has a nice sense of humor. Sometimes He molds a work of art and leaves it empty. You can't tell from appearances. I knew a woman once that I swore was more chaste than a vestal virgin only to learn that within she burned like the sun. There was another you'd think was made for love, luscious as Aphrodite, with a nun's purity." A frown flitted across his face. "It was she who brought me to this cursed ocean, her husband . . . But never mind. I'll risk this one's being worth a man's life, two men now. The question is, what am I to do with you?"

While he talked at such length, probably to gain time in which to plan his next step, I stared at the girl. Her eyes were the deepest blue I have ever seen, her hair, which fell loose below her shoulders, was blue-black, her nose was straight, her chin firm. Nor did the dress which Watling so disparaged quite conceal the promise of her body. She was young, too. I doubted if she was twenty. But it was neither her youth nor undoubted loveliness

324

that aroused in me the first generous impulse that I had felt since the hour I dove from Cousin's ship. It was her mouth, the one imperfection that marred breath-taking beauty. It was a large mouth, wide and heavy-lipped—Polly's mouth.

For the sake of that mouth I resolved to save her. But I was no knight errant to rush gallantly into adventure. I must live to kill Edward Cousin, consequently I would meet guile with guile. Like Watling I sparred for time.

"Why not take her back unharmed," I suggested. "I'd swear with you that the two dead men killed one another."

Watling simpered and sighed as was the fashion among the gallants of the time.

"Alas! Impossible. To do so after seeing her in the pool would be to insult divinity."

I was not deceived by his foppish airs. He was dangerous as a fer-de-lance, the poisonous snake of the Caribbean that strikes like lightning and more fatally.

"You are convincing," I retorted. "You even tempt me." I bowed in the girl's direction. "But what of Shea's companion?"

"You saw him?"

"Yes, hastening toward the beach."

"Perhaps I erred there, in not pursuing him. I did not think it worth while. The man's a coward."

"He was frightened," I conceded. "He warned me to avoid you."

"Good. I doubt if he will talk. He fears Tim's fate. But what of you?"

I was not yet ready to answer that question. In fact I did not know its answer. I continued to play for time.

"If the fact that you have her hobbled means what I think it does, and her eyes are not liars, the girl herself will talk. Unless, of course, you intend to kill her too."

"Kill her! Kill Venus? Aphrodite? Kill love?" he protested. "No, no. I'll teach her gentleness. She will coo like a sucking dove after a few lessons."

"Liar." It was the first time the girl had spoken.

"Angel," he retorted, giving her a languishing smirk before turning back to me.

"You're Bone, the madman," he said.

I nodded.

"But you are no more mad than I."

"You're discerning."

"I am a damned clever man. Yes, a damned clever man. I get what I want; and since it is evident that you too are a sensible fellow and, what's stranger yet, an honest one, I propose that you go now, after promising that you will forget what you have seen here. I, on my part, will forgive you for killing poor Arsène, though he was my dearest friend."

"If I refuse?"

"Then you will learn why I always get what I want. Why I have the reputation for being the cleverest man with a long knife in the Caribbean."

"Have you ever hunted wild hogs with one?" I asked.

"I've heard of that. Stupid of you for such a mean reward, but I'll grant you it must take skill. A fight between us would be interesting but stupid.

"Stupid," I agreed. "Why not continue with the dice?"

"You mean game for her?"

"Yes. You have spoken so convincingly, I long to taste her myself. You were willing to risk losing her to Roach, why not to me?"

He laughed patronizingly.

"Your innocence is refreshing, but I assure you I did not risk losing her. I admit it appears so. I was about to play with Arsène. You see it was he who persuaded her to come here. She is half Irish so would not trust an Englishman, but believed a Frenchman when he vowed he only wanted to walk with her. I followed them. It seemed a pity to kill him, so I left it to chance. If he lost and relinquished the wench, he might live."

"But if he won?"

"Then, of course, I would have been obliged to kill him. It would have grieved me, too. I swear I loved him like a brother. So you can readily see how useless it is to dice."

326

"Then," I said regretfully, "I suppose it must be the knives."

He hesitated.

"You really stick pigs?" he asked. "Or is it false, like your being mad."

"It is not false."

"Then I suppose I must be sensible. The game we were about to play is quite simple. Arsène had just won the dice. You take his place. You may roll one, two or three times, as you see fit. Then I must top your total in a like number of throws."

He handed me the dice. My first throw was a seven. If I stopped there my chances were even. I threw again, a nine.

"Sixteen in two," I said and passed the dice.

Watling made a four and a five. Nine. When he threw the second time one of the dice rolled to the girl's feet. She bent over it quickly.

"What is it?" Watling asked her. "The one here is a four. So if yours is three we roll again, above it you come to me, one or two, Bone takes you."

Instead of replying she snatched the die and threw it into the woods. Watling chuckled.

"So you didn't like the verdict. I wonder what it was. What do you say, Bone? Since she seems to have made a choice, shall we leave it to her?"

I assented. The girl only looked at us. Watling picked up the remaining die.

"She's stubborn and we waste time. Come, one roll each. High wins."

He rolled a two. I was confident. The die turned lazily. A one.

"Bad fortune," Watling said kindly. "But fate, I assure you. Destiny would not have led me to that pool only to deny me the treasures I saw there."

He started toward the girl.

"Stop!" I commanded.

He turned.

"Devil's name! What now?"

"I want the girl."

He drew his knife. We fought near the body of Arsène Roach.

He slipped on a tuft of grass wet from blood. Before he could recover his balance I killed him. The knife went through his heart.

"He slipped. You killed him unfairly," the girl said.

I concluded that the die she threw away was neither one nor two. It angered me. This was unreasonable on my part. I did not want her. It was only that she had Pol's mouth. Without answering I went to her. She did not move. I untied her feet. She walked to where Watling lay.

"Clever man, damned clever man," she jeered.

Then surprisingly enough she leaned over and made the sign of the cross on his bosom.

"Come," I grunted.

"Where?"

"Home."

She was incredulous.

"But you said you wanted me for yourself."

"That was to trick him."

"Like you tricked him when you killed him unfairly. Yet I am to trust you."

I lost patience.

"I killed him as I could. Maybe if we had fought fairly he would have killed me. Then he would have had his way with you. Would you have liked that better?"

She was not much more than a child. She was at the end of her endurance. She burst into tears.

"He was a beast," she sobbed, "and so are you. The Blessed Virgin saved me."

I was sick of the whole business and determined to put an end to it. I had never seen a woman so determined upon being raped. Very well. I crushed her to me. She screamed. I stuffed her mouth with kisses. When she ceased to struggle I threw her to the ground and crouched above her. She stared up at me, frightened, wailing softly, helpless.

"If I wanted you I could have you now," I told her harshly. "Now get up, Venus—Aphrodite—love. We are going back."

She flushed angrily, but she got up and walked beside me down

328

the trail. Her lips were quivering. I was afraid she would cry again. And she was beautiful. Her laughter was as sudden as her tears.

"The saints preserve me!" she said weakly. "I must have looked like a goose."

"A very pretty goose," I assured her, as I smiled for the first time in months.

While we walked she told me her story. Her name was Judith Mara. She was born on the islands, the child of an Irish sailor and a Spanish woman. Her father was lost at sea; her mother was poor. She was taken into service. Six months ago she had accompanied her mistress on a journey from Mexico to Cuba. On the return More had taken them.

"My mistress was ransomed," she concluded, "but they would not pay for me. Anthony More offered to free me anyhow, and pay the men their share from his own pouch, but I begged him not to. I hate being a servant. Let Dona Margaret buy a black to tend her."

This ended the tale.

"But what will you do?" I asked.

"Anthony More is a good man." Her voice said he was a god. "He will find me a husband."

"And until he does?"

She answered gravely. "They say you are mad, but I don't believe it. At least not very mad, though you do rescue distressed maidens in a queer way. I'll be your woman until Anthony More returns."

"I don't want a woman," I protested vigorously.

"Nonsense. Anyone wants a woman to cook and clean his house. I can trim your beard, too."

So that was what she meant. I burst into laughter. "Delilah," I roared. "You would shorn me of my strength; but I warn you fairly. You can't captivate me. I want no wife."

Her blue, blue eyes opened wide in astonishment. Her speech was blunt to the point of brutality.

"I shouldn't want you for a husband," she explained soberly.

329

"I want a handsome young man. You're old. You have gray hair. When you kissed me your beard scratched."

"I'm not that old," I exclaimed indignantly. "Barely forty."

## 2.

Judith came to live with me. So far as I permitted she kept her promises. She was not in the way. She cooked my meals and scrubbed my house until it shone; only firmness saved my beard from destruction. I had been existing like a beast in its lair; Judith forced me, half against my will, to live like a man.

But she could not save me from the destructive corrosion of my hate. In spite of intervals during which her high spirits and affection recalled me to the world of laughter and reason, I remained for the greater part of the time sullen, bitter, solitary. My body was on Tortuga's beach or in its jungle, but my mind slipped further and further into a world of its own creating, an ever darkening world, peopled by malevolent misshapen creatures, twisted by hatred.

In this land I found a solace that the world of my body denied me. There Edward Cousin was in my power. I devised tortures for him; I heard him plead for mercy and spit in his face; I kicked his quivering mangled body. Polly was with me. She joined me in my sport for I endowed her with my own wicked madness.

There can be no doubt that I was mad—then and for many months after. Not in the way that the poor wretches in bedlam are mad, for when it suited my purpose I could match wits with any man, as my meeting with Luke Watling proved; but no one whose spirit draws its only sustenance from hate is sane, and mine did that, or nearly so. Perhaps I was finally healed because I was not quite wholly lost to malice. If this be true Judith Mara saved me, for during all the dark days she was beside me, laughing at my humors, ignoring my sullen indifference and when the necessity arose pulling me back from the final fetid pool of destruction. She did this with no weapons other than the scorn of her Irish tongue, the pain in her deep blue eyes, and above all the shadow of Polly Bragg that hovered over her heavy red mouth. If ever a

330

mortal repaid an obligation Judith Mara did. I saved her from shame at the hands of Luke Watling, who, after all, was a likeable rogue, such as many an orphaned serving girl would welcome as a lover and protector. In return Judith accompanied me through a period of horror such as is unknown to most men, paying her debt, keeping tight hold on her own faith, never losing her brave hope for me, though God knows I strained it to the uttermost.

From the day she came to me she suffered for her loyalty. When she vowed she lived with me only as a daughter the men guffawed and the women sneered. They were the more cruel in their disbelief because they were so contemptuous of the moral habits of the outer world that they resented any pretentions to their observance. Or did they envy them? In Judith's case persecution took the form of jibes from the females and lewd advances from the men, who could neither credit her with virtue nor view me as a serious rival.

I put an end to the worst of her troubles by thrashing the more obnoxious among the men, but although this was effective it increased the unpopularity of both Judith and myself. We became pariahs among outcasts.

"Wait till Anthony More's home, filthy slut," I heard a woman say to Judith. "He'll teach you and your loony to mend your dirty ways. D'you think he paid your ransom himself so you could be meat for a lousy shipwrecked half-wit?"

"He did it because he is a kind man," Judith answered hotly.

The woman cackled derisively.

"Take off your clothes and look at yourself in the water and you will see why he did it. He was only waiting until that skinny carcase of yours filled out, and now that it has, he'll find the fruit got a worm into it as soon as it ripened."

"You're only jealous, Peg, because he doesn't fancy your fat thighs," Judith retorted.

Her antagonist sniffed and retreated, her broad buttocks undulating eloquent testimony to her profession.

As a rule I paid little attention to such passages. I knew that until Judith learned to ignore abuse it would continue, and that short of protecting her from physical violence I could do nothing.

331

Besides she must learn what life held, the sooner the better. But the suggestion that Anthony More might disapprove of her being with me was disconcerting. I had need of Anthony More; and I could easily conceive of his having designs on Judith. She was a lovely enough creature to tempt the jaded appetites of any pirate chief. I asked her about it.

"It was only Peg," she said. "She's jealous."

"But I never looked at the slut," I protested.

Judith's candid laughter was not flattering.

"Not you. It's Anthony More she wants."

"And he wants you?"

"No, he is kind to me, like a father."

Was Judith that innocent? She was nineteen years old, her life had not been sheltered. Her eyes were keen, her wits sharp.

"You collect too many fathers," I told her dryly. "Do as this Peg advised. Look at your own naked body."

She grinned impishly.

"I do. It's lovely, too. Not bulging like Peg's. But I am careful about the fathers I collect. You, for instance. Do you want me —for your woman I mean?"

"Nor any other way."

"Neither does Anthony More."

"The greater fool he," I said, somewhat to my own surprise. She made a face at me.

"No more a fool than you."

I was frightened at the vague stirring of my senses. I changed the subject hastily.

"What is this Anthony More like?" I asked.

"Nice."

"A nice pirate," I teased. "He's the greatest cutthroat of them all."

"You will see," she replied confidently.

"Will he be angry that you are with me?"

"Not when I explain."

"He really doesn't want you for himself?"

"No."

"Then he is blind. I know that much. And nice. What else?"

332

"Why, he is much like you," she said as if surprised at her own discovery. "Only he is not a coward."

"Neither am I!" I exclaimed indignantly.

"But you are. You are afraid of what makes you unhappy. Anthony More is not."

Anthony More came home.

One morning in early winter I was amazed to see that during the night a frigate had entered the cove. I had not believed the channel deep enough to permit it to enter. Small wonder that the Spanish found Anthony More so elusive.

On the beach I sensed that a new spirit gripped the settlement. Men who only yesterday had been pictures of sloth moved with decision. The women had buried their feuds; they smiled at one another and screamed profane pleasantries as they strutted self-consciously in their gaudiest finery.

The frigate was being unloaded. I watched the happy bustling scene sullenly. I resented so much merriment, and I was afraid that Judith might be right: that inexplicably Anthony More might indeed be a good man. I wanted no good man, no benevolent knight errant, no Robin Hood of the waves. My need was for an evil man, a coarse-minded, heavy-handed, greedy villain, a good average pirate chief. I could do business with such a creature, and I had my plans laid. I was wealthy. Besides a large amount of goods and valuable plate, I owned Saltash. I would give all that I possessed to More or any other man who would deliver to me the living person of Edward Cousin. It was a rich reward, more than enough to buy the King's pardon and settle down as a respectable planter and man of affairs. A tempting bait for any pirate. But would it tempt Anthony More? Who was this Anthony More?

He stood on the sand directing the work. I went to him. The years had etched the lines around his eyes and at the corners of his mouth more deeply; beyond that he had changed but little. I was stunned. Anthony More was Bill Smith. He *was* a good man, pirate or not. And even though I knew that Anthony More's implacable war on slavers proved that Bill Smith still hunted

333

Cousin, the knowledge did not console me. If he found him he would keep him for himself. He might even merely kill him. That was not enough.

He did not recognize me. As I waited for him to speak I searched my mind for the best means to turn him to my own purposes.

"Who are you?" he asked.

"A shipwrecked planter from Jamaica."

His interest quickened.

"Jamaica? Do you know the planter and slave trader, Edward Cousin?"

"Since I was a child," I said.

He was not concerned with my childhood.

"A West Countryman, eh. Sometime we must talk of the old country, but not now. I want information concerning Cousin. Have you been to his plantation near Spanish Town? Do you know anything about the movements of his ships?"

"No, but I knew him when his men killed my father, when he drove my sister to suicide." He gasped as recognition dawned in his eyes. "And when a man named Smith left Plymouth to pursue him," I concluded.

"Tom Bone," he shouted incredulously as he flung his arms about me.

I told him my story. He listened in silence save for savage cursing when I came to that part dealing with the capture of his own ship.

When I finished my narrative I made my plea.

"I do not know exactly how he wronged you," I said, "but it cannot have been so great as the injury to me. Give him to me. Take all I have for yourself or your men—only give me Cousin."

For many minutes he looked over the water.

"So you have followed me," he said at last. "I am glad for I feel my search is about ended, and yet I'm sorry, too. It isn't worth it, Tom—this dedicating your life to the destruction of one man. I gave you some books once. In one of them are the words, 'Vengeance belongeth unto me, I will recompense, saith the Lord.'

334

And again, 'the Lord shall judge his people.' They are wise words. It is not too late for you to heed them."

"Are you sorry that you have not?"

"No, but I am sorry for you who are starting on the barren trail that I have followed almost to the end."

"And still follow."

"Yes. I still follow it, but vainly, or so I now believe. If fate had willed it, surely I should not have had to wait for fifteen years. I have failed."

I urged that he tell me about those fifteen years, so that I might avoid his errors.

"Tonight," he promised.

He came to my cabin as the sun was setting. There, with a bottle of brandy at his elbow, and Judith Mara, wide-eyed, on a stool at his feet, he talked until dawn.

For me his tale was one of disappointment and failure. In adventure it surpassed the wildest flights of my fancy, but I listened unmoved to accounts of the most daring exploits. I was interested only in what had to do with Edward Cousin.

When Bill Smith left England he went to Tortuga, which was then the chief nest of the buccaneers and took service with a famous captain. While others gambled away their stolen profits, or threw their gold to trulls, or drank it up, Bill saved his. As a consequence it was not long before he could offer a substantial sum for a captured vessel. He raised a crew and became Captain Anthony More. Anthony More was his real name, the name by which Edward Cousin knew him. He was determined that his quarry should recognize the huntsman. But he did not altogether abandon Bill Smith, the fisherman. When he raised the red flag a tiny white fish was in one corner.

"I have heard that men say it is from pride," he chuckled. "That Anthony More wants to vaunt a coat of arms. Well, I have quarterings properly vouched for by the college of heraldry, but I prefer my little fish; although I am afraid that it does not much resemble the cod."

He had not found it difficult to pick up the trail of Edward

335

Cousin, who was well known as a slave trader of austere piety, cold ferocity and ever increasing wealth. Most of the private adventurers had been forced out of the trade by the King's grant of monopoly to the Royal Africa Company, but Cousin bribed the officials and expanded. He bought a plantation near Spanish Town, stocked it with slaves and became a planter of consequence, the more respected because he was seldom seen. Bill had approached that plantation and found it guarded as effectively as any medieval stronghold.

"I had heard in Port Royal that Cousin was there," he said, "so I resolved to find him and settle my score in his own lair. I was not ignorant of the rumors concerning his place, God's Acres, he calls it, nor did I discount them for I knew of what horrors Edward Cousin was capable. But I did not realize that the basis of all these tales was rooted in the suspicions that ever hover over mystery. As you know Jamaica is a place where there are no secrets. Greed is unashamed, crime flaunts its profits whenever fat Henry Morgan appears on the streets. Vice is an art to be cultivated, its rarer forms applauded. A man steals from his neighbor and kills him in 'honorable' duel if he protests. A fastidious mistress beats a black girl to death for having pulled her hair while dressing it; her husband parades his dark concubines openly, and puts her half-caste bastards to work in his fields, or sells the females to the brothels of Port Royal. The foremost planters fight and claw one another like savages for black flesh at the marketplace 'scrambles.' And all these things are done openly, without shame, even without thought. But Edward Cousin is mysterious, secretive. 'What evil is so great,' says rumor, 'that even in Jamaica it must hide its head?' For God's Acres is an unapproachable fortress, the last cultivated land beyond Spanish Town. Beyond it are the maroons and the jungle's terror. I was told that there is an overseer there, and, except for Cousin, no other white. I approached the place full of venom and hope.

"I wasted my time. Armed negurs met me, accompanied by vicious dogs. I was taken to the house and turned over to a negress. She was in the prime of life, comely too; but there was no joy in her. She was dressed like an English matron of Crom-

336

well's time. She kept her eyes demurely on the floor. She asked me what I wanted.

"I told her I was a trader come to see her master. She did not tell me if he was there or not, merely that he received no one at God's Acres. She gave me refreshment and gravely bade me God-speed. The guards and the dogs escorted me out.

"Nothing had occurred. Yet when I was well away from God's Acres I felt as though I were relieved of a crushing weight. I cannot explain it, I only know that it is a wicked place. It oppresses with evil, it is heavy with the stench of corruption. Possibly you might be more successful than I was if you went there. I did not try again. If my failure lies in that, I do not regret it." He shivered. "The Devil smiles on whoever lives there, for it's lost to God."

After his failure at God's Acres Bill haunted Spanish Town and Port Royal, but without success. Cousin did not frequent public places.

"I could have waited," Bill admitted, "until I met him on the streets. Sooner or later he must have appeared. I could have shot or stabbed him. But like you I have felt that death is not enough. You and I are not seeking justice, but revenge. Cousin has beaten us, make no mistake about that. You may find him and break his body, but he has beaten us. We are the reflections of his own evil."

I was impatient with his moralizing.

"What did you do after that?" I asked.

"Returned to the sea. Since then I have attacked every slaver that I came upon. But although I have captured his ships, killed his men, robbed him of his blacks, I have not found Cousin. I have only one small grain of comfort. I have made him afraid. The slavers are hard-bitten men as you have discovered; they stand and fight. But there is one ship of Cousin's, the largest of them all, that always runs when it sees the flag with the white fish."

He closed his eyes wearily.

"That is not a great reward for fifteen years as a blackguard."

"You aren't a blackguard," Judith protested indignantly.

"Thank you, my dear. Perhaps not altogether. I get drunk less

337

than most pirates, and take only the women that are willing for the sake of my gold. But I remain a blackguard. Any man who has been a pirate for fifteen years can be nothing else."

"What shall I do?" I interrupted. "It seems that even the great Anthony More cannot deliver Cousin into my hands. I had thought to buy him from you."

"Search for him yourself," he said gloomily. "I'll give you the next ship I capture."

### 3.

Bill Smith kept his word. He gave me a fully manned, well-supplied ship of forty guns. The articles under which I sailed were those usually entered into among the buccaneers: division of booty according to rank, but division of food, water and strong liquor equally; no man was to gamble for fear of fighting, drunkenness was to be above decks; withholding spoils from the common store, cowardice in battle, desertion of their posts were punishable by marooning; the settlement of all quarrels must be postponed until we reached shore.

Such regulations were customary, but there was another one peculiar to Bill Smith. He pointed to the white fish on the colors that floated at the masthead.

"No ship of Anthony More's attacks an English vessel, unless it's a slaver," he reminded me.

I promised him, although I did not share his scruples.

As I was about to sail Bill introduced another element unusual among pirates. He brought Judith aboard.

"You took her away from me," he said firmly. "You are her father, care for her."

I was dismayed at the burden he was placing upon me and angry at what I thought was in his mind—that I could thus be made to forget Polly and my oath to follow her into the sea.

"What would you have? Must I marry the wench just because I happened by in time to rescue her from Watling?" I demanded brutally.

Judith flushed angrily, but Bill was unperturbed.

"You could do worse, if she were fool enough to have you,

338

but she assures me that you are very old. So only talk to her when your mood is blackest. A man in your temper needs a friend."

"So that is it," I growled, not as mollified as I felt I should be. "I must have a guardian to watch over me. You, too, think that I am mad."

"No," he said soberly. "But you could go mad out there, I know. And remember that no man not fully possessed of his faculties will outwit Edward Cousin."

My men were experienced seamen and fighters. I let them guide me in our operations. "Attack all slave ships; other than that I leave matters in your hands," I told my mate. He followed my orders and exercised his authority shrewdly. He was neither afraid of a fight nor did he risk one in which the odds were too great. As a consequence my career as a pirate captain, measured by ordinary standards, was successful.

I was popular, too, for I led the attacks with a disregard for my life that was less credit to my courage than to a firm belief that I would live until I had met Cousin. Moreover, I gave the greater share of my loot to the men, keeping only such trinkets as caught Judith's eye. My generosity strengthened the belief that I was deranged, but my lunacy being of such a pleasant sort men were eager to serve under me.

But neither success nor popularity lightened the shadow that lay so darkly across my mind and heart. Each day was but another chapter in frustration. I sank deeper and deeper into gloom until in spite of Judith's undismayed efforts, I was once more the brooding obsessed creature that I had been on the derelict. My only relief from depression was in battle. Then the exhilaration of killing lifted my spirits on the wings of some dark ecstasy. This was heightened to a frenzy if the ship attacked was a slaver. At such times I hacked and slashed my way through the thickest fight, scarcely conscious of what I did, blind except for one hated image that was always before my eyes. I was in a terror of apprehension lest I should be too late; that Cousin might be killed before I reached him. As I fought I howled his name, hurling challenges and epithets from one end of the deck to the other. When the battle was over my despondency was deeper than before.

I often looked at the captive negurs and wished bitterly that I might change places with the most miserable of them. Attacking slavers as we did, the blacks constituted the bulk of our booty. We sold them at some convenient port. The authorities knew that they were stolen, but my quartermaster who managed the disposal of all goods blandly swore to the contrary, and cheerfully paid exhorbitant duties as well as judiciously placed bribes. The planters welcomed us. We sold cheaply.

The sales took the form of what were properly called scrambles. A flat price per head was fixed, regardless of age, sex or health. The blacks were then assembled in a half-dark shed and the buyers summoned. The ensuing scene reminded me of starving urchins fighting for coppers that were scattered by a drunken sailor. A few attempted to pick their wares judiciously but most clutched indiscriminately at whatever was at hand. Some brought ropes or long strips of leather which they would toss around a huddled group of negurs and haul them triumphantly from the pool in bundles like sticks of ebony. The whites cursed, scratched, kicked, clubbed and occasionally knifed one another; the blacks, panic-stricken by the pandemonium which they could not understand, increased the turmoil by wailing, struggling against their claimants and sometimes breaking out of the shed itself.

I watched these scenes with bitter complacency. The brutality, the confusion, the degradation of black and white alike harmonized with my own mood. Occasionally I kept a negur. I gave Judith four huge fellows to guard her against harm on shipboard or in the ports. She was kind to them and they soon became devoted to her beyond the limits of slavery. They ceased to be black chattels; they were men again, cherishing and protecting a woman. Matthew, James, Simon and John, she called them, and the apostles themselves were not more faithful and devoted to their Master than were these four to Judith Mara. I also insisted that she have a black wench to serve her, although she protested that she had no need of one. My motive in all this was not altogether generous; it amused me to exalt this former serving girl to the worldly station of a gentlewoman. And indeed as she passed through the dirty streets of a West Indian port, bedecked with the finery of a lady, adorned with jewels, accompanied by her black maid and the four black guards, she outshone the dames of the local gentry.

Occasionally I sent a slave to work in the fields at Saltash. Soon after leaving Tortuga I had sent word to Trigg that Polly was dead and that I did not know when I would return. Meantime he should continue to run the plantation. Actually I could not endure the thought of ever again going there, to be alone where Pol and I had been together; and yet I could not bring myself to dispose of the place. It was my one remaining link with the happiness of the past.

But under the merciless rack of my brooding even the past was tortured into a gruesome parody of the reality which it had been. Every injustice, every wrong, every disaster was exaggerated to fantastic proportions. The kindness of men, the loyalty of women, the smiles of fortune, all had combined to enable a penniless bound man, fleeing from misery and want, to become a free farmer in Virginia, and later a rich merchant and planter in Jamaica. I ignored it. Even Polly was transformed into an unreal image of the fleshly living Pol, whose memory I murdered as surely as Cousin killed her body. The ghost was an unsubstantial shadow, a martyr of passionate sweetness, born to be crucified by a harsh world to the sole end that poor misused Tom Bone might suffer.

Self-pity, hatred and failure to find Edward Cousin drove me from one excess to another. For months I was worse than Cousin himself. The first sign of the dissolution of whatever remnant of decency that I still possessed was the defiance of Bill Smith's command that with the exception of slavers no English ships should be attacked. Casting about for grievance I drew this prohibition from the murky depths of my discontent. Why, I asked myself, should I spare English vessels? Had it not been Englishmen who wronged me? Cousin was English, or half so; Berkeley and his gang were Englishmen, Mary Trigg was English. Must I grant such creatures mercy? Never—Bill Smith had no right so to bind me. He had not suffered as I had.

Judith protested against my decision. She was not outraged at the idea itself. To her piracy was piracy, and she found it no more evil than the legal pillaging and oppression to which she was accustomed in Cuba. Nor did she, the child of a Spanish mother and an Irish father, love the English. She had been nurtured on tales of the cruelty and wickedness of Englishmen, tales that the English buccaneers did little to abate. But to Judith a man was more important than his nationality. Anthony More had been kind to her, so she would have his wishes respected.

"You promised him," she reminded me severely.

"Only fools keep promises," I told her with conscious cynicism.

"Then Anthony More is a fool," she retorted hotly.

"That he is," I agreed. "Otherwise he would have found Cousin by this time."

Having failed in her appeal to decency, Judith flatly warned me that Anthony More did not tolerate disobedience. He had executed more than one man for disobeying him. This served only to loose the ever pressing floods of my self-pity.

"Tell him, then, that I defy him. It is only what I should have expected. I might have known when I saved you from Watling that you would betray me. Tell Bill, so that I may be hanged by the one man in the world that I still love. It will be a fitting end for me."

"You love him so much that you break the one pledge he asked of you," Judith retorted in disgust.

I was offended that she failed to show sympathy for my wrongs.

"I suppose you will abandon me now," I muttered.

She refused to grant me the satisfaction of another grievance.

"No. I said I would stay with you. I keep my word," she said contemptuously.

The men too grumbled. Like Judith, they were not concerned with Bill's scruples but they feared his wrath. I was able to satisfy some with the assurance that sole responsibility was mine and, as usual, all the profits from the new venture theirs. Others, however, rejected my argument. Desertions began. Despite them I clung to my determination. We looted English ships, held Englishmen and their women to ransom, killed any who opposed us, and a few whose only fault was inability to find ransom money. But I did not find ease in viciousness.

"Even as a brute you're a failure. You haven't the courage to

342

be a villain. Why not reform?" Judith reasoned. But although her mockery stung me it did not shake my resolution.

I, who had always been temperate, resorted to drunkenness. I hoped to gain the release from trouble that other men seemed to; besides it was a part of the design of a man ruined by circumstances that I was so busily weaving. I failed to find surcease. Drink only made me more morose when under its influence, and more deeply depressed during the periods of recovery. Nonetheless I kept doggedly at it. I sat in my cabin for days on end, sodden from drink. During these periods I permitted no one near me but Judith. I forced her to serve as cook, cabin boy, messenger and confidant. She submitted to my tyranny. She was not a patient girl, or a meek one, but she had courage. Bill had sent her to prevent just what was happening. She lost battle after battle, but she did not surrender. So hour after hour she catered to my needs, listened grimly to my abuse and scoffed at my maudlin pleas for sympathy. She awaited an opportunity to bring me to my senses.

Only word that a ship had been sighted diverted me. At such times I lurched to the deck, hoping wildly that it might be Cousin. After each disappointment I turned to the bottle. I no longer led the fights. The mate took my place. While my men boarded and captured the prizes I sat sullenly in my cabin. The men tolerated this only because I demanded no share of the spoils. Even so my original crew melted away. Each time we entered a port men deserted. Others were recruited easily enough, but a more vicious gang of cutthroats was never assembled. Bill had sent me to sea with the cream of the buccaneers; I ended with their droppings. Finally out of the original crew only Judith and the mate remained. He made no secret of his contempt for me, but continued to serve because he was growing rich.

"A little while longer and I'll buy the King's mercy and a farm in England," he often said.

"Why not a plantation out here?" I once asked him.

"Because I want the ocean between me and Anthony More when he learns what's happened under the sign of the fish that you keep flying up there," he answered dryly.

"I'll deal with Anthony More," I assured him.

343

"Maybe, but when that time comes I intend to be safe in England."

Judith stuck to her post from loyalty.

"I'll see you to Hell itself," she told me.

"And shove me through the gate, no doubt," I retorted.

The sickness that possessed me led me finally to women. Judith was at hand, young, lovely, loyal. I tried to take her.

"The first time I saw you you threw dice with Luke Watling with me as the prize," she reminded me. "One of the die rolled to my feet. I tossed it into the jungle. Do you remember?"

I did. I could even hear Luke's affected drawl. ". . . so if yours is three we roll again. Above it and you come to me, one or two Bone takes you."

"What was the number?" I asked Judith.

"A one."

I had thought that I was beyond pride, that I cared for no one's opinion; it was not so. I was hurt and disappointed.

"So you preferred Luke," I grumbled.

"Look at yourself," she replied. "Dirty beard, tangled hair, bloodshot eyes. And your heart is blacker than your louse-covered body."

In spite of her contempt I could have taken her had I been resolute enough to use force. But as she herself had said, I was a failure even as a villain. I turned to easier game, women of the ports, captives from the ships we looted.

Time passed and I became obsessed with the idea that among the women who offered themselves I might find Polly's body. After that I lived for my search. It was not mere lust, it was madness that possessed me. I quit drinking. I led my men to battle again so that I might claim as my share of the spoils whatever woman caught my eye. If my captive proved tractable I kept her. Each time I hoped that my quest was ended, each time I was disappointed. When I had done with my victim she was released without ransom. I threatened those who resisted, but I did not carry out my threats. My own indifference and Judith's mocking eyes saved them. They too were released.

Among the women of those months I can recall today only a

344

few: a Dutch girl with yellow hair, a Frenchwoman who was proud, and a common Portugee slut with mincing manners, a shrill voice, and a choice assortment of entertaining tales, all lies. And finally there was Maria Montijo.

Maria affected the airs and precious mannerisms of a certain type of gentlewoman, but she was not one. She had been the servant of the wife of a government official in Galicia. When the latter was sent to Cuba he left his wife in Spain, but took Maria with him. He was killed when we captured the ship upon which they traveled.

Maria readily accepted my attentions. I found her abandoned, knowing, and without scruples in the art of pleasing men. As the weeks passed and I made no move to get rid of her, Judith, who usually disregarded my women, showed concern.

"This Maria of yours hates you," she told me one day.

"I wished you could hate me that way," I retorted, as I remembered and licked my lips.

She sniffed.

"Any woman could do what she does. How many would bear with you as I do?"

She said it quietly with no undercurrent of meaning, but for some reason I did not believe that she was being entirely candid. I wondered if I had abandoned my suit too soon, and attributed Judith's dislike of Maria Montijo to jealousy.

"If you could see us sometime when we are alone," I boasted, "you wouldn't say that she hates me."

"And if you could see how she looks at you when your back is turned, you would not be so sure that she loves you."

Eventually I grew tired of Maria. She had nowhere to go so I gave her a little gold and left her in Kingstown on the Island of St. Vincente.

"Find a husband," I advised.

Her black eyes smoldered with passion that I took to be love. One arm was around my neck; her long thin fingers combed through my beard.

"Someday I shall do as you command," she whispered. "But

not until I have erased you from my heart. You will return to your poor Maria?"

She pressed against me. I was reluctant to let her go.

"I shall return," I promised, "and probably find that you are a virtuous wife."

Her lips sought mine. I could feel her sharp teeth. When she spoke she was panting heavily.

"Only ask for me," she whispered. "Whatever I am I shall come."

"My dirty beard and filthy body did not bother her," I bragged to Judith when we were at sea once more.

"Hatred is blind and can't smell," she replied.

"Then why is she so anxious that I return to her?"

"I can't even guess."

A few months later we were back at Kingstown. I had not put in there to see Maria Montijo, but neither did I intend to miss the opportunity. In spite of Judith's protests I proposed to enjoy the Spanish girl's company while in port. I inquired for her in a brothel on the waterfront. The proprietor admitted that he knew where she could be reached. For a piece of silver he agreed to fetch her. He was not gone long but he came back alone, leering.

"She says that she must have time to prepare for you. Tonight at the Oak and Vine."

I located the Oak and Vine. It was squalid, even for a Caribbean tavern. I thought with a slight pang that Maria had not done well in the profession. That night when I went to meet her I took a bag of silver.

The tap room of the Oak and Vine was small, dirty and badly lighted. There were two doors, one opening upon the street, another that led into a back room. Scattered about were a few tables. At these sat a dozen or so patrons. They belonged to the villainous, ragged brotherhood that are common to the lowest type of waterfront dive. As I stood in the doorway viewing the scene the host hastened to me. He pointed toward the door opposite.

"She is in there." His voice was oily.

I crossed the room and opened the door. Maria was waiting.

346

I strode toward her, but midway across the room stopped. She had raised a pistol.

"Sit down," she ordered.

I obeyed. As I looked at her I knew what Judith had meant when she said that Maria hated me.

"Why?" I asked, indicating the gun.

She told me why in brief measured words. When the vessel she traveled on was attacked and her lover killed, Maria Montijo's life had crumbled about her in ruins. When the sun rose that morning she had been secure. Her lover lay beside her. In a few days they would reach shore. She, the child of poor peasants, the serving girl, would be installed in what by her standards was magnificence with a house and servants of her own. She was savoring the fruits of luxury and love. That was at dawn. At noon her lover was a corpse, she was a captive of the pirates, with no one to ransom her, no hope of even returning to her former life.

"You left me no way of living except this," she told me coldly as her eyes swept the dirty meanly furnished room. "And only this for as long as I please such beasts as you and the host outside. I have hated you since the first day I saw you."

As she talked I realized it was no use to argue or plead. In this girl I saw myself, listened to my own words. I had done to her what I fancied the world had done to me—killed her lover, ruined her hopes.

"I understand," I told her. "Shoot me."

She laughed harshly and walked toward the door.

"I want you alive."

"Why?"

"I haven't decided, except so that I can hurt you. Do you know that there are white men in the islands who are slaves? When I am tired torturing you I may sell you as a slave, if you are still fit to work. Or I might put out your eyes. I could watch you then for years, creeping from place to place, a blind, crippled beggar."

She slipped out of the door.

I was sick with horror. She had revealed a portrait of myself. Her spirit of hate and bitterness was my own. I was her Edward Cousin. I was afraid, too, for I knew that she would do what she said. But after all I could still fight for my life and at the least gain a quick death. I unsheathed my sword with which I was by this time expert and followed her.

The tap room was as I expected. Maria was in one corner with the host. Between me and the outer door were the rogues who had been drinking. I closed the door through which I had just passed, put my back to it and waited. Maria looked at my sword.

"Surrender peaceably, and I'll spare you—a little," she said.

I did not answer.

"Take him," she ordered. "When you bring him to me helpless, Peter here will pay you. He has a bag of money, too. You can have that."

She was right. Without realizing it I still carried the bag of silver. The men advanced slowly. I resolved not to wait. My onslaught was so unexpected that I thought for a moment I might cut my way to freedom. Thrusting, parrying, slashing, warding off blows with the bag of silver I advanced. But they were too many. To prevent their getting behind me I retreated until presently I again stood with my back to the wall. There for the time being I was safe. Try as they would my assailants could not break through my guard. My blade met every attack. They fell back. Three were on the floor.

Maria came forward. The pistol was in her hand.

"Cowards," she spat at them, "are you afraid of a single man? Stand back. I'll cripple him."

She loaded the gun and pointed it at me. I could not reach her in time to keep her from pulling the trigger. Instinctively I used the only weapon at hand. I threw the bag of silver at her. At the same instant the pistol roared. Its charge hit the money bag. A shower of silver filled the air and rattled to the floor. It was too much for the bullies. For a moment in their scramble for the coins they forgot me. I darted for the door. I reached it but before I could pull it open they were upon me. Once more it was parry and thrust. Again I held them at bay. But I was growing tired. It could only be a matter of time before they pierced my defense. I resolved not to wait until exhaustion forced me to surrender. They must kill me or be killed.

348

"I'm coming now, Pol," I muttered and sprang forward. The die cast I was glad. My body felt warm, my heart was light as it had not been since the day Cousin captured us. "Pol," I cried as I fought. "Pol . . . Pol." Two were down, another. Then, although I was certain that no one had slipped behind me, my arms were pinioned from behind. At the same instant a sack was slipped over my head. I could see nothing, the sounds from the room were muted. Strong arms encircled and lifted me from my feet.

I felt fresh air and knew that they had carried me out of the Oak and Vine.

The exultation that I had felt during the fight ebbed. In its place rolled smothering floods of frustration and terror. I should not see Polly yet, nor would I ever avenge her. For Maria had outwitted me. I was her prisoner and whatever my fate I knew that she would not permit me to die; nor when she had worked her pleasure on me was it likely that I would be in condition to continue the pursuit of Cousin. Slavery on a sugar plantation, she had said, or a blind beggar, crawling from tavern to brothel beseeching charity from such creatures as she. I groaned as they carried me through the streets. Presently my captors halted and I heard a door open. Stale fetid air told me that I had been taken from one dive to another.

"Is he hurt?"

The sack over my head muffled the sound of the voice but I could tell that it was a woman's. Maria had come with us. She did not intend to postpone her sport.

"Release him," the voice said.

My captors loosened their hold; the sack was removed. I was staring into the eyes of Judith Mara. Beside her were Matthew, James, Simon and John.

"You," I gasped.

"Only me. I hope you will forgive me for tearing you from Maria's loving arms."

I was too relieved to feel resentment at her mockery, or even shame.

"How did you know that I would need tearing away?" I asked.

Her explanation was simple. She had always believed that the

349

Spanish girl hated me. Consequently when I had strutted on board that afternoon declaring that Maria was awaiting my pleasure Judith had been suspicious. When I left the ship she ordered one of her negurs to follow me to the Oak and Vine. When he entered I was in the back room but he saw the ruffians preparing for my return. He ran back to the ship and reported my danger. Judith armed the four of them and led them to my rescue. They arrived just in time.

"But why throw a sack over my head and carry me away?" I complained. "With the help of the negurs we could have thrashed Maria's bullies and taught her a lesson."

"Exactly," said Judith. "But I was not interested in Maria's lesson. I wanted to get you out of there, and you are such an ill-tempered brute that I could not be sure you would come willingly."

"Where were you?"

"Holding the door open."

"Did they try to follow us?"

"No;" and she added with what I thought unnecessary reluctance, "I will say you can fight, Tom Bone. They had had enough."

After we had talked a few minutes longer I suggested that we return to the ship. Judith shook her head.

"The ship is gone. The mate has taken it to England."

"And you didn't try to stop him?" I protested.

"Of course not. It was my idea. I am going to take you back to Tortuga."

"And if I don't choose to go back?" I asked her.

"Oh, but I am sure you will."

She smiled at Matthew, James, Simon and John. They grinned back amiably. They adored Judith. I knew that at a nod from her they would strangle me or slit my throat. I argued in vain. She had taken her measures only after careful planning. My rendezvous with Maria merely presented a favorable opportunity for the execution of her project.

"But why have you done this to me?" I asked indignantly.

"Because I had to. It is like Anthony More said. A man with a grievance as bitter as yours must be strong to be alone on the sea. He was strong. You aren't. He sent me to help you. I failed but at least I can take you back."

"So I am your prisoner instead of Maria's," I complained.

"If you like, but I promise I shall treat you more gently than she—though with less affection."

## 4.

I stared glumly at Tortuga's shore line. The moment I shrank from was almost upon me. I was not afraid to meet Bill Smith; I was ashamed. He had sent me forth in a stout vessel, well manned. I had vowed to find Edward Cousin, and promised that in doing so I would attack no English ships except slavers. I had lost my ship, broken my promise and failed to find Cousin. Most humiliating of all I was being brought back unwillingly, the prisoner of a girl hardly old enough to be called a woman.

I was Judith's prisoner; there was no doubt about that. I found it out even before we left St. Vincente, where both my demands and pleas had been firmly rejected.

"Anthony More is your friend," Judith told me. "He will know what is best for you."

"Damn you," I cried in a passion of frustration. "You treat me like a naughty child. Can't you realize that I am a middle-aged man? One who has fought Indians and captained a pirate vessel."

"Well, don't naughty children always play at pirates?" Judith asked tranquilly.

I glared at her.

"You really account me no more than a foolish child?" I finally managed to gasp.

"Haven't you been acting like one?"

All my melancholy wickedness and self-conscious vice had impressed Judith no more than that. I was overwhelmed and protested no more. As we approached Tortuga I half hoped, half feared that Bill would take a more serious view of the sins at which I had worked so hard. Both fears and hopes proved wasted. Bill was not on the island when we arrived; a few days later he

351

was brought ashore dying. He had been fatally wounded in a skirmish with a Dutch trader. He sent for me.

"I haven't much time," he said. "Stuck through the belly by their skipper. He was a stout man, that Dutchman."

I tried to tell Bill that he would not die. He silenced me.

"Don't waste my time. I want to talk."

All through a burning afternoon I listened to him talk away what was left of his life. There were times when the blood rose from his stomach and stood in bright bubbles on his lips as he gasped for breath. Each such attack left him weaker, but he clung to life until night. He did not waste time in reproaching me.

"Judith has told me what occurred out there," he said as he turned his eyes toward the sea. "It does not surprise me. I was attacked by the same malady when I first came out. My sickness was not so severe as yours, however, and I overcame it." He smiled thinly. "The reason for that is that I was well born. Gentlemen have their virtues, Tom. You should have learned that by now. But let it pass; it is done with. I wish to talk to you about yourself and Edward Cousin."

I thought he was going to try to dissuade me from further pursuit of vengeance.

"Nothing you can say will make me give up finding him," I warned.

There was no indication that Bill even heard me.

"Edward Cousin," he said in a hard controlled voice, "came to my home as a guest. He was a young man, ugly as the devil himself, and with the bestial fascination and wiles of the devil.

"Prudence, my wife, was only nineteen. While she was yet an infant her father was killed fighting with Cromwell. Her mother was a sectarian of strong will, harsh temper and fanatical religious zeal. Had Prudence been born two hundred years earlier she would have been dedicated to the church, and might have lived happily in the secluded half light of the convent. Instead she grew into girlhood under the shadow of her mother's imperious will. She was timid, overanxious to please and without a will of her own. As the result of an arrangement made when we were both young, she came to me as a bride at the age of seventeen. She was

352

a pretty child, docile and sweet, but so burdened with a sense of sin and tortured by the consciousness of evil that there was no joy in her. I loved her because she was so frail and helpless. For two years I nursed her. I began to see a happy woman emerge from the pale bud of frightened childhood. She even learned to laugh.

"Her mother saw it too. She grew afraid that her daughter might forget that the substance of life is corruption and its end death. So she sent Edward Cousin to remind her. He was a young man with a reputation for zealous piety.

"'I am afraid of him,' Prudence confided to me, but I only laughed. 'Your mother sent him. He is our guest!' So we welcomed him to our home."

Bill sighed and was silent for some minutes. I could see that the years had not healed his hurt. He was visibly wrestling with strong emotions. But when he spoke his voice was toneless.

"I need not tell you the consequences. It happened under my nose and I did not suspect it. When I detected the old fear lurking in Prudence's eyes, when she shrank from my touch, I only thought that Cousin was frightening her by renewing memories of the harsh teaching of her mother. I was angry that so much of my work must be done again, but did not doubt that it could be done. I remonstrated with Cousin, only to be deluged with a wave of dark prophecies concerning my own soul. Because he was my guest I tolerated him for a short time longer. But Prudence grew worse, so finally I turned him out.

"Charles II had recently mounted the throne of England. I learned later that Cousin was forced to flee the country. He had denounced too many of his neighbors during the years of his power to be safe when protection from London was withdrawn. So by the time I knew what he had done to Prudence he was gone. I found no trace of him until just before that day in Plymouth when we parted. My wife died still babbling of sin. Her mind wandered and turned toward Cousin. He had told her that he was going to the West Indies."

"So you followed him," I interrupted.

"You know that," he muttered impatiently, "but it is not what I am using my last breath to tell you."

He stopped. It was obvious that he found it difficult to find words for whatever it was he did wish to tell me.

"The evil did not lie in the fact that Cousin seduced my wife," he said at last. "She was young and had little knowledge of the world. I would have found ways to make her happy again. But it was not only her body that he defiled. He destroyed her spirit. He left her with such a burden of sin that like your sister she was crushed beneath it.

"She could not wait until death to enter the Hell which Cousin had revealed to her. Her mind gave way; she lived in a dark world of horror. I could not enter it with her. I was a man. I had tasted of her flesh and was wicked. The sight of me was abhorrent. If I touched her she recoiled in fright.

"A child was born, Cousin's. Prudence named her Camilla; it means attendant at a sacrifice. I had hoped that the baby would turn her mind away from her sins, but the result was the exact opposite. To her it was the living symbol of lust. We had to take it away from her.

"I have said that my presence was abhorrent to my wife. It made her fantastic world more dreadful. I provided for her care and left her. But I could not escape the ruins of my own hopes. The silent sympathy of friends was salt in my wounds. Their conversation, their manners, their happiness became unbearable. I resolved to flee a life that held only memories of a dead past. I had been a gentleman, I would be one no longer. I had lived on the land, I would go to sea. So Anthony More disappeared. I became Bill Smith. You knew me then. When the floods of memory ran too full I got drunk. I took women, as you have done, foolishly hoping that I might fancy Prudence was in my arms. And I waited until the day when I should find Edward Cousin."

Bill looked at me out of bleak eyes.

"Do you still believe that I would dissuade you in your search?" he asked.

I shook my head.

"Good. Listen, then. I have advice to offer you and requests to make. First promise me to give over your folly. It is Cousin

354

you hate, not the world. With good fortune you can avenge yourself on one enemy. You cannot do injury to all mankind."

"The world is as evil as Cousin himself," I muttered rebelliously.

"Maybe," Bill replied, "but you miss the point. Do you want Edward Cousin, or do you merely want to nurse and coddle your own wrongs until self-pity reduces you to the condition that you were in when Judith brought you here?"

I tried to defend myself. He halted me.

"I was wrong about you," he said. "Go away. Send Judith. When I die I want someone with courage near me."

He closed his eyes.

"No, Bill," I stammered. "I won't go. What is it you want of me?"

"To know, first of all," he murmured, "if vengeance against Edward Cousin means enough to you that you will give up your mawkish childishness and act like a man."

"Yes," I said, and meant it.

He opened his eyes.

"There is one way," he said, "only one certain way. I could never take it, because Cousin would recognize me. Do you think he would know you again?"

"I am certain he would not," I answered. "He was looking at Pol after the first moments when he was puzzled by some faint memory of me. And I have changed. This beard and the gray streaks in my hair."

"Good. That is what I thought. Now listen."

When Bill had told me how to trap Edward Cousin he appeared happier. It was as though he had transferred a great burden from his own shoulders to mine—which indeed he had. His mind turned to other matters.

"In the care of Samuel Hart of Jamaica I have considerable wealth," he told me. "Take him the papers that you will find in yonder chest. He will turn my stuff over to you. Find means to send it to Amy More, Ash Hollow, near Plymouth in Devon."

"Amy More, Ash Hollow," I repeated, and added curiously, "Did you have another daughter?"

"No. Camilla means attendant at a sacrifice. There have been enough sacrifices to the evil spirits that possess Edward Cousin. When my wife died I ordered her child's name changed to Amy. It means beloved."

He stared at me for some minutes. I knew he had a further request to make.

"What is it?" I asked.

"Amy is still unwed. Could you marry her, Tom?"

"Edward Cousin's daughter?" I exclaimed.

"No, Prudence's daughter." He laughed gently until he choked and almost smothered in his own blood. When he could speak again he explained. "I will not deny that I ask it chiefly for Prudence's sake; but it would be a subtle revenge on Cousin, too. Not so gratifying for the moment as to twist his limbs and tear his flesh, I'll grant that, but in the end more lasting. Think of it. A man's immortality is in his children; cherish Amy, make her happy, cleanse her of the dark spirits that have lived in her father, and you will destroy Cousin's soul as surely as the tortures that you plan will destroy his body. Can't you savor a revenge such as that?"

I told Bill that I could not. He sighed.

"I don't blame you; but for my poor wife's sake I tried. But at least promise you will see that my goods reach Amy, and that you will care for her."

I did promise that much, and he was content.

Anthony More died just after the sun had set. He was the last of the true buccaneers, and a very great gentleman. But as I cried like a woman over his dead body it was not for Anthony More that I wept, but for Bill Smith. And the tears washed out the dark folly that had filled my soul. My purpose was again a clear burning flame. I must find Cousin. When he was dead I would start on an even more dreadful and mysterious journey. I would go into the sea in search of Polly Bragg.

# XVI

## I.

We buried Bill on a hillside overlooking the sea. The next day the men held a meeting. A new leader was elected. He was a shrewd fellow who immediately demanded that every man swear to keep Bill's death a secret.

"Anthony More and his white fish on our flag are too valuable to let die," he explained. "Many a ship surrenders to Anthony More that would stand and fight another man."

I swore with the others because it was required of me, but I had no interest in the matter. Bill Smith was on the hillside; for me there had never been an Anthony More. Besides I was done with pirating and anxious to get away so I could put Bill's plan into effect. As soon as I could arrange it, accompanied by Judith and her four negurs I left Tortuga for Hispaniola. From there we sailed to Port Royal.

I took Judith to Saltash.

"This is her home," I told Trigg. "You manage the plantation as before, but the house is hers. Give her whatever she requires."

It had been hard to come home. But Bill's words on his death-bed, and the shock of his death itself, had completed the cure of my madness, a cure begun by Maria Montijo and Judith. All of them, in their own way, had borne home to me the consequences of my morbid folly. I was still determined to punish Cousin to the uttermost, and then to join Polly; but meantime I was as other men, capable of laughter and friendship and pleasure. And love, too. For two years my emotions had been wasted in sterile floods of brooding bitterness; now they found an object for their devo-

tion in Judith. I did not regard her as the daughter that she, herself, swore she would be to me—I was too conscious of her womanhood for that—but I was content to accept her placid affection and
leave her in peace; for no one could replace Polly, and in forty
years I had learned that there is more in life than getting a woman
into bed. So I took Judith to Saltash and installed her there.

I myself did not intend to stay. I had business in Port Royal
and on the sea and in Africa. I had business with Edward Cousin.

I took Trigg into my confidence. He admitted that the plan
was feasible, but opposed my carrying it out.

"Too dangerous," he said. "Stay here."

"What is there for me here?"

His face twisted into the sardonic grin that I knew so well.

"Wealth, comfort, a beautiful girl not more than twenty, I'd
say, tender—"

"Tender you think," I jeered. "Let me tell you that no man
living could say to me the hard things Judith Mara has said, or
treat me with half the contempt."

"For love of you, my boy."

"Boy to you, but to her I am as ancient as you yourself. Besides I don't love her."

"Pol?" he asked.

"Do you think I could forget?"

He shrugged.

"Men do."

"Not such women as Polly."

"She's not worth your loyalty," he said abruptly.

I had wasted too much anger in the past few months to spare
more on Trigg. I told him wearily that he could leave Saltash if
he found my wife's memory unpleasant. He refused flatly.

"I meant no harm beyond that she was, after all, only a woman.
I'll stay with you. You need your friends, and when more time has
gone by maybe you will change your mind about Judith."

I told him to suit himself. When he spoke again it was with a
queer hesitant defiance, as if he half doubted the wisdom of speaking yet found it impossible to remain silent.

358

"I still think you should give up your plan," he said. "If you must find Cousin, wait for him in Port Royal."

"Bill tried that."

"Then go to God's Acres."

"Bill did that, too. He found only armed slaves, dogs and a negur wench who fed him and sent him away."

"It might be different now. It's said in Port Royal that Cousin has recently taken a bride."

"A negress he has saved, no doubt," I sneered.

"Not if rumor is true. They say that she is a white woman guarded by a giant negur. Queer tales go the rounds in Port Royal. Contradictory, too. Some say that she is more pious than Cousin himself, and that she holds herself so close to Christ that her own husband dare not touch her; but others, chiefly negurs and half-castes, swear that she is a witch. All agree that she is white and beautiful, though I have found no man who has seen her. She never leaves God's Acres. Go there. Times have changed since Smith's visit."

After some thought I resolved to take Trigg's advice. Perhaps God's Acres had changed. It also crossed my mind that even though I failed to reach Cousin I might find his wife. If so I would kill her as he had killed Pol. If he loved her let him suffer as I had suffered. The more I considered it the more the idea appealed to me . . . kill Edward Cousin's bride.

I had a reason other than revenge for going to God's Acres. Upon my return to Port Royal I had sought for some trace of Abel and the negress, Evalyn. I was resolved to find them if I had to comb the Caribbean, and to purchase them from their new owners, whatever the cost. At first luck seemed to be with me. Inquiry proved that in the fall of 1683, only a few days after I had escaped from his ship, Cousin brought a cargo of blacks to Port Royal. Being an unusually fine lot they were sold at auction rather than in a scramble. All this was promising. Abel and Evalyn must be somewhere in Jamaica. But the trail came to an abrupt end. I found the auctioneer, the customs official. They could tell me nothing. I sent Trigg to visit the plantations of the island on the pretense of buying slaves. It was useless. I concluded reluctantly

359

that Cousin in a rage at Pol and me had killed Abel and the girl on shipboard. But when Trigg spoke of God's Acres another possibility presented itself. I would look for my negurs there. It would be like Cousin to keep them himself, so that he might have leisure to contemplate their wickedness and devise means by which they could be persuaded to repent.

When I was ready to go both Judith and Trigg wanted to accompany me. I rejected their offers. I was unwilling that Judith should run the slightest risk of falling under the shadow of Edward Cousin. I wanted Trigg as a reserve.

"I am going alone and, except for my long knife, unarmed," I told him. "If I am not back by tomorrow night you come with men and guns."

The morning was bright when I started for Spanish Town. The sky, the sea, the mountains were as beautiful as when Pol and I had admired them together. I spurred my horse that I might reach Edward Cousin sooner. At Spanish Town I asked how to reach God's Acres. A negur looked at me out of rolling eyes and babbled in the soft sibilants of Africa. A white man pointed to the west and spat.

"Last plantation," he muttered.

When I reached it I was surprised. Bill had spoken of it so vividly that I half expected a walled prison with moat and spiked portcullis. But God's Acres looked much like other plantations. Negurs worked in the fields, the birds sang sweetly, the sun still gleamed bright in the sky. But as I turned into a lane that led to a house set far back in the trees, two negurs appeared from the bushes. They carried guns. Fierce dogs bristled beside them.

"Where?" asked one.

"Is this God's Acres?"

He nodded.

"Then I am going to that house."

They did not answer but fell in beside me. Out of curiosity I made my horse trot. The blacks did not protest. They loped abreast me effortlessly, the dogs at their heels. These last did not bark at the horse as most dogs do, but their fangs were bared.

360

I was beginning to sense why Bill had not returned to God's Acres.

We reached the house. An iron knocker was on the door. I banged it furiously. A negress opened it.

"Is your master here?" I asked.

She shook her head.

"Your mistress?"

The blank curtain that had hitherto hid her face lifted for a moment. Fright spilled out of soft velvet eyes, her mouth trembled, her blank brow wrinkled. She only stared at me.

"I am coming in," I said.

She stood aside without protest. As I entered the door I looked back. The guards stood on the porch. Their guns were ready. The dogs crouched at their feet—waiting.

I stepped into a broad dark hall. Closed doors led to rooms on either side. I paused. The negress beckoned me to follow her. She led me into a large room. Thick curtains shut out the sunlight; the furniture was massive and ugly. In the center was a table upon which lay an open Bible. An inexplicable impulse led me to it. I picked it up. A passage was heavily marked:

> *"And he said unto me, Go in, and behold the*
> *wicked abominations that they do here."*

I looked up. The negress who had let me into the house was gone. Another stood in her place. She was dressed like an English servant in a severe puritan household of Cromwell's time.

"Who reads this?" I asked her, pointing at the Bible.

She showed no surprise at my question.

"The mistress left it for the master to read," she said. "Sit down, please."

Her voice was toneless yet oddly compelling, and I knew that I would get no information out of her. I sat down. We looked at one another. The wench who had let me into the house returned. She brought cakes and brandy. I waved them away.

"You will not eat?" the woman asked.

"I came to see your master."

361

"He does not receive guests."

"Is he here?"

"He is never here to guests."

"Your mistress?"

"She sees no one."

"But she at least is here."

The woman did not reply. I walked over to her.

"I shall look until I find one of them," I told her.

She did not answer but rose and preceded me into the hall. She pointed to a broad stairway.

"Up there," she said.

I thought that she meant Cousin and his wife were there. I started up. I had not gone halfway when I heard the door open. I swung around as the dogs burst in. Snarling savagely they rushed at me. They were fierce beasts but not as dangerous as the wild hogs on Tortuga. Moreover, they were forced to charge upwards. When the first leaped at my throat I side stepped and plunged my long knife into his belly. He yapped like any hurt puppy and died. The other hurled himself at me. I did not have time to use the knife again. I grabbed him by the throat and strangled him with my bare hands. Meanwhile my human assailants, the negurs who had escorted me to the house, were coming warily up the steps. They held their guns like clubs. I laughed. So Cousin did not trust them with powder and shot. My knife dripped with blood.

"Go back," I said.

They hesitated and obeyed. I followed them down. The young woman had disappeared but the other one waited quietly at the foot of the stairs. I locked her with the two dejected guards in a closet. Then I continued my search of the house.

It was a large house of many rooms . . . and empty. It was empty of more than human occupants. It lacked all sense of life, all feeling of being lived in. The furniture was scant and heavy and dull. There was not a picture on the wall, a book, except the Bible, or a vase on a table. There were no pipes or tobacco jars for the master, no needlework for the mistress' idle hours.

Upstairs in the bedchambers there were clothes. I found Cousin's first: hats, cloaks, doublets, shirts, breeches, shoes, boots. They were sober, well cut and of good quality. Another room, far from Cousin's, appeared to be that of the new mistress. And here was a puzzle. At first I thought it a servant's closet. It was small and as barren of comforts as a nun's cell. Its only furnishings were a bed covered with a quilt of some coarse material and a hard straight chair. I was about to leave it when I noticed two curtained recesses. I looked into one and saw what I expected: heavy shoes and clogs, modest kerchiefs and hoods of coarse ugly cloth, bodices of sober color that must hang loose as sacks, and chemises heavy and plain.

Indifferently I pulled back the other curtain and gasped in amazement. Chemises of the finest linen were here, with full sleeves ending in fashionable ruffles of lace, a scarlet cloak, gowns cut low and square at the neck, with long paneled trains. Magnificent riding habits, boots of finest leather. Shoes, too, elegantly made with jeweled buckles. A chest of drawers was in one end of the closet. I looked in it. There were hose of rich material, scarlet, black, white. In a case was gay jewelry of every sort: clasps, earrings, necklaces, strings of pearls for the hair. I found gum patches for the face too, and ointments and powder for the skin. I stared at the stuff in amazement. What sort of a creature was Edward Cousin's wife?

When I had finished my search I freed the negurs.

"What is your mistress like?" I asked.

"Good," muttered one of the men.

"A witch," spat the woman.

I could get nothing more out of them. At length I grew weary of the mystery. After all, Cousin's wife, witch or saint, was no affair of mine. Bill had been right, his plan was the only one that promised success. I would leave God's Acres. But I would also leave a momento for Edward Cousin. I drew my long knife from its sheath.

"Tell your master this came . . ."

I was about to say "from Tom Bone" when I recalled that Bill had said that Cousin fled from the blood-red flag which bore a

363

white fish in one corner. And no one but the pirates knew that Anthony More was dead. So in a split second I changed my mind.

". . . that this came from Anthony More," I said, "and that its mate will be carried naked until it rests in Edward Cousin's heart."

The old woman smiled.

"I will tell him," she promised.

I left God's Acres satisfied that I had accomplished all that was possible, and that on the whole the day's work had not been bad. But as I left the plantation my complacency was disturbed. From the hills behind me came the throb of voudou drums. They seemed to repeat the words of the negress at God's Acres. "A witch," they said, "a witch." I wondered uneasily if Cousin was now in league with a creature who had sold herself to the devil . . . and I urged my horse to greater speed. I wanted to reach Spanish Town before night came.

The next morning I lingered long enough to make vain inquiries concerning Edward Cousin and his wife. The people there knew, or professed to know, nothing. It was common knowledge that Cousin had recently taken a wife, but no one had seen her. Since his ship was at Port Royal one presumed that he himself might well be at home, but who could tell? The songs of the voudou drums? Maroons no doubt. Certainly no one could swear that they came from God's Acres.

I tired of vaporous nothings and turned my horse toward Port Royal. A few miles from Saltash I met Trigg. He was at the head of a cavalcade of armed negurs. In the forefront were Matthew, James, Simon and John. Judith led them.

Trigg was both relieved and abashed. He explained that though he knew I had told him to wait until night before coming to my aid, he had resolved to get in the neighborhood of Spanish Town, just as a precaution. I laughed at him and thanked him for his zeal; but I was seriously disturbed that Judith was with him.

"I will not have her near Cousin," I declared.

"Nor would I," Trigg agreed, "if I knew how the devil a man might pound some sense into her head. I left her safe at Saltash.

364

Not twenty minutes ago she caught up with us. Short of compelling her and her four bucks by force—"

"Which you could not do," Judith interrupted calmly.

"Which I could do by myself without straining a muscle," Trigg roared back, "but which would cause delay. Short of compelling her by force to turn back, I could do naught but let her come."

I turned to Judith.

"Have I told you that I love you, Judith Mara?" I questioned.

Her eyes fell. "As a daughter?" There was pleading in her voice.

"In any way you wish," I retorted, "so long as you understand that you are all that stands between me and the beast that I was when you first knew me. Now swear to me on the crucifix that you hold so dear that you will stay away from Edward Cousin and God's Acres."

"But there was no danger, with Trigg and the men."

"In this one matter I must have my way," I insisted.

She swore without further protest.

Trigg was anxious for news of my adventure, but when I had told my story he was downcast.

"So you didn't see Cousin," he muttered gloomily.

"There is still Bill's way."

"And now I suppose you will try it."

"As soon as possible."

He reverted to the subject of God's Acres.

"And you neither saw nor learned anything of Cousin's wife?"

"She is a greater mystery than before."

"So it seems. How about Abel and the girl?"

I had completely forgotten them. I admitted it and cursed myself roundly.

"Never mind," Trigg said comfortingly. "Some day I shall go for them myself. I am curious about your Edward Cousin and his wife."

"Especially his wife," I laughed.

To my surprise Trigg replied with the utmost gravity.

"Never in my life have I been so interested in a woman," he admitted.

Before continuing the pursuit of Cousin I called on Samuel Hart. He examined the papers that Bill had directed me to deliver.

"So Anthony More is dead," he said when he had finished.

"No," I replied promptly.

Hart frowned.

"But it says here that when I read these he will be dead."

I faced a dilemma. If I insisted that Bill was still alive Hart might refuse to turn over Anthony More's property to me. If I told the truth it might soon be common news that the great Anthony More was dead. I was not worried over the prospect of breaking my oath, which, in view of the fact that its sole aim was to facilitate robbery, I regarded lightly; but I was anxious that Edward Cousin should not be given the comfort of knowing that his enemy was dead. Yet, somehow, I must keep my promise to Bill. I asked myself if I could trust Hart. He was a Jew with soft-veiled eyes and heavy lips. His hands were narrow with long fingers; his hair was thin and gray. As a boy in England I had been taught to despise Jews and suspect them. Yet, as I looked at Samuel Hart I trusted him. There was patience in his voice and suffering in the lines around his mouth and eyes.

"Did you know Anthony More?" I asked.

"He would hardly have trusted me with his property otherwise," he answered cautiously.

"Don't fence with me," I begged. "Did you know him as anything other than a successful buccaneer?"

He weighed each word carefully.

"I knew him only as a buccaneer. I do not know if he could be called successful. He was a melancholy man."

"With reason," I exclaimed.

The Jew agreed.

"Do you know that reason?"

"He once told me that he had been deeply wronged."

"By Edward Cousin."

"I did not need to hear More's story to despise Cousin. He is

366

evil. He profanes God and uses His words to cloak hatred of all His creatures."

"Has he wronged you too?" I asked eagerly.

"No. I dislike him for what he is."

"Then you would not comfort him?"

"No."

I resolved to tell the truth. I admitted Bill was dead and explained why at first I had denied it. He promised to keep my secret.

"My people know how to keep silent," he assured me.

Upon his advice I decided to leave Bill's property with him, while he wrote to England to inquire after Amy More. When he received a reply he would send her the stuff.

Bill's business done I made a will. All that I owned I bequeathed to Judith Mara, only requesting that she give Trigg a home as long as he lived and continue the search for Abel. This done I was ready to enlist in the service of Edward Cousin.

That had been Bill's plan.

"The sea is too big," he had said. "One ship on it is like a fly speck in the heavens. I have searched for twenty years and failed. You might well search for twenty more to the same end. Give it up. Get on his own ship as one of his men. There, sooner or later, your opportunity will come. Aboard ship or in the jungles of Africa, sooner or later you will be alone with Edward Cousin. Perhaps not during the first voyage or the second. But if you have patience the time must come—and in less than twenty years."

"But how can I obtain service with him?" I had asked.

"Like all merchants he needs hands from time to time. You will have to use your own wits to persuade him that you are the man he wants."

It sounded easy when Bill said it in Tortuga. I was now ready to try it out. I knew that Cousin's ship, the *Pilgrim*, was in the harbor at Port Royal, where it was being careened and conditioned for a new voyage. I heard it said in the grog shops that his mate was looking for a man. I went to him.

He was the same giant that I had seen on Cousin's ship, but I felt sure that he would not recognize me. True, he had seen me

367

every day for a week, and, since I judged my attack on Cousin would create a deep impression, had reason to remember me. But I had been young then. A different man stood fingering a tattered hat and whining that he understood Master Cousin needed a man.

The mate shook his head.

"Too old, Uncle," he said.

"Barely forty-one," I told him.

He roared with laughter.

"With those streaks of white in your head and your beard half gray? Deep lines on your face, too. What caused those if not years? More years than forty, too."

For a moment I forgot my role.

"Suffering and grief caused them," I snapped angrily, and added truthfully, "And vicious living."

My irritation only amused him. He slapped a huge thigh.

"So, Uncle, you have been a misused man and a bad one besides. Go sit in the sun and dream about days gone by. Let young men sail the sea."

I discarded all pretense to humility.

"My face may be old," I retorted, "but my body is young and stronger than that blubber-bound carcase of yours."

He was still laughing as he stood up. A great hand, big as a ham, shot forward and grabbed me by the neck. He held me out and shook me like a puppy worries a dead rat. He set me down and stepped back.

"Blubber bound am I, Uncle," he roared gleefully.

"I am a small man," I told him. "Come nearer."

He grinned tolerantly and complied. I grasped him at the waist with both hands. I had seen Abel do it while scuffling with other negurs at Sidney. I prayed that God give me the strength. Slowly I lifted him. He did not struggle, but held his body tense. I strained to the utmost every muscle in my back and shoulders. I lifted him above my head until he was parallel to the floor. Then inch by inch I lowered him. When he was on the floor again I was weak as a kitten. I almost collapsed when he gave me a resounding slap across the shoulders.

"God damn me, Uncle. You are a man. And Jack Morgan is the one to admit when he has made a mistake."

"Then you will take me?"

He shook his head.

"And I am sorry, too; but Cousin wants not only a strong man, but one who can write and cipher. Someone to go with him and aid him when he chaffers with the negurs."

"I can write and cipher."

He rummaged in a drawer until he found writing materials. When I had satisfied him he asked my name.

"Tom Griffith," I said.

I hoped that a Welsh name might please him, and was not disappointed.

"A fellow countryman," he cried gleefully. "Well, Uncle, you are the man for me, but you must convince Cousin, too."

"When?"

"Not so fast. I'll ask a question or two. Not many want to sail with us. Did you know that?"

"I've heard things."

"And still want to come?"

"I want to learn the trade. Cousin knows it."

"None better," Morgan agreed grimly. "Who have you sailed with?"

"Anthony More," I said boldly.

His mouth fell open. Then he burst into one of his peals of explosive laughter.

"By God, Uncle. That's a rare joke. But don't tell Cousin. He'd have you hanged. He doesn't like the buccaneers . . . particularly your Anthony More. Many times we have run from him, although Cousin is no coward and fights others. But why did you leave More?"

"Pirates hang if they stay with it."

"I'll wager Anthony More will never hang."

"No, he won't hang."

A shadow crossed his face.

"If you have been a pirate maybe you won't want to come with us. A woman will be aboard."

"A woman?"

"A white one. Cousin has taken a wife. He ordered the cabin refitted for her."

My heart leaped. In a flash I knew what I would do. Somehow I would manage to keelhaul Mistress Cousin . . . before her husband's eyes. I would do it if I had to take the ship single-handed. I hoped that the woman was young and beautiful.

"Have you seen her?" I asked.

"Aye," he growled.

"Is she beautiful?"

"Cousin thinks so. He dotes on her." He went on savagely, "Oh, yes, she's beautiful. Beautiful enough to bewitch and damn Edward Cousin. Not that I care for that, if only he would keep her off this ship; but before she is done with him she will kill and damn us all. He was bad enough before, but since she has cast her spell over him he is a monster. With her on board again . . . God help us. If you are wise, Uncle, you won't sign with Edward Cousin and his bride."

"I am not afraid," I said confidently. "But, tell me, where does this mysterious creature come from?"

The great brute who had lifted me by the neck as easily as if I had been a pet rabbit trembled.

"How do I know where she comes from?" he muttered. "Cousin picked her up out of the sea. She is a witch, I tell you."

"A sea witch," I laughed, and as I thought of how I would keelhaul her my merriment increased. "Well, perhaps it will be best to dump her back into the sea," I chuckled.

A few days later I had an interview with Cousin. I had been schooling myself for it ever since I resolved to accept Bill's challenge. He himself had warned me.

"You are impetuous and lack discipline. Remember that the hardest part of your task will be to hide your feelings toward Cousin. You have grown into a strong man, but have you learned to master your own strength?" He smiled at me. "I think I have told you before that you are wrong to sneer at the gentle-born. You should copy some of their virtues. Most important of these is the art of governing oneself."

Although he was dying I protested. He answered me impatiently.

"How often I have said to someone that I have no time for this or that. Only now do I know the fatality that can dwell in those words. *I haven't time*, Tom, to argue with you, but remember this: a day will come when it will be your wits against the wits of Edward Cousin . . . your body, your spirit against his. On that day remember the words of a dying man—discipline, self-control."

Now the day had come, and as I stood before the dingy warehouse where Cousin had his office I did remember.

"Wherever you are, Bill, help me," I muttered, and knocked.

A negur opened the door. When I told my business he took me to Cousin. But instead of leaving us alone he stood behind me holding ready an unsheathed knife. I reflected that Cousin must have injured a great many men to make such a precaution necessary, and that while he took such measures it would be difficult for me to trap him.

In spite of all my resolutions to the contrary I almost betrayed myself during the first minute that I faced Cousin. I had believed that he could be no uglier, but I saw that I had been wrong. When I had last seen him he was merely ill-favored; now he was repulsive. His face was flattened and hideously scarred. Its flesh and muscles had been broken. His teeth were gone. I stared open-mouthed. My blood was warm. I once more felt my fist crash into his face and the flesh break and the bones crack under my feet. I had not dared dream that my mad attack on him aboard his ship had left such ruin. A small part, a very small part, of my debt was already paid. I could scarcely conceal my satisfaction.

"You are Thomas Griffith," he said abruptly.

"Yes, sir."

He asked the same questions that the mate had asked. I gave him the same answers until he wanted to know with whom I had last sailed.

"Captain Jonathan Reap, master of the *Topping Merchant*, out of Boston," I replied promptly.

I thought this safe because Reap had told us that he'd never heard of Edward Cousin. But Cousin had heard of Jonathan Reap.

"A cheating hypocrite," he declared. "Disapproves of the slave trade I am told; so he sells his rotten fish to the slave owners while he dares rebuke such men as I. But God will punish him. For what is the hope of the hypocrite, though he hath gained, when God taketh away his soul."

Cousin paused. He seemed to relish God's taking away the soul of poor Jonathan Reap. He had worked himself into such a fury at the insolent merchant that dared criticize him, that I began to think it would have been as well to name Anthony More.

"Why did you leave him?" he barked at me.

"Because he would have naught to do with the slave trade, sir. I am anxious to learn it."

This pleased Cousin as much as anything was apt to please him.

"You are old to be beginning," he grumbled, "but at least it shows that you have some sense." He fixed me with his cold stare. "And do not forget that Reap and the few other lunatics that presume to rebuke the trade are putting their judgment against Holy Scripture. 'Cursed be Canaan, a servant of servants shall he be among his brothers' . . . And note you, Griffith, that these blacks are the sons of Ham."

A few minutes later he signed me. I was told that I would be expected to make myself useful aboard the ship, but that my chief duties would be in Africa, where I was to act as Cousin's aide and agent in dealing with the native chiefs.

"My last agent cheated me," he said.

That was all, but I knew that I had been warned.

That night as I lay on the dirty mattress that served as a bed at the dive where I judged it best to stay while playing my rôle of Thomas Griffith, I reviewed the day's work and was content. I had gained employment with Edward Cousin, and more important still had faced him without betraying myself. I had only to be patient now and the opportunity I needed must surely present itself. But there was not as much time as Bill had counted upon. Weeks and months, but not years. After I had signed the necessary articles Cousin had looked at me dourly.

"You will have to learn quickly if you learn the slave trade from me," he said spitefully. "This is my last voyage."

During the next few minutes, despite the dislike and contempt that I felt for Edward Cousin, I was sorry for him. He was such a cheap piece of humanity: a little man whose willingness to abase himself before the most bigoted among the Puritan politicians had given him brief power. Thus clothed he strutted pompously across his little stage, scolding, croaking, admonishing in order that he might hide the poverty of his mind, believing all the while that the garb of authority made him something more than the mean creature he was. As a consequence he was so despised that when the winds of politics changed he ignominiously fled, leaving only a stench where memory of him lingered.

In the New World by entering a business where cheating, slyness and heartlessness supplanted decency and fair dealing he had gained success of a sort. He was a rich man and feared. But as he sat once more behind the desk of authority that makes little men big, he was still a poor cheap creature. A little man . . . without friends . . . lonely. It was this last that aroused even my pity. For there in his office he found the world so empty that he confided in me, a tramp seaman hunting a job—or so he thought.

"My last voyage," he repeated. "You see I have taken a wife lately. She wants me at home; women worry about a man when he's on the sea." His harsh scarred face softened a little, his cold eyes fired. His voice was wistful. "Women are like that, you know, when they care for a man."

Before I dropped to sleep I recalled that Cousin must have taken his wife after I had disfigured him. Could any woman, even a witch out of the sea, or, I thought, more likely out of a brothel, really want him at home? Could a woman even look at what I had made of his face without shuddering? Maybe a witch could.

Before I sailed I made a final visit to Saltash. I told Trigg to watch over Judith, although when she challenged me I had to admit that it would be more likely that she would watch over him.

"But just the same if I don't come back you will be needing another father," I teased. "Your third in less than three years. You take new fathers as other women take lovers."

She laughed with me, but her deep blue eyes were wet. She put her arms around me and kissed me. Her mouth was cool, but her voice trembled.

"Come back," she said.

The *Pilgrim* was ready to sail. The crew was assembled. Only Cousin was not yet aboard. The men went about their work, but from mate to cabin boy they were tense and uneasy. They were waiting for the hour when Edward Cousin would bring his wife aboard.

I was idly polishing a piece of brass when a fellow nudged me.

"There they be," he whispered hoarsely.

I looked over the water to the wharf. True enough there was Edward Cousin. He and his wife had stopped not far from the water's edge. The woman had her back to me. She wore the long red coat I had seen in the closet at God's Acres. A hood covered her head. From under it a few locks of brown hair had escaped. At least not tresses of seaweed, I thought. They were too far away to be heard but I judged that they were arguing. At least Cousin was gesticulating wildly. The woman did not move. Her arms hung quietly at her side. There was something frightening about her quiet figure. For the first time I felt the uneasiness of the men. Would I dare lay hands on that quiet body? Gradually Cousin, too, grew quiet. Finally he was as still as she. But hers was the stillness of power in repose; his the weariness of the beaten. He leaned toward her. For the first time she moved. She stepped backward and raised her hand. He stopped; his heavy shoulders drooped. She stood frozen for an instant, then stepped around him and walked away. He watched her until she was out of sight. She did not once look back. When she was gone he shook his head and walked toward the small boat that waited to bring him to us.

When he came over the rail his face was purple. Without meeting any man's eye he strode to the quarterdeck and gave the orders to sail. His voice was choked. A small negur girl came out of

374

the newly fitted cabin. Cousin himself had brought her aboard the previous day. A surprise for his wife. She had not seen the tableau ashore. She was young and artless. She trotted directly to Cousin.

"Where mistress?" she asked lightly.

Cousin glared at her.

"Where mistress?" the child repeated.

"On shore," he rasped. "Where you had best join her."

He picked her up and tossed her like a doll over the ship's side. From where I stood I could see her knife into the water like a fish that has wriggled off the angler's hook, struggle to the surface and swim easily toward shore. A sailor, not far from Cousin, could not see. He looked anxiously over the rail. Cousin knocked him senseless. The rest of us busied ourselves at anything that came to hand.

The voyage of the *Pilgrim* had begun.

### 3.

The *Pilgrim* was a frigate-built vessel of something over three hundred tons. She carried thirty guns and a crew of one hundred and twenty-five men. Except that the deck was raised a few feet so that there might be more light and air below, where the slaves were packed, she was an ordinary vessel, well built and sturdy.

I was determined to make as many friends as possible among the men, and, although they were a sullen suspicious lot, I was not entirely without success. This was due largely to Jack Morgan, the mate, who, perhaps in order to balance Cousin's complete isolation from the crew, mingled with the men more after the fashion of an officer of a pirate ship than a merchantman. If the stories told by the men were true, Morgan was a wild beast in battle; and of my own knowledge I can say that he carried out Cousin's most revolting orders with complete callousness. But at other times he was a good-natured likable brute and he had taken a fancy to me. He persisted in calling me Uncle and swore that I was at least sixty, but his chaffing was well meant, and the men followed his lead. I was immediately welcomed into the brotherhood of the forecastle—such as it was.

Two days out of Port Royal a suspicious-looking vessel was sighted. Orders sharp as pistol shots exploded across the deck. The men moved with a speed and discipline that I had never seen approached by pirates. The guns were manned, sharpshooters clambered into the rigging, a boarding party assembled. Cousin took his place on the quarterdeck. The *Pilgrim* held steady on its course.

The ship drew closer. "A pirate," shouted the lookout positively. A few minutes later we could all see the red flag. But suddenly the man aloft, who had been singing out his news in a full confident voice, changed his tune. "The white fish, sir," he called down tonelessly.

I looked at Cousin. He uttered no sound but his lips were moving. "Anthony More," they said. Without a word he turned and entered his cabin. Morgan took over.

"We'll show a clean pair of heels, lads," he shouted. "You know what to do."

The men showed neither elation nor disappointment as they went about their tasks, but here and there I intercepted a sneer or a sardonic grin. We outran the pirate easily.

That evening in the forecastle the men talked. A few of them had been with Cousin for years, but none could tell why he fled from Anthony More. He was not a coward; they agreed on that. They had seen him fight. They gave it up at length as an old mystery which they had vainly worried over before. But they continued to discuss Edward Cousin. As I listened I realized that they hated and feared him, but they admired him too.

"He's a man who knows what he wants and gets it," one of them said.

"The devil can't stop him," a fellow agreed.

"I've never seen him beaten," chimed in a third.

An old chap who had been sitting to one side nursing an extra ration of rum looked up. He spoke in a thick voice, but his words were clear.

"I have, and it didn't take the devil either. He was balked by a slip of a woman, and his face damn near beaten to a pulp by one of his own prisoners."

376

The old fellow cackled gleefully. The rest of them looked away from him uneasily.

"Some of you will remember," he insisted. "The woman he took off the pirate. She was in his cabin for a week, but by the looks of him when they came out I'm damned if he got what he wanted."

My heart was pounding. I clenched my teeth. Discipline, I told myself, discipline. Remember it is your wits against Cousin, your body, your spirit. Don't give yourself away. Discipline, Bill said . . . But in spite of everything I found myself breathing hard. If they touched Polly with their foul tongues . . .

"Shut up, Jack," one of the sailors said.

The old fellow only laughed.

"God damn me if he didn't get down on his knees to her. Right there on the quarterdeck, and he grabbed her around the middle. She just shoved him away. He had her keelhauled then, but he wasn't lookin' when we took her up, because by that time her husband had damned near killed him. His face looked worse than hers."

I was about to cry out when a heavy fist caught the fellow flush on the jaw. He slumped to the floor. Morgan stood above him, glaring at us. But he seemed less angry than afraid.

"Why didn't one of you stop him?" he asked nervously. "You know the Old Man will half kill him if he hears about it. And have we ever talked about that day without bad luck falling on us? Forget, damn you, forget it, forget him, forget her."

I was bewildered at his intensity. His voice was shrill, almost hysterical.

"He didn't say much," one of the men declared sullenly. "He'd but started. We hadn't time to stop him. And the Captain needn't hear."

"Needn't hear," Morgan retorted contemptuously. "You're a fool, Ned Jenkins. He hears everything that is said on the *Pilgrim*. The man who forgets that doesn't live long."

He stamped out.

I was pleased. It seemed that Edward Cousin did not revere the memory of Thomas Bone and his wife. Like Anthony More's

377

white fish, we frightened him, although we were only ghosts.
From that hour my fear of Edward Cousin diminished. I saw
him in his true character: a bully. He was a wicked man; there
was no doubt of that. Cunning too, and resourceful. Dangerous
as a poisonous snake. But he was not invulnerable. Like a snake
he could be crushed. I recalled everything that I knew of him.
It had always been the weak or defenseless that he overcame. Old
women like Jenny, men like my father, alone against armed thugs,
girls, not over-bright, such as Evalyn my sister and, I suspected,
Bill's beloved Prudence. Negurs, ignorant and in bonds. He had
his will with such as these. But Polly alone, defenseless, his captive, had reduced him to ridicule; that he killed her only under-
scored his impotence. And he turned tail at the mere sight of
Anthony More's banner. Even I, condemned for piracy, his prisoner, had beaten him down, trampled him under my feet. Yes,
Edward Cousin was wicked, formidable—but he was not invulnerable.

So far as I know Jack did not suffer for his indiscretion, nor
did we encounter ill fortune. But a few weeks later I learned that
what Morgan said about Cousin knowing all that was said aboard
his ship was not idle talk. One day he ordered a sailor flogged.
He watched the beating. God knows it was brutal enough, but
it did not satisfy Edward Cousin. Muttering incoherently he
snatched the knout from the hand of the man appointed to ad-
minister the punishment. Before he had done he had half killed
his victim. The most frightening aspect of the thing was that he
was not angry. I doubt if he felt the least resentment; it was pure
blood lust.

That night the men talked about it. They had all witnessed
similar incidents; nonetheless they were resentful. I judged it an
opportune time to discover if their temper could be turned into
mutiny. I had been waiting for such a chance, for of all the
projects which I had turned over in my mind mutiny suited me
best. Other schemes limited the time I could hope to have Cousin
in my power, but if I could make myself master of his ship as
well as his person there would be no end to my opportunities for
hurting him.

378

"I am but a new hand," I said cautiously, "and have no complaint against Cousin, but after hearing you talk I wonder that you still serve under him."

"The pay is good," someone muttered.

"Not good enough to transform men into whipped curs." I deliberately disregarded an angry murmur and plunged on. "Or maybe I am unjust—to curs. A cur would fight back."

The murmur stopped. There was a long uncomfortable silence.

"Fight Cousin?" someone finally gasped incredulously.

At the actual words a frightened quivering sigh drifted through the forecastle. It was man's sound. Under similar conditions animals whine. They *were* curs, soundly thrashed and cowering under the lash. I knew that my hopes were futile. There would be no mutiny. I hastened to retrieve my position.

"Whose talking about fighting," I cried in pretended dismay. "I only say that if I felt like some of you seem to, damn me if I wouldn't quit Cousin's service. Personally I'm satisfied. It was you gave the Old Man Hell, not me. As for that little affair this morning, you're lily-livered women. I've sailed on ships where worse was done regularly—and no harm done."

It was the best I could do. Nevertheless during the rest of the evening no one mentioned Cousin's name. I was conspicuously ignored.

Cousin sent for me the next day. I went to his cabin. As I passed along the deck men looked at me queerly. Cousin sat on a heavy stool. The negur bodyguard that I had first seen in his office at Port Royal was present. Once more he stood directly behind me. I wondered if my adventure was to end with a knife in my back.

"I have been told that you do not approve my service," Cousin said.

I was puzzled at the mildness of his voice. I had steeled myself against anger. But although his tactics upset me I clung to the resolution I had made the day that Cousin fled from the pirate. He is a bully, I decided then, cowering before such creatures does not appease them. It only invites their blows.

"You have been told a lie," I said.

379

He frowned in annoyance.

"Do you deny that last night you said that my men were worse than dogs?"

"No. I did say that." I spit on his well-scoured floor. "Your crew isn't worth the floggings you give them. They have no spirit. That little affair of yesterday morning, for instance. They did not like it; it turned their delicate stomachs. And so they whine."

"What would you do?"

"Me? Why should I do anything? I'm not paid to snivel over other people's troubles. But if I felt as some of them seem to, I'd quit your bloody ship at the first port."

He looked at me thoughtfully.

"There is something to be said for candor," he murmured reflectively, more to himself than to me, I thought. "Candid men are seldom dangerous."

He lapsed into silence. I judged that he was turning something over in his mind.

"You don't like my crew and you do only what you are paid to do," he said finally.

"I don't dislike them," I said. "I just don't think they are worth the ship or its master."

"Be frank," he purred. "Perhaps you will tell me your opinion of the *Pilgrim's* master."

"I'm not sure I have one, but you are not weak-kneed like the crew. You know enough to be strong."

That pleased him.

"A wise man is strong, yea a man of knowledge increaseth strength," he declared, and added unctuously, "The Lord has sent you to serve me."

I did not answer. He continued, watching me keenly while he talked.

"You are a shrewd observing fellow. What you just said is true. The crew are cowardly rats. But even rats can be dangerous; so I can use you. Continue to talk as you did last night. If any of them shows signs of heeding you tell me his name."

I knew then how it was that Cousin heard everything that was said aboard the *Pilgrim*. Treacherous himself, he was naturally suspicious of everyone else, so he had spies among his own men. Well, so much the better for me. I wanted to gain his confidence. Here was an opportunity to do so. Moreover, although I had small hope of success, I could use his own orders as a cloak to foment trouble. Possibly I could stir up a mutiny after all.

Cousin seemed to read my thoughts.

"You are a clever man, Griffith," he said. "Clever enough to know the difference between giving disgruntled men an opportunity to reveal themselves and stirring up trouble among the well disposed."

For a moment I was frightened, but then I realized that this was no exhibition of occult powers. Cousin was merely acting in accordance with his own suspicious nature. I replied boldly.

"As you say I am a clever man, and I shall tread the line shrewdly. But what do I get paid for all this? Informing was not mentioned in the articles I signed."

That reassured him. Self-interest was a thing that he could comprehend. He promised to pay me well. I was about to leave when he called me back.

"A crew of mine did mutiny once," he said softly. "It was only a few years after I came to Jamaica. I was inexperienced, but even so I triumphed over my enemies, for my cause was just. But although the law of the sea gave me the right I did not hang the mutineers. I remembered that the Lord is long suffering and of great mercy, and spared their lives. God has rewarded my humble effort to follow His example. For even after all these years there are still blind maimed beggars scattered throughout the ports of the Caribbean who whisper tales of the one mutiny against Edward Cousin. Perhaps my present crew may have seen one of these poor fellows and heard him talk. You might ask one of them to repeat the story."

"It will not be necessary," I assured him.

"Good. I had hoped not. We shall both be better served by reason of your ready comprehension. And now I am sure that you will see the need of some slight punishment in order that the men will not be suspicious. They expect something, you know. Shall we say fifty strokes?"

I recalled how, as I approached the cabin a few minutes before, the crew had looked at me. It would take more than fifty strokes to convince them. The stakes in this game I played were high. I could not afford losing them because of a pinch-penny wager.

"Out of respect for your reputation and that of the blind maimed beggars I would suggest at least seventy-five," I said.

A slight smile lightened Cousin's misshapen face. For an instant I think he actually admired me.

"You are a man after my heart," he said almost jovially. "Shall we make it a hundred?"

"Agreed. But in that case might I be so bold as to beg that you consider the possibility of being elsewhere during the ceremony?"

His smile deepened. In another man the thin snort that escaped him might have been laughter.

"You are an uncommonly understanding man, Griffith. Uncommonly understanding." He grew thoughtful. "I only hope not too understanding. I cannot possibly grant your request. You see, I have always felt it my duty to personally supervise the punishment of the erring children that the Lord has seen fit to put under my care, painful though it has been. If I neglected to appear it would arouse speculation. But I promise that I shall leave the rod of chastisement in other hands, even though they prove lax."

I was flogged that afternoon. Cousin kept his word. Morgan administered the hundred lashes and although I should not say that he was lax, neither, by the standards of the sea, was he unduly rigorous. Although I was still conscious when it was over he threw a couple of buckets of water over me.

"Hell, Uncle," he growled, "you were lucky. The Old Man has left you your skin. Only a hundred lashes, and he didn't take a hand himself."

Weak and in agony though I was I remembered my rôle.

"The devil with your Old Man," I groaned. My fervor was sincere.

I played my part until we sighted the coast of Africa, but I

382

drew no spark from the men. I told Cousin so. He appeared satisfied but not surprised.

"You have been zealous, too, I understand," he said.

"I told you I'd play the game shrewdly."

"So you did and so you have. Continue to do it. The real opportunity for a trouble-maker comes when we are loaded with seven hundred and fifty blacks."

That gave me an idea.

# XVII

DURING THE Eastward Passage a large supply of horse beans which Cousin had intended to feed to the blacks on the return voyage spoiled. This misfortune compelled us to stop on the West Guinea, or grain, Coast where we bought provisions. From there we made our way eastward, picking up elephants' teeth and additional corn until we reached Axim, a Dutch fort on the Gold Coast. Here we bought our first negurs.

The Gold Coast blacks are bigger, stronger and more intelligent than those further east. Moreover, because they are vain and hold less-favored tribes in contempt, they can generally be persuaded to act as informers. In a business where the most dreaded disaster is mutiny this quality (and the higher price they bring in the West Indian market) causes Gold Coast slaves to be highly prized. Unfortunately the native kings know this and bargain shrewdly.

Cousin had worked out a clever scheme for making the most of this situation. It was his custom to buy a hundred or so men on the Gold Coast and fill out his cargo with the cheaper wares further east. By thus leavening the mass he made sure of all the spies that he needed, and at the same time laid a foundation for the claim put forward in the Caribbean that he sold Gold Coast negurs. This enabled him to fix a higher price per head at the scrambles where he disposed of his slaves.

Since the Dutch are a sensible people, and not strangled by trade laws as we are under the English, we were greeted courteously by the factor at Axim. He advised Cousin to buy from a near-by native chief. Cousin accepted this suggestion but he did not visit the King himself. Natives were frequently treacherous and the African jungle was full of fever. Cousin stayed aboard the *Pilgrim*. I visited black royalty. I had been employed for that.

I took a dozen men with me and native guides supplied by the Dutchman. The village was two days' journey. It was a mean place but the King greeted us civilly. He was a fantastic sight: a good figure of a man, dressed in an ill-fitting buff coat which boasted cuffs of the heaviest, filthiest lace that I have ever seen. On his head was a magnificent cocked hat with a dashing plume; around his neck he wore a heavy gold chain. But alas! His glory ended abruptly at his knees. His legs were bare; he wore no shoes, and his dirty splayed feet were in incongruous contrast to his European finery. He had less dignity of bearing than the red Indians of North America, and at times acted like a buffoon. Nevertheless I found him a cunning trader.

He assured me with an eloquence which my translator did not fail to reproduce that slaves were exceedingly hard to get. There had been no wars of late and consequently there were no prisoners to sell; food had been plentiful, too, so a man would not dispose of his wives and children at a reasonable rate. Only kidnaping remained and kidnaping was a slow business. Dangerous, too. He laughed a deep laugh, straight up from his belly. He would show me. A big black was brought before us. The King looked at him appreciatively and laughed again.

"Tell him," he ordered.

The prisoner complied. He needed no translator. He had learned English from traders. His story was simple. He lived further east. A Frenchman had come to his village for slaves. His King had sent him to kidnap some. With a small number of companions he had set out. They had been ambushed by my host's men. They themselves would be sold as slaves. That was all. He was taken away.

"You see how hard and dangerous it is?" the King asked.

We dickered all day. Unlike the European slave trader, who has a variety of manufactured articles with which to tempt the negurs, the American merchant is limited to a few products. The most important of these is rum, but Cousin also had a quantity of coral of excellent color and weight. This is highly prized in Africa. I had samples of both coral and rum with me. The King examined them. I looked at his captives. Finally we agreed on terms. The exchange itself would not take place until the negurs were brought to the shore. There the slaves would be examined, Cousin's products tested again and if both parties were satisfied the business would be concluded. We passed the night in the village and returned to Axim the following day.

Cousin was satisfied with the bargain I had made. A week later the King brought the captives to market. Each one was subjected to the most rigid examination. They were made to run, jump and hop on either foot. If this tired them unduly they were rejected. Only the young were taken. It was not unusual for a black trader to shave an old man's gray beard and hair, oil his body and give him liquor to stimulate his spirits. Thus doctored he might be foisted upon the unwary buyer. In order to detect such tricks the mouth of each slave was carefully examined. If his teeth were missing or decayed he was not accepted. When the examination was completed those who had been approved were branded on the breast or shoulder. This was done to prevent substitution before they could be loaded on the ship.

I took no part in these activities but watched them with considerable interest. The blacks were almost all half paralyzed from fear. They submitted dully, obeyed without question. Only the big fellow whose capture had so amused the King was unafraid. He accepted his examination quietly. When he saw me he bowed with a natural dignity and smiled sadly.

Cousin noted this and asked the reason. My explanation pleased him.

"Treat him well," he ordered. "He will be useful."

The next day the blacks were brought aboard. Their previous indifference gave way to hysteria. One broke away and threw himself into the water. To prevent similar accidents the others were put below. Only the former kidnaper was excepted. He was

386

allowed to stay on deck. Cousin charged me with the task of watching over him. I called him Jim.

"Would your people really jump overboard if we let them on deck?" I asked him one day.

"Some."

"Why?"

"Afraid."

"What of?"

"They think white men eat them."

I laughed, but when I considered how the poor devils below must feel it did not seem so amusing.

"Explain to them," I suggested.

"What?"

"The truth. Surely you know our purpose in buying you."

"You sell us across the water. We work for white man."

"That's right. Tell them."

His eyes were somber.

"Maybe they rather you eat them."

"Nonsense," I exclaimed sharply. "Many slaves are happy. Why Abel and Matthew—"

I stopped. How could I explain to this free man of the jungle that slavery was pleasant? Besides I knew that it was not. Abel, Matthew, a few others . . . but I saw the cane and tobacco fields broiling under a hot sun. I heard the crack of the overseer's lash. Jim was looking at me.

"It isn't always so bad," I said lamely.

"They never come back home," he murmured.

"Of course not. They make new homes there."

"They never come back home," he repeated.

After that I saw Jim in a new light. He was no more resigned than the others. In his way he was just as frightened. But he was afraid of the truth. If he was quiet it was only because he was too intelligent to struggle blindly. A new possibility began to shape in my mind.

One afternoon Cousin summoned me to his cabin. In a day or two we would arrive at New Calabar where the balance of the cargo would be picked up. Then the long voyage home . . . St.

387

Tomas . . . the Middle Passage. This was the period of peril. Disease: flux was the most dangerous . . . sometimes half the slaves would die of it. There was danger of fever and smallpox too; and the clap that spread even on Cousin's ships, despite all efforts to keep men and women apart. But sickness was the ship's surgeon's business, Cousin said, and with his skill and God's blessing too many would not be lost. Violence was another matter. It was time to use the negur I called Jim. Did I have his confidence? I said that I did not know.

"You're a fool then and have wasted your time," he growled. "Send the man to me."

Jim was gone a long time. When he appeared he was grinning.

"I go home," he confided to me. "Big master say it. I tell him if negurs plan mutiny. Then I go home."

My heart sank, but I could find nothing to say. For the moment, at least, Jim belonged wholly to Cousin . . . but not quite wholly it appeared.

"I believe in white God, too," he said.

"What?" I gasped.

"Praise God who punish sinners, but help black children go home if they obey big master."

To Jim religion was that simple.

Jim carried the word of God below decks. As a missionary he was evidently both zealous and effective, for in a few days he reported that most of his fellows understood about the partnership between white God and big master.

"Do they all believe they will go home?" I asked.

"They all go home," he said firmly. "Big master use Gold Coast men as shepherds for Calabar negurs. When flock is safe in big master's land he take shepherds home."

When I repeated this to the mate he grinned.

"Cousin always does that. He gets their help that way. You should see them at the other end when they find out that they are to be sold instead of taken back home. If they could get their hands on him they would tear him to pieces."

I had known negurs in Virginia, the West Indies and Africa and found them, with a few exceptions, tractable.

388

"Can they really be dangerous?" I asked doubtfully.

"Haven't you heard of the maroons?"

"Old wives' tales. Whispered horrors. I doubt if the maroons ever did more than steal a few animals."

"That's possible," he admitted, grudgingly, "but I've seen negurs on shipboard. Was in a mutiny once. They aren't scheming bad like the whites. They're crazy bad. They go berserk. And it's a dangerous game Cousin plays."

"Mean rather than dangerous," I protested.

"No, dangerous. Take this Jim you've been nursing. He was quiet enough when they brought him aboard because he understood the whole game. He was in the business himself. He kidnaped blacks, sold them to whites who took them away on ships. His turn to be kidnaped came. Unlike most of them he even knew what would happen to him. The blacks practice slavery among themselves. Jim knew he was to be a white man's slave. He was resigned and therefore not dangerous. The worst that he might do was jump overboard. But now Cousin has given him hope. He also made a bargain with him. The negur will keep his end of the bargain only to learn that he has been duped. How would you feel?"

"Like Jim will feel," I admitted. "But what can he do?"

"Nothing probably. None of the others ever got a chance. But I wouldn't want to be the planter who buys him. He's going to be a mean negur."

"I suppose it would be dangerous if they found out that Cousin was deceiving them before we reached home."

I was thinking aloud.

"My God," the mate yelped, "don't even talk about it. But they won't. How could they?"

"I guess they couldn't," I said.

The negur women were separated from the men by a stout partition. One afternoon the sound of wailing, screeching and moaning came from their quarters. To my surprise no one heeded it.

"Aren't you going to do something?" I asked Morgan.

"About what?"

389

"Can't you hear? There's trouble among the women."

"The Old Man is only saving them," the mate said.

"After which he will bring up the handsomest one and take her to his cabin for special instruction," a nearby seaman added, "but he won't let us near them, though there's plenty of decent captains in the business who give their men the run of the wenches. And why not, I'd like to know? Doesn't a heifer with calf bring a better price?"

He smacked his lips.

He was mistaken about Cousin. When the latter appeared, sweat poured off his forehead and ran down his bare chest and arms; he was breathing hard and his hand trembled so that he could hardly hold the heavy whip he carried . . . but he was alone.

"Well, I'm a whoreson," muttered the seaman.

"You'll be worse than that if he hears you," warned Morgan. "Besides you're a fool. He hasn't taken one of them since he married."

"I'd forgot that," confessed the sailor. After a moment he added fervently, "By God, what a woman his wife must be."

"She is," declared the mate with conviction. "That is if she's a woman at all."

"And why shouldn't she be a woman?" I asked.

"Because she's alive for one thing," he retorted cryptically, and changed the subject.

I did not share Morgan or the sailor's reverence for the attractions of Cousin's mysterious bride. I felt certain that wife or not, sooner or later the lust that I had twice seen take possession of him would again have its way. When it did I intended to take advantage of it if possible. At the first opportunity I questioned the sailor. He proved voluble.

"He goes down with the Bible in one hand and a whip in the other," he said a little wistfully, "and it used to be you never could tell what he'd bring up. Sometimes fat and round and soft as a suet pudding, sometimes skinny girls of fifteen or sixteen; then again a wench of thirty or more, almost too old to be shipped. Sometimes they was what I'd call handsome, other times not.

390

No, damned if you could tell what it would be, except black and female."

"How did he treat them?"

"Hell, I wasn't there. But from the way they looked when he sent them back it couldn't of been very gay. They'd come out like limp black rags . . . no life in 'em at all . . . except a couple that had just enough guts left to jump overboard before anyone knew what they was about."

Although I had expected some such answer I was disappointed.

"Didn't any of them gain any influence over him?" I asked.

"Not in my time, but I guess one did once. It was when he first came out, I'm told. He didn't sell her like the others, but took her home with him to God's Acres. I saw her once at that. Mistress of the place she seemed to be, with rich clothes and jewels."

I recalled Evalyn's pitiful reign of glory and remembered the drab dress of the negress I had met at God's Acres. Was she the seaman's richly appareled mistress of Cousin's home? What tales could she tell?

"So you have visited God's Acres," I said.

"Just that once. The Old Man caught fever on the home voyage, so some of us took him to his plantation. The wench met us at the door. One of the lads remembered her, but if she recognized him she didn't show it. She gave us good rum and food and sent us on our business . . . I wonder how *she* likes Cousin's bride."

He told me more but none of it helped. It was evident that I could not reach Cousin through a black woman. Regretfully I relinquished the idea.

As we sailed along the coast of Africa we stopped at a number of trading stations where we took on food, water, a little gold, more elephants' teeth and a few blacks. Each time we anchored I prayed that Cousin would land and, alone or with a small party, accompany me into the jungle. But he stayed safely aboard ship. The day before we reached New Calabar, which was the last stop before we headed westward, I had to admit that so far my plans had proved futile. For the first time since Bill had given me hope

391

I felt again the black fog of frustration that had enshrouded me for so many months.

Since the day that I launched Bill's project I had been pursued by bad luck. When Cousin signed me he announced that it was his last voyage. After that I had taken heart from the news that he had a wife who would be aboard. I thought I might hurt him through her. I saw her leave him at the waterfront. My hopes turned to mutiny. The men were afraid. Meantime, Cousin never moved without his negur guard. Of course I could kill him. There was nothing to prevent my shooting him . . . almost any hour that I wished. If necessary I would. But it would not satisfy me. Edward Cousin dead was a small matter; Edward Cousin alive and suffering was my goal. I could now see only two paths that might lead to it. One, if it existed at all, would be found at Calabar where the bulk of the negurs would be bought. I thought it possible that Cousin would leave the ship there and assume personal direction of the negotiations. If he did, an opportunity might come. If not . . . I shuddered at the one remaining way: a mutiny of the blacks. I shuddered, but I went in search of Jim. He stood at the rail gazing toward the low-lying shore line.

"Home," he said. "You know there is belief that when black man die his spirit go home to jungle. That why some jump in water and drown rather than go to white man's country."

"But you don't have to worry. You are coming back some day," I reminded him.

He agreed without much enthusiasm. I was pleased. He was in a receptive mood.

"The big master has come to Africa many times," I said.

Jim agreed again. He even smiled wanly and confided that he himself had seen Cousin before, had been present when he bought slaves from his King.

"I suppose he wanted them to act as shepherds for the Calabar negurs," I suggested.

"Yes. That what he use Gold Coast negur for."

"They must have come home with interesting tales to tell."

"They never come home," he said mechanically, and stopped.

392

"Never come home," he repeated. "Never heard of one that come home."

He stared blankly toward the shore line. I left him. It was enough for the present. There was still Calabar.

## 2.

The Guinea Coast of Africa is not always hot. The day that we cast anchor in the muddy sand off New Calabar was cold and dismal. A number of the crew were already racked with fever. One man had died from the flux. Cousin was sullen, Morgan frightened.

"Bad luck hangs over us, Uncle," the mate complained.

"Nothing too bad yet," I pointed out.

"Maybe not. But I feel trouble."

"Well, don't borrow it."

"I won't have to. It will come aboard of itself—with the negurs, most likely. I'm surprised that you, being Welsh like me, don't smell it."

We were interrupted by a message from Cousin. He wanted to see me. When I waited on him he announced that he himself intended to visit the King of Bandy, William by name, at his town of Great Bandy, which lay some miles up the river. I was to pick and properly equip a score of trustworthy men. While we were gone Morgan would get the *Pilgrim* over the bar and await us at the mouth of the river.

I chose the men from among those who grumbled most and seemed least afraid of Cousin. I no longer believed it possible to persuade them to mutiny, but I did hope that if I took things into my own hands they might remain aloof. By sunset I was ready and anxious to go. But Cousin was in no hurry. A messenger had been sent to King William. It was necessary to await his reply. Meantime the mate visited the factor at the English fort and made arrangements for the use of his barracoons. He bought additional stores, too. Yams, plantain, bananas, malegetta. This latter is a pepper much used to prevent flux and dry bellyache. I watched all this impatiently. I wanted to be with Cousin in the jungle.

393

At last we set out. We went up the river in long narrow canoes, hollowed from cotton trees. One of these carried our whole party. Another was filled with negurs sent by King William as an escort. We were on the river for three days. During that time Cousin sat with his guard in the rear of the canoe. The jungle appeared to depress him. He stared alternately into the thick yellow water and at the swampy shore. At night he stayed close to the fire. My hopes sank.

The village of Great Bandy is on a small, low-lying marshy island. We arrived there at an opportune time as the King had just waged a successful war, capturing hundreds of prisoners. He called our attention to a platform upon which were stacked innumerable severed heads. Some were already bare skulls, dry, white and grinning, but others were fresh with the flesh still rotting. The whole village stank from them. But King William was proud of his trophies. I gazed at them and hoped that my grunts of admiration might atone for a queasy belly. Cousin stared impassively.

"Too old for slaves," the shrewd King assured us. "I do not kill strong ones."

The strong ones were apparently kept somewhere off the island. That evening they were brought from the north shore in huge canoes, some holding as many as eighty people. Cousin looked at two or three hundred of them and signaled that he had seen enough.

"Buy them," he told me. "Seven hundred if he's reasonable."

Because the King had so many captives and was anxious to sell I was able to drive a close bargain. I arranged that seven hundred in the ratio of four men to one woman should be delivered at the fort of New Calabar. In return the King was to receive goods to the value of three pounds for each man and two pounds four shillings for every female. I reserved the right to reject any that the ship's surgeon found unfit.

After the business was out of the way the King entertained us. A dinner was served which consisted principally of the putrid flesh of some unrecognizable animal and plantains that were covered with flies that could not be driven away. Then the negurs danced. This would not be worth recording except for the girl.

She was one of the captives from the recent war. King William was keeping her for himself.

"She dances," he said, and leered.

I do not care for the dancing of the blacks, but the wench was big, with good features and a strong well-shaped body. She was lithe and graceful. Like those of so many of her race her brown eyes were bottomless, but they were not soft, they were hard and bold. Her dancing was the most abandoned I have ever seen, her contortions seeming to spring from sheer joy and pride in the flexibility and strength of her muscles.

The men watched hungrily.

"A man could have some bloody fun with a piece like that," one of them finally gasped.

"Aye, he could," another agreed. "She's havin' that much fun herself."

The King beamed proudly, but Edward Cousin sprang forward snarling like a beast. Even yet I cannot recall without horror what followed. I have heard of greater cruelty among the savages, but nothing more wanton. King William and his natives watched with apparent indifference. The girl, intoxicated by her own rhythms, did not even stop dancing. Cousin's men obeyed him slavishly. The two poor devils whose only fault was that they were men with a man's desires were thrown to the ground by their fellows and securely bound. Cousin himself gouged out the right eye of each of them. Then glaring madly at us he chanted in a voice that was deep and savage as the jungle that pressed around us.

*"And if thine eye offend thee pluck it out, and cast it from thee: it is better for thee to enter into life with one eye, rather than having two eyes, to be cast into hell fire."*

He was breathing hard. His own eyes glittered.

"Is there any man here who would deny the words of the Savior?" he shouted.

No one spoke, but after that we did not relish the black girl's dancing, though so far as I could see her own spirits were in no way cast down. When at last she was exhausted she threw herself at her master's feet where she crouched like a great black dog that fawns for favors; but as her eyes roved boldly over the white strangers, she seemed more like a sleek cat. She looked at Cousin and held him in perspiring agony.

"Now that wife of whom I have heard so much had better look to her witchcraft," I said to myself. "If she has magic it must travel fast over the sea."

But as yet there was no evidence of Mistress Cousin's powers.

"Will you sell her?" Cousin shouted hoarsely.

The King laughed and fondled the wench carelessly, possessively. He owned no other woman who danced so well, he explained, and followed this with a candid full-bodied description of her other skills.

As the King talked Cousin grew more avid. I was afraid he would leap at the negur chief as he had at his own men. If he did I knew that our heads would soon be on the drying table with the others. But I underestimated Edward Cousin. His brutality was always measured, even his lust was controlled by cunning. He would cover himself with a cloak of piety and believe he was cozening God, and preserve his own skin by caution. But he would also have the woman.

*"Look not upon me because I am black, because the sun hath looked upon me: my mother's children were angry with me; they made me the keeper of the vinyards; but mine own vinyard I have not kept."*

Cousin's voice rang deep and sweet into the night. Even the negurs who could not understand the words were charmed by the magic of the sound.

The spirit of exaltation faded. He turned to me.

"I brought you here to buy negurs. Buy that one," he said. "Pay any price, but do not fail. Bring her to me that I may cleanse her of sin and make her fit to be a handmaiden of the Lord."

He walked heavily toward his quarters. "To get knout and

396

Bible," I wanted to shout; but I remembered the men recently blinded and was silent.

I bought the wench. It cost fifteen pounds in rum and coral which were paid over immediately out of the stores we had brought with us. Even at such a price the King refused to deliver the girl until the next morning. He bade us good night and left us, the wench trotting obediently in his wake.

I went to tell Cousin. As I had surmised the heavy whip and the Bible were ready to his hand.

"Where is she?" he muttered. His voice was thick like a drunkard's.

When I told him he did not censure me. He merely swore that we must immediately rescue her from iniquity. I was frightened. We were a score of white men surrounded by hundreds of negurs. I told Cousin so. He reminded me that we were supported by the strength of the Lord. It occurred to me that men frequently try to make their God into a panderer, but I did not press the point.

"You will have her tomorrow," I urged, not very hopefully.

"But she sins tonight."

He was adamant. It was useless to point out that the King had possessed her for weeks, and that these negurs were heathen savages who did not possess the white man's theory of chastity.

"The white lamb of Christ must not be further sullied," he insisted.

In spite of my fear I laughed at the idea of the lusty black animal of a woman we had watched as the white lamb of Christ. And as I laughed I thought of how Polly would have laughed too, and then I forgot my fear and remembered why I was in the jungle. My opportunity had come.

"Very well," I said. "I shall get her tonight. Go to the south bank and wait for me. Meet us as we come ashore."

"You will do this alone?" he asked suspiciously.

"Alone or not at all. Twenty men are no good here. We would need hundreds to take her by force."

He considered this, looking at me out of hard eyes that stared from under red-rimmed, drooping lids.

"Why do you risk your skin?" he finally asked.

397

"In order to save it," I replied promptly. "You are so bent on folly that I must take a hand to prevent you from getting us all killed."

"Is that all?"

"Not quite. I expect a reward."

He could understand that.

"How much do you want?"

I had not even considered the matter. A quantity of coral was in an open box. I pointed to it. He gave it to me without quibbling.

"In an hour on the south bank," I promised.

But as I started to leave he stopped me.

"I shall go now. Come with me. You can watch and see where I land. Then we shall not miss one another."

I cursed under my breath. His caution had already wrecked my plans. However, I controlled myself. "You would be proud of me, Bill," I breathed to the sky as we walked toward the river bank. Negurs moved about the village and along the bank. They looked at us curiously but neither asked us our business nor interfered with us. I wondered if they would stand idly by if I attacked Cousin, but decided not to risk it. Canoes of all sorts were drawn up on the shore. Cousin shoved a small one into the water.

"I'll go with you," I said as casually as I could. "Then I shall know precisely where to come."

He laid the knout which he had brought with him in the bottom of the boat. Beside it he put a long knife.

"Just watch where I land," he said as he picked up the paddle. "I shall be looking for you. And don't fail to come, or I shall make King William a parting gift. He would undoubtedly be pleased to have a white slave. And do not come alone. If you do I shall shoot you as you step ashore."

When he was gone I considered my problem. Cousin's caution had upset the simple plan that had come to me when I thought of Pol. This had been to precede Cousin to the south bank of the river, overpower him as he stepped ashore and carry him into the jungle where I would not be disturbed. But he had gone ahead of me. He could hide and wait. He would see any boat that left the island. I had no choice but to get the girl—or one that looked

398

like her. That was it. It was not a bright night. Cousin would be unable to detect the fraud until I was upon him. All that I needed was a woman of more than average height. I went to King William.

His Majesty was in his house. The wench lay asleep in a corner. I told the King I wanted a woman for the night, and showed him the coral. He looked at it and put out his hand.

"Take her." He pointed at the sleeping girl. "I'm done with her and your chief won't know." He yawned in heavy content. "But I doubt if she'll be worth much tonight."

"She will do," I said hastily.

He walked over and kicked her. She rubbed her eyes and sat up.

"Go with him," he commanded, pointing at me.

Smiling she came to me. I led her away. As the moonlight struck and slid off her velvet-black skin my blood turned hot, but I mastered my desires. No woman save Polly Bragg could stir my emotions as powerfully as the thought of Edward Cousin. I remembered the whip that he had put in the boat, in anticipation, no doubt, of the struggle for the black girl's soul. I would find a use for it. I looked at the wench again. This time my heart was quiet. I was reflecting how well she would look with a fresh-flayed white hide draped across her comely shoulders. I was so pleased with the idea that I tried to explain it to the negress. She could not understand. Resorting to signs I threw an arm across her shoulder. She smiled and drew her lean black belly taut. I gave up and hastened toward the river where I shoved her into a canoe. She picked up a paddle and looked at me for further orders. I pointed toward the opposite shore. Obediently she bent her back. Strong steady strokes sent us into the river.

When we emerged from the shadows of the shore, pale moon-light bathed the black girl opposite me. She paddled with easy graceful strokes. Her muscles rippled under smooth shining skin. I watched her and was moved as I have sometimes been moved by Polly when she leaned over a hoe or lifted a mattox. No lady, however elegant her toilet, no prostitute, bedecked though she

399

may be in gaudy finery, can make a man conscious, as I was then conscious, of the beauty that is in a woman's body.

As the canoe touched the river bank the girl leaped ashore. For a moment I was afraid that she might flee into the jungle, but she waited smiling good-naturedly as I clambered after her. The exhilaration which I had felt when it dawned upon me that the opportunity for revenge was at hand was gone. In its place was stale tasteless determination. Even this was soon shattered.

While we still stood in the thick matted grass that grew at the river's bank, Cousin's voice, low yet clear and cold, came from a tangled thicket a few yards away.

"Get back in the boat, Griffith."

As I look back upon my life there is little of which I am ashamed, and still less in which I take pride. But that night I did well. Even as Cousin spoke, two courses flashed through my mind. I could obey Cousin, take credit with him as a successful pimp and use his increased confidence in me to trap him at some later time. It would be a shrewd move and the proper one for a man who had dedicated his life to revenge. But if I did it, I knew that before the sun rose the barbarian who now stood beside me, her whole body alive and pulsing with animal joy, would be worse than dead. She would be a broken, sin-conscious woman . . . another victim of Cousin's perverted lust and warped piety. And I was responsible for her being within his grasp. I had brought her with me as bait. I could not abandon her. Not even to avenge Polly. Polly was dead . . . this woman alive. I resolved to follow the other course: to stay and fight my final battle with Edward Cousin on grounds where I was doomed before the struggle commenced. As I made this decision I felt Polly's presence near me for the first time since she had gone overboard. I believed that she was waiting for me to join her; I was content.

I had no idea how I was going to fight.

"In the boat?" I echoed.

"Immediately."

"Why?"

"Do you question my orders?"

"Not aboard ship, sir."

"You came to Great Bandy on duty."

"This night's work is no part of that duty."

Cousin's forbearance came to an abrupt end.

"My pistol is primed and pointing at you," he said. "Get into the boat."

I thought I was going to die, and at the same time realized how doing so would serve my end. I flung my words at him in triumph, rather than with any hope that they might prolong my life.

"When you shoot me," I cried, "this girl will take fright and run as an animal does when it hears gunfire. You will never catch her in the jungle."

I moved in front of her and waited. I could hear Cousin mumbling to himself. Gradually the words became audible.

"For her soul's sake I must spare him," he muttered.

Presently he spoke to me.

"What is it you want?"

The trouble was I did not know; or rather I knew well enough that what I wanted—to send the girl back to the King with whom she had apparently been happy—was the one thing that Cousin would not grant. I remembered Judith and Luke Watling. I smirked.

"I thought I might share in the fun, sir."

I doubt if Cousin had ever before been spoken to as if he were a common rapist. I am sure that he did not so regard himself. He came out of the thicket choking with rage. With his gun pointing at me and a knife in his hand he explained my errors. He did not lust after the flesh, or so he said; he only longed to save a human soul.

"As you have other souls," I said meaningly.

The gun in his hand was steady as his voice.

"As I have other souls," he declared.

"The negress at God's Acres perhaps. She is old now, but once she must have been young, like the wench here. Did you save her soul?"

"She is now a Christian."

I knew I was about to die. I stabbed blindly.

"And your wife? She whom I saw with my own eyes turn and

leave you at the wharf, without so much as looking back. She who men say is a witch out of the sea. Is her soul saved? Or has she sold it to the devil?"

The pistol roared. I felt a dull shock. Before I could regain my balance he struck me. I fell to the ground. The long whip lashed out and curled about my waist. A flayed white skin . . . The phrase flashed crazily across my mind, and I turned my head instinctively toward where the girl had stood. To my horror she was still there. Standing quietly, watching.

"Run," I cried. "For God's sake, run."

She bobbed her head amiably and smiled her lack of comprehension. But Cousin, who had been reloading his gun, was diverted. Once again the whip sang. This time it curled around the negress' shoulders. With an expert twist and jerk he brought her to her knees. He forgot me. I tried to get up but my head swam so that I could rise no further than my knees. I crawled toward them . . . painfully . . . inch by inch, knowing that when I did reach Cousin I could only die.

The heavy whip snapped and sang and whined. The sounds that issued from Cousin's throat were not human; they were the screams of a beast of prey, or, for aught I know, the jabbering of devils. Only occasionally was a word recognizable . . . sin . . . flesh . . . repent . . . Hell. The black girl rocked back and forth under the lash; and as I crawled toward them I saw that there was beauty even in her agony. She swayed rhythmically . . . her cries were like the keening of the wind through the forest.

I stopped crawling. There was another sound. I do not know how long it had been sobbing through the jungle. But the girl had heard. She was swaying to its beat. I had heard such music in Virginia, in Jamaica. Now I heard it in the land of its birth. It was the throbbing of the voudou drum. While I listened Cousin paused. He had remembered me. He turned, fingering the pistol. Then he heard. His mouth dropped open, fear burned through the frozen curtains of his eyes.

"Voudou," I muttered.

He did not even hear me.

402

"She," he babbled. "She warned me."

The whip dropped from his nerveless hands. He ran screaming into the jungle.

Perhaps the strangest of all the strange things that occurred that night was the quieting of the drums. Cousin was scarcely out of sight before their throbbing faded away. I shivered. "She," he had cried. "She warned me."

The negress swayed back and forth for a moment longer before she got to her feet. She started toward me, stopped, picked up the whip. Like Cousin she made it sing through the night air. Then she talked to it. She confided some secret to it, cajoled it, laughed softly and placed it in the boat. After she had disposed of the whip she turned her attention to me.

Cousin's bullet had lodged in my shoulder. The girl took my knife and cut it out. Then she bound up the wound and helped me into the boat. She paddled us back to the island where she took me to a clean small shack and undressed me and put me to bed. As she leaned over me I lifted my hand and touched one of the welts that disfigured her fresh smooth skin.

"Sorry," I said.

She shook her head and laughed and pointed at my own waist where Cousin had caught me with his whip.

"Go back to the King," I said, and pointed toward his quarters.

Again she only laughed. I did not know if she understood me. I did not care. I was too tired and hurt to argue. When I awoke the next morning she was curled up on the floor opposite the pallet that served me as a bed. Evidently since she had seen me buy her she regarded me as her master. This faithfulness was not necessarily a sign of devotion. Among the natives of Africa, prisoners of war suffer either slavery or death. Although this was my first voyage with a slaver I had already seen men, and women too, who had been rejected by the ship's surgeon killed on the spot by their native captors. If they could not be sold they were not worth keeping. But although I could understand the girl's attitude I did not propose to be burdened with her. The King was fond of her. Let him have her. Though stiff and weak I managed

403

to get up. I nudged the wench with my foot as I had seen the King do. She stirred and groaned. I was ashamed. She was a mass of angry welts. When I examined her I realized that the King would not accept the return of goods so badly damaged. She sat up, stretched herself, grimaced in pain and finally smiled at me. I repaid her courage with a frown. What was I to do with her? My own future was extremely doubtful; certainly I was in no position to take care of anyone else. I made a motion for her to stay where she was, and went out to inquire after Cousin. In the village I learned from one of our men that he had come back after daybreak.

"Been out all night and was fair whipped by the jungle," the fellow said, evidently savoring his master's discomfiture. "Scratched and bruised he was, his clothes ripped to shreds, and his crocodile eyes damn near swoll shut. I never saw him in such a bloody mess or bloody temper. Damn me if I don't believe the devil himself was chasin' him through the woods."

As the man talked I heard the drums again. I heard Cousin shriek "She."

"Maybe the devil did, or his voice or his dame. But where is Cousin now?"

"In his quarters with his bodyguard. He left orders that we start down the river in two hours."

I knew that Cousin would not forgive me the previous night's adventure. Even if he overlooked defiance of his authority he would still hate me because I had witnessed his bestiality and panic. Nevertheless I was determined to remain in his service. In the first place, unless I wished to flee into the African jungle I had no other choice; secondly I still intended to kill him. But although I knew well enough what I wanted I was far from certain how Cousin felt. Would he order me killed out of hand? Sell me to King William as he had threatened? Either course was possible, but I felt that it would be more like him to dissemble until an opportunity arose to teach me my lesson at his own leisure. If he did adopt such a policy I would be safe until we were at sea. After that it would be merely a matter of which of us struck first, with all the odds in Cousin's favor. I was willing to risk those odds but first I had to find out if the game was to be played. I went to Cousin.

As the sailor had said he looked as if he had been literally whipped by the jungle. He was scratched and even yet blood oozed from some of the cuts. His hands were bandaged. A patch was over one eye. I stood in front of him and because the negur with the long bare knife did not plunge it into me at once, I breathed more easily. It seemed that for the time being I was to be spared.

"What do you want?" Cousin demanded.

His voice was under perfect control. "Your wits against his," Bill had said. Never before had it been so true. I could not reply that I wanted to kill him, or learn if he planned to have me murdered immediately or at a later date. I said the first thing that came to mind.

"About the girl, sir."

He was too shrewd to pretend ignorance.

"What about her?"

"She is in my quarters. What shall I do with her?"

"Spawn of Satan," he muttered uneasily.

"Yes, sir, but I bought her with the coral you gave me."

"You bought her?"

"As a gift for you . . . for us . . . sport . . . you know."

"If you bought her she is yours. My advice is kill her."

"I can't do that. Last night, after you were gone, she got me back here. Saved my life, for all I know."

"Last night after I was gone, you say?"

"Yes. On the river bank."

He did not lie to deceive, but as a warning.

"I was not on the river bank last night, nor did I see you. I judge that you took this slut somewhere for your own lewd purposes and had an accident. A blow on the head of some sort. At any rate you are suffering from delusions."

"Possibly," I agreed. "But the girl did bring me back."

Cousin made a sign to the guard. I felt the knife's point prick gently under my left shoulder blade. For what seemed an interminable time no one moved or spoke. Then Cousin said smoothly:

"You may take your wench. When we get aboard ship put her with the others. And now that that matter is disposed of, tell me why you came here this morning. Not to talk about a negress, I think."

The knife bit delicately as if to hasten my reply, but I spoke as quietly as had Cousin himself.

"To find out if last night was real, sir, or, as you suggest, only the consequence of a deranged fancy."

"And are you satisfied?"

"Oh, yes. You have helped me wonderfully. I remember it all now. I did like the girl's looks and I took her across the river. There I received a blow, two blows in fact, one from some heavy instrument like a whip, the other sharper, more penetrating, on the shoulder. Knocked me silly, I suppose, because this morning when I awoke I thought it was you who had delivered them."

"And now?"

I laughed.

"Oh, now I know better, sir. Why, if it had been you, you would be angry with me."

He managed a thin smile.

"Quite right, Griffith. I have said before that you are a shrewd man. By the way, have you ever seen my place in Jamaica? Or met my wife?"

I regretted that I had baited him the night before about my visit to God's Acres, but it was too late to withdraw.

"I went to God's Acres when I was hunting a job with you. Unfortunately you were not at home, nor was I so lucky as to see your wife. An old slave received me . . . treated me handsomely, too."

"And you repaid this hospitality by killing two of my mastiffs and locking my servants in a cupboard."

"God, sir, why would I do that?"

"I have wondered why any man would. But someone did, and you admit that you were there."

"Aye. But I wouldn't be the one you spoke of."

406

"Yet my negurs reported no other visitors. Ah, yes, a knife was left with some vainglorious message purporting to come from the scoundrel Anthony More."

"Anthony More! Knife!" I exclaimed.

"Yes. An excellent blade. You now feel its point at your back."

"I've heard of Anthony More," I admitted.

"No doubt. Most men have also heard of the devil."

We looked into one another's eyes, and both knew that it was a fight to death. Cousin lacked only one advantage. He did not know who I was, or if I were acting for myself or as an agent for another . . . Anthony More for example. He would wait a little in hopes of finding out. Nevertheless, when I left him I knew that my life hung by the thinnest thread.

On my way back to my own quarters I picked up one of the native translators who had been loaned us by the factor at the fort. I wanted him to talk to the girl. She was still waiting.

"Tell her she is free to go back to her own people," I said.

Upon receiving my message the girl threw herself upon her knees, sobbing and kissing my hands and even my feet. Then she burst into a torrent of words. At first I thought this was gratitude but I was soon disillusioned.

"Her people were all killed by King William's men," the translator explained. "If you do not take her with you the King will have her killed. Her head will be thrown with those of the other useless ones."

I thought of Jim.

"But does she wish to leave Africa . . . to go across the water and never come home?"

Upon questioning it appeared that she did. She was my slave. Her body would heal. She would dance for me.

I surrendered.

"Tell them to bring her down with the others that the King is sending. And tell her not to be frightened. I shall take care of her."

She kissed my hands again and went away smiling. Nor, when I thought the matter over, was I altogether displeased. True, I did not want a black dancing girl or a concubine, black or white, but the thought of Jim had reminded me that I needed friends among the slaves who were to be shipped on the *Pilgrim*. Like Jim, this girl had spirit. She would need a name. Martha, I decided.

The return to the mouth of the river was uneventful. The slaves arrived a week later. The busiest days of the voyage followed. Seven hundred negurs had to be examined, branded and transferred to the *Pilgrim*. Once aboard the men were stowed forward, the women behind the mast.

I had little to do with all this business, but with the other members of the crew was kept busy preparing the ship for the long voyage home. However, I found time to look after Martha. At our first meeting she handed me a knife. How she had kept it during the voyage down the river God knows, but she had. It was the one Cousin had dropped that night on the river bank. Her eyes flashed as she gave it to me. She pointed to a scar that still disfigured her shoulder. Her meaning was clear.

I arranged with the factor to keep her in the barracoon at the fort until just before we sailed; and I took pains to send Jim to visit her there. I wanted the two to become friends, and I hoped that the girl would infect Jim with her own hatred of Cousin, and shake his faith in the "big master's" promise of freedom. I was not disappointed. A few days after he first talked to Martha Jim came to me.

"Martha say big master bad," he said.

"Martha knows," I replied.

"They don't come back," he muttered gloomily.

"No, they don't come back."

He looked at me in agony.

"Not even the shepherds from Gold Coast?"

"They are sold into slavery across the water."

"Just like Calabar negurs?"

"Yes."

He struggled with his problem. On the one hand were the deep impression Cousin had made upon him and his desire to believe

408

that he would be set free; on the other hand were Martha, my assurances, and the testimony of his own eyes.

I watched the conflict in Jim's open face. It was desperately important for me to gain his support. I threw away all vestiges of caution.

"Listen, Jim, big master *is* bad, as Martha says. He is a liar. Think, how many negurs from the Gold Coast have been taken away? You yourself have captured them . . . seen them sold. Some of them to Cousin himself. But none came back. Have you seen even one who came back? Have you even heard of one who came back?"

He shook his head.

"They don't come back," he said heavily. Anger flashed in his eyes. "I go talk to big master."

I caught hold of him.

"No. That won't do any good. He will put you in the hold with the Calabar negurs."

"What can I do?"

"Help me. If you will I'll see that you *do* get home."

"If big master lie, I guess all white men lie."

Here was a new difficulty, but I still had one card to play.

"You like Martha?" I asked.

"Good girl," he told me.

"She wouldn't lie to you, would she?"

"No."

"Then go to her. Ask her if you can trust me. Follow her advice. And if you help me, and we succeed in my plan, I'll give Martha to you when it is time to go back home."

"You give me Martha?"

"If she'll have you."

"I talk to her."

He was back in a few minutes.

"I help you," he said.

"Good."

"What you want?"

"Wait until we are at sea."

I could tell that he did not like that, but after a moment's hesitation he surrendered.

"Martha say to do as you want. I wait."

So it was that when the *Pilgrim* weighed anchor for the homeward voyage I had two allies aboard, though they were only black savages.

# XVIII

## I.

WHILE WE were in sight of land the slaves were shackled in pairs and, except for a few trusted ones such as Jim, still kept below decks. This prevented them from falling into a frenzy as the shore line of their homes faded in the distance. But once well out to sea most of them sank into an apathy so deep that both their spirits and bodies required that they be brought into the fresh air and forced to exercise. Since their market value depended largely upon good health their needs were given consideration. Morgan explained to me the routine on Cousin's ships.

"All the crew but you know the Old Man's little tricks, Uncle. Tomorrow we start bringing the negurs up. They are fed at ten in the morning and again at four in the afternoon. First they clear out the filth from below. After that, while they eat, some of the crew sprinkle fresh vinegar in the hold. It's sour stuff but it helps keep the cargo sweet."

He laughed at his little joke, but I was in no mood to appreciate such wit.

"Then they exercise?"

Perhaps he was disgruntled at my lack of humor, maybe I spoke too eagerly. Morgan checked his laughter in mid-air.

"Now what makes you suppose that?" he grunted.

"Why—I thought it was the custom—with all slavers. In order to keep the negurs in health."

He thawed.

"And you're right, Uncle. But the exercise is maybe not just what you think."

He paused so long that I was afraid he had finished.

"I've heard that they dance," I suggested.

"Aye, that they do on merrier vessels, but not aboard the *Pilgrim*. Here, when they are fed the Old Man reads to 'em out of the Scriptures and leads them in sacred song."

"But they don't know English."

"Right, Uncle. Not a blasted word, most of them, but with the aid of a whip and that magic voice of his, Cousin soon has them running and twisting and screaming. 'Sin' and 'Jesus' are about the only words they learn on the whole voyage, but they are quick at picking up a tune and they make sounds of one kind or another."

He chuckled.

"The Lord doesn't get quite all the profit either, because during his soul-saving the Old Man manages to give his blacks plenty of exercise. Wait until you see it. Cousin speaking with the voice of an angel and laying on the knout like Satan, and all the while the savages writhing and screaming until you forget that they are men, and can half believe they are already black, charred, damned souls. It's a picture out of Hell."

"Isn't there danger of mutiny in all that excitement?"

"On a slaver there is always danger of mutiny, but the *Pilgrim* runs less risk than most."

"Why?"

"For one thing Cousin has spies. For another he's careful."

"I know about the spies, but what precaution can he take in the face of confusion such as you have just described?"

"Well, the women are kept together on the quarterdeck. That's partly to separate them from the men. Also it is so they will be in easy reach when Cousin starts laying around with his whip. In addition to the women there are two small guns on the quarterdeck. They are loaded and trained on the deck below where the men are. I stand behind one of those guns with a lighted match in my hand. Someone else mans the other. Our orders are . . . in case of trouble blow the Hell out of everyone on deck."

"Including your own crew?"

He grinned.

"Including the crew. That's why I'm telling you all this. You are going to be one of them on deck. The Old Man thought you ought to know. He said it would keep you careful."

"I'll be careful," I promised, "but I'd like to be at that other gun with a lighted match."

Morgan's grin faded. He regarded me soberly.

"There was a time I thought you would be, Uncle, but the Old Man doesn't seem fond of you any more."

"We had a little trouble at Great Bandy," I admitted.

The mate put a heavy hand on my shoulder.

"Be careful, Uncle. It's not healthy to have trouble with Edward Cousin."

Then as if ashamed of even such a slight show of kindness he added ferociously, "And remember this, Tom Griffith, if the Old Man orders it, I myself will hang you, or have you keelhauled."

"I believe that," I said. "Especially keelhauled. I suppose you'd even keelhaul a woman."

The last words welled out of me in a wave of bitterness that washed through my whole being at the reminder of Pol's brutal death. I did not expect them to affect a man hardened by years of sailing with Edward Cousin. But to my astonishment the blood drained from Morgan's cheeks. His face twisted in fear. He clutched me convulsively.

"Don't talk about it," he muttered. "Don't even talk about it."

His grip relaxed. His voice was normal.

"You have your orders, Uncle. When we bring the blacks up tomorrow, you are to stay on deck with them. Move around and keep *them* moving. If anything looks wrong come to the quarter-deck."

That night I laid my plans. The next morning I explained them to Jim. He had been sunk in despair since Africa disappeared; my message set him almost mad with joy. I had to restrain him from attempting the mutiny at once.

"There is no hurry," I insisted. "It is two weeks' voyage to the island of St. Tomas. Any time before we arrive there will do . . . and we must not fail. Take care . . . move cautiously. Get six men that you can trust. Be sure that none of them know Eng-

413

lish, then they cannot betray us even if they would. When you are ready let me know."

He agreed to get the men, but was worried about Martha. Black men were not allowed to mix with women.

"I'll manage to see her," I promised. "But can I make her understand me?"

Jim looked doubtful.

"I taught her a few words. She can say 'damn big master, beat big master, kill big master' . . . and maybe—"

"That is enough," I interrupted. "Martha knows all the English she ever need know."

Five days later I was standing at the ship's rail. Although there was only a moderate breeze I was, for the first time in my life, sick at sea. I had retched until I was weak and dizzy. The negurs had just been brought above decks. As I watched them they seemed to melt together, fade into a wavering fantastic mist, then suddenly resolve themselves back into human beings. I gradually grew aware of someone nudging me impatiently. It was Jim.

"You do not hear me," he complained.

I found it difficult to focus my attention.

"I hear," I managed to say.

"I got men. We ready to take ship from big master. You make it go back to Africa."

"Good," I murmured. "Good, Jim . . . Martha . . . tomorrow . . . tomorrow . . . tomorrow . . ."

The last thing I remembered was Jim's staring anxious eyes. They were big. They grew larger . . . larger . . . until I felt myself slipping, falling, into their soft bottomless depths . . . down . . . down . . .

Jim caught me as I fell. They carried me to the forecastle where I lay racked and wasted by fever. By the time I recovered we had left St. Tomas far behind.

"You're lucky to be alive," Morgan told me. "You wouldn't be if the Old Man hadn't let Jim and your black wench take care of you. And I must have been wrong about him not liking you any more. I never saw him take so much interest in a sick man. Used to sit by your hammock by the hour. Left orders to be called whenever you started talking."

"That's when he sat by me?"

"Mostly."

"What did I say?"

"Ask him or the negurs. I've got more to do than listen to every sailor that goes out of his head from fever."

"But you must have heard something."

"Not a word that I heeded. Cousin asked me once though if you had ever talked to me about a woman you called Pol or a man named Smith."

I could get nothing more from Morgan and had even less success with Jim.

"You don't talk plain when sick," the latter explained.

"You didn't hear me mention your name or Martha's . . . or our plan?"

He looked anxious.

"Not that I could understand. When can we take ship?"

"Not until I am stronger and have had time to think."

"We get farther from Africa every day."

"I'll get you back."

The truth was that for the first few days after my return to consciousness I was ready to give up all thoughts of mutiny. We were in the Middle Passage now, and I was not sure that my navigation, good enough for coasting from island to island in the Caribbean, or a short run to a continent, was equal to mid-ocean. It might be better to return tamely to Jamaica, where I could buy Jim and find some means to send him and Martha back to Africa. I was too tired to fight.

But once on deck again my determination for revenge reasserted itself. Each day it grew stronger as my body regained health. Moreover, I doubted that Cousin would permit me to reach Port Royal alive. I reconsidered my original plan. In its chief features it was as good as before. Only the timing would have to be changed. Instead of seizing the *Pilgrim* and making for Africa, I must wait until we reached the Caribbean. I realized that this

415

was dangerous because Cousin might strike first, but as we were in mid-ocean there was no help for it.

Jim was gloomy and suspicious over the delay.

"You sure you won't be like big master?" he asked.

I reassured him as best I could. In the end he accepted postponement largely because there was no other course open to him.

The days that followed were, according to Morgan, about what might be expected in the slave trade. A number of negurs died of flux, and, despite the surgeon's vigorous examination, there was some pox. A few blacks died of broken hearts. Morgan laughed at this. He said it was impossible, that they were no better than beasts, but I have known caged beasts to die, and Jim said it was so.

One afternoon two women threw themselves overboard. This brought the sharks to my attention. Of course I had known they were there. Whenever a dead negur was thrown into the sea they took the body. Cousin and certain members of the crew seemed to enjoy the spectacle, but I had avoided it. However, when the women jumped I ran with the others to the rail. I saw a flash, heard a scream . . . that was all.

"It's him," screamed a sailor. "It's old Dan'l."

"Old Dan'l?" I repeated uncomprehendingly.

"The shark. Been after us ever since we left Africa. Gets more bodies than any of them. I call him Dan'l after my old man. Dan'l was his name . . . damned bloody brute . . . flogged me senseless, he did."

"How do you know this is the same shark?"

The fellow looked at me in disgust.

"Think I don't know old Dan'l? I been watching him ever since we left Africa. Watched particular when we thought you was about to die. Wondered if he liked white meat."

Later I asked Morgan if the sharks followed the ships.

"Most in the trade think so," he replied. "The Old Man says not."

"Yet they are always around," I mused.

"Maybe they smell the blacks. Anyhow they're well fed."

Ten weeks out of Calabar, ophthalmia broke out among the

416

slaves. This is a disease which affects the eyes. It is common among the slave ships, striking both blacks and whites. As a rule it runs its course in a week or two and the victims recover, but occasionally sight does not return. In such cases it was Cousin's custom to throw the blind negurs overboard with the dead. The sharks took them. After the first instance of this I protested to Morgan.

"Most captains do it," he said. "A blind negur can't be sold."

I recalled the shrieks as the sharks struck.

"At least knock them in the head first."

"The Old Man won't allow it."

"In God's name, why not?"

The mate winked.

"He says it would be murder. In my opinion he enjoys it."

All this would not be important, but for Martha. She went blind. Ten days passed, two weeks. Morgan approached me.

"We throw your wench overboard tonight," he told me.

"The devil you do."

"The Old Man's orders."

I went to Cousin's cabin. He was sitting at a table. He looked anxious and distraught. His eyelids were puffed and inflamed. He did not recognize me at first, but when he did he seemed pleased. I told him my mission.

"A mistake," he said. "If you want a blind slave it is your affair."

I thanked him and started to leave. He stopped me.

"Why are you on this ship?" he asked.

"To learn the slave trade."

He knew I lied. He even knew that I realized that he knew it. But for the moment he pretended to believe me.

"Ah, yes, I remember," he said affably. "You told me that before. You said you were from the West Country, too. We should talk. Sit down."

I obeyed and waited. His thick lips were moist, his red eyes gleamed, but his voice remained kind.

"You talked when you were sick."

"Men often rave when they have fever."

417

"No doubt. But sometimes they speak the truth. For example you called constantly for a woman, Polly Bragg. I'll wager there is such a person."

"A girl I knew once," I said levelly. "Dead now."

"How sad. There was another . . . Betty, I believe."

"My wife."

"Dead, too?"

"The Indians took her."

"Your luck is bad with women. And how about men? Do you know Anthony More? I am told he too comes from the West Country."

In my anxiety to disown Bill I overshot the mark.

"How could I have known him?" I asked. "I was a fisherman's lad. Anthony More was a gentleman."

As I said it he raised his hand. The black guard grabbed me from behind. In a minute or two I was trussed like a fowl and lying at Cousin's feet.

"So Anthony More did send you," he gloated.

"I never knew him, I tell you."

"But you knew somehow that the pirate blackguard was born a gentleman. Strange knowledge. I thought I was the only man in the West Indies save More himself who knew that."

I tried to repair my error.

"I heard of him as a boy in England. I lied because I knew you were afraid of him."

He prodded me with his foot.

"I am afraid of no one," he shouted.

You lie, I thought. You are afraid of the devil, Anthony More, and, unless I am mistaken, your mysterious wife. I thought this but I did not say it. Cousin was still talking.

"You came to see me about your negur wench. I am touched by your solicitude . . . tonight I'll have you tied back to back and tossed overboard together." He laughed. "Back to back but your bellies will be bare and soft. There's a shark . . . I'm told one of the men calls him Dan'l . . ." His voice trailed off into a gentle purr.

He kicked me into a corner and left me there. Fear spurred my

418

brain to furious action. I must save myself. There must be some way of reaching Edward Cousin. Bill had done it, his wife . . . His wife! All through the day I recalled every word I had heard of her. Out of the fragments I pieced together a desperate plan.

Just before sunset Martha was brought to the cabin. They had stripped her. A weight was already tied to her feet. Her eyes were swollen and discolored. Otherwise she was a magnificent creature. Even Cousin thought so.

"A sweet bride for Dan'l," he said.

"Martha," I called.

She recognized my voice and started toward me. Cousin stopped her.

"You will be close enough presently," he said.

She spit in the direction of his voice. The spittle caught him full in the face. He only laughed.

"Damn Edward Cousin," she said distinctly. "Kill Edward Cousin."

"You've taught your wench pretty habits and talk," he said to me.

At this moment Morgan came in.

"Strip him and tie them together," Cousin directed. "After that a hundred lashes apiece."

Morgan came toward me.

"Wait," I cried, as if overcome by fear, and to tell the truth I was. "Don't let him do it, master. I'll tell what you want to know."

"No need. I already know."

"I swear you don't."

It amused him to humor me. He dismissed Morgan. It was gloomy in the cabin. My own eyes were burning but I could see Cousin at his table. Near by Martha stood motionless as an ebony statue. The negur guard was almost as still, but his eyes betrayed him. They roved hungrily over the girl. It was a strange setting and a queer audience for a mortal struggle between an English lad from Cornwall and a gentleman of Devon. My weapon was no less queer.

"Well?" Cousin said.

"More didn't send me."

"Who did?"

"Will you spare my life if I tell you?"

"I promise nothing."

I did not care if he promised or not. I only demanded it to make my game appear real. For the same reason I pretended stubbornness.

"Then I'll tell you nothing."

"Morgan," he called.

"No," I cried in real panic. "I'll tell."

Morgan was at the door.

"Wait outside," Cousin ordered. "I doubt if it will be much longer."

When the mate was gone he bade me be quick.

"It was your wife."

Crying like a wounded animal he leaped from his chair. He started toward me and ran headlong into Martha who stood between us. She stepped to one side as he raised his fist. He struck out and hit only air. He stood there for a moment arm outstretched, mouth working.

"You lie," he finally mumbled and turned back toward the table. He *felt* his way back to the chair.

I laughed. With a little luck the game was in my hands now. Edward Cousin was blind. There were still grave dangers, but surely God would not have so stricken him without reason.

"You lie," Cousin muttered for the third time, but his voice shook.

"Can you see?" I retorted. "Or are you blind because someone has stuck pins through the eyes of a waxen image?"

"Tell me the truth," he groaned.

"Will you spare me?"

"If you tell the truth."

"And the girl?"

"Yes."

I told him the tale I had worked out during the long afternoon. It had seemed desperate then, but now with his blindness to play

420

upon he must believe me. Unless of course he had been with his wife that day . . . I had to risk that.

"It began at God's Acres," I explained. "I went there just as I told you. And it was true that I only wanted a berth with you that I might learn the trade. Everything else was like I said, too, until it was time for me to go. Then I got angry at being balked and searched the house. The negress set the dogs on me. I killed them. I'd heard Anthony More was the one man you feared so I left the knife and the message. I started back to Spanish Town, but as I left your house I heard the voudou drums. Maroons, I thought. At your gate a negur stepped from behind a bush. He told me to follow him. I didn't want to but something forced me. I was afraid to refuse. He took me to the mountains. There were maroons there . . . and a white woman. She said she was your wife."

I paused. If he had been with his wife all that day I was ruined.

"What did she look like?" Cousin muttered.

I had foreseen this question and realized its peril. But I had at least seen the woman's back at Port Royal. I knew she was rather small and slender with brown hair. For the rest I recalled how Polly had looked that night when she acted the part of a voudou priestess in the Virginia wilderness. The description was good enough.

"It was she," Cousin groaned. "What did she want of you?"

"She knew who I was and my business, though how, God only knows. She said you would never take me unless she came to my assistance, but that she was prepared to do this by means of a charm. I was to wait two days and go boldly to your office at Port Royal. At first I was afraid but she promised to protect me from you even if you found out. I finally consented. You know the rest."

Long minutes passed while Cousin sat silent. In spite of the confidence with which I had begun my tale I waited with bated breath. Could he find a flaw which would deliver me to Dan'l?

Finally he spoke.

"But why did she want you on the *Pilgrim*?"

"I never knew rightly. All she said was that she had promised to go herself, but business in the mountains prevented it. I was to watch over you and see that nothing harmed you."

I knew this was weak, but I could do no better and it proved good enough. Cousin's ugly face lighted up.

"You mean she was anxious for my welfare?"

He was pathetic. Maybe I should have pitied him, but I did not. Instead my wits were sharp knives with which to probe his wound.

"I wouldn't say exactly that," I replied judicially. "It seemed more like she was saving you for some purpose of her own. The goat without horns, maybe."

He seemed to shrivel and grow small.

"I'll punish her. I'll kill her with my own hands," he growled; but for once his marvelous voice failed to carry conviction. It was curious to hear Edward Cousin talk of punishment in such luster-less tones.

"Kill her when you reach her," I said indifferently, and as the woman meant nothing to me I meant it. "But now do I go free or do you want her black magic to pursue you further?"

"The slaves often fall blind," he argued, and it was evident that he was trying to convince himself, not me. "The sickness comes out of Africa."

"So does your wife's witchcraft."

"God will give me strength to oppose it," he replied without conviction.

"That is as may be; but she promised me that if I die the devil will keep you blind."

"How am I to know you are telling the truth?"

"You may learn in one of two ways. Feed me to the sharks and continued darkness will teach you. Permit me to live and in a few days you will see again."

He capitulated.

"Untie him and the woman, too," he told the guard.

As I left he gave me a final grim message.

"If I do not see soon, before I am done with you you will long for Dan'l's caress."

As Martha and I left the cabin I knew that I had very little

422

time left. Edward Cousin was not a patient man, nor was he a fool. Consideration might bring to light the flaws in my fairy tale.

Morgan was on the quarterdeck. When we appeared he whistled in surprise.

"Not many persuade the Old Man to change his mind, Uncle," he said good-naturedly.

"Most of you are afraid to try," I retorted. "Where is Jim?"

"On the deck somewhere, but before you look for him put the woman below."

"She isn't going below."

"Don't be a fool. You know Cousin's orders about black women."

"I just told you his orders. This one doesn't go below."

He stared at me in amazement.

"Do you mean to say that the Old Man says you can keep the wench with you all night?" He laughed derisively. "Hell, Uncle, that's sin."

I grinned. "Do you blame me?"

"Not I. Jack Morgan was never the man to begrudge a sailor his fun. But I'll just speak to the Captain, to be sure you understood him right."

"I wouldn't," I said. "He has just gone blind."

"Blind," Morgan echoed stupidly.

"Why not? Others in the slave trade do."

"But not the Captain."

I managed a laugh.

"He's just an ordinary man like the rest of us, although you don't seem to believe it. For that matter neither does he. To hear him you might think the Lord's particular job is to look after Edward Cousin's health."

Morgan looked at me shrewdly.

"You aren't trying any tricks, are you?" he asked.

I shrugged.

"Go on in and see. I only warned you to be friendly. You know yourself that he damned near threw me to the sharks. Over nothing, too."

423

"Then why does he let you have the girl?"

"He mentioned two reasons. 'She'll give you the pox,' he yelled, 'and send your soul to Hell.'"

Morgan relaxed and laughed.

"Not half in a temper, is he?"

"Go look for yourself. Maybe you will be lucky and only get Dan'l instead of disease and damnation."

"You blasted whoreson," Morgan chuckled. "I don't notice you letting your black curse far out of reach. Now get off the quarter-deck, and don't take the wench to the forecastle. I don't want the lads fighting over her."

"Then you are not going to Cousin?"

"Tomorrow will do."

Tomorrow.

## 2.

The crew was used to the sight of naked black women; but to see one alone with a white man after her sisters had been returned to the hold was unusual. And Martha was uncommonly handsome. As I walked along the deck I winked, grinned, spat and handled the girl. I met their envious jibes good-naturedly.

"Tomorrow, maybe," I promised the more pressing. "But I'll knife any bastard that interrupts us tonight."

For the next few hours I wanted to be undisturbed. Jim and I had last-minute plans to make and Martha, too, despite her blindness.

Martha went into action first. She knew the cost of failure but she had no fear. She was confident of her womanhood.

"That man," she said contemptuously, or at least Jim so reported. "That man. I'll have him kissing my mouth so hard he won't know it if the jungle is on fire."

We left her just before dawn scratching softly on the door of Cousin's cabin.

They brought the slaves on deck at the customary hour. As they ate their morning meal I surveyed the scene. Everything was as usual. Although there had been no whisper of trouble Morgan stood beside one gun; an old hand of Cousin's was at the other.

424

Laxness was not permitted on the *Pilgrim*. Although the women were on the quarterdeck Cousin did not appear. I prayed that he would stay away a few minutes longer.

The bowls from which the slaves fed were being collected. There was a sudden scuffle. Two negurs were quarreling. A member of the crew hastened to them. They forgot their own difference and turned on him. Jim and I went to the rescue.

"Under control," I called, glancing up.

The little guns on the quarterdeck looked very big. Morgan's hand held the match steadily.

"Bring them here," he ordered.

It was customary. They would be severely whipped as an example. I had counted upon it. We shoved our captives through the crowd and up the few steps to the quarterdeck.

"Take the others below."

The mate's order was just too late. As we reached the top of the steps I lunged for Morgan, and Jim rushed at the guard beside the other gun. Our two erstwhile prisoners sprang toward Cousin's cabin. Below us the remaining mutineers summoned the women from the quarterdeck, thus jamming the steps, and harangued the men. In a few seconds pandemonium gripped the ship. I knew I must win quickly. If I did not the negurs would get completely beyond control. I knocked the match out of Morgan's hand. To my surprise he grinned.

"It's a pleasure to split you open, Tom Griffith," he said.

There was no malice in his words. Here was a man who enjoyed a fight. He had his knife in his hand. We circled warily. I was lighter than he, quicker on my feet, and although he would not believe it, younger. But he towered a full head above me, and his reach was longer. Moreover I could not waste time in cautious maneuvering. I slipped in and thrust. For a man of his bulk he moved lightly. As I dodged back I felt my shoulder burn.

"Blood," growled Morgan contentedly.

I did not reply. I was desperate. Not from the wound, which was a mere scratch, but for lack of time. The turmoil on deck was mounting. I resolved to hazard everything on one stroke. I threw my knife. It missed its mark but as Morgan ducked I sprang at

425

him. My fist caught him squarely in the belly. While he gasped for breath I closed in. We grappled. For a moment we stood there, straining muscle against muscle. Slowly I lifted him as I had done that afternoon at Port Royal. Except now he was struggling. With my last ounce of strength I heaved him forward and threw him to the deck below. Without waiting to see the result I sprang to Jim's assistance. As I did so I observed the two negurs who had made their way to the cabin hurling themselves at its door. Cousin had apparently locked himself in. With a fleeting prayer for Martha I attacked the gunner. In less than a minute we were masters of the quarterdeck.

"Quiet them," I yelled at Jim.

He tried. He shouted from the quarterdeck. He rushed among them. He may as well have attempted to quiet black tossing waves. I looked down in despair. Morgan, unhurt, grinned up at me sardonically.

"The gun," he suggested.

I realized that it was our one hope. I rushed to it. Because Cousin did not wish to destroy too much valuable property it carried only a light charge. Even so a dozen or so fell before it. There were wild cries, cursing, moaning, then quiet. I stood beside the other gun with a lighted match in my hand while Jim talked. He told the blacks not to be afraid. They would be free. They would go home. Soon they were laughing and singing. Those from Calabar went peacefully back to the hold. The ones from the Gold Coast were kept on deck. With the crew still under my gun I explained that I only wanted Edward Cousin. Unless they resisted no one else would be harmed. I ordered them to lay down their arms. One by one they did so. Only Morgan refused.

"I'll see you in Hell first," he said grimly.

I could afford to be generous.

"Do as you like, Jack. And when I am done with Cousin we can finish our little game with the knives."

"I'll remember it."

"Good. Meantime, I'll have to lock you up."

"Who are you?" he asked unexpectedly.

I was going to say Tom Bone. The men below were looking

426

at me expectantly. My name would mean nothing to them. But there was one that would.

"Anthony More," I cried boldly.

A gasp followed by low curses and awed whispers swept the deck. Even Morgan was impressed.

"So you have the Old Man at last," he muttered.

I glanced toward the cabin door. The two negurs had stopped trying to break it down. Like all the rest they were watching me. As I looked the door swung open. Cousin stood there, his sightless eyes fixed straight ahead.

"Mutiny." He did not ask, he stated a fact.

"Yes, sir," Morgan replied. "They've taken the ship."

"Who?"

"Anthony More."

Cousin shrank back. The door slammed. Jim started toward it.

"Let him go," I told him. "He'll wait."

"Martha," said Jim.

I had forgotten her; but even as I ordered the door to be opened she appeared from somewhere behind the cabin. Following her, grinning foolishly, was Cousin's once fierce bodyguard. The tension snapped. Morgan laughed first, the crew followed, the negurs chimed in out of sheer sympathy. Only Jim refused to join in the merriment. He was scowling.

"Where was she?" I gasped.

He spoke to her. She answered volubly.

"It's like she said," he explained gloomily. "He was kissing her mouth."

"Through all the fight?"

He nodded.

"Now I kill him."

He started toward the negur.

"No, Jim."

"She's my woman."

"No fighting now."

He hesitated.

"Wait," I urged, "and if she is willing I'll give her to you. Then she will be your woman. You'll own her."

427

He spoke to her. She came to him. He took her in his arms, slowly, almost experimentally it seemed.

We did not have to break into Cousin's cabin. When I called to him he opened the door without protest. I shoved Morgan in and posted Jim and three of his friends outside. The negur guard was put in the hold with the other slaves. I then told the crew to sail the ship as before and no one would come to harm. They appeared docile. At last I was ready for Edward Cousin.

I was ready and yet I delayed. The days passed and I did not even visit the cabin. I told myself that I was savoring my coming triumph. It was not so. I felt no triumph . . . no exultation. Victory had come too late. I had not forgiven Edward Cousin. I loathed him no less than in my bitterest moments of insane rage; but with the rod of chastisement ready at hand I realized that it was too frail for my purpose . . . or his deserts.

"Vengeance belongeth unto me . . ."

I came to know why God claimed such an awful prerogative. Man is not august enough to hate.

What good was there in torturing the bleak sightless creature who sat in the cabin, helpless and in my power? If every wave of the sea echoed his agonized shrieks would Polly sleep more quietly? I doubted it. Would my own life be less empty? I knew that it would not. Nor could any bodily suffering atone for Edward Cousin's wickedness. Anguish of spirit . . . loneliness . . . frustration . . . heartbreak. These were the things that I wanted for Edward Cousin. What good merely to break his bones? Better to send him back to the witch he had wed. She, it appeared, knew how to wring his black heart.

But I had gone too far to retreat. The safety of the negurs who had joined me required Cousin's death. And I myself required it. Not for revenge, but because if he lived innocent people who crossed his path would suffer in the future, as they had in the past. So because I must kill him and because death was not enough I put off settling my account with Edward Cousin.

However, he did not entirely escape punishment during those days. Jim asked for the whip that Martha had given me on the beach at New Calabar.

"Are you going to beat your woman?" I teased.

"Big master whip Martha on river bank. Now Martha whip big master."

Glad that there was someone aboard to solve so simply and directly the complex problems of justice, I gave him the whip and my blessing. Each afternoon he and Martha went to the cabin. I did not accompany them but later Morgan described the scene to me.

"She laid on with a will. Enjoyed it like a child that's getting even with someone. Sometimes she sang as she lashed him, or maybe she called him strange heathenish names. She never seemed exactly mad though, so much as just having fun. Jim would stand and watch the wench. He was proud of the way she could swing the whip. He never said a word . . . just enjoyed himself quietly."

"And you?"

The mate grinned.

"Hell. You had me tied up like a hog on the way to the sticking pen, so I couldn't do anything but sit there helpless and watch. It did sort of break the day's monotony though."

"How about Cousin?"

"Never uttered a sound while they were there the first day; after they were gone he asked who it was. I told him. He prayed a lot those days, and he never failed to mention Martha and Jim when he was reminding the Lord that the lot of you deserved damnation. But he didn't whimper in front of them."

This strengthened my conviction that it was sterile revenge to inflict pain on Edward Cousin. The whippings stopped the day Martha's sight returned. She was so happy that she threw the whip overboard. Jim, who was devoted to the girl, was as pleased as she.

"Big master's curse gone," he said with satisfaction.

This was the first time I heard that the blacks were attributing their blindness to Cousin. But it was so. The evil eye, they said. They were also convinced that when Martha spit in Cousin's face she had brought his own black magic to bear against him. Was he too not blind? Meantime I was making a discovery of my own

429

concerning ophthalmia. I had put a stop to throwing those who did not recover overboard.

"The others will get it from them," the surgeon protested.

"Leave the sick on deck then. They can do no harm."

To the doctor's amazement they all recovered.

"You weren't giving them time," I suggested.

He swore that Cousin was a cautious man who kept his damaged property longer than most slaving captains.

"Then it's getting them out of that stinking hold that does it."

The surgeon only grunted. He himself finally attributed it to his own skill. The negurs gave me credit. My magic was stronger than Cousin's, they declared. I didn't and do not know. But since that time I have directed ship captains to bring the afflicted on deck and keep them there . . . and I've never lost one from blindness.

But if I cured the negurs I was less skilled in caring for myself. The responsibility for the vessel, the fear that the crew might be plotting to recapture the ship, the burden of carrying Cousin's fate on my mind all combined to make day and night one long ordeal of watchfulness and anxiety. I could neither eat nor sleep. As a consequence by the time we entered the Caribbean I was a sick man.

Weak and still irresolute I finally went to the cabin. Cousin sat at his desk. His hands and feet were bound.

"Tom Griffith," he whispered, though I had not spoken.

"Anthony More," Morgan said from the couch where he lay tied.

"Griffith," Cousin repeated.

My head ached, my eyes burned. I dropped wearily on a stool.

"Don't you believe I am Anthony More?" I asked.

"No."

"Why not?"

"I knew Anthony More. He was bigger than you, and he was a gentleman."

"A man bends under the years and coarsens."

"Anthony More would not bend."

"You knew the girl who was his wife, too."

"A weak creature of the flesh."

"Yet she bore you a child and went mad from the sin you left on her soul."

"A weak creature," he repeated indifferently.

"True. She was weak. But her weakness gave me the strength to follow you. And she did not sin alone. When you are dead she will rest in peace, but God will exact punishment from you."

"I have walked in the ways of the Lord."

"With the wife of Anthony More?"

He was silent.

"Know ye that the unrighteous shall not inherit the Kingdom of God? Be not deceived: neither fornicators, nor idolators, nor adulterers . . ."

It was not hot, yet sweat stood on Cousin's forehead. He was a coward after all. He was afraid of Hell. But I was too tired to press my advantage. Let him settle his sins with his God. I got up.

"You keelhauled a woman once," I said heavily; "for that—"

I was interrupted by a low cry.

"No," he whimpered, "no."

I wondered if there was, after all, a degree of brutality which offended even Edward Cousin's conscience. Did he suffer remorse over murdering Pol? It did not matter.

"You keelhauled a woman," I repeated. "It was just before sunset. At that time tomorrow you will be keelhauled. Morgan will take charge. As he took charge then."

"No," protested Morgan from the couch.

"Then you will join him."

The mate said nothing. I turned back to Cousin.

"If you survive you will be hanged at sunset. Your body will be thrown to the sharks."

When I had left the cabin I felt no satisfaction, but only a weary disgust . . . with Cousin . . . with the coming day's work . . . with myself. The next day the depression deepened, but at mid-afternoon I returned to the cabin. Cousin was at the desk again, Morgan on the couch.

"Will you help me or be keelhauled?" I asked the latter.

"You leave me no choice."

"Good."

I loosened him.

"Sir Anthony."

I knew that Bill had been a baronet, yet the title sounded strange. But even more strange was the note of uncertainty in Cousin's voice. I thought that he was breaking. I did not answer.

"Sir Anthony." He spoke with such urgent appeal that I relented.

"Yes."

"You say that I must die because a woman was keelhauled."

"I said nothing of the kind. You must die at a certain time, in a certain manner because you brutally murdered that woman. But you would die anyway . . . for your wickedness."

He brushed this aside.

"Did you know that woman?"

"Yes."

He was breathing so hard that he could only speak in gasps.

"In the name of God tell me what you know?"

He was sobbing, pleading. Edward Cousin humble was a new Cousin. I looked at him. To my amazement he looked back at me. The blindness had left him.

"You can see," I exclaimed.

He shook his head impatiently.

"Since morning. Does it matter to a man about to die? Tell me about the woman."

"She was—"

Cousin's face blurred, his form grew dim. "He's going blind again," I told myself, then I realized the truth. It was I who was blind.

Cousin noted it first.

"He's lost his sight," he called sharply to Morgan.

Before I could recover from the shock the mate's hands were pressing at my throat.

"If you move or cry out," he muttered, "I'll break your neck before help can reach you."

They tied me. Then they talked. As I listened my mind began to work. I would not be defeated by Edward Cousin. I would not permit him to avenge himself upon the blacks who had helped me.

"Four negurs are outside the door," I said. "At sunset they will come in."

"You will be dead by then," Cousin sneered.

"We can deal with four blacks," Morgan added.

"Possibly. But on the deck outside are a hundred more, all armed."

They considered that.

"What do you propose?" Cousin finally asked.

"Tomorrow we pass Tortuga. Land me, the wench Martha and the Gold Coast negurs. You recover your ship and the rest of the blacks."

We bickered, but as sunset approached Morgan grew nervous.

"If those black devils come in here they will not wait for explanations," he warned Cousin. "I can kill More, right enough, but you and I will follow him damned quickly."

Cousin granted my terms.

"But how do we arrange the transfer?" he asked.

"You release me immediately," I replied. "When we reach Tortuga I'll get off with the slaves and the arms. After that the ship will be yours."

"Why should I trust you?" he demanded.

"Because I pledge the honor of Anthony More."

"A pirate."

"A gentleman."

"*I'll* take your word," announced Morgan.

Cousin protested. The mate was respectful but firm.

"I've stuck with you, sir, but my skin is at stake as well as yours, and I won't lose it needlessly. It's better than twenty years since I first heard the name Anthony More, and I have yet to see the man who calls him a liar."

He aided me from the chair and guided me to the door.

"Till tomorrow, sir."

He said it respectfully. I was no longer "Uncle," but a great name to be treated with deference. I offered him his freedom, but he refused it.

433

"I'll stay with the Captain while the ship is in the hands of mutineers," he explained.

"Tomorrow, then."

I sat on the deck all night considering my course. Edward Cousin was in my power. Was I to let him go unscathed? Must a promise to such a creature be observed? Not Tom Bone's promise . . . of that I was certain. But I had pledged the honor of Anthony More. What would Bill himself want me to do? He, who had spent a quarter of a century hunting Edward Cousin . . . and in all that time, the mate declared, no man had called him a liar. That was the honor of Anthony More. I heard his voice.

"Gentlemen have their virtues, too, Tom," he had said.

Bill had been proud that he was a gentleman.

When Martha came to me with word that it was dawn I was startled. I had even forgotten that I could not see. But although I was blind I had never perceived my way more clearly. I sent Martha to get Jim.

I explained to those two what we must do. They accepted my leadership unquestioningly.

"You get us home," Jim said cheerfully.

"But not the Calabar negurs," I reminded him.

"They are no good," he declared contemptuously.

Fortunately Martha, who was from Calabar herself, could not understand him. However, she seemed content to share his fortune and was unmoved by the fate of her people. I recalled that the blacks were accustomed to the thought of slavery. They had practiced it among themselves long before the first Portuguese trader came to Africa.

When Jim and Martha had gone I sent for Morgan. We talked all through the forenoon. He told me why he was faithful to Cousin. The great brute had a sentimental core; there was a farm in a Welsh valley . . . he fancied himself there with a red-cheeked girl such as he had seen in the village before he ran away to sea. To realize his dream he was ready to sell his soul. Cousin paid well.

"And this is the last voyage, Sir Anthony. If I was going to keep to the sea I'd be proud to join you; but I'm done with wandering, and the Old Man has all my savings at Port Royal."

Morgan told me many other things that morning, among them how Martha had whipped Edward Cousin. Finally I came to the purpose of the interview. I summoned the courage to ask him what had occurred when they hauled up Pol's body. Without his knowing it, I think, his voice dropped to a hoarse whisper.

"It's an evil thing to talk about, sir," he said fearfully, "but I'll tell you this. Since that day we've been cursed, Edward Cousin and all aboard his ship."

I did not press the question. Indeed it had taken all my courage to ask it. I had no desire to know if the corpse they brought up had been robbed of life by bruising from the ship's keel, drowning or sharks. Polly was gone. I could not join her yet. Cousin and I were about to part . . . to meet again.

# XIX

I FOUND BILL's pirate nest abandoned. Either the new leader had been unable to hold the men together or the Spanish had cleaned out the place. However we found shelter in some of the shacks which were still standing, and the jungle provided sufficient food. With a hundred-odd negurs for company I settled down to wait for my sight to return, and for word from Joseph Trigg, to whom I had sent a message by Morgan. I saw again in less than a week; a few days later a small ship picked its way into the cove. Trigg himself came ashore. Judith was with him.

"She wouldn't stay home like a respectable female," he complained, but it was evident that he did not find her unmaidenliness altogether disagreeable.

Judith looked at me out of wide grave eyes.

"Are you really blind?" she asked abruptly.

"Do I look it?"

"Jack Morgan said that—"

She burst into tears. Crying women render me helpless and angry, sympathetic and awkward. I lifted Judith's bowed head the more roughly because I wished to be tender.

"My eyes are good enough to make out a foolish lass blubbering over nothing. Could a blind man see so much?"

She sniffed once or twice more.

"And I have wasted tears on you," she said severely.

"Not at all. I was blind until a few days ago."

She kissed me then, but despite the tears shed for me so recently

436

that they still trembled on her long eyelashes, her lips were not so ardent as they had been six months before.

We held a council that night. I told Trigg and Judith of my voyage and all its incidents, and of my promise to send the blacks back to Africa. After considering the matter Trigg suggested that he take charge for me.

"You can't take them to Jamaica," he pointed out. "That many slaves landed would be observed, and it's possible that Cousin may be watching for just that. If he caught you he could claim the negurs, and have you hanged for piracy besides. But from what you tell me he does not know that you are Tom Bone the planter, and owner of Saltash. So let me go to Port Royal alone and there in your name, and with your credit, fit out a vessel for the slave trade. I'll pick up a discreet crew and captain from among the lads I've sailed with, and ship myself as your factor. From Port Royal we will head here, pick up the blacks and take them to Africa. We can drop you and Judith at San Juan. From there you can go home as Tom Bone, and Edward Cousin will never be the wiser."

I could find no flaw in the plan save the expense of fitting a ship as a slaver. It would be costly and unnecessary.

"Very necessary," corrected Trigg, "because I intend to bring back a cargo of blacks."

I protested that I had seen enough of the trade, but Trigg insisted.

"You are a rich man, but not rich enough to send a ship to Africa and back without a cargo."

"Dispose of Saltash," I suggested.

He stared at me.

"What do you intend to do?"

I could not say that I intended to swim into the sea in search of Polly Bragg. It sounded foolish even to me. Besides I was beginning to doubt if I ever would.

"I don't know," I mumbled.

"Well," he said dryly, "Judith is young, and I am getting old. We need Saltash if you don't."

So I entered the slave trade. When I told Jim he was en-

437

thusiastic. He swore that he would kidnap the finest negurs in Africa for me.

"Be careful yourself," I warned him. "I cannot afford to ship you back and forth across the Atlantic another time."

Later I asked him if he had no compunctions in helping to send men over the sea from whence they never come home. I could not even make him understand what I meant. I have known a few whites, such as Jonathan Reap, who have scruples about the slave trade, but never a negur.

Trigg returned sooner than I had expected. To my dismay he had chartered the *Pilgrim*, with Jack Morgan in command.

"But Morgan is loyal to Cousin," I protested. "Besides, he intends to leave the sea."

"Talk to him," Trigg advised.

Cousin had refused to give the man who had worked for him so many years his savings. His excuse had been that in permitting me to leave the ship Morgan had joined the mutiny.

"The bloody bastard threatened to turn me over to the courts for piracy if I protested," the mate said bitterly. "So what could I do? I heard that the *Pilgrim* had been chartered and applied to the new master for a berth. I didn't know until we sighted Tortuga that I was working for you."

But he professed himself pleased at the arrangement.

I asked him about the farm in Wales.

"Wales," he snorted. "I'm too used to the smell of salt to settle down to cows and chickens and one woman. I'll die at sea."

The blacks trooped on board joyfully and the *Pilgrim* headed east. Judith and I left her at San Juan.

Jim and Martha waved to us from the ship's rail.

"I send you good negurs," shouted Jim.

"Kill big master," Martha screamed genially.


I came back to Jamaica in September of 1686. Through the fall and winter I lived quietly at Saltash with Judith Mara. Inquiries revealed that Cousin was at God's Acres. He lived there with his wife. I sometimes wondered how she had explained away the tale I had spun; but if rumors were true perhaps it had been unnecessary. Men whispered that she had bewitched him. I intended to go to God's Acres some day and find out. But I put it off. Peace was good after the years of pain. For the first time since Polly's murder I was happy. I told myself that I loved Judith Mara. I told her, too. She laughed at me and asked if my heart beat faster when she was near, if my body ached from loneliness in her absence. I remembered Pol. But how did Judith know love like that? I asked her. She laughed again, but there was little joy in her mirth and her eyes were wistful.

In February I asked her to marry me. After a week she said she would, and cried and clung to me, and swore to be a good wife. I pitied and envied her. How young she is, I thought, and innocent and in love. And how beautiful. I was very proud that she was going to belong to me. But when she suggested that our marriage should not take place until after Lent I consented. I was not impatient.

I felt tenderly toward Judith. I wanted her to be happy. Because she was young I believed that she would enjoy society. Such as there was in Port Royal we became a part of. There were balls and entertainments at Saltash. The Governor came to us and old Henry Morgan once again honored our drawing room. The latter, never noted for tact or grace in speech, clapped me on the back one night.

"You've a good eye for women, Bone," he roared. "The girl here is more beautiful than your former lady."

Judith, who hung on his arm, winced and looked at me humbly, as if asking forgiveness. It flashed over me that she knew that no one could ever be as beautiful to me as Polly Bragg. I smiled at her.

"At least she is too beautiful for an old rogue like you to tamper with," I told Morgan.

He guffawed gratefully. He regarded himself as a gallant, and his taste for young females increased with his years.

Judith had younger admirers too. She flirted with them lazily and kept them at arm's distance. I admired and rallied her upon her skill.

439

"It's your Irish blood that outwits them," I told her. "A timid Spanish señorita would need a duenna."

"They are tasteless," she yawned. "Young gentlemen are tasteless. They do not interest me."

I considered my own maturity, and the well-aged sap rose warmly to my heart.

"Quite proper when your future husband and servant is at hand," I declared with complacent gallantry.

She laughed and gave me a fleeting kiss.

The *Pilgrim* returned in March. Jim, true to his promise, had loaded her hold with a fine cargo. Every negur aboard was from the Gold Coast. Morgan declared them the best lot of blacks he had ever seen.

"I'd like to have a partnership with you, sir," he said wistfully. "With me to handle the ship and deal with Jim in Africa, and you at this end, we could make a fortune. I would be content with a third of the profits."

Because I did not wish to be burdened with the responsibilities of a business, I rejected the suggestion. However, when the blacks from the *Pilgrim* were sold at auction the profits were so great that I changed my mind. But in one respect I modified the plan. Trigg was to manage in Jamaica. The three of us would divide the profits equally.

"When I die," I told Judith, "you will be not only the most beautiful but also the wealthiest widow in the West Indies."

To my consternation she burst into tears.

"I don't want to be a widow," she sobbed.

I looked at her in helpless irritation. She was carrying devotion too far. I preferred the bold-tongued courageous creature who had fought for my sanity at Tortuga and aboard ship.

"I was only teasing you," I assured her, "so stop your sniveling and think of the riches. There at least you can find nothing to cry over."

She dried her eyes. When she raised them they were smoldering hot. Her voice carried in it a spark of the old fire.

"And I don't want to be rich either, Tom Bone."

She left me without explaining, nor did she give me her customary light kiss. It was the first cloud that had come between us since I had asked her to be my wife. It bothered me. I told Trigg. He looked at me so sardonically that I regretted confiding in him. After all, Judith's vapors were her affairs and mine. I had been wrong to expose them to the contempt of an embittered old man. I tried to make amends.

"She is young, of course. It's but natural that a girl her age should occasionally fall into queer moods, especially with marriage approaching."

"Especially then," Trigg agreed.

Although I did not like his tone I blundered on.

"It was foolish of me to talk about dying, even in jest. It upset the child. Later when we are wed and settled down she will be sensible again—and happy."

As I said this last I realized for the first time that Judith was not happy.

"God grant that you may be right," Trigg snorted.

As the days passed Trigg's mood grew even more fretful. I observed him following Judith with anxious hurt eyes . . . or glaring somberly at me. At length I concluded that he was in love with the girl himself. I pitied him, and was a little amused that one so old should be so absurd. Easter had passed, the wedding was only two weeks away when he finally brought himself to explain.

"You've done more for me than any man alive," he told me unhappily, "but Judith is the daughter that I saw in my own Mary, when she was yet young, and I can't sit idly by and permit her to ruin her life."

That was the preface. The body of the tale was a love story, a very ordinary one about a girl and boy who fell in love . . . only the girl was Judith Mara and the boy a sailor named Harry. It had occurred while I was away, and he had gone to sea just before my return.

"Why didn't Judith tell me when I first came home?" I demanded.

"She wanted you to see him first."

441

I considered the matter coolly and, I thought, sensibly. But the years, and a measure of good fortune, make a man mean. I was neither hurt nor jealous that my betrothed should prefer an ordinary seaman. I was outraged. I was fond of Judith Mara. I even loved her. I wanted her to be wealthy and idle, to wear costly clothes, to eat rich food. I wanted her to live at Saltash where she would be waited on by blacks brought from the jungles of Africa to serve her.

I did not want her to be the wife of a poor sailor, wearing out her body working for him when he was ashore, and her heart longing and fearing for him when he went to sea. That she should want such a thing was absurd. I told Trigg so.

"You have two weeks to consider it," he said. "But while you are thinking, remember this. She is a fine girl, and she will break her heart for the duty she thinks she owes you."

"It is how fine she is that I am remembering," I insisted. "Can I let her throw herself away on a penniless sailor?"

For the first time in weeks Trigg broke into explosive laughter.

"By God, I should have guessed it. You care for her as a father, not a suitor." He quit laughing and leaned toward me eagerly. "Confess it, Tom, you love the lass only as a daughter."

Controlling the first flush of indignation caused by such an attack on my manhood I forced myself to consider the matter carefully. The problem was not so simple as it sounded. The instinct to protect Judith . . . the determination that she should not be hurt . . . the desire that she should find only laughter and ease in a world that I knew held more of tears and hardship . . . these were undoubtedly the feelings of a father. But there were moments when I looked at Judith and felt other things . . . not fatherly.

"How can I tell how I love her?" I said.

"Did you ever doubt how you loved your Polly?" Trigg asked gently.

"That only happens to a man once."

"And when it has happened does he dare ask another woman to accept what is left?"

442

I recalled how Judith had looked as Henry Morgan spoke of the days when Pol was mistress of Saltash.

"I must think about this," I muttered.

Trigg spoke hesitantly.

"There is something else . . . Tom. That is . . . Polly . . ."

All the doubts and irritations of the past weeks crashed together in a sudden thunderhead of temper.

"I've stood enough of your interference," I shouted. "Leave Pol in peace."

Trigg had said that I had two weeks to decide. Two days were enough. Polly's ghost brought me to my senses. Wrestling with my problem I had gone to the spot where she and I once lay planning a new life in Jamaica. Our prospects had been no brighter that afternoon than were the present ones of Judith and her Harry. But Pol, who had tasted luxury at Denham and solid comfort with James Lester, had not been afraid. Judith Mara was of the same stuff as Polly Bragg. Only I had changed. I was fat and sleek. Blinded by increasing wealth I had called it youthful folly to trade luxury and ease for love. I had offered Judith the wisdom that lies in living safely . . . I had told myself that a full belly was more important than a singing heart. But Polly's ghost whispered no. It whispered other things, too. It showed me the way to happiness for Judith and a measure of contentment for myself.

I returned to Saltash and Judith.

"Kiss me, my dear," I said.

She did.

"Again. Not with the cold rim of your lips, but hard with your mouth."

She flushed.

"Do you know what I mean?"

"Yes," she admitted in a low voice.

"But you can't do it?"

She raised her head proudly.

"I'll never kiss you that way, nor for that matter will you me."

I took her hand.

443

"You are right, Judith. For me there is no comfort, for Polly's dead. But your lad's alive. You must marry him."

When I had convinced her that the world was in truth paradise, and she had gone into the tropical sunshine to add to its warmth and dazzle it with her brilliance, I found Trigg.

"I must go to Port Royal," I told him, "but first, do you know where the rum is?"

"I always know where the rum is."

When he had fetched a gallon jug and two ale mugs, the latter Joseph Trigg's idea of the proper receptacle for hard liquor, he looked at me questioningly.

"It's not often you call for rum."

"I want to drink a toast."

"A toast?"

"To Cupid."

He beamed.

"God bless you, Tom."

"Not me. You and Polly's ghost."

When I had finished my drink and Trigg was settling to his third I explained how I had reached my decision and confided to him my plans for the future. He did not try to dissuade me.

"I'll miss you," was all he said.

At Port Royal I visited Samuel Hart. I had not done so previously because I believed it unnecessary. The Jew had impressed me as an honest and shrewd man. I assumed that he had disposed of my business long ago. But now that I was about to leave Jamaica I resolved to make sure. Hart's greeting was slightly reproachful.

"I expected you sooner," he said.

I thought that he wanted payment, but he brushed the suggestion aside.

"That can be settled later. The affair has proved more difficult than we anticipated."

He drew a large sheaf of papers from a drawer. There were letters, legal documents, court records. They told a strange tale, one that was not pleasant. As I read and pieced it together I felt a burden of responsibility settling on my shoulders. When I had

444

killed her father I must go to this daughter of Edward Cousin.

After Bill disappeared the grandmother of Amy More asserted her rights. She took the child away from the kindly people with whom Bill had left her. She reared her as she had reared her own daughter. There was nothing in the document to indicate what manner of child developed from the seed of Edward Cousin . . . or what woman grew out of the child. Neither her appearance nor her character was discernible. At twenty she married a suitor selected by her grandmother. He was a sober, substantial Dorsetshire widower, fifty years of age, with sons older than his bride. As a boy he had fought with Blake against the Dutch and served Cromwell in Ireland. England changed but Jonathan Felton remained the same. When Charles II came to the throne he retired to his land where he stayed, stern, unbending, incorruptible. Amy lived with him there. I do not know if she was happy. In later years she refused to speak of him, or of her life as his wife. Like Jahve of the ancient Hebrews the name was too sacred to be profaned by utterance.

In the year 1685 Charles II died and his brother, Catholic James, prepared to mount the throne. But a pretender challenged his claim. This was the Duke of Monmouth, bastard son of Charles and Lucy Walters. He was a selfish man, not very brave, not very intelligent, not loyal at all . . . but he was a Protestant. So when he landed at Lyme Regis and raised his banner Jonathan Felton took his two grown sons and went to war. He died at Sedgemoor, but the boys came home. They hid in a barn. Amy fed and kept watch for them, but her vigilance was to no avail. The rebels were ferreted out, captured and hanged. Jonathan Felton's property was confiscated by the crown, his widow arrested and tried for giving shelter to traitors. She had the honor of being tried by Bloody Jeffries himself, and was one of the relative few so distinguished to escape with her life. Samuel Hart had gotten a copy of the record of her trial. It was a curious document.

"Before he departed," Amy had told the court, "my husband instructed me in my duty."

"Indeed," sneered the judge, "and might we know what a traitor's concept of duty was?"

"He said if aught befell him I was to care for his sons."

"You failed," gloated Jeffries.

"Yes, my lord."

"So now we must stretch your neck."

"My fault was indeed grievous, my lord."

"Ah! You confess yourself at fault."

"Surely it is a great fault to fail one's spouse, my lord."

So through four close-written pages Bloody Jeffries and Amy Felton discussed wifely duty.

"Odd's blood," the exasperated judge finally shouted, "the woman is a fool. Deport her."

As I laid the account of the trial aside I thought how curious it would be if Cousin's daughter were in Jamaica. A number of the unfortunate rebels of 1685 were. They worked in the fields with the negurs, and lived with them. Englishmen and white . . . but slaves.

Amy, however, was not among these. She had been sentenced to twenty years' hard service and sent to Carolina where she was indentured to a family by the name of Todd. A year later her master moved to Boston, in Massachusetts. She went there with him.

"It must have been difficult to trace her," I said to Hart.

"We are a patient people."

"You have not sent Anthony More's property?"

"No. Amy Felton is no ordinary bound wench. She is a convicted criminal serving a sentence. As such she must be entirely at the mercy of her master. He may be an honest man, but we do not know him."

"What do you suggest?"

"Wait. I know many of the New England captains who trade here. Perhaps we can learn more."

"Meantime the girl suffers."

"We do not know that. Besides what else can you do?"

"I can go to New England myself."

Until that moment I had thought to go to England. But what did it matter? Before I left Samuel Hart I arranged that he should procure me passage on a ship that was expected to leave Port Royal in three weeks' time.

At Saltash I rallied Judith.

"Is your Harry a good sailor," I asked her, "or can he only make port in a woman's arms?"

"Of course he is a good sailor," she pouted.

"Then I must have him on the *Pilgrim* where Jack Morgan will make him a better one. When he knows enough he will have a ship of his own."

Judith's eyes sparkled.

"Meantime," I continued, "you are to live here and watch over Joseph Trigg, lest he drink himself to death."

"You mean we are all to live here at Saltash as before?"

"You and Trigg are, and your Harry when you can keep him at home. I am going away."

Judith's face clouded.

"Not to her . . . not to the sea."

"No."

"Then what *will* you do?"

"There are other lands to see, new adventures that await a man yet in his mid-forties."

"Will you come back?"

"Who knows? Meantime I wish to give a farewell ball . . . the most notable in the history of Jamaica. We shall announce your betrothal."

"But Harry is not here; and if he were, what would a common sailor lad do at a grand ball?"

"What I, a fisherman's son, or you, a former serving girl, will do I suppose."

Judith flushed.

"I did not mean I was ashamed, but Harry would not be happy at such an affair."

"Then it's a good thing he is at sea . . . for I must have my ball."

"Of course, if you wish it."

"Good. See that invitations are sent to everyone of consequence . . . the officials of Port Royal . . . the planters both here and around Spanish Town. But one you must leave to me . . . that of Edward Cousin and his wife."

Trigg readily agreed to go to God's Acres for me.

"I've always wanted to see the place," he said cheerfully, "and most particularly to get a look at Mistress Cousin. I can convince them that Anthony More will be here, too. I've cozened sharper people with my glib tongue . . . All the same it's a fool's project, Tom."

"Why?"

"They won't come. He is well-nigh a recluse and it's said no white man has seen his wife."

"I don't care a hang if she attends or not, but he will if you do your part. Remember it is the one appearance of Anthony More . . . Cousin's one opportunity to denounce him and thus get him hanged. And demand a fat sum before you give up your secret . . . that is the sort of gesture Edward Cousin understands."

"Maybe you are right," Trigg admitted, "but if so, what then? There is law even in Jamaica. You can't kill a man in your own garden with all the island's dignitaries as an audience."

"I think I can."

2.

Judith worked herself and the negurs so remorselessly that by the time the first guests arrived the ball did promise to be the most magnificent in the history of the island. But it was not this that brought people streaming to Saltash, punctual beyond the hopes of the most demanding hostess. For a week rumors had spread in Port Royal and even Spanish Town. One said that Mistress Edward Cousin would be at Saltash, another that the great Anthony More himself might be on hand. A witch and the last of the buccaneers . . . tidbits for the most exacting palates.

The Governor himself saw fit to speak to me about More. He was considering the dispatch of a file of soldiers to Saltash. I discouraged the idea, and promised to take ample precautions of my own. Sir Henry Morgan was more difficult to soothe.

"Damn pirate," he roared in a fine rage, "damned thieving pirate."

I could not be sure if he was envious or merely the victim of the excessive virtue that so frequently afflicts the reformed.

"At least we shall have you to protect us if he does show up," I declared cheerfully.

But when I left him Sir Henry was still mumbling "damned thieving pirate."

The women were harder to be rid of. Some tittered, made languishing eyes and sighed as they demanded to know if that awful desperado was really a friend of mine. Others were more intrigued by the thought of Mistress Cousin. As the evening passed and neither of the celebrities appeared the atmosphere grew more tense. Rumors ran wild: More had been apprehended and shot; a gentleman declared that his lady insisted Mistress Cousin was in the garden with the devil, who was her lover. Judith informed me with twinkling eyes that Sir Anthony and Edward Cousin had run afoul one another at our gate. One was dead, the other mortally hurt.

Joseph Trigg stirred his mess with expert hand.

"When they find Cousin's body they will swear Sir Anthony More killed him," he assured me. "Why, half of 'em will say they saw it done."

"Excellent," I admitted, "but where *is* Cousin?"

"He will be here. I told him the assignation was not till midnight."

"Is Judith ready?"

"She will be when the time comes."

I felt quite calm. Edward Cousin would soon be at Saltash. "It is our last meeting," I thought.

They were in the center of the room. I suppose the footman announced them, but for a moment I was ready to credit witchcraft. They had not been there before and now they were. Voices, shrill a moment earlier, were still. There was a murmur . . . a whisper . . . silence. Anthony More was forgotten. For the first time in my knowledge Edward Cousin seemed insignificant. All eyes were on the woman beside him . . . the slight figure . . . the brown hair. She was gowned in barbaric magnificence . . . she carried herself with the easy insolence of a queen. The eyes that swept the assembly were cold gray ice; her heart-shaped face might have been a frozen mask. Her heavy mouth had never been more sensuous . . . had never promised less . . .

My head spun . . . my throat grew dry. I tried to cry her name but no words came. Trigg and Judith were beside me. They drew me into an anteroom.

"Careful, Tom," Trigg said in a voice tender as a woman's.

"You knew?" I gasped.

"I suspected. I tried to tell you."

I could stand it no longer.

"Polly," I cried, "Polly Bragg."

But the devil laughed and the fiends echoed Mistress Edward Cousin.

I wept like a woman and like a woman fainted. When I opened my eyes a few minutes later Judith leaned over me, her cool hand stroked my forehead. Trigg stood by. The old man and the girl were staunch and wise. They gave me their presence and were silent.

"How did you guess?" I finally asked Trigg.

"Little things. After you came home from your pirating and told me all that had happened I recalled that the stories of Cousin's wife began to circulate soon after you and Pol disappeared. Then one of the commonest rumors was that she was a witch out of the sea. You had said that Pol was keelhauled. Could any woman save a sea-witch survive an ordeal that kills the toughest men? Ignorant sailors might say no. There was the voudou, too. I remembered the part Pol played among the Indians in Virginia. Finally I could not find Abel and the wench. I'll warrant both are at God's Acres."

As Trigg told it it seemed that an idiot must have guessed. And I had had even more proof than he. Cousin's fear at the mention of keelhauling . . . Morgan's even greater terror. I had actually seen Polly on the docks the day that the *Pilgrim* sailed. Why had I failed to recognize her? Because I had been so certain that she was dead? Because I had been too full of hate and self-pity? Perhaps, but surely there was some excuse for me. How could I have looked for Polly Bragg in Edward Cousin's wife?

"What can it mean?" I asked dully. "Pol . . . his wife . . ."

"He must have forced her to marry him and kept her prisoner at God's Acres," Judith ventured. "That is why no one has seen her."

"You are being kind, Judith, but it is not true. You never knew Polly Bragg but you have just looked at her. Is she a woman compelled against her will? Did Cousin look like a man who had mastered her?"

Judith was silent. I turned the knife in my own wound.

"And she has not been kept captive. No man saw her merely because no one looked for her. But I saw her. I saw her leave him on the dock at Port Royal. She was her own mistress then."

Judith's voice trembled. She blinked back the tears.

"Don't, Tom, don't torture yourself." Then suddenly her Irish temper flared. "I'll kill her with my own hands," she cried.

It was no idle threat. Judith meant it and was capable of trying to do it. It brought me out of my misery.

"No," I protested.

"But think what she did to you. Not only tonight . . . Tortuga . . . the months on the pirate ship . . . the creature you were then . . . all from loneliness . . . from sorrow for her . . . Polly Bragg." Her young voice burned with indignation. "Polly Bragg," she repeated, "filthy bitch."

I struck her. She recoiled, more from surprise than the force of the blow, and stood glaring at me out of hot angry eyes. Trigg stepped between us.

"Forgive him, Judith," he said heavily; "you see he still loves her."

The anger drained from her face.

"May a man love me so," she murmured.

Trigg turned to me.

"What you say is true, Tom. You and I who know her well know that no man could force Polly to do aught against her will."

"Why then?" I muttered.

He continued heedless of the interruption.

"Not the Polly that we knew and loved. But who can say what happened to her during those minutes when, with her body bent back like an Indian bow until it must have almost broken, she was pounded between the water and the ship's keel? Who knows what happens to a woman's soul when her lungs are bursting from want of air and, for aught we know, sharks flash past her tortured eyes? It is a miracle that she was alive when they brought her up, but maybe she was not all alive. Maybe our Pol stayed somewhere down there."

"You mean she has been mad since then?"

"Would your Polly—yes, and my Polly too—marry Edward Cousin?" he asked.

"No."

"Then call her what you will, she is not the woman you loved."

"I cannot explain it," I admitted, "nor is there need to. She is Polly, that is enough. And she must still love me. We shall carry out our plan tonight. Tomorrow Polly will be mine again. Bring Cousin to the grove as arranged."

Trigg assented.

"I'll meet you in an hour's time," I told Judith, and left them. I wanted to be alone.

An hour later I walked into the grove. A bench was there in the clearing. Judith was waiting. She looked at me in bewilderment for an instant. She had never seen me without the full beard I had worn since the days on the derelict. I had changed my dress, too. I wore my most magnificent clothes and carried a sword at my side. Under my arm was a hat that boasted a splendid plume. Judith gasped. For a moment I was afraid that she might betray herself, but she recognized me quickly and fell into her part.

"Sir Anthony," she cried and ran to me.

I took her in my arms.

"I never knew you were so handsome . . . and young," she whispered.

There was so much surprise in her voice that I almost laughed aloud.

"You, my dear, are very lovely and brave to come here."

452

I said it aloud, for the benefit of Cousin hidden in the bushes, but I meant it, too. We sat on the bench.

"Is he here?" I murmured for her ear alone.

"I believe so. I heard a slight rustle soon after I came."

"Then we had best play our game."

We kissed and murmured. I fondled her. My blood grew hot, and although my thoughts were for Polly, the body under my hands was Judith's. She pushed me away, half angry, half amused, and not wholly unmoved.

"That's enough. I must save something for my bridal night."

She said it loudly and firmly. I had started to stammer an apology when Cousin stepped from the bushes.

"Anthony More," he said in a voice that was redolent with unctuous self-congratulation.

I jumped from the bench.

"At your service."

"Not *my* service, the hangman's."

"Are you quite sure?"

"Certainly. The old rogue who acted as your panderer in arranging an assignation with the trollop yonder betrayed you to me two weeks ago. I have dispatched him to the house to inform the Governor of your presence. All the gentlemen gathered there will soon be hastening here to take you."

"Aren't you afraid I shall flee?"

"Anthony More will not run away."

"How long since your messenger left?"

He smirked knowingly.

"I only revealed myself when sufficient time had passed to guarantee the arrival of assistance."

"And yet, though the house is but a little distance, they have not come, nor do I hear any disturbance."

Some of Cousin's aplomb seemed to ooze away but he was not seriously concerned.

"They are probably organizing."

"Joseph," I called.

Trigg stepped from behind a tree.

"Is this the 'old rogue' that betrayed me?"

Cousin was disconcerted, but not to the degree that I had expected.

"Treachery," he exclaimed angrily and barked a command.

Three negurs appeared. One was the bodyguard that I knew so well, the other two were the ones that I had seen at God's Acres. All three carried knives.

"I trust no one," Cousin explained, "so I had these fellows follow me."

I was cursing myself roundly for so underestimating Cousin's cunning when Judith spoke.

"Up, lads," she said sharply.

Matthew, James, Simon and John appeared as from nowhere.

"A little precaution on my own part," the girl told Cousin as her blacks attacked.

The negurs, fighting silently, moved smoothly as great black panthers; their knives gleamed wickedly in the moonlight. The struggle was short and decisive. One of Cousin's men died with a knife under his ribs, the others fell to their knees. Matthew, James, Simon and John looked to Judith; Judith looked to me.

"Take them to one of the sheds," I suggested. "Hold them there. Trigg will show them."

Judith pointed to Cousin.

"Him, too?"

"No."

She nodded. Trigg and the negurs took their prisoners away. I turned to Cousin.

"There are just the two of us now," I said, and drew my sword.

"I can't fight Anthony More," Cousin cried in a panic-stricken voice. "I fear no other man on earth, but I will not fight Anthony More."

Pol slipped from the shadows like a ghost.

"Tom," she said in a flat voice.

I started toward her.

"Stop," roared Cousin, but it was not his command that checked me.

"Stop," Polly had echoed.

As I stood in a daze Cousin spoke. He was as bewildered as I.

454

"Do you know Anthony More?" he asked Pol.

"This is not Anthony More."

"But—"

"It is Tom Bone, my husband, the man that you swore was dead."

Her voice was still flat. Her face under the pale moonlight was like carved marble. I recalled stories whispered by the blacks of bodies that are resurrected and live on without souls.

"I swear," Cousin was saying, "that he is dead. I saw him die."

I thought then that I knew why Pol had stopped me. She was possessed of just such fantastic horrors as had attacked me. She believed that I was dead. I turned furiously on Cousin.

"You lie," I shouted. "You saw nothing. You were lying on the deck where, despite your whole damned crew and your negur guard to boot, I knocked you. Your lying mouth was filled with blood, your eyes were already swollen shut when I leaped over the rail . . . But enough of talk. You just boasted that you feared no man save Anthony More. Very well, Anthony More is dead, but Tom Bone is alive."

The moon was soft that night. The clearing in the grove was small, yet large enough for courting a maid or killing a man. Polly had laid it out. It was edged with bright flaunting blossoms; there was a fountain in the center with a bench beside it. Just for us, Polly had said of the bench. But it was Judith who sat on it as we fought. Polly stood motionless where she had first appeared.

Cousin drew his sword. He fought after the Spanish fashion, treading cautiously in a circle, following an almost formal pattern in his strokes. I had encountered this mode of fighting on the ships of the Dons. To the uninitiated, because it was based on a sound defense, it seemed timid, but many an unwary Englishman had discovered too late that in that defense lurked death. "Protect yourself," a Spanish pirate once said to me, "wait for an opening, then one thrust and that one fatal." There was no joy in it, no bravado, no singing blood; only cold, grim, determined steel.

I fought after the manner of the English, though I am told

they borrowed it from Italy by way of France: attack, parry only to save yourself for another thrust. War is a merry business and the greatest game that man has invented, but one that palls quickly. Kill or be killed and have an end to it. Life waits with love and food and drink and the song of the nightingale and the smell of a wet meadow.

For me Polly waited, cold as stone but only needing to feel my flesh and my pulsing heart to know that I was real and alive. I pressed the fight . . . and in doing so laid myself open. I saw Cousin's blade soon enough to escape death, but too late to go unscathed. The point bit into the flesh of my left side, well below the heart. Cousin, the death stroke having failed, moved back.

"Are you hurt, Tom?"

The voice was charged with anxious affection, but it came from Judith, on the bench behind me. I could see Pol. She had not moved or spoken.

I laughed angrily and attacked. Fury at Pol's indifference gave me new strength and new recklessness. Perhaps because I cared little if I lived or died my arm was stronger, my feet nimbler. My sword found its mark. Cousin grunted and sank to the ground. I stood over him. He was unconscious. My sword's point pricked his throat.

"No."

Polly had at last spoken. I turned incredulously.

"You want me to spare him?"

"Yes."

I clung desperately to reason.

"But I am alive, Pol. Tom Bone."

"Alive," she repeated impersonally. "Yes, alive . . . warm, loving and alive. I know, Tom Bone is alive."

"And you still say I must spare Edward Cousin?"

"Yes."

I threw myself at her feet.

"But why? For the love of God tell me why?"

She looked down at me. For a moment I thought I saw the old Pol stirring, but my hopes were dashed. She spoke slowly.

"If he dies I shall have nothing left to live for."

456

I stared up at her in horror.

"You mean that?" I gasped.

"Yes."

"Would to God you had died that day."

It was torn out of my deepest being.

"Would God I had," she agreed simply.

Judith was beside me. She raised me to my feet. In her hand was a fragment of her most magnificent gown. She had torn it to bind my wound.

"Come, Tom."

Her voice was warm and kind. I pushed her away and seized Pol's hand.

"Polly," I cried once more. "It's Tom . . . alive . . ."

She withdrew her hand from mine, walked around me and leaned over Edward Cousin.

"Please release his blacks," she said over her shoulder, "and send them here at once. I must get him home."

Judith urged me gently toward the house. I last saw Polly kneeling beside Edward Cousin, cradling his ugly head in her arms.

"Tom," Judith murmured as she dressed my wound. "Poor Tom . . . poor Tom Bone."

"There is no Tom Bone," I told her woodenly. "Tonight Tom Bone died."

# Book Four

# XX

## I.

I HAD SENT orders to Trigg to release Cousin's negurs as Polly had requested. After doing so he hastened to us, but Judith dismissed him.

"I was with Tom before," she explained.

I knew what she meant. She thought that the demons that had possessed me during the Tortuga and pirate days would return. She was mistaken. A man does not suffer such an ordeal twice. In the four black years during which I had believed Polly dead something within me had hardened . . . or died. So as I sat staring blindly into the tropical night I was not angry or vengeful or bitter. I was empty.

"Tonight Tom Bone died," I had said to Judith.

It was true. Not the body; nor did I feel the slightest urge toward self-destruction, for I knew that no Polly awaited me in Heaven or Hell . . . but nonetheless Tom Bone had died.

"If you will still have me," Judith said toward dawn, "I will be your wife."

While I sat numb she had waged and won a gallant battle . . . and a useless one. I rejected her sacrifice. It was not generosity. What did a ghost want of a radiant creature such as Judith Mara? I tried to explain to her that I wanted no person or thing from the past near me. I do not know if she understood, but my self-absorption was not so great as to blind me to her relief. She even attempted to infect me with a measure of her own warmth.

"You are right to refuse such a shameless forward creature," she assured me. "Your need is for new faces, and that reminds

461

me that your own face is new. I was quite startled in the grove. Without your beard you are a handsome man. You will yet find a proper maiden to love and breed you a fine lot of children."

"Do you believe that?" I inquired somberly.

She stood by her guns.

"Of course, and I hope it with all my heart."

I would not permit Trigg or Judith to come with me to Port Royal.

"I would rather see you for the last time here at Saltash, where we have been so happy," I lied to them. The truth was that I had come to Saltash with Pol. Since I must leave without her, I would go alone.

In Port Royal I went to Samuel Hart. He gave me Bill's stuff and prepared to take me aboard a waiting vessel.

"Have you told the Captain the name of his passenger?"

"I thought that might wait until you went aboard."

"Good. My name is Thomas Bond."

"Very well," he replied. But after a moment he added quietly, "Man does not escape sorrow through flight."

"What do you know of my sorrow?" I exclaimed involuntarily.

"Only what I guess. But for many months I have known the identity of Mistress Cousin."

My choler subsided almost as quickly as it rose. It had been impossible to unburden myself to Trigg or Judith—they were too close to me, their pity was too hard to bear—but this grave old man was almost a stranger and impersonal as a priest in the confessional.

"Since you guess so much, would you have me stay in Jamaica?" I asked.

He threw out delicate nervous hands in a quick gesture of denial.

"By no means. I only say that when you have taken a new name . . . fled thousands of miles to a new land . . . that sorrow will remain in your heart."

"I expect that, but what more can I do?"

He smiled ironically.

462

"My people suffer and grow wealthy."

"I am already rich."

"Add to your riches."

"Do you then believe that I can buy surcease of pain?"

"No. Your wealth is useless for that; but in the work of accumulating it you can sometimes find forgetfulness. You do not now believe that, but later you will remember what I have said."

In spite of myself I was impressed.

"And if I should, what could I do?"

"Ah! There you are fortunate. You are already in the slave trade between Jamaica and Africa. Extend it to include New England. Rum for slaves, slaves for sugar, sugar into rum, with a profit on each transaction. It is a new trade but the New Englanders are already growing wealthy on it."

I thanked him for his kindness. A few hours later I was aboard the *Gull*, bound for Newport in the plantation of Rhode Island.

Roger Arnold, captain of the *Gull*, was ambitious. During the five weeks that I was on his vessel he showed no curiosity whatsoever concerning my past, but inasmuch as Hart had informed him that I was a man of substance, he was very willing to play a part in my future. He did not attempt to conceal his motives. He was doing well enough selling fish and barrel staves to West India planters, but he longed to enter the Africa trade. To do so required capital. He hoped that I might be interested.

My first impulse was to reject his overtures, but recalling Samuel Hart's advice I temporized by explaining that I had business in Boston. After that my plans were uncertain; I might not remain in New England. If I did I would consider his offer.

"That's as fair as a man could ask," Arnold said. "Meantime make inquiries concerning Roger Arnold. You will find no reputation better for honesty and thrift."

I conceded this hastily for I had no wish to hear a catalogue of his virtues, but he would not be denied.

"I am a godly man, too, though it may be that I do not call on the Lord to witness my piety and trouble Himself with my affairs as often as some of the canting captains who sail out of Boston." A shadow clouded his good-natured face. "If you do decide to remain in New England, I hope for your sake that it will not be Boston."

"What is wrong with Boston?" I asked idly.

He snorted a Newport man's contempt for Boston and all Massachusetts colony besides.

"By accident the wind blew the *Mayflower* there. Later vessels followed her so Boston grew fast. Why, they boast that there are seven thousand souls there, though I doubt if they have above five. But despite its size it has only a past, sir. Now Newport looks to the future. The slave trade is barely beginning, but already we have the lead. We'll pass Bristol herself before we've done. That is why I long to be in it," he wound up wistfully.

Presumably the fear that I might succumb to the wiles of Boston continued to haunt the mind of Captain Arnold, for a few days later he returned to the subject.

"Smallpox," he barked at me across the dinner table.

"On board?" I asked, startled at his ferocity.

"Boston, and two great fires in late years."

"Newport is free of such inconveniences, I presume."

He replied to my irony with an open grin.

"Completely, sir. Only health and opportunity at Newport. But, laugh as you will, Boston is cursed. Even her own clergy admit it. They blame the ill fortune on the ungodliness of the people."

I solemnly promised to beware pitfalls in Boston; and thereafter, until the day I left the *Gull*, I was obliged to vow that if I remained in New England I would give Newport and Roger Arnold my gravest attention. Nonetheless upon landing I made my way straight to Boston.

David Todd, a mild-mannered man, heard my errand and called his wife.

"A gentleman is here on business concerning your servant Amy," he explained.

"Humph!" grunted Mistress Todd, scrutinizing me suspiciously.

"May I see her?" I asked.

"What is your business?"

"It is with her."

464

"That is as may be, but the law gave her into my keeping for twenty years. She is a wicked creature, or she would not be in her present condition; so why should I expose her to the first stranger who announces he has business with her?"

There was no doubt that Mistress Todd controlled the situation. I swallowed my dignity and pleaded humbly, explaining that I had been a friend of Amy's father.

"He disappeared," she interrupted severely; "abandoned her when she was but a baby, I am informed."

"Ah, yes, ma'am," I admitted, "and a shameful thing to do it was, one that he repented bitterly. That is why on his deathbed he made me promise that I would repair the wrong."

"Did he give you anything for her?"

The hard eagerness in the woman's voice attested that Samuel Hart was a wise man.

"No," I lied.

She glared at me suspiciously.

"If he did, it is my duty and right under the law to care for it," she reminded me.

Mistress Todd no longer controlled the situation. I had found her master. Greed owned her as surely as she owned poor Amy More. I realized, too, that it would be foolish to give the girl's legacy into these people's keeping.

"Your wench's father left nothing," I repeated curtly, "but he once saved my life, and I am a rich man. I'll buy the remaining years of the girl's service."

The mere claim to wealth transformed Mistress Todd into a whining beggar.

"Why, master, I couldn't part with Amy," she declared. "I've trained her to my ways like she was my own daughter and cared for her too."

"How much?" I interrupted.

"And if she was to leave us I must get a new wench and train her to our house, and then she will serve but five years, while Amy's sentence still has well over fifteen to run."

"Buy a black," I suggested. "They are yours for life."

465

"They cost too much," Mr. Todd interposed nervously. "Besides I do not . . ."

His wife merely looked at him, his voice trailed off, his eyes dropped. I gathered that what Mr. Todd did or did not was of small consequence, and continued to address myself to his wife.

"I'll buy you the finest black woman you can find and pay you whatever money Amy cost you in the bargain," I said recklessly.

Mistress Todd shook her head.

"It's not money I am thinking of, master, it's my feeling for the girl."

I picked up my hat.

"Well, I call God to witness that I have done my best to fulfill my vow to Anthony More. And to be honest with you I do not want a young woman on my hands. I am pleased to leave her in such fond care."

The woman was so alarmed that she grasped me by the arm.

"You can have her," she cried.

So Edward Cousin's daughter became my servant . . . but Polly was Cousin's wife. Fate weaves strange patterns and in this one I found neither comfort nor satisfaction.

Amy More, or rather Amy Felton, was an ugly graceless woman. She possessed her father's jutting features, spotted skin and broad-shouldered, thick-trunked body. Like him she too feared God and saw in Him a stern unloving Master. But with this the resemblance between daughter and father ceased. Amy did not wrestle with the flesh, for unlike Cousin she was not tempted by it. When I took her from the Todd household she was only in her mid-twenties, but she was already a harsh woman of unforgiving virtue. There was no joy in her and no sorrow. She lacked both laughter and tears. She resented the world and repulsed it. She did her duty and made duty unpleasant in doing it.

I sometimes wondered if the revulsion to the flesh that Bill's Prudence experienced after her lover was gone seared with its agony the child that she carried in her womb. Whatever it was, Amy was a damned soul. She could not even suffer. Her flesh was non-sentient, her mind thick and heavy as her body. Yet to

466

save her soul she felt sin necessary, so she fancied the crimes that she was too dull to commit.

Naturally I did not know all this when I took her from Mistress Todd. I only knew that she looked like Edward Cousin and that I had assumed a heavy, disagreeable burden; for I learned that since she had been sentenced for crime I could not free her.

I took her to an inn and explained this. Then I told her of Bill and the legacy that I held for her.

"My father was a wicked man," she said when I had done. "I will not touch his wealth."

I argued, pleaded, threatened. It was futile. She resisted me with flabby, impenetrable stupidity. At the end of an hour I knew how Bloody Jeffries had felt when he presided at her trial for treason.

"You have bought me," she said stubbornly, "and are my master. You may treat me as you will but you cannot make me sin."

Sin! I was torn between tears of vexation and lewd laughter.

"I would beat you," I finally gasped, "if I did not suspect you would enjoy it." I thrust some Spanish coins on her. "Go buy some decent clothes."

She looked at the money. Suspicion glowed in her dull eyes.

"Why are you trying to be kind to me?" she asked.

"Not for your sake," I assured her testily, "but because I loved Anthony More."

"My father was a wicked man."

"The vilest I ever knew," I agreed readily.

"But you loved—"

"I loved Anthony More. Now as you profess yourself my servant, for God's sake obey me."

She stood her ground.

"You too must be wicked," she declared almost joyfully, "but perhaps God has sent you here that I may redeem you."

"Too late," I assured her in something of a genuine panic. "I *am* wicked. In fact I have already sold my soul to the devil, sealed the bargain in my own blood and celebrated the black mass. Now

467

if you do not leave me I shall call my master, Satan, to send demons to possess you."

She paled and hastened away, but I was not entirely reassured, for I thought I detected a gleam of missionary zeal that was almost warm steal into her muddy eyes.

"Seventeen years," I groaned when she was gone.

I broke faith with Captain Arnold and remained for some months in Boston. The inn where I was proved pleasant, and there were no signs of either smallpox or fire. For the time being I was without purpose, while a decision involved some sort of disposition of Amy. I could think of nothing to do with her and was unable to bring myself to enter upon a life in which she would have a share. But witchcraft finally drove me out of Massachusetts. Such learned men as Increase Mather to the contrary, I do not believe in witches and witchcraft. As a boy I had seen Old Jenny burned as a witch and known that she was nought but a harmless old crone. I had heard the voudou drums in Virginia and seen Pol and Abel work their charms. It was a very gallant fraud but it was not magic. True, the drums of Africa had had their way with Edward Cousin on the banks of the Bandy River, but his panic had come from within. Certainly I, who knew Polly, could scoff at Cousin's fear of his wife. In Jamaica it was whispered that Pol herself was a witch. What the frozen creature who had stood in the moonlight at Saltash was I did not know, although I had racked my brain for an explanation . . . but she was Polly Bragg . . . and not a witch. I did know that. So out of my experience came the conviction that though men and women undoubtedly sell themselves to the devil, they get no extraordinary gifts in return. Satan seems entirely willing to leave them to their own devices, which sometimes, as in the case of Cousin, are hellish indeed.

Entertaining such sentiments I had little patience when Amy brought home tales that witchcraft and evil were sweeping Massachusetts, and especially Boston. I told her so.

"The Scriptures themselves say thou shalt not suffer a witch to live," she retorted in triumph.

"The Scriptures also say that God takes no pleasure in fools,

468

and if He lacks patience for them, how can a mere man such as I have the strength to tolerate your folly?" I answered wearily.

"Do you mock the Holy Word?"

"No, but I marvel to hear it used so often to excuse lack of charity. Jehovah is obeyed slavishly by people such as you, but in your harsh virtue you crucify Christ a hundred times and glorify it; whereas Judas Iscariot betrayed his Master only once . . . and hanged himself."

"I will not—"

I was tired of argument and I too could use Holy Writ to my purpose.

"Servants be ye obedient to them that *are* your masters according to the flesh," I roared. "Now get out and do not annoy me with further gossip."

She left and did not again mention witchcraft; but a few days later I received a call from a delegation of worthies, high in the Councils of both the Church and the colonial government. They were circumspect but firm. They understood that I had denied witchcraft, blasphemed and even sold myself to the devil. I admitted the first charge, whereupon they read Mather's *Essay for Recording of Illustrious Providence*. I still demurred. After some hesitation they abandoned the subject and turned to more serious charges. Amy was summoned. She admitted that she had informed the authorities that I had confessed selling my soul to the devil. To her dismay I denied the whole matter and swore solemnly that she, a convicted criminal, was acting from sheer malice. God did not strike me down and Amy retired discomfited. Nonetheless when the delegation left I felt that they were still suspicious and that sooner or later I would again run afoul of them. I resolved to leave Boston. This resolution was hastened when Amy came to me in a state as near hysteria as was possible in so phlegmatic a clod.

"She cast her eye on me today," she said, shuddering.

"Who?"

It was a mean tale. A family living in South Boston declared its members bewitched. In searching for a victim they went to the home of the laundress who washed their linen. The woman her-

469

self was not there, but her mother, a toothless bent ancient, flew into a temper at the slurs cast upon her daughter, and cursed the visitors soundly, calling them, they swore, "bad" names. The men of God and of the law, to whom the matter was referred, did not appear to consider that the poor old creature was herself only resenting the bad name that threatened her daughter. She was poor, had a reputation for drunkenness and did not belong to the Church. They tried her for witchcraft. Amy had attended the trial and while there felt the black shadow of the woman's magic.

I heard her with what patience I could summon, and when she finished tried once more to reason with her. She only resented my refusal to give credence to her affliction. I finally lost my temper.

"I myself am at fault," I told her. "I have let you live here idly at the inn. As a consequence your servant's soul has found its scullery maid's level . . . and your head is filled with nonsense. We shall leave Massachusetts immediately and live some place where I can find work for you. Then there will be no time for witches' trials."

We went to Newport where by good luck I learned that Captain Arnold was ashore.

"Do you have witches in Rhode Island?" I asked half in jest.

"The only place in New England free of them," he responded with sober pride. "Not a single witchcraft trial in the plantation's history."

"The only place in New England where men are sensible," I suggested.

He would not have this, for to admit it would clear Boston of the cloud that darkened its name. There were witches, he insisted firmly, but like other vermin they remained in Massachusetts.

"Well," I told him, "so long as you keep them out of Newport I shall follow your advice and make it my home."

"And the slave trade, sir?"

"To tell you the truth, I am already in it, but I believe we can make room for you."

His broad face beamed.

I built a house in Newport. It was a two-story frame affair,

470

such as the prosperous merchants of the town boasted. Its mere possession established me as a man of substance. I installed Amy there as housekeeper. Under her severe eye my home was perfectly run. That it was, meant nothing. No memories from the past haunted it, no dreams for the future had gone into its creation. I slept there and ate my food; I intended to die there . . . but I did not live in my fine house. Instead I took Samuel Hart's advice and found a measure of forgetfulness in a small untidy office near the waterfront. From there I directed a trade in blacks that made the name of Thomas Bond familiar from Trinidad to Newport and all along the Guinea Coast. I instructed Trigg and Morgan to expand their operations, gave Captain Rogers the help he required, and later financed other ambitious New Englanders.

By accident I had news of Betty from one of these latter. He had just returned from a voyage during which he had taken a part of his cargo to Virginia. I was checking his report. "Five slaves, sold to Ernest Jackson, overseer at Sidney plantation near Jamestown" an entry read.

"Do you know the plantation's master?" I asked the captain.

"I have dealt with him."

"And the mistress?"

"Only by repute, sir. Both she and her husband are well spoken of, and Sidney is said to be one of the fairest plantations on the James."

"Have you seen their son?"

"I have heard it said that the lady gives her husband one each year. If you will tell me which of the lads you are interested in I shall make inquiries on my next visit."

"By no means," I hastened to say. "The mistress of Sidney is a kinswoman of mine, in a manner of speaking, but I doubt if she would be glad to have the relationship brought to attention. The plantation's name aroused my curiosity for a moment . . . that is all."

But it was not quite all. When the Captain was gone I remembered and was faintly stirred by jealousy. Ned had taken such complete possession of the woman who had been my wife. And remembering Betty's fierce maternalism I could not but admit that he had probably given her a fuller measure of happiness than I, and found for himself the contentment that had eluded me. I compared my lot with his. For Ned: Betty, children, Sidney; for me: figures in a ledger and a house presided over by the warped daughter of a man I hated. But the brief moment of self-pity passed. I had chosen freely, nor did I regret my choice. Those years at Saltash with Polly beside me were worth any price. Those years . . . I beat back the rising tide of the past and turned to my work.

One day news came that James II had been driven from the throne of England, and a few weeks later that Bloody Jeffries was in the tower. I thought that Amy would be glad, but though others in Rhode Island shouted for joy at the fall of the Romish King and the imprisonment of his chief butcher, this strange woman who had suffered so much at their hands showed no satisfaction.

"Aren't you pleased?" I asked.

"Justice is the Lord's," she responded severely.

"But," I protested, "the Lord also endowed mortals with the capacity to love and hate."

She looked at me with such an utter lack of comprehension that I was moved by an impulse to stir her. What would she do if I seized her in my arms? Was she capable of any emotion but turgid piety? What sort of wife had she been?

"Did you love your husband?" I asked.

"He walked with the Lord," she said drearily, "and I was his handmaiden."

Such conversations as this were frequent, but I never learned much of what went on beneath Amy's bleak exterior. I doubt if there was much to learn. I forced her to accept slaves to do the work in the house, but she was not grateful.

"I could do the work," she told me. "Why else am I your servant?"

"To please me," I said mildly, "and it pleases me that you should act as my daughter, rather than servant. You will manage my home but not toil in it."

472

She compromised with her conscience by declaring herself my housekeeper. As the months passed I grew a little fond of her for no better reason than that I had no other companionship and that it amused me to try to dispell the fog that surrounded her. So as my wealth grew and I learned the power of money, I paid certain people, and the law relinquished its grip on her.

"You are free," I explained.

After pondering the matter for some time she informed me gloomily that she must find work, and could only hope her lot would fall among godly people. I told her to give over her nonsense, she must remain with me, only to learn that such conduct on the part of a free woman would be wicked in the eyes of God and scandalous to the neighbors. I had difficulty in persuading her to remain as a paid housekeeper; and even so she was restive. Her dull soul stirred, I think, with a sense of sin. I resolved to find a husband for her. I knew that I had the money to buy a proper one.

She protested vehemently.

"Men are evil," she declared. "I'll have none of them."

I let her have her way.

Trigg wrote me regularly. In the first of his letters he explained that he had gone to God's Acres, but Pol had refused to see him. She had also forbade future intercourse of any kind. I resolutely seconded her command. I wrote:

> "Do not mention her name, it is as you once said: the Polly we knew died under the ship's keel. She is dead. Tom Bone is dead. Our child is dead. Between Mistress Cousin and Thomas Bond there is nothing."

After that, except for messages of affection from Judith who, not knowing how to write, depended upon Trigg, the letters concerned only the slave trade. So when three years after I had settled in Newport one of my ships brought a letter in Trigg's hand I opened it indifferently. As I had expected it contained reports on business and Judith's fond remembrance, but it closed with something else. I read it with a sense that it was unreal and then read it over three times.

"An agent of Cousin's came to me some months ago, with the suggestion that the merchant Thomas Bond (you are famous out here) would find it to his advantage to visit Edward Cousin. I gave the fellow scant courtesy, pointing out that you lived in Rhode Island and would scarcely come to Jamaica merely to call on Edward Cousin. He left but returned a few days later with the suggestion that I go to God's Acres. I was tempted, but refused because I knew that I would be recognized, and that Cousin's wife, if not he himself, would guess that Thomas Bond was Tom Bone. I did not believe that you would want that.

All this was some months ago; I have not told you sooner for reasons over which I need not waste time. You know them. But a few weeks ago the agent returned with a demand that I transmit to you an offer of a business alliance with Cousin. I laughed at him and turned him out. Three days ago he was here again. He informed me that Edward Cousin is himself going to Newport to consult you. His wife will accompany him.

I can only add what I learned from Samuel Hart, whom you advised me to consult if I needed shrewd counsel. He, Hart, who seems to know everything, informs me that when Cousin retired from the slave trade he placed large sums of money in certain commercial ventures which have turned out badly. Furthermore God's Acres is not doing well, although the sugar plantations in general prosper. It is Hart's opinion that Cousin aims at recouping his fortune by re-entering the slave trade, and seeks capital or a partnership from you because it is known that your interests have expanded rapidly and that you have not hesitated to place money with men who knew the business.

You will know how this has troubled me, and how heavily the burden of decision has weighed upon me. Judith urges me to inform Cousin who you are, and I grant that common

474

sense is on her side. But you and I (yes, and Pol too) have never been notable for our common sense, so I have resolved to leave the decision with you. Cousin does not sail for six weeks. I have no doubt you can find a ship leaving Newport or Providence that will reach here before that time. If you want them stopped tell me."

A ship was sailing the next day. I wrote Trigg a letter instructing him to act on Judith's advice. But I tore it up. Polly was coming! It was unthinkable that I should stop her. My heart sang; the pale winter sun of New England seemed warm and bright. I wrote another letter, ordering Trigg to send word that Thomas Bond would be honored if Edward Cousin and his wife would be his guests while in Newport. Then, although it would be at least ten weeks before they could arrive, I began to make plans for their entertainment.

## 2.

Outside, a brief day had died. The snow and mud lay heavy in the street. The gray of the ocean penetrated the land so that it was scarcely possible to tell where the swirling mist ended and the tossing water began. Yet it was spring and for a few brief moments at midday the sun had shone and I had felt life stirring about me.

"Spring, the beginning," I told myself. I stretched my arms and flexed my muscles and laughed aloud at the strength that I felt surging through me. In the full noontide of my manhood it was spring . . . the season of adventure . . . and before another hour had passed Polly would come.

The ship had arrived during the afternoon. I immediately sent word that my carriage was at the disposal of Mr. Cousin and his wife. She had replied graciously that my hospitality would be gratefully accepted.

Now, outside the brief day was dead. It was cold and dark, but in my house it was warm and bright. The finest of wax candles gleamed softly, in the fireplace great logs crackled bright defiance to the night's chill. Sleek, well-trained slaves moved noiselessly about their affairs. A table covered with massive silver awaited its burden of food and drink. Even Amy was richly, although soberly, dressed.

"You are acting as the mistress of my home," I told her, "and are of gentle birth. Try to conduct yourself in accordance with both obligations."

"Are these people godly?" she had asked.

"Edward Cousin talks of God more than any man I ever knew," I assured her.

This pleased her. She even caught some of my fervor. I watched her and reflected for the hundredth time that it would be an amusing moment when father and daughter stood face to face. We were on the threshold of that moment.

The negur footman announced them. Amy and I waited under the chandelier, its bright light fell on us. Pol entered a few steps ahead of Cousin. I heard her gasp. She threw out her hand as if warding off a blow, but, with only the faintest trace of hesitation, she continued to walk toward me.

Prepared as I was for the meeting I was unnerved. Whatever Polly's life with Edward Cousin might have been it had not, in my eyes, lessened her desirability. The years had not thickened her body; she moved with the same lithe grace that I had watched so proudly and possessively at Saltash; her face still held the promise of all that woman can ever mean to man.

"Mr. Thomas Bond," she murmured, and curtsied deeply.

I bowed low over her hand and pressed it to my lips. It was colder than the winter's sea. When I straightened up Cousin was beside her. We glared at one another. I felt the hairs on the back of my neck rise. Like two game cocks, I said to myself, wary, but for the moment immobile. Polly, however, though her cheeks were flushed, still smiled.

"Mr. Thomas Bond," she repeated in a clear, firm voice.

Cousin and I bowed to her will. We nodded stiffly. My heart sang no more. So Tom Bone *was* dead, and Polly Bragg as well. Thomas Bond, merchant, and Mistress Cousin looked into one another's eyes and mumbled conventional phrases. I presented

Amy as Mistress Felton, which indeed was her proper name. As I looked at Cousin and his daughter the resemblance between them was startling, but naturally the others did not observe what they did not dream existed.

Cousin kept his eyes fixed on me with the vigilance of a soldier in enemy country. Amy stared at Pol in fascinated disapproval. Presently we went to dinner. I placed Pol at my right, Amy presided at the foot of my table. Polly was obviously puzzled.

"I hope Mistress Bond is not ill," she ventured at last.

"Mistress Bond?"

"Your wife."

I wondered what sort of sport she considered this.

"Alas! madam," I said slowly, "my wife died at sea, brutally murdered."

Cousin muttered something unintelligible. Pol paled but pursued the subject.

"I have some knowledge of that tragedy," she said softly, "and believe me you have my sympathy." Her eyes had been downcast, but now she lifted them and for an instant I saw the old Polly. "I have heard it said she loved you greatly." Her eyes did not drop but a curtain fell over them. Once more I was shut out; her voice continued impersonally, "But it was rumored in Port Royal that you were wed again."

"Thomas Bond has never been in Port Royal, madam."

"Indeed," she murmured; and the conversation drifted to other subjects; but a few minutes later she returned to the attack.

"Your Jamaica representative has a place called Saltash," she said.

"Yes."

"A beautiful place."

"I am told that love went into its building."

Her lips trembled but her voice remained steady.

"I was there once. It happened that I overheard its master talking to a young girl. His words were very tender, but his hands were bold. She was forced to check him. There was something said about the approaching bridal night."

As I listened horror crept over me. Polly had witnessed the

comedy that I played so fervently with Judith. She had supposed the wedding Judith spoke of was mine. No wonder she had stood in the moonlight like a frozen statue. I was about to discard the transparent disguises that we were employing when Cousin spoke.

"My *wife* was outraged by the indecency of that couple," he purred.

The words made me pause. She *had* consented to marry him. That was not yet explained, or why she had begged for Cousin's life. I re-adjusted the mask.

"Perhaps it was a game they played," I suggested.

"To what end?"

Pol's voice was eager. I shrugged.

"There may have been reasons. I heard a tale once of a pirate who lured his enemy into his reach by sending false information that he would meet a trollop at midnight by a certain fountain."

"A clever scheme. If our friend at Saltash employed it he played his part well; but I hardly think the explanation will do. As I said the girl talked of marriage."

"From what you tell me she said she would save herself for her bridal night. Is it not possible that she was outraged at this fellow's boldness because he was *not* the prospective groom?"

Pol lifted a glass of wine.

"Possible," she confessed. "But the subject begins to pall on me. Tell me more about your pirate. Did he kill his enemy?"

"No. He had his sword at the villain's throat when the latter's wife appeared and swore her husband was all that she lived for, so my soft-hearted buccaneer spared him."

Wine splashed over the goblet's edge. Pol shivered.

"New England nights are cold," she said.

For a week Polly evaded me though she and Cousin lived under my roof. I saw her daily but never alone. I worried the problem of her conduct like a dog with a bone, but found no answer. It was evident that Cousin was as puzzled as I. He made no pretense of friendship or even courtesy, and did not mention the business that brought him here. When Pol was present he sat in gloomy, watchful silence. At other times he avoided me, but as days slipped into weeks I saw him more and more frequently with Amy. On such occasions I could hear his voice rise and fall in the fervid cadences which I well knew, and Amy's dull face fairly glowed. She spoke of Cousin with more enthusiasm than I had ever known her to exhibit. I thought them a good pair and attributed their friendship to the natural bond that might be expected to exist between father and daughter. But one day I found Amy crying.

"He kissed me," she sobbed; "I am a wanton."

I shook her so roughly that her teeth chattered.

"Is that all?" I demanded.

She twisted from my grasp and shrank back, glaring at me out of swollen red-rimmed eyes. I raised a clenched fist. Her mouth fell into a loose ugly leer. She appeared to forget the self-recrimination of the moment before as she directed a torrent of abuse against me. As I listened I realized that her animosity was not the product of a sudden rage. It was poison distilled by a master chemist. The voice was the voice of Amy, but the sentiments came out of the brain of Edward Cousin. He had twisted her to his will as he had so many women before her. At first I thought it was only her body that he wanted, and wondered that a man with Pol for wife could glance at Amy. It flashed through my mind, too, that if I did not interfere he would debauch his own daughter, and that this would be a far more diabolic vengeance than any my hatred might devise. But I rejected such a horror. Amy belonged to Bill's Prudence as well as to Cousin; and Bill had not directed me to her for such an end. Moreover, I felt an impatient affection for the poor graceless thing.

When she was exhausted I questioned her as gently as I could. There had been only a kiss. She had torn herself away from him and fled in an ecstasy of sin. But he had followed her and agreed that she was a wanton, and that only some great act of penitence could atone for such wickedness as hers. As she said this last I detected malice creeping back into her voice. The whole affair puzzled me. It was not like Cousin to demand penance of his victims before he was done with them. Unless he was merely amusing himself by playing upon Amy's emotions.

I pointed out this latter possibility to Amy, suggesting that one kiss does not make a wanton, and consequently whatever atonement might be required could not be great, since it must but fit the sin. It infuriated her that I should regard her lust lightly.

"You are right," she spat, "it was a small fault to let a wedded man hold me in his arms and press his mouth to mine . . . small as adultery which from the way you look at Mistress Cousin is no doubt but an evening's sport to you."

She burst into hysterical laughter. More to quiet her than out of anger I struck her. Her laughter died and left her gasping for breath, but her cheeks glowed, and when she was able to speak she did so with the venom of a poisonous snake.

"A small sin," she repeated, "one that requires but a small penance! Would you like to hear the penance that Edward Cousin requires for our very small sin?"

"No," I replied in disgust, "I have already heard that tale too often."

She ignored me.

"He is a good man; and though the flesh is sometimes too strong for him he does not belittle the temptations of Satan, and like you he believes that atonement should fit the sin. He says that I must kill you, because you are evil and your death would be pleasing in the eyes of God."

Her words had gathered fury like a gale, and, having reached their full force, like a spent storm they died into nothing. She sank back with a sob and regarded me out of dull frightened eyes.

This new proof of Cousin's wickedness did not shock me. But as I looked at Amy I pitied her. I sat down.

"Would you murder me?" I asked her quietly.

She only stared.

"Have I been unkind to you?"

"He says you are evil."

She said it with such stubborn conviction that I knew Cousin had taken her as surely as he had taken the others, although he had disdained her body.

I left her and went to my room where I took from a chest a long knife that I had kept from my pirate days. I found Polly and Edward Cousin. With the knife naked in my hand I told them what I had learned. Cousin denied it; Polly said nothing, but she knew that it was true.

"In Jamaica I granted you this man's life," I finally said to her, "now I am going to take back that gift."

Cousin had courage of a sort.

"You will murder me in cold blood," he said disdainfully, "while my wife looks on."

No words of Cousin's could have lengthened his life by a single second, but as I approached him Polly spoke. Her voice was soft.

"But, Edward, what would you expect of Tom? Have you forgotten that day when you stripped and bound me and had me drawn under the ship's keel? Murdered me, or so you thought, and he thought so too. Were your feelings so delicate then?"

I stared at her. She came to me and stretched out her hand. I gave her the knife. She continued to talk to Cousin.

"And you forget another thing, my dear spouse. Tom Bone can scarcely regard you as my husband, nor can I, nor can you yourself. We all know that I am his wife."

Cousin, who had shown fortitude when he faced mere death, wilted. He seemed suddenly old and tired. He groaned. Pol was without pity.

"No, Edward. We are not wed. Adultery. Sin." Her words were no longer soft. They crackled like fire and seared him like flames out of Hell. "Sin before God. Sin for which we will surely be damned. You have been afraid to say it, Edward, but since that night at Saltash you have known that you lived in adultery. And yet you have not put your wickedness behind you. And even now, though you are staring through the very portals of Hell, if I will it, you will sin again."

As I listened Pol's secret was revealed to me, and the bitterness I had felt for her dropped away. I never loved her more or felt greater tenderness. For the first time since our childhood I was stronger than she; she needed me.

"Pol," I cried.

She ignored me. With the knife balanced expertly in her hand she approached Cousin. The blade flashed, a trickle of blood appeared on his throat. Pol laughed softly. I shuddered. There was a warmth of passion in her laugh that I had not heard since she lay in my arms under the stars of Saltash.

"Not yet, Edward," she mocked, "I am not through with your soul yet, so I only scratched your ugly neck. But see how expert I am. You should see me in the mountains, Edward . . . the goat without horns . . . it's a pity you are such a coward."

She turned her back on him and faced me.

"Killing him will wait, Tom. I think the time has come when we must talk."

We left the house and the town. The day was dull, there was a brisk chill wind. As we walked along the seashore I contrasted in my mind the gray skies and leaden waters of the North Atlantic with the depthless blue of the Caribbean. I was somewhat surprised to realize that I preferred New England. There was peace here. The blood was cooler; and the same piercing winds which blew mist in from the sea cleared fog out of the brain. Pol seemed to read my thoughts.

"It is like a winter day in Devon," she said wistfully.

"Good?" I asked.

She nodded.

"Gray clouds that race across the sky, only to dissolve into mist. The ocean leaden, or green or black . . . anything but everlasting gleaming blue."

"There is blue in England, too."

"And we love it because though it is generous it never holds itself too cheap. But it is the wind that I like best of all . . . damp and cold and clean. Clean," she repeated, "clean." She turned to me fiercely.

"Do you know what the word means, Tom?"

"Yes," I replied. "Clean of hate and endless tormenting schemes of vengeance."

I took her hand. She jerked it away. Her eyes were dark as the sea.

"I shall never be clean of that," she cried.

We found shelter behind a rock. She pulled me down beside her.

482

"Since I came to your house I have been trying to decide," she said vaguely. "I now know what I must do, but first we shall talk. Tell me all that has happened to you since we were parted on Cousin's ship. Tell me everything, but especially about the girl you called Judith and held so close in your arms."

"She—" I began eagerly.

Pol smiled wanly.

"From the beginning, Tom. If you tell me that she was merely an actress playing a part and that there was nothing between you, I shall not believe it. You cared for one another. I saw and despite all that is said to the contrary jealousy is not always blind. But if I know everything perhaps I shall understand."

"Yes, we cared for one another," I admitted, "but—"

"From the beginning," she repeated.

So I told her from the beginning. I told her of the crazed creature on the derelict, how I was saved and how I met Judith Mara. I explained how I found Anthony More, only to learn that he was my friend, Bill Smith. I told of the days of piracy and my debauchery, and how Judith Mara fought so steadfastly that in the end she triumphed. I told her of Bill's death and of his scheme to trap Cousin, and of the charge to care for Amy More that he laid on me.

"She is Cousin's child," Pol asked incredulously, "and you care for her and are kind to her?"

"I am even a little fond of her."

She stared at me broodingly.

"Go on," she said at last.

I described the voyage of the *Pilgrim* and how I had taken Cousin's ship only to lose it because I became blind. I told her of the months at Saltash and how I at last asked Judith to marry me, and that only Trigg's intervention prevented our wedding. Finally I told her of the night upon which she herself came to Saltash.

I explained how Trigg pretended to Cousin that he was a disgruntled servant of Anthony More, and offered to sell information that would lead to the buccaneer's capture. Cousin paid and was told that his enemy would be at Saltash the night of the ball.

483

To lend his tale color Trigg related how Judith Mara, the mistress of Saltash, had once been More's prisoner and had become so enamored of her captor that though she had long since been ransomed she remained his doxy. Cousin was interested but wary. He said first that he would consider coming to Saltash, then rejected the idea, finally accepted it. But he was cautious. He must see More with his own eyes, and see that he was indeed bent on amusement not fighting. Moreover, Trigg must remain with him that there might be no treachery. So the scene at the fountain was arranged.

"It was only to convince Cousin that I was defenseless and an easy prey," I told Polly earnestly.

"You played your part ardently."

"I am a man. Besides I had seen you but an hour before. While I caressed her Judith was only your shadow."

A smile played fleetingly at the corners of Pol's mouth.

"A lovely shadow, Tom, and substantial."

The smile was stillborn. Pol stared broodingly at the horizon.

"It is my turn now," she sighed. "Love kept me alive under the ship's keel," she said slowly, "but as they pulled me onto the deck I lost consciousness. When I opened my eyes it was to a world of hate. You were gone, our child was gone."

The ship's surgeon had cared for her. Cousin himself attended her. She had been taken from the ship to God's Acres, where after many weeks she recovered. Her body was not even scarred. Cousin regarded this as direct intercession from Providence. Naturally the Lord would desire Edward Cousin's mate to be unblemished. He explained this to Polly the day that she was able to get out of bed. When she pointed out that keelhauling her and murdering her husband were strange ways to gain a woman's affections, Cousin blandly shifted the responsibility to God. The one was doubtlessly an ordeal to test if she were worthy to be his, Cousin's, wife. As to her husband, he had leaped overboard of his own will, and that too was surely the hand of God, so that Pol might be free.

Joseph Trigg had been right when he said that the Polly Bragg who married Cousin was not our Pol. For during the weeks that she lay in bed, those same weeks that I drifted, half crazed, on the derelict, hate mastered her, as it mastered me, and took possession of her. Her body was soft and unmarked, desirable as before, but her spirit was warped and hideous.

"When they told me that you had jumped overboard and drowned I knew that I had murdered you," she explained. "I had been a coward as they led me to the ship's rail. I was afraid of death, but I was even more afraid of being alone at the bottom of the sea. I wanted you with me. So I asked you to come. You obeyed . . . died . . . and I was still alive.

"During the weeks that I lay in bed I turned over in my mind means by which I might make Cousin suffer. I could kill him easily, but it was not enough. He must live until his body knew the agony that mine had known; he must suffer the emptiness that I suffered. Then one night as I lay sleepless, almost retching from hate's bile, it came to me that the greatest cruelty to Edward Cousin would be to tear from him the mask of piety by means of which he had blinded himself to his own wickedness, and make him look at his naked soul and realize that it is black and damned forever; to make him live with that knowledge . . . tremble at the Hell that awaits him . . . until he suffered as the poor creatures such as your sister suffered.

"So I married him," she continued tonelessly, "I married him that I might torture his body through imposing upon it the frustration that mine suffers in your absence, that I might convince him that his soul is damned; and finally that when I had done with him I might kill him with my own hands and send him to the tenderer mercies of the devil. Only then would I be free to join you."

As I listened to Polly I marveled that her thoughts had been so similar to my own. But her weapons were far more subtle, their edge sharper. Beside hers, my own schemes of vengeance were those of an awkward child. She was still talking.

"Before I married him I made him vow with his hand on the Bible that he would be patient . . . not force me to his will . . ."

"You trusted him to keep such an oath?" I exclaimed.

Her smile was dark as the dark sea.

485

"Do you forget that while you were still on the ship I had been alone with him in his cabin for a week? At the end of that time he had gotten so little comfort, though no oath bound him, that he could only resort to the angry petulance of an ill-natured child who smashes the toy it cannot possess. Furthermore as he leaned over my bed at God's Acres he drooled hollow prayers to God, but his real adulation came not from his mouth, but from his eyes . . . and they rested on my body. I knew then that I need not fear Edward Cousin. When you made him a figure of such great wickedness you created your own monster, Tom. Evil, vile, venomous . . . but not great. He bent to his will only those feeble in mind or body. When circumstances put strong men in his power he could only kill them. He is not an angel of darkness, rebelling grandly against God. Edward Cousin is only the devil's pimp . . . a procurer of the weak-minded and unfortunate."

I nodded. I too had realized it on that day when the *Pilgrim* fled before a ship bearing the standard of Anthony More. Pol paused for a while . . . then continued in the same flat monotone.

"I told my husband that I had been a wicked woman . . . a wanton who had given herself freely through sheer frenzy of the flesh. As I described my sins his hands trembled, the sweat stood on his forehead, spit leaked out of his heavy broken mouth. But when he attempted to take me in his arms I repulsed him.

"I see the light now," I told him. "I have received grace. You were indeed the instrument of the Lord. The ordeal at sea has cleansed me and I am resolved to do penance until I receive a sign that I may be yours in fact as well as in name."

"How soon did that time come?"

The question was wrung from me. Polly ignored it, and hastened grimly on. She had played on Edward Cousin with diabolical skill and merciless ferocity. She took for herself the smallest, meanest room at God's Acres. There she lived austerely as if indeed she did penance. Her clothes were plain and ugly, her food simple. She shut herself in solitude for days at a time. Cousin believed that she prayed.

"But it was not so," she assured me. "I was cursing him and

486

pondering new measures against him; and sometimes I permitted myself to think of you."

But at intervals barely frequent enough to keep Cousin aroused she abandoned her rôle of penitent. On such occasions she called in the wench Evalyn, who, with Abel, she had insisted upon having, and together they garbed her as the courtesan that she pretended to have once been. Thus prepared, she beguiled her husband with every art she knew. She explained this change by swearing that she could keep herself from him no longer, that though her soul be damned for it, her lust must be served. But always when Cousin was fairly aroused she drew back. Sanctity descended upon her.

"Dangerous," I asserted.

"Not very. I told him that I would destroy myself rather than submit to him until I heard the command; and at the same time suggested the joys of that day. He protested, he even wept, but he waited."

"If he had not?"

"It would not have mattered. I had no feeling. I was already dead."

I recalled the women I had taken as I sought forgetfulness, and knew that what Pol said was true; but the knowledge did not diminish the fierce jealous anger that had been gnawing at my vitals ever since I saw Pol as Cousin's wife at Saltash . . . and which had burst into an almost unbearable flame since they had been living under my roof.

"But you surrendered," I reminded her. "Just now in his room you taunted him with adultery."

"Wait," she commanded.

Pol played her game skillfully, but it did not satisfy her. She discovered the possibilities of voudou by accident. One night the drums of the maroons had sent their throbbing message out of the hills to God's Acres. Cousin had shuddered and expressed the opinion that those who embraced magic sold themselves to the devil and would surely suffer the worst tortures of Hell. From that moment Pol was determined that Cousin himself should practice black magic. She moved cautiously. First she sent Abel to the mountains. It was a dangerous mission because, though the maroons welcomed fugitives, they despised any black who would return tamely to his bondage. But Abel disarmed their doubts by stating frankly that he came at the behest of his mistress who, though a white woman, was possessed of more magic than the most powerful witchdoctor, and who foresaw a time, not too far distant, when with the blacks as her followers she would drive the white man from the island and the negurs would rule under her, their priestess.

I was appalled. The possible rising of the slaves was a horror that hung over the Indies; and I had lived in them long enough to share it. But when I pointed this out Pol was unmoved.

"Does it matter?" she said drearily.

When Abel had prepared the way she went with him into the mountains. At first she remained in the background, but when she had seen enough to be sure that priest and priestesses of voudou were only crude fakers, she allowed herself to be drawn into their rites. Meantime Abel renewed his declaration concerning the white priestess' ultimate intent. The negurs crowded around her, clamoring to know when the moment for the attack would come.

"The master of God's Acres is a powerful priest," she told them. "He alone stands in our way. We must first win him over. When I have done that and learned his secrets you shall sacrifice him and eat of his flesh . . . then you will have the strength to conquer the white man.

"You see," Polly said to me quietly, "when I have persuaded him to accept the snake god in the place of Christ, and have tired of torturing him with the knowledge that his soul is damned, the negurs will eat him."

As she spoke my own heart sank. I mastered myself with difficulty . . . forced myself to speak quietly.

"You speak of the future," I said.

She nodded morosely.

"Go on. Tell me how you can persuade him to practice voudou."

"He wants me even worse than he wants his soul."

"Must you continue?" I asked her. "Let me go back now and kill him, and trust to the devil for the rest."

488

"Men say there is a Hell," Polly said slowly, "and I feel that it must be true, else why should there be such wickedness on earth? But no man has seen it . . . or its punishments. What if Edward Cousin should merely sink into a deep, dreamless sleep?"

For the moment I gave up argument and urged her to finish her story. She picked up the threads wearily.

She had arranged that Cousin should hear from others that she had visited the maroons. Abel whispered dark hints to blacks who he knew would spread the rumor. The plan worked. Cousin grew more and more morose. Finally he charged his wife with witchcraft. She denied it, but made certain that he should hear more and darker reports.

This had been the situation when he proposed that she go with him on the *Pilgrim*. This threatened her plans. She had counted on his months of absence to make her final arrangements with the maroons. If she accompanied him all her work might be undone. Nevertheless she consented to go. She even went to the docks, where I had seen her. At the last minute she refused to sail. She told Cousin that the sight of his ship brought back too vividly the memory of her torture. She could not go aboard. He must leave without her . . . but perhaps when he came back she would be waiting for him in the way which he most desired. He had argued in vain, pleaded, commanded. Finally he threatened to use force. For the first time she half confessed witchcraft.

"Would you take me to the very heart of voudou?" she asked. "Must I thus add to my peril? Leave me this once; then give up the sea and protect me with your strength from evil."

He stepped toward her. She drew back and walked around him.

"Cousin was not sure if you were a witch or not," I interrupted. "When I invented my yarn about his witch-wife protecting me with her magic, it was final proof that you were in league with the devil."

"I suppose so," Polly agreed. "In any event your tale served my purpose. When my husband returned to God's Acres he told me what had occurred. I was puzzled, of course, but I knew that Abel's rumors, concocted for Cousin's ear, had spread over the island, so I guessed part of the truth . . . that someone had twisted gossip to his own purpose. For my part it suited me well enough. I admitted the truth of your whole story and boldly confessed that I had given up the struggle for virtue and made a pact with the devil. But though a voudou priestess I still loved Cousin and had sent you to watch over him.

"He was so frightened for his own salvation that for a few minutes I believed he might kill me. But his lust fought with his fear—and triumphed. That day was the crisis. Since then I have owned his body as completely as he ever owned the meanest of his blacks. I did not even permit him his reward.

"My body is the devil's," I told him, "and he shares his mistress only with his own vassals. Renounce God, come to the voudou rites, eat of the goat without horns, and I shall share with you pleasures taught me by Satan himself.

"I no longer wore dull clothes but tempted Cousin with every device known to woman. He groaned and groveled before me, begging alternately that I renounce voudou, and that I come to him as I was. Many times my feet have been wet from his tears as he embraced them and pleaded for pity. But he would not sell himself to the devil. He has been able neither to put me away nor accept my terms. For a few weeks I was content. He writhed from fear and frustration and I poured acid in his wounds. But I grew weary. I wanted his soul, then his life. I was tired. I wanted to go to you, Tom.

"Then came the invitation to Saltash. By that time Cousin dared not move without seeking my consent. Abject fear was piled upon infatuation. My magic had sent him reeling drunkenly through the African jungle, it had struck him blind aboard the *Pilgrim*.

"At first I forbade going to Saltash. I was afraid that Anthony More might escape the trap laid for him and rob me of my vengeance by killing Cousin. But I changed my mind. I do not know why unless it was that I longed to see Saltash once more before I ended the game at God's Acres and died. So I ordered Cousin to take his blacks for protection, and even accompanied him to the trysting place myself, though Trigg tried to dissuade me.

"There I saw you and the girl and heard her speak of her bridal night. I naturally believed that you were to be the groom. I had thought that my heart was already carrion, that I could no longer feel, but when I saw you with her I discovered that I had been wrong. Misery's scalding waters washed me anew."

A note of appeal crept into Pol's voice.

"You must try to understand how I felt, Tom. I saw you strain her to you, kiss her . . . heard her speak of marriage. I had abandoned the world, had myself proclaimed a witch, had even wed Edward Cousin . . . all to avenge you. Then I saw you alive, holding a beautiful girl, half my age, in your arms."

"I can understand," I said grimly. "Do you forget that not two hours before I had looked at Mistress Cousin . . . and seen you?"

She sighed.

"If you had only come to me then instead of letting me find you with her."

"I was waiting until I killed him. I did not know you would go into the garden with him."

"But I did go, and when you were on the point of killing Cousin I stopped you. Surely you understand why. I believed my love was lost . . . even its memory was curdled. You were worse than dead. I was determined that you should not rob me of my hate. It was all I had left."

"And I was such a cursed fool that I believed you cared for him," I muttered.

"We were both cursed that night," Pol said sadly. Then as she resumed her narrative her voice was once again flat and impersonal.

"I nursed Cousin jealously. Love was never more devoted than my hate. When he was strong again I at last gave him his way with me."

"Why?" I cried out.

"In part because I am a mean creature . . . that is to say, a jealous woman in love. If he can take a beautiful girl,' I told myself, 'I can at least degrade his love by surrendering what was once his to his enemy."

491

"But even that night you must have known I loved you," I protested.

"I think I did; but jealousy was not all that blinded me. There were the years of hate, too. I could not give up my revenge. Since you were alive I was not wed to Edward Cousin. Each time he took me I taunted him with the sin of adultery. He cringed but could not master his passion."

She shook herself and passed her hand across her eyes.

"Since then there have been moments when I almost felt sorry for him. Think of him now . . . for weeks he has stayed under your roof because I will it, though he believes that whenever I am out of his sight I am in your arms. Is he not to be pitied?"

"No," I said. "He himself never knew mercy; and even during these weeks that you speak of, he has played upon Amy in order to persuade her to murder me. Do not pity him. Do not regret any of the punishment you have inflicted upon him . . . but for your own sake, let me kill him now. You cannot go on. Some day you will drive him too far."

Her hand moved listlessly in the sand.

"The game is about played, Tom. He is afraid that I shall stay with you. That fear has smashed his last defense. He has promised that if I will return with him to God's Acres he will renounce God and join in the voudou rites."

"You can't go back," I insisted. "You know yourself it is madness. We are together again. We can have the old days as at Saltash. What is revenge or hate compared to that?"

"For the past weeks I have been saying to myself what you just said. That is why I remained in your house. I wanted to convince myself, to make myself give it up. But it is no use. Perhaps I am sick. Until the sickness is gone I am unclean. Only Cousin's blood can wash me. The days of Saltash are gone forever. If there are to be other days for us they must be built on new foundations."

"You are more than sick, you are mad," I said.

"Mad," she agreed. "And past redemption. So leave me to my deserts."

As she spoke a strange thing happened. The dull sea seemed to turn to cobalt . . . the gray skies were deep blue. I stood at a ship's rail . . . dirty, unkempt, red-eyed . . . my full beard filthy and uncombed. My mouth was dry. I had just left Maria Montijo. I was looking into Judith's mocking contemptuous eyes, trying to drive her away from me that I might be alone with self-pity and hate.

"I am past redemption," I cried, "leave me to go to the devil in my own way."

Judith's voice was clear and hard. She made the sign of the cross.

"No mortal is past redemption," she said.

The moment passed. I was on the New England shore again. Pol was looking at me. Her face was cold as the stone against which we leaned.

"Come," I said. "We must go home."


### 3.

We walked along the shore and through the town. By the time we reached home darkness had fallen. A pale moon was on the horizon.

I went directly to Amy's room. There were things I must tell her before I finished the night's work. Pol went with me. I did not bother to ask why. Amy's door was open. A half-consumed candle shed a fitful yellow light. Beyond it, casting a shadow against the curtain, was the body of Amy Felton. She had hanged herself.

Pol reached the body first.

"Wait," I exclaimed.

A note, addressed to me, was beside the candle. I read it. The words were graceless as Amy herself, but they brought tears to my eyes. It was a pitiful thing that any creature should live and die so harshly.

"He came to me here after you were gone. I now know that he is an evil man, but it is too late. I know, too, that I am doing a wicked thing, but I am not strong enough to bear the burden of my sin. You tried to be kind to me, and I should feel gratitude, but I do not. You should have left me with Mistress Todd. She is a good woman."

"Get Cousin," I told Pol.

"What are you going to do?"

"Nothing I had not resolved to do when we were still on the beach."

She hesitated a moment, then turned toward the door.

"No tricks," I warned. "Mad or sick or both, you may be, and whatever you are I love you. But at this moment I will brook no interference."

While she was gone I fetched swords and waited.

When Cousin came I handed him the letter.

"She hanged herself," I said.

He read the letter and stared at the twisted blotched face of the corpse.

"Mad," he said coldly.

"A little, I think."

"Then why send for me? This letter is a part of her madness."

"No. In that she was not mad. Listen, and while you listen look at the corpse of the woman you drove to death. You knew her as Mistress Felton. The lips you kissed were hers, the body you pressed to you was Mistress Felton's body. But Mistress Felton is dead. Look at her . . . look at her carefully: the coarse black hair, the thick lips, the muddy skin, the thick powerful body. Do you recognize her? You should, for you knew her mother. Her mother was Anthony More's wife, but Anthony More was not her father."

I saw Cousin's body grow rigid. His hand clenched. I heard him gasp.

"That is right, Edward Cousin. The woman you drove to her death is your own daughter. I do not expect you to pity her, but while you face death, think of your own soul—and the crowning sin with which this night you have burdened it."

I handed him a sword.

We faced one another. In the brief seconds before the necessity of killing or being killed engaged my whole attention, I re-

494

called the evil that Edward Cousin had done. Polly, Bill, Evalyn, Jenny, and finally and most vividly of all I remembered that day upon which I first heard Edward Cousin's name—the day that his bullies murdered my father. I was a small, helpless boy again. I felt Ned Bone's hand clutch mine more tightly as he died . . . and my own hand grasped the sword hilt with new determination. I advanced slowly. Cousin stood still, eyeing me warily.

It must have been a fantastic sight. The moon drew a narrow ribbon of silver across the room, the candle flickered upon the table. That was all the light there was. Pol said later that it was as if she were watching a duel of ghosts, shadows that lunged, thrust and retreated. And in the background was the corpse of Amy Felton. Someone brushed against it. It swayed gently to and fro.

Retreating toward the center of the room I reached the ribbon of moonlight. As if it had been a chasm of death, I leaped over it into the gloom beyond. Cousin came forward slowly until he reached the light. After that we each clung to the shadows, only our swords venturing out of the darkness to flash white against the moon's glow—hot steel that only blood could cool.

As a boy Cousin had not worked on the docks and in the stable; as a youth his muscles were not hardened by a ship's tough rigging, an ax's weight, and the icy waters of the North Atlantic; as a young man he lived on inherited fields instead of wresting them from an unwilling forest and cultivating them under Virginia's broiling sun. He was a gentleman who deemed it ignoble to toil with his hands or bend his back to labor. So he had to die.

Imperceptibly—at first I sensed rather than felt it—he grew weaker. I pushed forward until I stood full in the moonlight. I could hear Cousin breathing heavily. It was evident that he grew wearier each minute. He must kill me quickly or he was doomed. He pressed forward. A sudden thrust, a clashing of steel and the hot hissing of one blade sliding off another. Cousin thrust again; this time I followed parry with riposte. As the swordsman's art goes, it was a sorry stroke. It was slow and awkward, but it was untired and strong. And it was death. Death to Edward Cousin. His last human sound was a grunt as he collapsed.

495

We left him there, his daughter's corpse still swaying gently, casting its shadow over his lifeless body.

"Why did you do it?" Pol asked when we were out of the room.

"I couldn't allow you to go back to Jamaica with him, the horror—"

She threw out her hands in protest.

"I don't mean that. I know the reason you killed him. But why in that way? He didn't deserve a kindly death."

"I know it. When I decided out there on the beach to kill him I didn't intend he should have one, but Amy's death changed things. It meant I had failed in my promise to Bill Smith. So, though I killed Cousin to avenge a dozen people, and most of all to keep you from killing him, I chose the manner of his dying for Bill. He would have wanted it in a fair fight. Bill was a gentleman."

Pol smiled a little.

"So you finally say a good word for gentlemen?"

"Bill's sort."

After that we talked about the bodies. Pol wanted to get rid of them, but I had a better way.

"I'll put a knife beside Cousin," I explained, "and call the authorities. The knife and note will tell their own tale. Cousin sneaked to Amy's room for another visit, found the dead body and the note intended for me. He read the letter, realized that he had driven the girl to her death, and killed himself in a fit of remorse."

Pol sighed.

"You have grown clever since I knew you," she said.

"I have dealt with clever men."

Her eyes were somber.

"Don't be one, Tom. Be like you were."

"With your help," I promised.

The authorities accepted the evidence of their eyes. The next day we buried Amy. Pol and I were the sole mourners at the grave of Edward Cousin's daughter. After the funeral Polly told me that she was going away.

"Not now," I protested. "It is over, and we are together."

"We shall not be together until I have forgotten a little that I lived as Edward Cousin's wife."

It may seem strange that I let her go so easily, but my own suffering has brought me some wisdom, and her eyes were clouded with misery.

"Where will you go?" I asked.

"Only to Boston, now. When I first came here and saw you I thought I might give over my revenge and stay. So I sent for Abel. He should be here in a few weeks. I shall wait for him."

"And then?"

"Into the forest . . . somewhere in its depths there must be peace."

"But the savages."

"I will be safe with Abel."

She reached out and touched me.

"I am sick as you were sick. Perhaps, like you, I shall be well again. Surely you can wait."

"I can wait," I promised.

I saw her once more. It was when I took Abel to her in Boston. The shadow of the past was still heavy upon her.

"Care for her," I told Abel.

He nodded.

They left me and disappeared into the wilderness.

# XXI

Two weeks ago a trapper knocked on the door of my fine mansion in Newport. He told me a strange tale. The previous winter his zeal for furs had carried him beyond the farthest limits of English settlement, across the mountains and into the country claimed by France. At last he came to a river that the Indians call the Wabash. There on a bluff he found a cabin. Back of it was cleared land. He knocked and a woman came to the door. Behind her, a long knife in his hand, stood a giant negur. The woman welcomed him; and after he had eaten and rested the black showed him a pile of the heaviest pelts he had ever seen. But when he offered to buy them the woman refused. Later she asked him from what part of America he had come. He told her Virginia. She had looked out over the river.

"If ever you pass through Henrico County and come to a ruined plantation called Hickorywood, tread the ground lightly," she murmured.

They had kept him with them all night. The next morning while he was preparing to leave the woman asked him if he would go to Newport, in the province of Rhode Island, for the gift of the furs. He accepted eagerly.

"Take them then, and when you reach Newport find the merchant, Thomas Bond, and tell him what you have seen."

There was no message for me the trapper said. He was just to tell me what he had seen.

As the man talked I saw Pol as I had last seen her.

"Were the woman's eyes clear?" I asked. "Was there peace in them?"

498

"Curious you should ask that," he replied thoughtfully, "for I could not help noticing her eyes. They were the clearest and most peaceful I have ever seen."

It was two weeks ago that the trapper told his tale. Tomorrow with a gun and a long knife for company I shall turn my back on Newport and go into the wilderness . . . toward the West . . . toward the river called the Wabash . . . toward Polly Bragg.

**THE END**